THE BLUECOATS SEARCHED RUTHLESSLY
FOR INDIANS . . .
BUT A WARRIOR WOMAN WAS
READY TO DO BATTLE

A jagged streak of lightning struck the ground like a snake uncoiling. Stands Shining waited for the boom of thunder. It came, blotting out all other sound.

For a moment, nothing changed. Stands Shining bit the inside of her lip, her eyes fixed on First Cloud, who was still riding toward the bluecoats. Slowly he began to slip sideways. She caught her breath. The warriors around her did the same.

She saw First Cloud fall, topple from the black and white horse. He made no move to catch himself. When he landed on the ground, he lay still, his riderless horse breaking into a gallop and racing to the south away from everyone.

Stands Shining blinked in disbelief. For a moment she connected the lightning blast with what had happened to First Cloud. But the lightning had been nowhere near him. The bluecoats milled about. She smelled the faint tinge of gunsmoke wafting toward her on the wind.

First Cloud had been shot! She understood that now.

With a shriek of defiance and rage, she urged her horse ahead and galloped down the hill, bow in hand.

Kill them, she thought. Kill every bluecoat. . . .

ARAPAHO SPIRIT

JANE TOOMBS

A Dell/Banbury Book

Published by
Banbury Books, Inc.
37 West Avenue
Wayne, Pennsylvania 19087

Dell ® TM 681510, Dell Publishing Co., Inc.

ISBN: 0-440-00272-9

Printed in the United States of America

First printing—August 1983

Chapter 1

1833

Rainy wakened to the touch of a gentle hand on his shoulder.

"The sky," Mother said. "Come, see the sky."

Mother didn't speak as well as Father. She often used strange words. Rainy had learned in his five winters that these were secret words not to be repeated to anyone. To hear such words made Father hit Mother with sticks until her blood flowed.

"Meteors," Mother said.

A new secret word. Rainy tried it in his head. Meteors.

Mother tugged at his hand and he rose, wrapping his rabbit-skin robe around his shoulders. He was getting too old for rabbit skin, but Falling Leaf Moon had ended and the night was chill. He'd already shot his first bird with the bow and arrows Father had made him, but he didn't dare ask Father for a wolf-skin robe like the other boys his age wore. Father was like the grizzly, easily angered.

Rainy followed Mother as she raised the tepee flap and walked outside. He stopped short, staring in amazement at the sky. Brightness streaked across the darkness. Here, there, everywhere he could see, there were fiery trails of light that changed the night to frightening brilliance.

The stars were falling!

He straightened his shoulders and tried to be brave. "Will they fall on us?" he asked.

"No," Mother answered, but her voice was uncertain.

Murmurs of disbelief wove all around Rainy. They came from the other women and children standing in the circle of tepees. Most of the warriors had left the village to hunt. His father had left with them.

Were the stars falling on the warriors, too?

A man shrieked somewhere in the pines behind the village. Rainy knew the cry had not come from one of their own warriors. It had come from an enemy and it was a war cry. Women screamed and ran. Some hid in their tepees. Others darted away from the village. His mother stood frozen.

"Utes!" Rainy shouted at her. Still she didn't move.

Armed Ute warriors dashed from the trees. As they raced between the tepees, Rainy grabbed his mother's hand and tried to pull her. She stumbled after him. Finally she began to run.

A Ute with white lines like claw marks painted onto his cheeks lunged at them, seizing Rainy's mother by her long hair. Crying and shouting, Rainy hurled himself at the warrior. He bit the Ute's arm. He kicked at his legs.

The warrior fended off the boy, losing his grip on his mother. She scrambled away. The Ute snarled and grabbed Rainy's arm. He raised his tomahawk. Rainy stared defiantly into the painted face.

As the tomahawk came down, he heard his mother cry out his name. He was flung aside with such force that the breath was knocked from him. When he could think clearly again, he found himself on his back, gazing up at the fiery sky. He sprang to his feet and looked around.

The Ute warrior knelt beside Mother, who was sprawled on the ground. Blood smeared her face. The warrior grasped her hair in one hand, his knife in the other. Before Rainy could howl out his rage and anguish, a man loomed up behind the Ute and smashed his war club onto the warrior's skull with such force that Rainy heard the crunch of bone. The warrior slumped sideways and lay motionless.

"Boy," the man with the club said. "Boy, help me."

Rainy recognized Early Snow, one of the Water Sprinkling Old Men. Together they dragged Rainy's mother into a clump of bushes. Early Snow broke off a branch and went back to brush the sign of their passage from the dirt. He didn't return. Rainy crouched beside his mother. He couldn't see her because light from the falling stars didn't penetrate through the bushes, but he could feel the stickiness of blood on her forehead.

Was she dead?

A lump rose in his throat and tears scalded his eyes. He buried his face in his hands to muffle his sobs. What would he do without Mother? A picture of his father's furious face flashed before him. Perhaps Father would beat him with a stick for not saving Mother from the Ute. Father had never loved him as Mother had.

Many others feared Father. Bad Hawk, Our People called him. No one liked to think what Bad Hawk's wandering left eye saw while his right eye looked at you. Some whispered that it could see into the spirit world. They said that was why Bad Hawk was so cruel—he was tormented by the spirits for spying on them.

Rainy dabbed at his wet face, telling himself he must make his heart strong. But the sounds of fighting and death beyond the bushes scared him. A gun cracked and he tensed. Another crack, then another. White men's guns.

A hairy-faced man with pale eyes had come to the village last summer with two Cheyenne warriors and Rainy had seen such a gun. Often he had marveled with the other boys how its loud roar could bring down an elk from so far away. None of Our People had such a thing. He didn't think the Utes had guns either.

Carefully Rainy eased forward until he could part the bushes to look toward the village. He stared into the face of a white man struggling on the ground with a Ute warrior. Fascinated, Rainy watched the pale-faced man plunge a knife into the breast of the warrior. The Ute choked and fell back. He didn't move.

The white man stood up. When he knelt to retrieve the knife, Rainy saw he had fingers missing on one hand. Before Rainy could draw back, their eyes met.

Tom Fitzpatrick reached into the bushes and yanked out a blood-smeared Arapaho boy. The child tried to pull free, but Fitzpatrick held him firmly with one hand. With his crippled hand, he made signs. Are you wounded? he asked the boy.

After a moment, the boy raised his right hand palm up, then turned the palm down, meaning *no*. He stared into Fitzpatrick's face.

Friend, Fitzpatrick signed.

The boy took a deep breath. *Mother hurt,* he signed. *Help Mother*.

Fitzpatrick glanced swiftly about. He'd heard no shots for several minutes and there were no more sounds of fighting. What was left of the Ute raiding party had turned tail and fled. Hell of a thing he and his three companions getting mixed up in a Ute-Arapaho quarrel, but the Ute war party had fought them and they'd had no choice. Probably thought we meant to help the Arapahos, Fitzpatrick thought.

He let go of the boy. The mother must be hiding in the bushes. Near the bodies of a Ute warrior and an old Arapaho man, Fitzpatrick had seen a partly obliterated trail indicating where something had been dragged into the bushes. Following it, he had come on the Ute he'd been forced to kill. The warrior was sniffing along the same trail. No doubt he was after the woman.

Well, he'd do what he could for the boy's mother, then they'd have to be getting on. He was overdue for a meeting in St. Louis. Fitzpatrick took another look at the streaks of light still brilliantly etching the sky. He had never seen anything like it in the old country or America.

"Meteors," the boy remarked unexpectedly. Fitzpatrick's jaw dropped.

The boy turned and plunged into the bushes. Fitzpatrick followed him. In the darkness, he saw the form of a woman on the ground. He lifted her as gently as he could and carried her toward the village. The boy ran beside him.

Find a squaw to care for the injured woman, Fitzpatrick told himself, then move on. He shifted her weight so he could see her face. There was blood all over her. It looked like some Ute had tried to scalp her. She moaned and opened her eyes. When she saw him, he felt her body tense.

"Who are you?" she asked. "Where is my son?"

Fitzpatrick stopped, nearly dropping her. The Indian had spoken in English! After he gathered his wits together and told her who he was, she asked to be put down. Then she sat on the ground hugging the boy.

"My name is Elizabeth Hampton Abbott," she told him. "I've been held captive here. Please take me with you."

"And the boy?" Fitzpatrick asked, looking at the five-year-old, his light eyes set deep in the dusky face of an Indian.

"He must come too. I can't leave my son."

The woman told her story. She explained how she had accompanied her husband on a trading expedition to New Mexico along the Santa Fe Trail and that the wagons had been attacked by Arapaho and Cheyenne near the

Arkansas River. Her husband, Lester Abbott, had been killed. She'd been taken prisoner and forced to become the wife of an Arapaho named Bad Hawk. His harsh treatment had caused her to miscarry the child of her white husband. Later, Bad Hawk had taken her north and she'd borne him a son.

Elizabeth smiled at the boy. "His name means Rainy in Arapaho," she whispered lovingly, "but he's been sunlight to me, the only thing that's kept me alive." She stared up at Fitzpatrick. "Don't bring us into the village. Let them think we're dead. That way, Bad Hawk won't come after us. He's a terrible man. Evil."

When the trappers left the village an hour later, they stopped at the tepees to pick up the woman and the boy. Elizabeth rode unassisted, a crude bandage of scarlet flannel binding her head wound. But when the trappers camped near dawn, she collapsed onto the ground and Fitzpatrick shook his head, doubtful that she would be able to go on.

She was a pitiful sight, even with the blood cleaned from her face. Old burn scars puckered her right cheek and neck. Her left forearm was crooked as though a broken bone had healed badly. He noticed she could scarcely use the arm and moved like an old woman though she still must have been in her twenties.

Will power alone must have kept her on a horse that far. Could she summon the strength necessary to get her to her father in St. Louis? Judge Douglas Hampton was well known there. Fitzpatrick had seen him several times, a proud, dignified, older man. What would he make of a half-Arapaho grandson?

Judge Hampton turned away from his daughter's bedside to look out of the long window facing the side garden. The promise of spring had encouraged a few blooms. He could see the yellow heads of daffodils nodding in the flower bed that circled the birdbath.

"Where is he?" Elizabeth asked weakly.

"Hampton is fine," the judge answered, sensing her intense concern. "Jerome's keeping an eye on him. They're in the back meadow and Hampton is riding the pony I gave him."

"He loves horses."

"Yes. And he's good with them. I don't doubt he'll be ready for a jumper soon." And boarding school, although the judge didn't mention this aloud. Elizabeth would be upset. But she mustn't be allowed to turn the boy into a pantywaist. After all, he'd soon be six.

Dear God she was thin, he thought. Skin and bones. And those hideous scars on her face and neck, her maimed arm. He could hardly bear to look at her.

Damn savages. There was no room in this country for both God-fearing men and heathen redskins. He'd have raised an army big enough to wipe every last Indian off the face of the earth if he ran the government. None of this nonsense about setting aside land for them. Land for the devil's children? No!

As the boy galloped around the side of the house, the pony's hooves threw chunks from the damp lawn. The judge's face softened. A crackerjack rider, his grandson. Too bad Lester Abbott hadn't lived to see his son.

Hampton Abbott. A fine name for this sturdy, handsome lad. He grew more civilized every day. Thank God he'd been rescued from those filthy savages before they ruined him.

Boarding school for the boy. A good one. Get him ready for West Point. Make a soldier of him. Cavalry. An officer to lead men against the Indians. Wipe them out. The judge smiled.

Hampton Abbott crept up the stairs, avoiding the boards that creaked. Grandfather didn't like him to be in

Mother's room—he was well aware of that fact. But Mother needed him.

Even she called him Hampton now. He answered readily to the name. Here in this vast village of white men, he could no longer be Rainy. But his grandfather kept telling him about a dead man he said was his father, a white man called Lester Abbott. Grandfather was wrong, though. He clearly remembered Father's angry face, his left eye that never looked at you but saw into the land of spirits. Surely his father had been one of Our People.

Yet he said nothing of these memories to Grandfather. The old man sternly bade him be quiet if he spoke at all of the time he and Mother lived in the village of Our People. And he never spoke the language of Our People except when he was alone in his room at night. Then the whispered words seemed to ease the loneliness of being shut away. He was grateful for Jerome and the ponies. He'd hate it at his grandfather's if they weren't with him.

Hampton slipped into Mother's room and tiptoed to her bed. Sometimes she didn't wake when he came to her but tonight her eyes were open and she smiled at him. He sat on the bed and she drew him down and kissed him. She smelled wrong, something like sweet flowers. Yet the odor of decay lay underneath the sweetness and frightened him.

"So solemn," she teased. Her voice was small and tired.

He couldn't smile, even for her.

"Hampton," she soothed, "don't be afraid."

He couldn't help it. Being brave wasn't so hard when you faced an enemy. A warrior faced even death with a strong heart. But to face his mother's death was not easy and he knew she was dying. What would happen when she was gone? How could he live in this house without her, with just Grandfather and the old man's black-skinned slaves? He had only Jerome, who worked with the horses.

Jerome was his friend, but he was a slave, too, and had to obey Grandfather.

"Let's go back to Our People," he whispered in Arapaho.

His mother's eyes widened. She looked very unhappy, then angry.

"Evil," she snapped bitterly. "Your father's an evil man, a cruel man. How could you ever think of returning to such a monster?"

Rainy blinked in confusion as she went on.

"He may be your father but he has no right to you. Never!" His mother's voice was fierce. "You're *my* son. A Hampton."

"Hampton Abbott. Grandfather told me."

She sighed and shook her head. "You're not an Abbott."

"Grandfather said I was."

"He's confused. He believes what he wishes." Again his mother sighed. "Perhaps it's for the best he accepts you as an Abbott. Otherwise . . ." She bit her lip, then took his hand and held it to her scarred cheek.

"I'm going to die. You know that," she told him after a moment. "You must make me a promise, Hampton. A vow." She eyed him. Then she pulled his head down and whispered a word in Arapaho. "Vengeance."

She let him go. "Not now," she cautioned, "you're a little boy, only six years old. But you must remember. As you grow up, when you become a man, you must carry out this wish of mine. I can't die in peace unless you promise me."

Hampton's grasp of the white man's language was improving daily, but he wasn't completely certain he had understood his mother. "Vengeance," he repeated in Arapaho, frowning.

"Your father!" his mother exploded. "Bad Hawk!"

Yes. Bad Hawk was his father, he knew that despite Grandfather's words.

"Look at me!" she cried. "See my face." She threw back the coverlet to expose thin legs marred by healed cuts. "This your father did to me." She thrust out her deformed arm. "This, too."

Rainy's ears roared with her words. He stiffened his legs to keep them from trembling.

"Find him," Mother rasped. "Find Bad Hawk and kill him. For me. For what he did to me."

Hampton stared at her.

"Promise me," she pressed. "Lay your hand on your heart and promise me that when you're a man you'll hunt your father like the animal he is. Hunt him and kill him."

The hair rose on Hampton's neck as he listened to the savage hatred in his mother's voice. Father had beat her often with sticks and with his fists. He was afraid of Father. But kill him? He closed his eyes for a moment. He wasn't Rainy any longer. He was Hampton. Hampton Abbott. Even his mother called him by that name now.

She wanted Father dead, like the man named Abbott was dead. And he must kill Father. He must promise her he would.

Hampton opened his eyes. He swallowed to try to moisten his dry throat. He put his hand over his heart and felt its rapid beating.

"I promise," he told her.

Chapter 2

1840

Pony Girl clutched her hands together as she watched the coal-black stallion rear, then buck violently. With the final lunge, the boy riding him flew over the horse's head and landed almost at her feet. Then the black stallion snorted. He tossed his head as he galloped away.

"First Cloud!" Pony Girl cried as she ran to kneel beside the thrown rider. "Are you hurt?"

The boy blinked up at her. Pony Girl saw he was dazed and bit her lip. In the four years she'd lived in the Kiowa camp, First Cloud had been her only friend. Despite being older than she was—he'd seen thirteen winters to her nine—he'd taught her how to watch and care for the horse herd and how to ride. How could she bear it if he were badly hurt?

The muscles tightened in First Cloud's face as he clenched his teeth. He pushed himself erect, saying nothing, beads of sweat on his forehead. Pony Girl could tell it was an effort for him to stay on his feet. But she pretended not to notice how he wavered. She did not want him to fall and be humiliated in front of her. To save him embarrassment, she turned away to look for the stallion.

Dream Runner. She'd named him that in secret, for

he wasn't hers to give a name to. He was the most beautiful horse she'd ever seen, not large, but fiery and faster than any other in the herd that belonged to First Cloud's father. First Cloud had no reason to feel shame. No brave had ever ridden the black horse more than a few paces without being thrown.

Dream Runner stopped and watched Pony Girl as she walked very slowly toward him. She began to chant the song that honored him, the words coming softly from her lips as she approached. She made no sudden gestures and sang all the while.

> Black
> Night black
> Coal black
> Swift as the wind
> He runs
> Dream Runner flies
> With Thunderbird
> Dream Runner
> Swift and black.

All thoughts of First Cloud faded from Pony Girl's mind. There was nothing on earth except her and the stallion. A power stretched between them, keeping him still, her almost unbreathing. Closer and closer she came. Her hand reached out to Dream Runner and he tossed his head and stamped but did not bolt. Reverently she touched the soft sheen of his coat, leaned close to blow her breath into his nostrils.

A sweet grassy odor mingled with his horse scent. A vision of herself racing across the plain beside Dream Runner flashed before her. She was no longer Pony Girl but a graceful sorrel mare, her spirit a horse spirit. Together they ran, free as the wind, over spring-green lands. The sorrel mare. The black stallion. . . .

*   *   *

First Cloud tensed as he watched Pony Girl clutch the black stallion's mane. He tried to shout to her but his breath was too weak to carry his voice. As she scrambled onto the horse, First Cloud tried to force his still-trembling legs into a run. Hadn't Pony Girl seen how he'd been thrown? The horse would kill her!

In his heart he knew he couldn't stop her. Pony Girl had a way of doing as she wished. He might not have been able to stop her even if he hadn't had the breath knocked from him by the fall.

He remembered how he'd taken pity on her soon after his father brought her to the Kiowa camp. She had been captured in a raid against the Arapaho and she wouldn't obey the women of his village. Sometimes they beat her. Time and again First Cloud had found her huddled among the horses. Finally he'd talked to his father, who'd agreed to let the Arapaho girl learn to be a horse herder. The name his father had given her was Pony Girl.

She had learned quickly and had an amazing way with horses, but even Pony Girl wouldn't be able to stay on the black stallion. No man could ride him, much less a little girl.

But Pony Girl was still on his back, her hair flying loose. The horse galloped toward First Cloud, seeming not to notice he carried a rider, seeming not to care. He raced like the wind and First Cloud's mouth gaped open in astonishment. How had Pony Girl worked such power?

"Ho, First Cloud!"

The hail made First Cloud whirl around. His cousin, Many Arrows, rode from the direction of the Kiowa lodges. First Cloud was ashamed he hadn't heard Many Arrows approach. What kind of a warrior would he become if he allowed a brave to ride up and surprise him?

"Send the girl to the women," Many Arrows called. "She's to be returned to her people before the sun falls in

the west." He wheeled his horse and loped back toward
the camp.

"No!"

The cry came from Pony Girl. She slowed the stallion
and slid from his back. Then she ran to First Cloud. He
put an arm around her and they both stared at the vast
array of lodges nestled along the distant river, many circles
of tepees etched against the cloudy sky.

Not only Kiowa camped here along the Arkansas, but
Comanche, Cheyenne, Arapaho, and even a few lodges of
Apache. For this was a peace council, the largest First
Cloud had ever seen.

"It is well we will no longer war against the Arapaho
and the Cheyenne," his father had told him. "They live
on one side of the Arkansas River, we on the other.
Besides, it is not wise to have such valiant warriors as
enemies. As for the Comanche, we've never had a bad
heart toward them."

"I want to stay with you," Pony Girl pleaded urgently, looking up at First Cloud. "Keep me here with you."

First Cloud turned her so she faced him. "Don't you
understand? Father gives you back to the Arapaho nation
as a sign that the Kiowa mean the peace to last forever.
You must go. It is for the benefit of all."

"I don't want to leave you." Pony Girl burst into tears.

First Cloud looked helplessly at the sobbing girl. She
had taken the place of the sister he never had. And yet she
wasn't really a sister. She did no women's work, only
tended the horses like a boy. It was true she was his
friend. But she was still a child, even if she could ride a
horse no brave had mastered.

He touched her wind-blown hair. "You must go to the
women so they can dress you in new clothes. It isn't
proper for the Kiowa to send you to your people with your
hair tangled and your skirt torn."

She covered her face with her hands and wailed even more pitifully.

"Think how happy your relatives will be to see you again," First Cloud comforted, but he wondered if her mother and father were still living. They could well have died in the raid that made Pony Girl a Kiowa captive.

Pony Girl dropped her hands and stared forlornly at First Cloud, her cheeks wet and dirt-smeared.

"I'll come to your village and visit you," he told her. "Kiowa and Arapaho are friends now."

"You won't. You'll forget," she pouted, wiping at her eyes.

He drew himself up. "I make a promise not to forget you. I vow to come and see you. You know I speak truly."

Pony Girl sat hunched on the dun horse she rode to the sprawling Kiowa camp on the south bank of the Arkansas River. Her heart was as sad and grey as the sky. Though her mount walked slowly, she made no attempt to urge him to hurry. She had to leave First Cloud. There was nothing she could do to make him let her stay.

She'd been with the Kiowa four winters, but it wasn't their camp she would miss. Sometimes the women hit her and made fun of her.

"This girl is foolish enough to think she'll grow into a man instead of a woman," they sniped scornfully. "She is worth nothing."

But it was having to leave First Cloud that made Pony Girl's heart heavy with misery. She had thought she never would be parted from him. She loved him for his kindness and she respected him. He was the best bowman among the younger men and was also the handsomest and the finest horseman. She sometimes felt she'd burst with joy because he'd chosen her as a friend.

Now again she sniffed, holding back tears. Instead of

crying, she could remember First Cloud's promise to visit her. First Cloud would keep his word. She knew it.

When she neared the Kiowa lodges, the woman called Seven Stones ran to her and yanked her off her horse.

"How dirty you are," Seven Stones chided, pulling her toward a tepee. "We'll have to wash your hair. Even then I'm not sure that you'll look right." Her fingers dug into Pony Girl's shoulder. "Why can't you ever behave in a proper manner?"

Pony Girl didn't bother to reply. She kept her silence as she was scrubbed and her hair oiled. Finally her tangles were worked out. Without protest, Pony Girl let the women arrange her hair so that it came forward in neat braids. Afterward, they dressed her in a white deerskin wrap-around skirt and loose shirt with delicate beading.

They hung shells around her neck, put new knee-length moccasins on her feet. Pony Girl was so loaded with finery that she rattled and clinked when she moved.

"See," Seven Stones commented, "she is quite pretty. Who would have thought it?"

The women led Pony Girl from the tepee and brought her to where First Cloud's father, Antelope, smoked around an outdoor fire with other Kiowa band chiefs and the great war chief Sitting Bear. There the women left her. Pony Girl stood waiting for the men to be ready. Instead of bowing submissively, as she knew she was expected to do, she kept her head up.

Sitting Bear's long, thin mustache had always fascinated her. She'd never seen a warrior with hair on his face before she came to live with the Kiowa. The men continued to smoke. They paid no attention to her. Pony Girl gazed across the river where dogs barked among the circles of tepees, belonging to the Cheyenne and the Arapaho. The Kiowa didn't put up their tepees in such fashion.

After a long time, Antelope motioned Pony Girl to come closer.

"This is the Arapaho girl," he explained to Sitting Bear. "She is not so valuable as a horse, but I thought to give her back."

Sitting Bear glanced at Pony Girl. "It is good," he agreed. "We will announce her return to the Arapaho before we give everyone the sticks for the horses."

Pony Girl knew how the giveaways worked. Each warrior carried a bundle of sticks and handed one or more to every person he intended to give a horse to. Pony Girl's eyes widened when she saw the great bundle of sticks next to Sitting Bear. It was true his herd was large, but there were more sticks in the bundle than she could count. Did Sitting Bear plan to give a horse to each person at the peace council?

Antelope rose and placed a hand on Pony Girl's shoulder. Her heart began to pound in her chest as he guided her toward the long rows of people who sat waiting by the river. The men were in front, the women behind, and then the children. Pony Girl had never seen so many people together in one place before. The faces blurred as she looked at them. For a moment she thought she might disgrace herself by vomiting.

Antelope stopped. He pushed Pony Girl in front of him.

"I give you this girl," he announced to the assembly. "I give her back to the Arapaho who are her relatives. I, myself, took her from a village beside Wolf Creek four winters ago. Who claims her?"

For long moments no one spoke, though a buzz of low murmurs ran through those seated.

Pony Girl swallowed. Maybe no one would claim her. Could she then stay with First Cloud? She wished for this and yet—did no Arapaho want her?

An old man rose to her left. Pony Girl stared at him. He was a stranger to her. But would she recognize any Arapaho? Her mother had died when she was a baby and she scarcely remembered her father. This man, though, was too old to be her father.

"I claim the girl," the man declared. "She is the daughter of my nephew. He is dead."

Antelope pushed Pony Girl toward the man.

Reluctantly, Pony Girl stepped in that direction. She felt the grey sky was pressing down on her, making it hard for her to breathe. As the many eyes watched her, she noticed now that the man she walked toward gazed at her from his right eye only. The left looked somewhere else, at something she couldn't see.

She was afraid. Her legs felt as if they wouldn't hold her. There was power in the air and it was threatening. But suddenly she was bathed in light. Ahead of her, beside her, behind her, the people sat in dimness. Light flowed to her only, touched her, warmed her. Her legs stopped trembling. She was no longer frightened.

Voices cried out in awe. Pony Girl heard but didn't move, standing instead in her circle of light, looking up, seeing the sun send its rays through the clouds as a gift to her alone.

"A sign!" a voice called out. It was the voice of the man who claimed her.

"I, One Claw, say that this girl's name shall be Stands Shining," he proclaimed. "I say she carries powerful medicine. Her medicine comes from Father Sun himself. Great good will come to Our People through Stands Shining."

Chapter 3

Crying Wind put her fist to her forehead, signing that she was angry. But Stands Shining had already seen anger in the narrowing of her great-grandmother's eyes. They had become mere slits in the ancient wrinkled face. Besides, though she was still more fluent in Kiowa, Stands Shining understood the language of Our People much better than she let anyone know.

"Living with those others has turned you sour," Crying Wind accused. "I tell you, I show you, what is proper for a woman of Our People, and you can't understand." Her black eyes glinted. "Or maybe it's that you won't understand. I don't believe a girl of my blood can be so stupid."

Stands Shining did not reply. Her four winters in the Kiowa camp had taught her the value of silence. She had been back with the Arapaho a full two moons now and found that a woman's work among the *Inunaina*, Our People, as the Arapaho called themselves, was much the same as a woman's work among the Kiowa.

Women were expected to carry water from the stream to the tepee—this being a girl's or young woman's task. Stands Shining liked filling the buffalo paunches or bladders with water. Doing that, she was outside and away from the tepee. What she hated was being forced to sit and bead moccasins or to sew skins together to make clothes.

Other girls laughed and chattered as they worked. Stands Shining didn't understand. How could they be so happy doing such uninteresting tasks? Every time Crying Wind's attention was diverted, she would throw down her sewing and run off to find the horse herd. This sun, Great-grandmother had caught her just outside the tepee.

"My heart was light with gladness when my grandson brought you to our tepee," Crying Wind lectured. "I am an old woman and believed that here at last was a girl to help me with my work. Here was a girl for me to teach the ways of a woman of Our People. Here was a girl who would grow up to marry a great warrior who would hunt for us so we should never go hungry."

Stands Shining shifted uneasily. She longed to speak, but Great-grandmother didn't understand how she felt any more than the Kiowa women had.

Crying Wind's face softened seeing the girl's discomfort. She patted her cheek. "You look like your father's mother," she sighed. "She was a handsome woman, one who quilled designs no other has yet matched. She was also an excellent wife. Your grandfather was much envied."

The old woman sighed once more. "They live in the spirit land now. Only One Claw is left. And now you. But I'm coming to believe your return is a doubtful gift."

As she spoke the last words, One Claw entered the tepee.

"What is this?" he asked. "Every time I come near you are scolding the girl. Is everything she does wrong?"

"She does nothing—that's what is wrong," Crying Wind replied. "If I take my eyes off her she runs to the herd. Better you should have brought me a Pawnee slave to help with the work than this girl who prefers horses to people."

One Claw looked at Stands Shining. She kept her

head up, forcing herself to return his gaze. He signed that she should leave the tepee, then followed her.

"We will walk to the horses," he told her.

Stands Shining had not conquered her fear of her great-uncle. He was the band's medicine man and medicine men were powerful and dangerous. Besides, his wandering left eye frightened her every time she looked at him. But she trotted along, hurrying to keep up with his rapid pace, and all the time wondering what he would do to her when they reached the herd.

Would he punish her?

She hadn't been beaten since coming to Our People's village. Crying Wind lashed her with words, not sticks, and One Claw had never hit her. A medicine man didn't have to hit anyone. He had strange powers more deadly than any blow.

Hair rose on the nape of her neck and she felt a sudden chill despite the heat of the sun. One Claw could change her into an animal. A weasel. A snake. She grimaced. Or, worse, he might make her a stone to be walked on forever. If she became a stone, never would she race the wind astride a galloping horse. Never again would she feel the strength of the animal below her, making her a part of him, or experience that marvelous sensation of power. . . .

Stands Shining clutched at her great-uncle's hand, stopping him. "Pity me," she begged. "Don't turn me into a stone."

He stared at her, frowning, and she watched him warily.

"What would you have me change you into?" he asked.

"A . . . a horse," she stammered. She remembered her vision and added, "A sorrel mare."

"You are very particular."

"I can't be any different than I am," she cried. "How can I?"

One Claw said nothing for a time. Then he motioned for her to continue on. They walked in silence until they came to the hill where One Claw's herd grazed.

"Is it true you like horses better than people?" he asked.

As she tried to find the right words, Stands Shining kept her eyes fixed on a frisky pinto colt. "Horses understand me," she answered at last. "People don't."

"I will try to understand you," One Claw promised.

Stands Shining turned to look at him, not believing her ears.

"Tell me why you upset your great-grandmother."

"I want to be with the horses and . . ." Stands Shining hesitated before blurting out, "I want to learn to hunt—like a brave. I do not want to do the work of women." She clapped her hand over her mouth. Never had she admitted this to anyone. Not even to First Cloud. Now to have told One Claw, of all people!

He gazed at her for a long time and inwardly she trembled. Had his left eye looked off to see how he would punish her? She jumped when suddenly he pointed to a tree forty paces away.

"Do you see that cottonwood with the double trunk?" he asked.

"Yes."

"If you stood at that tree and I stood here where I am and it was so dark no light showed, could you walk in a straight line from the tree to me?"

"I don't know." Stands Shining hesitated. "I think maybe I could."

"We will see."

One Claw led her to the tree. He unfastened a shiny green trader's cloth he wore about his neck and bound it around her head so it covered her eyes.

"When I tell you, you will start counting your fingers and your toes aloud and slowly," he ordered. "As you count, I will go back to stand exactly in the place where I was. I will turn you now so you face directly toward that spot. When you finish counting, walk to where I am."

Stands Shining counted her fingers and toes carefully. When she was done, she stood listening. Birds called in the cottonwoods. To her left a horse snorted. All was darkness behind the blindfold. She began to walk. It was very hard not to put out her hands to feel in front of her, but One Claw had not said she could and she didn't dare.

Fear struck at her. Had One Claw covered her eyes so she couldn't see what he was going to do to her? He might have changed into a bear—medicine men could do that. What was she walking toward?

Her steps faltered but she gritted her teeth and forced herself on. She thought she must be close for she'd walked forty paces. She stopped. Where was he?

"Uncover your eyes," One Claw's voice came from her right.

Stands Shining pulled off the cloth and found herself four paces away but even with him.

One Claw strode to her and took the cloth from her fingers. "We will try the Dark Walk again," he said. "If you learn to walk straight to me, I will know you can be taught. Then I will help you make a bow."

The next sun, after she'd failed again, Stands Shining spoke with a boy called Keeps Moving who sometimes walked with her when she went for water. He told her that all the Arapaho boys had to try the Dark Walk and that some never did walk a straight line to their teacher.

Stands Shining failed once more. But on the third sun, something in her head led her straight to One Claw.

One Claw fashioned the bow himself, using wood he'd received in a trade with the Osage. "Cottonwood isn't good enough," he told her. "Cherry is best for a hunter's bow, ash for a warrior's. But this orange wood from the country of the Osage is the best of all."

He measured the wood against her reach, making it long enough for her to grow into. Then he smoothed it on a rough-surfaced rock, held it over hot coals, and bent the heated wood into shape.

"You must make your own bowstring," he informed her.

Stands Shining took sinew she'd been using for making moccasins. Under One Claw's direction, she split it with the point of her knife. When she had a pile of sinew, she twisted the pieces into a cord by rolling them between her palm and her thigh. Each end had to be chewed until it was thoroughly moist. In that way, all the ends would hold together.

Once the sinew had dried overnight, One Claw showed Stands Shining how to fit the string to the bow and bind it.

"Now you must learn to make arrows," he told her.

He showed her how to look for straight, knot-free saplings and small branches. When she had collected several bundles of these, they were tied up to smoke above a fire for half a moon. While they were drying, Stands Shining fashioned her own wooden shaft straightener by making a hole in a piece of seasoned wood.

When the sticks were ready, she removed the bark and greased all the crooked places. She heated the sticks and cooled them while they were held in her shaft straightener. Before gluing on the feathers, she polished each stick until it gleamed. She marked each stick with her own special sign, a circle with a dot inside. All tribesmen marked their arrows so they could be identified.

"You will use blunt heads until you learn to aim properly," One Claw told her. "Sharp iron heads are for hunters."

Pulling the bowstring of the completed bow was harder

than Stands Shining had imagined it would be, and nocking her first arrow was even harder. One of the boys who watched her teased, "A squaw can never send an arrow straight." The other boys laughed in agreement.

"Trouble will come of a girl shooting arrows," Crying Wind predicted.

Avoiding the boys and Crying Wind, every sun Stands Shining splashed across the creek to practice. Patiently she retrieved each precious arrow and tried over and over again. One Claw had told her to paint a tiny circle on a small piece of buffalo hide, tie the hide to a cottonwood trunk and aim at the circle. When she could consistently hit the circle from farther and farther away, she told her great-uncle and he came to watch her.

"Yes," he consented, "you are ready for sharp iron arrowheads. I will trade with Little White Man for some and we will replace these blunt ones. Then I will take you into the hills to hunt deer."

The cool weather of Leaf Turning Moon changed the aspens in the foothills into glowing yellow flame trees. Pines rose green and tall around One Claw and Stands Shining as they climbed into deer country. Going on foot and leading their horses, One Claw showed Stands Shining a deer trail.

"Sometimes a hunger hides near such a trail and waits," he explained patiently. "These bushes make good cover."

Stands Shining plunged eagerly toward them and a loose rock clattered from under her foot.

"Noise tells the Utes we approach their land," One Claw warned. "And noise frightens our brother the deer so the hunter never sees him. Step carefully. Watch what is underfoot."

Stands Shining knew the Utes were enemies of both the Arapaho and the Kiowa.

"My arrows will shoot as straight at an enemy as at a deer," she vowed.

"We are not far enough into the mountains for the Utes to find us, little warrior woman," One Claw said, smiling. "I think you had better kill your first deer before you talk so big."

I could shoot a Ute warrior, Stands Shining told herself. I know I could.

She raised her head suddenly and listened to a sound she couldn't identify—a chomping, grating noise. Beside her, she felt One Claw stiffen.

"Be ready!" he hissed.

As she reached for an arrow, a gigantic animal burst from the bushes no more than ten paces away. It paused, swinging its massive head from side to side.

Grizzly!

Desperately, Stands Shining nocked the arrow, her eyes never leaving the huge brown beast. Just as she heard the snick of the arrow leaving One Claw's bow, the bear roared and plowed toward them. Stands Shining aimed for his eye. Then she shot her arrow and stood frozen as the grizzly tossed his head and came on, snarling. In an instant she smelled the dead meat stench of his breath.

When he was within an arm's length the bear faltered. He tried to rise onto his hind legs. Then he pawed at his face and tumbled sideways.

Stands Shining eyed the bear's bulk unbelievingly. It twitched and lay still. One Claw edged closer, prodding the bear's body with a long stick. The bear didn't move. Stands Shining saw two of One Claw's arrow shafts protruding from the grizzly's chest and knew they must have pierced the heart.

She gasped as One Claw reached down and yanked the bear's head around. Her own arrow was embedded in the bear's right eye!

One Claw grinned. "A brave hunter," he praised her.

Stands Shining swallowed. "I was afraid," she confessed. "I couldn't shoot after the first arrow."

"No matter," One Claw declared. "We will eat well tonight."

Stands Shining stared at him in horror. No one ever ate bear meat at a Kiowa camp. Bear was taboo.

One Claw knew what she was thinking. He reminded her sternly, "You are *Inunaina*. You are of Our People, not a Kiowa who's afraid to eat bear."

Stands Shining knew this was true. She was *Inunaina*, Our People, though some called them Arapaho and others called them Blue Cloud People. She would eat with One Claw that night.

The haunch of bear smelled appetizing as it roasted over the coals of One Claw's tiny fire. But when Stands Shining put her portion to her lips, her throat seemed to close. She forced herself to take a bite, to chew and swallow the morsel, but her stomach revolted and she spewed up the bear meat.

When she was able to stop vomiting, Stands Shining hung her head. She had disgraced herself.

"It is time to move our night camp away from this fire," One Claw said placing his hand gently on her shoulder. "A hunter never sleeps beside the fire where he cooks his meat. An enemy may locate the fire and wait to creep up and kill him while he sleeps."

That night Stands Shining woke to the sound of wolves fighting over the bear carcass. She slipped back to sleep, then woke again before dawn, starting up in alarm when she saw in the dim light that One Claw was nowhere nearby. After a moment, she heard his low chant and knew he was someplace close, greeting the sun. Before readying the horses for their return journey, she, too, rose and greeted Father Sun.

When he came into sight, Stands Shining saw that her

great-uncle wore the claws of the grizzly strung on a thong about his neck. He approached her, his hands cupped.

"Your arrow sped true," he told her proudly. Then he opend his hands and put a thong over her head.

She looked down and saw a single claw hanging from it. As she reached up to touch the claw where it lay on her chest, her heart swelled with pride. One Claw was giving her credit for helping to kill the grizzly, though they both knew it was his two arrows in the heart that had dropped the bear.

"I am hungry," Stands Shining announced, trying to keep her voice steady. "I will eat some of the bear meat before we leave." She knew that this time she would keep it down.

As the moons came and went and one winter passed and another and another, Stands Shining became a proficient, skilled hunter, supplying Crying Wind's tepee with all the food that was needed. Because of her, One Claw didn't have to hunt. He could devote himself to his medicine. And always Stands Shining gave meat freely to any in the village who needed it.

"We eat well, I grant you," Crying Wind grumbled. "But it is not seemly for a girl to hunt. You have seen twelve winters," the old woman told Stands Shining. "Soon your moon times will begin—you are almost a woman. Your blood will taint your arrows. Then how will you hunt?"

Stands Shining scarcely heard her great-grandmother. She was thinking about the warriors gathering for a raid on the Pawnee. Not only warriors from her band but from all the Arapaho who lived in the villages in the foothills near the Arkansas. By the time the next moon began—Black Cherry Moon—they would be riding toward Pawnee country.

The last time warriors had ridden against an enemy, Stands Shining had asked to go along, and the warriors had laughed at her. This time she'd go without asking. After all, every boy her age in the village had already gone on at least one raid, if only to carry water.

Stands Shining knew she would willingly carry water for the warriors, help at any task, if only they'd take her with them. But there were ceremonies and purifications for boys who wished to go. Stands Shining sighed. She knew better than to try to be included in those male rituals. Still, she wouldn't give up her plans to join this war party against the Pawnee.

She hadn't told anyone what she meant to do, not even One Claw. Certainly she could never tell Great-grandmother. If only Crying Wind could accept her as she was. She'd become fond of the old woman and hated to cause her distress.

"Shall I fetch water?" she asked, feeling Crying Wind's eyes seem to pierce her, to be divining her thoughts.

"I could use some," Crying Wind answered. "But I won't ask what in your heart made you offer to fetch it—some boy, no doubt."

Stands Shining walked to the creek, the paunch on a carrying stick on her shoulder. On her way, she passed two boys who were slightly older than she was. She really hadn't planned to meet a boy, but had to admit that her heart fluttered at the sight of the taller one, Keeps Moving. He reminded her of First Cloud, whom she'd never forgotten, but had almost given up hope of ever seeing again.

"I ride with the warriors," Keeps Moving told her proudly.

Stands Shining knew Keeps Moving liked her. He'd never jeered at her as the other boys had. He was the son of a respected war leader and had already ridden on two raids. During the last, he had even counted coup by touching a downed enemy with his lance.

Stands Shining was glad for Keeps Moving. But when she tried to congratulate him on riding with the warriors, the words stuck in her throat. Keeps Moving deserved to go. She didn't begrudge him his place in the war party. She merely wanted room to be found for her, too.

"May good medicine ride with you," she managed to say.

Keeps Moving smiled, gazing deeply into her eyes. At once something within her warmed. Yes, she liked this Indian boy very much.

That night Stands Shining made up her mind. She would trail the warriors, staying out of sight when there was cover and riding at night if she had to. When they were deep in Pawnee country, she would appear and they would have to let her join them. No Arapaho warrior would force one of Our People to ride alone in the land of the enemy.

She left the village before dawn with a parfleche, a buffalo-skin carrier. It was filled with provisions. She located the horse her great-uncle had given her when they came home from the grizzly hunt, the feisty pinto colt she'd noticed her first summer in the village. He'd grown into a small but sturdy stallion, not as fast as some but long-winded and dependable. She'd named him True Arrow.

Though True Arrow was not a fiery war steed, Stands Shining knew he'd take her wherever she wanted to go and bring her back. His coat shone from her brushing. And he never suffered with sore feet, for she spent hours making him buffalo-hide horseshoes. He was hers and she loved him.

It was three sleeps to Pawnee country. The warriors traveled east, away from the foothills of the mountains. When they weren't beside a stream, only thistles grew— buffalo grass, too, was already yellowing in the hot summer sun. Cliffs rose with nothing growing on their bluffs.

Stands Shining found it difficult to avoid being seen by the Wolves, the Arapaho scouts escorting the war party. She lagged far behind during the second sun, planning to catch up at night. Since Black Cherry Moon had barely begun, there was only starlight to travel by. But she felt confident.

She set True Arrow to a steady pace as soon as it was dark. As she rode, she tested the night air for scents, listening for any sound. A wolf howled and she checked the horse, scanning the horizon—the Arapaho Wolves used the same call to send messages.

Another wolf answered. She caught sight of him. The wolf was real, and stood on a hill to her left where his body blotted out the stars. She urged True Arrow on. While she didn't fear wolves, she didn't like riding alone at night. Evil spirits roamed in the dark. She was concerned that her grizzly claw necklace wouldn't be charm enough to ward them off.

After a time she stopped to check the ground for sign. As she slid from True Arrow's back, he whuffled. Stands Shining tensed, and before she could vault back up again, a dark form rushed at her.

She stifled a scream. Belatedly she reached for an arrow as a strong grip pinioned her arms to her sides. There was no chance to touch the arrow shaft.

And the hold on her flesh felt like the skeleton hands of an evil spirit.

Chapter 4

Stands Shining choked out words through a fear-tightened throat. "*Maheo*, Man Above, take pity on me."

Whatever held her shifted its grip and shook her. A man's voice spoke in the language of Our People.

"Why do you follow us, foolish one? Don't you know I might have sent an arrow into you instead of capturing you?"

The man sounded as if he were one of Our People, but it was well known that spirits could take any form. Stands Shining moistened her lips.

"Boy," the man scolded, his hands digging into her arms, "if you wanted to join the war party, you know you should have asked beforehand."

Hope warmed Stands Shining. It must be one of the Wolves who held her, not a spirit of the night. Still, she didn't relax. "You would not have taken me," she answered cautiously.

The man yanked her closer to peer into her face. Despite the darkness, she recognized Winter Bull, one of the older warriors. He thrust her back and let her go.

"One Claw's girl," he smirked in disgust.

Winter Bull brought her to the night camp of the warriors. Fifteen were in the party and they crouched in a circle, excluding Stands Shining, discussing what should be done with her.

"It's too late to send her back alone," the war leader, Heavy Pine, advised. He, too, was one of the older warriors. In addition, he was chief of the band.

"A girl on a war party makes bad medicine," Winter Bull grumbled.

There were grunts of assent, complaints because the Wolves hadn't spotted Stands Shining, also caustic comments about a girl who didn't know her place. No one offered a solution.

Finally, Keeps Moving broke into the silence. "I would speak," he offered tentatively. "Perhaps the girl could hold the horses in my place. She is good with them."

Stands Shining knew that many times the warriors left their horses some distance away before creeping into an enemy village on foot. Part of the reason for any raid was to acquire more mounts. So each warrior tried to bring back as many enemy horses as possible. War steeds tethered beside their owners' tepees were considered more valuable than those animals running loose with the herd.

"If Stands Shining watched our horses," Keep Moving continued, "I would be free to help go after the Pawnee horse herd."

Heavy Pine muttered after a time, "It is good." No one disagreed.

Dawn was considered the best time for an attack. But the next afternoon, the Wolves came back to report that many of the Pawnee braves were gone from the village, leaving it poorly protected.

"We will go in now," Heavy Pine decided. He led the party into a small depression between two hills.

Stands Shining's heart raced as she watched the warriors paint for battle. Keeps Moving rode to the south, circling to get below where the Wolves had told him the

Pawnee herd grazed. The other warriors set off on foot, going east, staying in the cover of a line of cottonwoods along a sluggish stream.

Stands Shining longed to be following the warriors into the village. But she was to watch the Arapaho horses to keep them from straying, and she remained on True Arrow, determined to do her best, even though she was disappointed. Keeps Moving's task, she knew, was hardly more exciting than hers, but there was always the chance he might be spotted by a Pawnee and have to fight.

Because many of the war horses were still tethered in the village, the Wolves believed the missing enemy braves were hunting. They reasoned that if the men had gone out as a war party, their best horses would be gone, too. Had the Wolves circled wide enough to test their theory? Had they spotted sign that told them which way the men had gone? Stands Shining wondered. And how long ago had the Pawnee braves left? Heavy Pine hadn't asked this question.

For a moment Stands Shining put aside her criticism. Who was she to question? After all, the Wolves hadn't found her until it was too late to send her back to the Arapaho camp.

On the other hand, she had little respect for Winter Bull. He was a braggart, most likely getting too old to scout quickly and thoroughly. He had gone with the warriors once Keeps Moving offered to run off the Pawnee horses. The other Wolf, Bright Dawn, was a man who always kept to himself. She hardly knew him at all.

Heavy Pine's roan stallion made a break for the stream on the other side of one of the hills and Stands Shining rode after him. After herding him back, she quieted the other horses.

Small clouds scudded before a wind from the north, lending a hint of coolness to the day. Stands Shining listened to hear what she could from the direction of the village but the hills blocked sound as well as sight.

The grass had already been cropped by the Pawnee herd, so the horses remained restless. Luckily, True Arrow seemed to know in advance just what horse would try to bolt. Without any sign from Stands Shining, he moved to head off the stragglers. Stands Shining patted his neck each time and leaned to murmur words of praise in his ear. Then she heard faint yells from the village. Her breath quickened at the hint of fighting.

True Arrow pricked his ears and swished his tail. At first, Stands Shining thought, he, too, was excited by the yells. Then she noted how he turned his head toward the west, away from the village.

Her skin prickled and she tried to reassure herself. Perhaps True Arrow was hearing Keeps Moving heading west with the Pawnee herd. But her uneasiness persisted. One Claw's words came into her mind.

"Heed not only what you see and hear but what you feel."

Stands Shining slid off the pinto's back. Trusting that True Arrow would hold the others, she climbed the hill to the west, crouching near the top so she wouldn't be seen. Stretching onto her stomach, she snaked up to peer over.

Four men on horseback rode toward her. They followed the trail left by the Arapaho war party.

Pawnees!

Stands Shining slid back down the rise, vaulted onto True Arrow and prodded the other horses into motion with the end of her bow. They'd be captured by the enemy if she didn't get them away. She drove the horses from the hollow between the hills toward the Pawnee village, hearing the bloodcurdling shouts of the enemy as they spotted her.

She knew she must get the horses to the Arapaho

warriors. If they hadn't all found mounts they stood little chance of survival.

Stands Shining pounded into the village, the Arapaho horses scattering in front of her, the Pawnee warriors close on her heels. She caught a glimpse of Heavy Pine on a dun horse and saw Winter Bull cutting the tether of a rearing white stallion.

A Pawnee riding after her shrieked in rage, then abruptly changed course to head for Winter Bull. The Arapaho jumped behind the stallion and reached for an arrow. The horse kicked and a hoof caught him in the head. Winter Bull fell and the Pawnee loosed an arrow that grazed his shoulder. The dazed Arapaho struggled to his feet. He was helpless.

Stands Shining wheeled True Arrow and raced toward the Pawnee, shrieking a challenge. Quick as thought, the Pawnee whirled and let fly his arrow.

Stands Shining's little pinto stumbled beneath her. He quivered and dropped to his knees, the shaft of the arrow protruding from his neck.

"No!" she cried.

Winter Bull scrambled behind a tepee, the mounted Pawnee charging after him. Stands Shining leaped from the stricken True Arrow and raced to the snorting white stallion. She grasped his head and brought it down to her despite his effort to break free.

"You must carry me," she crooned. "Carry me, brave horse, strong-hearted horse." She blew into his nostrils, then let go of his head.

In a flash she was astride him, leaning to murmur in his ear. A moment later she was riding him after the Pawnee who'd shot True Arrow. The stallion was skittish, but he obeyed her.

When howling Pawnee warriors galloped into the village, Stands Shining knew the main party had arrived. She heard the screams of women and children, Arapaho war cries. The smell of fresh blood mingled with the dust raised by the horses' hooves. Dogs snarled and barked as they dodged between the tepees.

"Ho!" Stands Shining shouted, spotting the Pawnee warrior she sought. "Horse killer! My arrow seeks you, Pawnee."

The brave turned and saw her. In one motion he wheeled his horse and slid to the far side of his mount. There he hung on by one foot. Stands Shining whirled her horse around at almost the same moment, realizing he intended to shoot at her from under his horse's neck. Somehow she was certain the white stallion was his. She counted on his not wounding the magnificent war horse and figured she'd be safe enough if she hung over the far side of her mount.

But she didn't want safety. She wanted the Pawnee dead. She wanted to dance with his scalp. A haze of red dimmed her vision, the blood of rage.

Crouching low on the horse's neck, she drove straight toward the warrior, bow in hand. A piercing whistle cut through the battle noise. Beneath her the white stallion quivered. Instantly she understood the Pawnee's plan. He'd taught his horse to obey whistled commands. She clutched at the mane as the stallion reared. She clung to the horse's back, desperately whistling herself, as close to his ears as she could get, hoping to confuse the signals.

"Strong Heart, Strong Heart, you are mine," she chanted as she fought for control. "Mine, Strong Heart. Mine."

The Pawnee bored in from her right, arrow nocked. But the white stallion shied away, his eyes rolling, his nostrils flaring. As the Pawnee leaned and readied to let his arrow fly, the stallion reared again and danced on his hind legs. When he came down his hooves clipped the Pawnee's shoulder and knocked him from his mount.

Stands Shining whooped with delight and maneuvered

the stallion closer. But suddenly, her urge for blood fading, she reached down to touch the stunned Pawnee with her bow tip.

"Coup!" she cried. "I count first coup!"

"Ho!"

Stands Shining whirled to see Heavy Pine pounding toward her.

"Ride!" he shouted, then gestured west with his bow. Stands Shining kicked the white stallion into a gallop and followed the Arapaho war leader.

The raid was over.

Much later, at the rest camp, Heavy Pine handed his paints to Stands Shining. "It is not right that one who counts first coup on a Pawnee chief should ride his white war horse with her face unpainted."

As Stands Shining traced circles on her cheeks with red, her spirit was as bright as the paint that she wore. No one ever again could deny her right to ride with the warriors.

Her thoughts turned to True Arrow and she bowed her head to hide the tears. The white horse she'd captured was handsome, but she had loved her pinto pony.

After her triumphant return to the Arapaho village, it was some time before Stands Shining noticed that Keeps Moving no longer lingered to wait for her by the stream. Soon she saw he smiled at Yellow Leaf, a girl not much older than she.

"What would you expect?" Crying Wind asked. "You own the best horse in the camp. How could any brave hope to impress you by bringing you a pony? Did Keeps Moving count coup on the raid? No. But you, a girl, did. Do you expect him to court you after that?"

Stands Shining told herself she didn't care, that she was too young to think of marrying. Let Yellow Leaf have Keeps Moving, she told herself. But her heart ached a little every time she saw them together.

* * *

On the next raid, Stands Shining spoke up as the warriors sat in a circle at the night camp before the attack. She offered to lead half the men down the bluff to the south of the Pawnee village during darkness so that when the Arapaho attacked at dawn, they'd come in from two sides of the village, trapping the Pawnee warriors.

"My medicine from Father Sun will keep us safe," she assured everyone.

After some argument, her suggestion carried—partly because Heavy Pine supported the idea and his opinion was respected.

Stands Shining felt no fear. She was, she believed, as invincible as the wind when at dawn she urged the white horse she'd named Strong Heart toward the Pawnee lodges. Behind her pounded Arapaho warriors.

"Hi, hi yah!" she cried in challenge as they raced into the village.

Riding home, the war party counted two Arapaho slightly wounded. None were lost. Ahead of them they rode half the Pawnee horse herd.

By the time Stands Shining had seen sixteen winters, the Arapaho warriors were seeking her suggestions, following her advice.

Heavy Pine no longer led raids, though he was still band chief. And he saw that Stands Shining was taken into the Kit Foxes, the Age Society for all Arapaho boys who'd reached seventeen winters.

"True, she is a woman," he admitted, "but she is also a warrior. With her along, our war parties conquer every enemy."

Woman Who Rides The Ghost Horse, the Cheyenne allies called her. They came to ask her to ride with them on their raids against the white wagons that had begun to arrive as thick as summer flies on the hunting plains of Arapaho and Cheyenne country.

"Their pale faces frighten the buffalo," Sees Crow Flying, a Cheyenne war chief, told Stands Shining. "Their mules and oxen eat the grass so that our ponies go hungry. Even the pronghorns run from the sound of the wagons. What would we do for meat if we didn't rid our land of these pests?"

Heavy Pine had warned it was best to avoid conflict with the whites, but Stands Shining, like most of the young warriors, found herself angered by the intruding wagons.

"Who will ride with me when we join the Cheyenne to make war on the whites?" she asked in her village. She had just gone through the proper ritual and given presents of tobacco to each tepee that housed a warrior.

Keeps Moving was the first to volunteer. He'd become a Wolf and was an excellent scout. Since he and Yellow Leaf had married, he seemed to find it easier to be Stands Shining's friend again.

"I follow no woman," Winter Bull muttered. He had never forgiven Stands Shining for saving his life on her first raid. And though she was happy not to have him along, his words made her flush in annoyance.

She was a warrior first and foremost. Many counted her as one of the bravest. What difference did it make that she was also a woman?

She sat proudly on Strong Heart as she led twenty-five Arapaho warriors over the hills to the Cheyenne camp. This was her first time as war leader.

One Claw rode with the party, but not as a warrior. Medicine men fought not with arrows but with secret powers. He urged his horse to the front.

"Your medicine grows stronger with each moon," he told Stands Shining. "Arapaho and Cheyenne alike respect the way you ride and shoot. The Pawnees fear you. Now you ride against the whites.''

Stands Shining glanced at him warmly. One Claw had supported her all along, and she loved him as she would have loved a father.

''Do you disapprove?'' she asked.

''I had a dream,'' he admitted. ''I saw you afoot, alone and weeping in the darkness. In my dream, Father Sun, from where your strength comes, was shut away from you.''

Stands Shining slowed her pace. ''Do you say we must turn back?'' Her tone was edged with regret.

''No. The dream concerned you but not this war party. Still, I came along to do what I could to help.''

Stands Shining smiled at him. ''I'm glad you're with me,'' she said, telling herself she wouldn't think of the dream. But it shadowed her heart so that she rode in silence.

''I was once a war chief,'' One Claw said after a time. ''Many are the enemy scalps I've taken.''

Stands Shining turned to One Claw in surprise. Her great-uncle rarely talked of himself.

''Did you think I was born a medicine man?'' he asked.

''I wasn't sure. But I suppose it takes many winters to acquire your knowledge and power,'' she told him.

''No. It takes a vision striking into your heart, destroying your life. Then you know what you must do, what you must be.''

Stands Shining didn't know what to say.

''If you live long enough, this will happen to you,'' he went on. ''I foresee it.''

''Is this what your dream of me means?''

''The dream was of darkness. That is all I know.''

One Claw found all signs favorable for attacking the wagons they sighted late the next sun. The whites driving the oxen and mules were circling into their night camp.

Grey Beard, the Cheyenne medicine man, agreed with One Claw, but Stands Shining argued against an immediate attack. Reluctantly, all listened.

That evening, Stands Shining lay on her stomach and peered over the top of a bluff. Ten wagons stood in a circle below her. Livestock was guarded in the center of the circle. The men would be able to use the wagons for cover and that was why she wanted to wait. Only rarely had she come up against rifles in warfare, but she knew that white men had many of them. She'd seen white traders shoot their guns, heard the roar, found the bullet of metal inside the animal that was killed. Always, she had watched closely to note how this was done and longed to have a rifle of her own.

Sees Crow Flying had a rifle, but lacked the bullets that it needed. It was useless. For the present, Stands Shining decided she would depend on her bow and arrows.

In the morning, the white men would hitch the oxen and mules to the wagons and form a single line to head west. The extra horses and the cows would be herded alongside. Stands Shining knew that. That's why she thought early morning was the time to attack. There would be confusion during the hitching. The wagons would no longer be in a protective circle. If the warriors could get close enough before the wagons were strung out, arrows would be as good as rifle bullets. A warrior could shoot many of them in the time it took to reload a rifle to shoot again.

In the night camp circle of warriors, Stands Shining spoke boldly of her attack plans. "If you listen, each warrior will have his chance to show bravery. It is like a buffalo hunt where, if one man rides too soon, the herd scatters and everyone loses because one man couldn't wait. If we fall upon the white man's camp together with no warning given until our arrows fly, all will share in the glory of battle."

Before dawn, Stands Shining concealed her warriors

in the cottonwoods below the wagon circle. As the sun reddened the eastern sky, the whites began to break camp. Stands Shining waited until some wagons were hitched to mules and the circle was broken. Then she motioned for the warriors to fall on the wagons.

The surprise attack confused the whites. Though their rifles roared, only four warriors fell wounded before they were completely overcome.

Stands Shining watched while the braves argued over the surviving women and children. How strange these palefaced women looked with their light hair and eyes. Why would any warrior want one?

One Claw rode among the warriors. "Taking a white woman as wife is bad medicine," he warned. "If you want to lie with one, have her here, then leave her. Our women don't like the palefaced ones. Having them in camp makes trouble."

Sees Crow Flying grunted loudly in agreement. "No white woman comes with the Cheyenne," he ordered. "We are not Comanches to have our warriors rape women until they die, but that doesn't mean one can't warm a warrior's robe for the night. Afterward, however, all will be left behind. Hear what I say."

In the end, no women and only three children were taken by the departing warriors. The Cheyenne chose a black-haired boy of about nine and a girl with hair the color of grass in late summer. She looked almost ready for her moon times and Stands Shining knew some warrior had his eye on her for a wife despite the words of Sees Crow Flying. The Arapaho took a boy baby whose mother had been killed.

"He will make my wife's heart glad," Spotted Dog declared.

All of the Arapaho village praised Stands Shining's leadership. But as she walked toward Crying Wind's tepee after the dog feast and the dance, she thought of the other warriors going home to their wives.

She had heard the pleasure grunts of the braves lying with the white women after the battle and had hurried away until she could no longer see or hear them. She had never been with a man. Restlessly, she had wondered what it would be like to join together with one in love.

The warriors praised her but the unmarried braves made no attempt to court her. Was she so ugly no one would ever want her? She sighed heavily.

Crying Wind looked up from her sleeping robe as Stands Shining came inside the tepee. She studied her great-granddaughter's face. "You come from a victory feast unhappy?" she asked.

"I should have my own lodge," Stands Shining replied.

"With a husband to join you, you mean," Crying Wind added as she sat up. "I've warned you from the time you held your first bow and now it is too late. No brave will have you for a wife. Never mind that you're as pretty as any woman in the village. What man wants a wife who won't cook for him or make his moccasins? Worse, who would want a wife who outrides and outfights him, who is a braver warrior than he can ever hope to be?"

Stands Shining did not answer, but when she lay against her willow backrest, her heart ached with the truth of her great-grandmother's words.

No brave wanted a warrior for a wife.

Chapter 5

"Ten to one on the bay with the left hind stocking," the man with the ginger whiskers called. He smoothed his yellow satin vest. "Ten to one, gentlemen."

Nineteen-year-old Hampton Abbott glanced at his grandfather, but either the judge hadn't heard—he was getting quite deaf—or he didn't care to comment on the long odds against his horse. Hampton grinned. He would be riding that bay in less than an hour, riding him and winning.

He and the judge stood near the stables at Riverview Race Track. It was a warm June afternoon. The wooden stands, painted white and gold, were filled. Those observers without seats strolled about appraising the horses or, in the case of the ladies, showing off their new summer clothes. A sultry breeze blew off the Mississippi.

Hampton eyed a honey-blonde young woman. The scooped neck of her green plaid gown was low enough to show the tops of her breasts. The tilt of the woman's chin indicated she was well aware of her attractiveness. But Hampton decided she couldn't hold a candle to Roseann Young. He doubted that any woman could, for that matter.

Hampton had caught a glimpse of Roseann earlier, escorted by her father, Colonel Young. She'd been wearing a pale rose muslin that set off her strawberry blonde curls and her blue eyes. At the same time, it had showed off her curves to advantage. Colonel Young had nodded to Hampton. Roseann had slanted her eyes his way and then pretended not to see him.

Sometimes her coquettish ways drove him wild with desire and anger. But he knew she liked him, that he intrigued her. Hadn't she let him kiss her last month? He drew in a deep breath remembering that embrace. Then he sighed.

"Bookmakers never have the odds right when a horse hasn't run for a year," Judge Hampton remarked. "Don't you fret about it." The judge had heard, after all. "I know we're going to win," he went on. "Hyacinth is the finest horse I've ever owned. That Chambers nag is no match for him. Anyway, I expect you'll enjoy beating the pants off Steven." The judge paused, waiting for his grandson's reaction.

Hampton smiled sardonically. It was no secret how he felt about Chambers. They'd been enemies from the moment they'd met in boarding school at age ten. Now Steve would be riding High Stepper, a fine horse despite what his grandfather said. Hyacinth had been injured last season but had completely recovered. Hampton felt a sudden surge of power. He would beat Chambers. He *knew* it.

His grandfather's voice pulled him from his thoughts. "Now listen, boy," the judge said. "I won't have you two brawling in public, no matter what the provocation."

"I don't think Chambers and I will meet before we're mounted," Hampton assured him. "I plan to concentrate on winning the race."

Grandfather was always cautioning him about his temper. He'd been in trouble in school for fighting, but what else could he do when some lout called him a dirty nigger?

It was because of his dark skin, he knew that. Grandfather might insist again and again he was the son of Lester Abbott, but he knew that couldn't be true. He'd never been able to forget that his father was an Indian named Bad Hawk. Mother had said so before she died. That made him half-Indian. But he never mentioned this knowledge to Grandfather. The mere mention of Indians infuriated the old man.

What was between Hampton and Steve Chambers wasn't as simple as a matter of name-calling. Chambers had done his damnedest to make life miserable for Hampton all through school. He'd even lied to get him into trouble.

A flame of hatred glowed between them that could never be quenched, and the fact that Roseann seemed to smile at Chambers as often as she did at Hampton did nothing to help. To promise Grandfather he'd hold his temper where Chambers was concerned was clearly impossible.

"We'll win, boy, no doubt about it." The judge patted Hampton's arm, then looked past him to smile and nod at a portly man with white hair.

Hampton recognized Thomas Hart Benton, senator from Missouri to the United States Congress. Senator Benton tipped his hat to the judge.

"How are you, Doug?" Benton asked as he passed. Hampton got a nod.

"Old Tom's as good as got you that appointment to West Point," the judge chuckled. "Makes me proud to think of you becoming an officer in the U.S. Army. Yes, boy, it does. Your daddy would have wanted it, too, if those red devils hadn't cut his life short."

Hampton was well aware it was Senator Benton's life-long friendship with Judge Hampton that had prompted the West Point recommendation. He also knew that Chambers was Benton's second choice.

"I'd better check on Hyacinth," he said to his grandfather.

"Oh, he's ready, boy, he's ready. But you go ahead."

The stallion stomped nervously as Hampton entered

his stall. There was no sign of Jerome. Hampton frowned. It was unlike Jerome to leave Hyacinth alone. The black man had been his friend ever since he first came to St. Louis. He loved horses as much as Hampton did. Where was he?

"Jerome!" he shouted.

Hyacinth whuffled, shifting position. He seemed upset. Hampton began to run his hands over the horse. Last, he touched the left rear leg with the stocking, and the horse danced sideways.

"Now easy, now easy," Hampton crooned over and over.

After a moment the stallion let him handle the leg. Just under the fetlock, Hampton's fingers touched metal. He drew in a breath. Wire. Someone had wound a piece of thin wire around the bay's leg so tightly it was cutting into the flesh.

As quickly as he could, Hampton unwound the wire. Hyacinth blew softly. How long had the wire been on the horse's leg? he wondered. He had only left the horse half an hour before and Jerome had been with him then.

Where the hell was Jerome? He was devoted to the stallion. He would never deliberately injure any horse, much less Hyacinth.

Hampton unfastened the stall door and led the stallion out, trying to see how badly the leg was injured. Just then, Jerome came panting around the corner of the stable.

"Massa Hamp," he gasped, "here you be."

Keep your temper, Hampton cautioned himself, but he demanded, "Why did you leave Hyacinth?"

"Why, a man come, told me the judge be wanting me, say I got to come right now, never mind the horse."

"What man?"

"He wear a shiny yellow vest, got whiskers looks like bad honey. Don't rightly know his name. He say I got to hurry."

The bookmaker, Hampton thought.

"Judge be powerful mad. He yell at me to get back here quick." Jerome shook his head. "That man be fooling me, looks like."

"Someone tried to hurt Hyacinth," Hampton explained, his voice breaking. He showed Jerome the leg with the wire cut, then had the black man mount the stallion and walk him in a circle. The horse didn't seem to favor the leg.

"Reckon he gonna race," Jerome announced. "Gonna win, too," he added happily.

When Hampton walked the bay to the starting lineup, he was certain he'd untwisted the wire before real damage had been done. Hyacinth pranced with his usual pre-race eagerness. Chambers was atop his chestnut horse. Hampton shot him a measuring glance. Could Chambers have had anything to do with the wire? After the race, he'd find that bookmaker and shake the truth out of him.

Right now he had to forget about everything but winning. As the flag went up, Hyacinth broke cleanly and fast, as usual, and took an immediate lead. Except for the Wilkins black and High Stepper, the other entries gradually dropped behind after the first turn. On the back stretch, the black pulled even on the outside. Hampton felt Hyacinth ready himself to speed ahead.

High Stepper came up on the inside. From the corner of his eye, Hampton saw Chambers' right hand dart out and up. Instantly, Hyacinth stumbled, fought to recover, but couldn't. Not being able to stop himself, he collided with the black and both horses fell, Hyacinth's scream of pain mingling with the cries of the man tossed from the other horse.

Hampton had been thrown free. He leaped to his feet and the black was up almost as quickly. Hyacinth struggled to rise. At that moment, Hampton noticed the splintered bone in the animal's foreleg and groaned in horror. Hyacinth would never get up again.

Hampton whirled to look at the track behind him. A short link of chain lay in the dirt like a coiled snake.

Chambers!

The other horses pounded past, veering clear. "My arm, my arm," the black's rider moaned, writhing on the ground.

Hampton stepped around him and caught the reins of the black horse. He vaulted into the saddle and quirted the animal.

"Faster, damn it, faster!" he yelled as the black raced around the far turn.

Ahead he saw Chambers cross the finish line on High Stepper and turn the chestnut to return to the winner's circle. Hampton pounded on, the high-pitched cries from the grandstand in his ears. When he came even with Chambers, he slowed and wheeled the black so recklessly that the horse kept his feet but slid in the turn.

Side by side with Chambers, Hampton flung himself from the black, glimpsing Chambers' startled face as they both plunged to the ground. Hampton shouted but had no sense of the words he yelled. As he landed on top of Chambers everything seemed etched in red. Chambers twisted to throw him off, but Hampton gripped his neck with both hands, fighting to keep him down, thirsting to kill him.

He felt hands on him soon, pulling him, yanking him up and away from Chambers. He writhed and turned, struggling to break free, but there were too many stopping him. They pried his hands from Chambers' neck. Men's voices shouted, their words muddled in the confusion. Someone said his name over and over. It was his grandfather.

"Is he dead?" a man asked as Hampton finally stopped fighting.

Chambers lay still, his face dusky. His eyes opened, then closed again. Hampton gritted his teeth. The bastard was alive. Why couldn't he have killed him? Hampton thought, berating himself. Then he looked up and caught the cold glance of Senator Benton.

The day of the funeral was hot and humid. Though the cemetery was thick with mourners, no one joined Hampton on the far side of the open grave.

He was an outcast and the terrible grief he felt ran deep. He'd killed his grandfather just as surely as if his hands had closed on the judge's neck.

No doubt Chambers was attending the funeral with his parents. Everyone in St. Louis, it seemed, had turned out for it. Or Maybe Steve was home packing to leave for West Point.

Hampton knew that's what had killed the old man, that after the fight at the racetrack, Senator Benton had withdrawn his name. Everyone in the stands had seen the two horses collide. Then they had seen the attack on Chambers.

No one believed the story about Chambers throwing a chain at Hyacinth's legs. The rider of Wilkins' black had seen nothing and the chain was never found. Yes, people were saddened that Hyacinth had to be destroyed, but it didn't stop them from unleashing their anger.

Hampton stared down at the dark grain of the walnut lid on his grandfather's coffin. The minister's words droned in the air like bluebottle flies.

As the first clump of dirt hit the coffin, Reverend Franklin didn't look at Hampton. The minister had avoided him as much as possible, Hampton noticed. Yet being set apart didn't bother him terribly. He'd never felt he quite belonged in the Hampton house, in St. Louis, in his private schools. He'd never felt at home. Always he'd sensed that he was too different to be acceptable.

Only Grandfather had accepted him, and now he was dead.

When the service finally ended, the crowd drifted away. Hampton stood by the grave alone. Reaching into his pocket, he brought out a dark rosebud he'd picked from the garden that morning. Carefully, he laid it on top of the raw earth.

"Good-bye," he whispered.

A hand fell on his shoulder and he whirled around.

"I didn't mean to startle you," Colonel Young interrupted. "My apologies."

Hampton stared at the colonel's red face from where keen blue eyes surveyed him. The colonel was running slightly to fat, but still looked trim in his army uniform.

"Come along, Hampton," the older man coaxed. "We've important matters to discuss."

Hampton followed Colonel Young without speaking, grateful that anyone at all wanted to talk to him. At the same time he was wary.

"I took the liberty of sending your carriage home," the colonel stated as they came to the drive where only the Young carriage waited. The Negro driver touched his fingers to his hat when he saw the two men approach. Where was Roseann? Hampton wondered.

"Take us home, Lucas," the colonel ordered.

At the Young house Hampton followed the colonel to the library. Once they were inside, Colonel Young closed the door behind them.

"I'd offer you a bourbon," he began, "but I know the judge didn't hold with liquor. Would you like something else—a lemonade?"

Hampton shook his head.

"Then sit down."

Hampton sat in a leather-bottomed straight chair. He watched the colonel pour himself half a glass of whiskey from a cut-glass decanter.

"I talked to the judge's lawyer," Colonel Young reported after he had sipped from his drink. "Son, there's no money. None at all. The house and what's left of the land will have to be sold to meet outstanding debts.''

Hampton had known his grandfather had sold off land bit by bit over the years. Nevertheless, the colonel's words jolted him.

"Yes, well, finding out surprised me, too," the colonel mentioned, noting Hampton's shock. "I knew old Doug had had some trouble, but I wasn't aware of anything like this." He looked sharply at Hampton. "What are we going to do about you, son?"

"I . . . I don't . . .'' Hampton stammered.

"It's a lot to grasp, I know that," the colonel commented. "You have to think about it, though. I mean to help you if I can." He finished the whiskey and touched his lips with his handkerchief. "I've got a little influence here and there and I've thought of a plan I think the judge would have endorsed fully. Yessir, fully. Your grandfather wanted you in the army and I think you'd be wise to stay with that plan. The army's a good career for a man."

The colonel poured himself another glass of whiskey and Hampton frowned, puzzled. West Point was out of the question now. What kind of army career was the colonel talking about? Was he expected to enlist as a dragoon? No, Hampton thought, I don't want to be a soldier. Most likely, I'd have to take orders from the likes of Chambers. Or Chambers himself for that matter. Never.

The colonel stared into his almost empty glass of amber liquid. "What I wondered, son, was how you felt about going west. Do you think you could work with Indians?"

Hampton's eyes widened.

"You're a born horseman, son. You handle yourself well and you're a crack shot. I've heard, too, that you have the knack of learning other languages. Heard you speak French, German and know your Latin. You've the makings of a first-rate scout, I'd say. The army always needs them. You work for the army, but you're your own man, too. Thought that might appeal to you. Of course, you'd need to learn more about the Indian business. You think it over." The colonel came over and clapped Hampton on the back. "You'll stay for dinner," he announced. "I insist. Afterward, we'll talk again."

That night at dinner, Roseann acted as her father's hostess. Mrs. Young had died years before and the young girl handled responsibilities well. She was lovely in her sheer white muslin gown and Hampton, watching her, almost forgot his misery.

After the meal, Roseann disappeared. While Hampton waited for the colonel to finish his after-dinner brandy, he went outdoors for a stroll in the garden. There he discovered Roseann sitting in the grape arbor.

The grapes, still green, had only just begun to turn color. They smelled of summer. In the fading light, Roseann was pale against the dark green leaves. She smile as Hampton came up to her. Seeing that, his heart hammered in his ears.

"Roseann." He caught her hand.

She pressed his, then gently pulled hers away. "I know how sad you're feeling," she murmured. "I just loved the judge."

I loved him, too, Hampton wanted to say, but the words wouldn't come. "Your father wants to send me west," he told her instead.

She clapped her hands. "How exciting!"

He blinked. Exciting? He felt numb, as though nothing would ever excite him again. "Wouldn't you miss me if I went?" he asked as he looked down at her.

"I always miss seeing a friend." Roseann lowered her eyes as she spoke, then glanced up at Hampton from under her lashes. She stood and turned her back to him.

Hampton caught her shoulders then, turning her around. "Would you wait for me if I went? Would you, Roseann?"

She began to laugh, a charming, light laugh like crystal lusters tinkling. Scowling, Hampton dropped his hands and stood back.

"Oh, Hamp, you look so very fierce," Roseann tittered. She came close, stood on her tiptoes and before Hampton knew what she intended, she'd kissed him quickly on the lips.

"There," she teased, pirouetting out of reach. "I don't intend to wait for any man, ever. But it isn't every man I kiss, either."

Her father cleared his throat. Hampton turned. Neither he nor Roseann had seen the colonel, and the expression on his face was grim. It told Hampton more clearly than words what the colonel was feeling. If Roseann's father had his way, Hampton Abbott would never be his son-in-law.

Chapter 6

Hampton put off giving his decision to Colonel Young and asked for a few days more to think about his future. A week came and went. No one came to call except John Evstone, the judge's attorney. He confirmed all that Colonel Young had said.

There was no money. The estate was in debt.

Obviously, Hampton thought, he had to make up his mind to do something, but lethargy gripped him. He roamed the grounds, often standing in Hyacinth's empty stall. Over and over he relived the day of the race, trying to imagine how he could have altered what had happened.

"Massa Hamp," Jerome told him on the second Sunday after the judge's funeral, "you ain't doing yourself no good. The devil done took yesterday and packed it up and you can't no way get it back."

Hampton turned to look at Jerome. The slave was standing in the stable entrance, his white hair touched by the sun. With a jolt, Hampton realized Jerome was part of the estate. He and the other slaves would have to be sold to help pay the debts. There was nothing that could be done to prevent it. Jerome wasn't a young man. What kind of life would he have with a new master?

"Jerome," Hampton blurted out impulsively, "how would you like to travel west?"

The Negro stared for a moment. Then he grinned. "Mighty well, Massa Hamp. Mighty well."

Hampton nodded. Taking a deep breath, he smelled horse and old wood, familiar odors. He strode from the stall and Jerome moved aside to let him leave the stable.

"I'll see what I can do," Hampton promised, gripping his shoulder for a moment. "Bring the carriage around in a little while."

Hampton went to his room and changed into his black suit. Though it was hot, he knew he'd have to wear it. As he shoved his feet into the new black shoes that pinched his feet, he hesitated. Then he crossed to the chest of drawers along the east wall. Pulling it away from the mahogany paneling far enough to wedge himself behind the chest, he ran his fingers down the wood of the wall until he felt an unevenness. Then he carefully prodded and pulled until a section of the maghogany lifted free.

When he was seven, he'd found the loose board. At once he'd made a hiding place, but he hadn't thought about it for years. Now he lifted out the buckskin pouch between the studding and took it to the bed. He dumped the contents on the green coverlet.

Mildew had all but ruined the pouch and its contents. Hampton lifted the items and stared at them, the feel of each one in his hands somehow threatening. He touched the faded quillwork on a small moccasin, held the remnant of a neck thong in his hands.

What the tiny quilled lizard-shaped sack was meant to contain he no longer remembered. The only thing he recalled was hiding the pouch when his grandfather insisted he rid himself of everything Indian.

Rainy had known, though. Rainy, who had run and played in these moccasins, who had worn the thong around his neck with the mysterious lizard pouch dangling on his chest.

But he hadn't been Rainy for a long time.

Hampton shook his head. Then he put the relics back into their hiding place and left the room, only to pause on the curving staircase.

"Your mother had her wedding reception here in this house," his grandfather had told him. "She came down those stairs in her wedding gown. I tell you, boy, she was a beautiful sight. Beautiful."

What kind of a wedding had it been when his mother was married to the Indian who fathered him?

Hampton ran down the rest of the steps. In the foyer, the huge brass and crystal chandelier hung motionless over his head. There was no breeze that day to set the prisms shimmering. Velvet and brocaded chairs and settees lined the foyer walls. Hampton studied the dining room, then went into the front parlor. From there he peered from the long and curved front windows to the drive where Jerome sat in the driver's seat of the carriage pulled by matching greys.

He took a deep breath. None of this was his. And he didn't really want any of it—except for Jerome. And he was going to fight for him.

Colonel Young stood in greeting when Hampton was shown into the library.

"I'm sorry I've been so long responding to your offer, sir," Hampton said. "It was most generous of you to want to help me."

"I can understand how you feel," the colonel replied. "None of us expected the judge to go so quickly. I knew you were close to your grandfather."

"You're right. Well, as you said, Grandfather wanted me in the army, and I'd like to try to learn scouting—but I do have one request before I leave St. Louis."

Hampton saw the colonel stiffen and felt a bitter amusement. Does he think I mean to ask for Roseann's hand? he wondered.

"And what is it you want?" Colonel Young asked.

"Jerome, sir. He's good with horses. If you recall, he's always worked in the stables. If he came with me I think he'd be of use. I realize I don't own Jerome because of the estate debts but . . ." Hampton stopped. "Is it possible you can arrange for him to go west with me?"

The colonel's relief was evident. "Well," he muttered. "Jerome must be getting on. What is he, fifty, maybe fifty-five now? Folks generally want a younger hand in the stables. Can't see that he'd bring much cash. I'll talk to Evstone, but I don't think he'll object. Lord knows you deserve a little something from your grandfather's estate." He rose and came over to Hampton. "You won't regret this, son. What you've agreed to do would have made old Doug proud, I know that. Forgive me, but I was so certain you'd do the right thing that I've already spoken to the superintendent of the Indian Agency here. Superintendent Harvey's enthusiastic. Thinks you might be of use as an interpreter once you learn the Indian tongue. He'll be glad to arrange for you to stay with friendly tribes along the Missouri River."

"When will I be leaving?"

"I'll speak to Harvey about it. Soon, I'd say. No point in dallying in St. Louis, is there, son?"

No, Hampton thought as he left the house. No point. Except for Roseann. He was determined to see her. But old 'Lijah, letting him out, had mentioned she wasn't at home that day.

Hampton jumped into the carriage. "They're going to let you go with me, Jerome," he told the black man. "We're heading west together."

"That be good news, Massa Hamp. Purely good."

As their carriage passed through the gates of the Young estate, heading homeward, Hampton saw a gig approaching. Roseann was in it. He started to lean out to wave to her, then drew back when he recognized her companion.

It was Steve Chambers.

Hampton clenched his fists, fighting down his rage. He saw Jerome's anxious face peer into the carriage. Got to hold on to myself, he thought as a shimmer of red began to cloud his vision. I'll ruin everything if I jump that bastard.

The carriage swayed as Jerome whipped the greys into a fast trot. Hampton breathed deeply. Wait, he urged himself. Not now. Someday. But not now.

Without warning, his mother's voice sounded in his head.

"Hunt him and kill him," it echoed. "Your father. Find him and kill him. Promise me."

Hampton's eyes widened in shock as the vision of that last night in his mother's room came flooding back. The memory of her death had remained locked away until that moment.

"You all right, Massa Hamp?"

Hampton stared at Jerome's black face, unable for a moment to understand where he was. The carriage had stopped and Jerome had opened the door.

They were home.

Hamptom pored over maps of the Indian Territory. He and Jerome would be heading up the Mississippi from St. Louis to the Missouri River, then up the Missouri to Independence. At Independence they'd disembark and ride north and west to one of the Potawatomi Indian villages near the Missouri.

The two great trails west also began at Independence, the Oregon Trail north and west to the Pacific coast and the Santa Fe Trail south and west to Mexico. Traders and emigrants traveled on them regularly through Indian Territory. Some, like the Bents and St. Vrain of St. Louis, even lived in the territory at their trading posts. Otherwise, only Indians lived in those lands between the Missouri River and the Rocky Mountains.

Hampton had seen Indians on the streets of St. Louis, but now he'd be living on their land, not they on his.

"It'll be some adventure," he remarked to Jerome.

"I 'spect it surely will," Jerome agreed.

Hampton touched the map with his forefinger. "Here's where we're going. First with the Potawatomi Indians north of Independence, then with the Delaware Indians west of them, near Fort Leavenworth."

"The colonel say they be friendly, right 'nough?"

Hampton nodded. "The Indians who attack the emigrants and traders are farther west. Pawnees, Sioux, Cheyenne. Arapaho." As he said the names, his skin tingled with excitement. He could hardly wait to leave.

He went to see Roseann the day before he boarded the steamboat.

"Why, I do declare you're a positive stranger lately," Roseann told him as they sat on the side veranda where three immense magnolias cast a cool, dense shade.

"You've been busy enough," Hampton returned sharply. "I'm sure you didn't have time to miss me."

"Whatever do you mean?"

"What I mean is your riding out with Steve Chambers."

"What if I have ridden out with Steve?" Roseann tossed her head. "I can do as I please and I certainly shall."

Her pink lips pouted as though ready for a kiss. Hampton set down his glass of lemonade. Then he got to his feet and reached for her, pulling her from the chair into his arms.

He kissed her fiercely, holding her tight, feeling the softness of her breasts against him, smelling the delicious scent of her body. She pressed close and for a long passionate moment her lips answered his demand. Then she began to struggle.

Hampton's arms closed around her desperately, trying to force her to respond again. But she fought to free herself and he had to let her go. She backed away, face flushed, blue eyes wide.

"You certainly have your nerve!" she cried. "Who do you think I am?"

"The woman I intend to marry!"

"You! I'm not going to marry anyone." Roseann smoothed her dress. "At least not for a long, long time."

"I can't ask you to marry me now," he blurted out in frustration. "I don't have any money. But when I—"

Roseann put her hands over her ears. "Don't you understand?" she interrupted, her voice rising. "I don't want to listen to you! I told you I wouldn't wait for you or for any man!"

Hampton pulled her hands to him, but Roseann wouldn't let him hold them. "You liked it when I kissed you," he declared.

"I did not!" She stamped her foot. "You'd better leave, Hampton Abbott. I think you've stayed long enough."

"You know I'm leaving St. Louis tomorrow," Hampton continued desperately. "Promise me you won't see Steve while I'm gone."

Roseann glared at him. "Are you out of your mind?" she asked. "I won't promise you one thing!"

Hampton reached for her again but she darted behind a chair. Her chest heaved. She looked both excited and afraid. Hampton took a step closer. He longed to smash the chair out of his path, grab Roseann and ride away with her. Her lips parted.

"Roseann . . ."

"Don't say one more word to me," she commanded, "except good-bye."

Hampton's shoulders slumped. He'd certainly made a

mess of everything. Sighing, he swung around and headed for the steps leading off the veranda.

"Hamp," Roseann whispered coyly.

He turned.

"You can come and see me again when you return to St. Louis."

He took a step toward her, but she immediately retreated.

"Good-bye, Roseann," he snapped, hurrying down the steps.

It was difficult to keep himself from glancing back, hoping against hope Roseann would run after him and kiss him good-bye. When, at the gate, he did look around, she was nowhere in sight.

Hampton had taken three horses with him on his trip: his favorite stallion, a young chestnut named Ares; a smaller dun gelding to use as pack horse; and a sturdy mare, Eurydice, for Jerome.

"Used to be I paid no mind to a horse kicking his heels," Jerome chuckled. "I hung on, talked sweet, and didn't get het up. He always settled down." Jerome shook his head. "Nowadays I picks a horse like Dicey. She don't get up to no foolishness to begin with."

The steam packet heading up the Mississippi toward the mouth of the Missouri was crowded. Mules, horses and wagons were crammed with traders' goods in the hold. On the upper deck, Santa Fe traders, gamblers, and mountain men in buckskins rubbed elbows with a party of priests and French-Canadians.

In the week it took to get to the Missouri, Hampton learned that the priests planned to stop at St. Mary's Mission before heading on up the Missouri—it was one of the Potawatomi settlements. Hampton introduced himself to Father DeSmet and asked about the Potawatomis.

"They are a good people," Father DeSmet told him.
"Naturally pious. They've taken well to farming."

Hampton concealed his disappointment. Whatever he'd
expected to hear from the priest, it hadn't been that he'd
be spending the next year with a village of farmers.

It was a stifling July day when they arrived at the
Potawatomi village. Hampton stared at the rounded huts of
bark, the yipping dogs, the dark-faced Indians.

You were a fool to expect to recognize anything, he
told himself. Taking a deep breath and ignoring the snarling
dogs, he strode over to an Indian standing near a hut. The
Indian's arms were folded stiffly.

"I'm Hampton Abbott," he announced.

The Indian looked Hampton up and down, but his
expression didn't change. Leaning to one side, he examined Jerome, who'd come up to stand behind Hampton.
After a time, he unfolded his arms and gestured to them to
follow him.

The Indian wore moccasins and a breechcloth, nothing
else. He led the two men between the domed lodges. Small
cooking fires burned here and there. Children stared, the
younger boys and girls peeping from behind their mother's
skirts. The women stared, too, but more at Jerome than
Hampton.

The Indian called to one of the women. He gave
orders and she hurried into a hut. Then their guide led
them past the village to a grove of large cottonwoods. At
that point he sat, gesturing that they should sit to his left—
Hampton first, then Jerome.

Soon five Indian men appeared and sat down near
them, forming a circle. Two women hurried up, one carrying a long-stemmed pipe with a red stone bowl that she
handed carefully to the first man. The other woman held a
bundle of twigs and a smoking stick. She knelt in the
center of the circle of men. With clumps of dried grass,

she started a tiny blaze, adding the twigs until a small fire burned.

When both women had left the grove, the first man pointed the stem of the pipe up, down, then north, west, south and east. He lifted a burning stick from the fire and touched it to the bowl of the pipe. Hampton smelled the sweet scent of tobacco mixed with a more pungent odor he didn't recognize. The Indian took a puff and passed the pipe to his left. Hampton took it, suddenly feeling a kinship with the ritual. He took a puff and passed the pipe to Jerome.

"Draw on it before you pass the pipe to the next man," he whispered. And Jerome did.

Summer gave way to fall. Gradually, Hampton and Jerome became accepted in the Potawatomi village. The chief, Three Buffalo, thought it a great joke to be teaching them his language. Eagerly, he initiated them into behavior appropriate for braves.

"They don't be all that strange," Jerome said to Hampton one fine September day as they watched the women come in from the gardens carrying corn and squash. " 'Most like regular folks."

Of the two of them, Hampton thought, Jerome was adapting more quickly to Indian life. He knew Jerome spent much of his time in the wigwam of a Potawatomi widow, who, because of Jerome's visits, became the envy of her friends. Hampton had found some of the roundfaced maidens attractive, but, unfortunately for them, he compared each one to Roseann and wasn't interested.

Winter swept down from the north. Inside the wigwam with Three Buffalo, Hampton learned how to make a bow and how to fashion arrows. Three Buffalo also taught Hampton Indian sign language.

"Every tribesman understands signs," Three Buffalo emphasized. "Friends. Enemies. All understand."

The chief's wife made moccasins for Hampton as well as a buckskin shirt with a beaded leaf design. He declined the offer of a breechcloth, preferring trousers.

When spring came, Hampton and Jerome packed to leave. They planned to head south to Westport for supplies before traveling northwest to the Delaware camp. It was there that they would spend the next year learning scouting with the Delaware.

Three Buffalo looked pensive as he watched them saddle up. "Delaware and Potawatomi are allies, it is true," he told them, "but you should stay here with us. You are friends."

Hampton was grateful, but he rode off with Jerome as planned.

"Gonna miss that widow woman some," Jerome sighed.

Rumors of California gold discoveries had trickled into the Potawatomi village. Like many others, Hampton had toyed with the idea of heading for California, imagining that if he returned to St. Louis laden with gold, he might convince Roseann to marry him.

But to go to California would mean betraying his agreement with Colonel Young. The colonel had taken it upon himself to outfit both himself and Jerome. He had seen to it that Jerome was allowed to make the trip.

Superintendent Harvey had arranged for him to spend these two years with the Indians. In return for his trouble, Harvey expected Hampton to be an interpreter for the Indians. Then there was that appointment with the army commander at Fort Leavenworth the following year.

These men trusted him. If he rode off to California, he'd be disappointing them. The judge had told him enough times, "A Hampton never breaks his word."

Well, he was a Hampton at least, even if he wasn't an Abbott.

As he and Jerome neared Westport, both stared in

disbelief at the hundreds of wagons crowding the open land near the town. Hampton read aloud the words painted on the canvas of one wagon.

"California or bust!"

"All them people be looking to find gold?" Jerome questioned disbelievingly. "Surely ain't gonna be 'nough to go 'round."

Hampton shrugged. Neither of them would be finding out how plentiful the gold was.

They left Westport the same day, both oppressed by the crowded streets and the noise. As they entered the woods bordering the Missouri, it began to rain. By the time they emerged from the trees and came in sight of the rolling prairie stretching in front of them to the horizon, it was pouring. Wagon trains ahead of them had left the ground rutted. Mud slowed the horses. The wagons lurched and rattled.

When they turned north toward Fort Leavenworth, they left the Oregon Trail and the wagons behind. The rain persisted but it was easier going without the deep and muddy ruts. By afternoon they rafted across the Kansas River into Delaware country, where they were welcomed.

Almost immediately Hampton was introduced to a brave named Deer Track, who had scouted for the army.

"Southwest country bad," Deer Track told him. "Cheyenne, Comanche, Kiowa, Arapaho. All enemies. Sun very hot. Sometimes no water." He gestured to the northwest. "Good country. Streams. Trees. Much game. Like my ancient home." His face was solemn and he did not look east.

Hampton learned from Deer Track how the Delaware had been moved westward from the Atlantic coast until at last they'd been forced to live in Indian Territory west of the Missouri. Three Buffalo, too, had told of being pushed from the Potawatomi ancestral lands near the Great Lakes.

Yet he had been east, to New York, with the judge a

few years before. It was made clear to him that the Indians had been asked to move west to make room for other people. Now he wasn't sure. Still, the relocation of Indians was a reality. And the Potawatomi, anyway, seemed happy where they were. The Delaware were another matter. They were more aggressive, eager to travel as scouts.

Hampton liked Deer Track. "Teach me everything you know," he told the Indian. And Deer Track taught Hampton how to read sign, how to locate himself in open land, as well as the many tricks of finding food and water in barren country.

"You learn more quickly than any white man I have heard of," Deer Track laughed one day to Hampton. Hampton laughed, too, but even then did not feel as close to the Delaware as he had to Three Buffalo.

In the middle of July, Three Buffalo appeared with ten Potawatomi braves and an invitation for Hampton and Jerome to come along on a buffalo hunt. Two days later they rode out with a hunting party of Delaware and Potawatomi. There were eighteen men in all.

They headed north for two days, traveling over the yellowing grass of the prairie already seared by the hot summer sun. There were no trees except for the cottonwoods and willows along the streams.

"Sioux country," Deer Track announced at the night camp. "Enemies."

Hampton knew the Potawatomi's sign for the Sioux was a wavy motion with the hand that meant snake.

"We bring back Sioux horses," Deer Track stated determinedly.

Hampton blinked. "No! We hunt buffalo!"

Deer Track smiled. "Maybe. And maybe Sioux horses."

Angry, Hampton went to find Three Buffalo, who was washing in the stream. "You told me this was a buffalo hunt," he accused the Indian. "I can't join in a raid against the Sioux."

Three Buffalo shrugged.

"Jerome and I will start back to Fort Leavenworth in the morning," Hampton declared.

But before dawn, the crack of a rifle brought him to his feet, groping for his own gun. He gaped in shock at the sight of Deer Track lying on the ground, an arrow in his breast.

Then an earsplitting screech made him whirl. Indians with paint-smeared faces leaped at the Potawatomi and Delaware, clubs and hatchets swinging.

Hampton caught a flicker of motion from the corner of his eye. He tried to turn and jump aside at the same time, but something smashed into his head.

Instantly, he fell into darkness.

Chapter 7

The ground throbbed under Hampton. Drums thundered in his head. Lying on his belly, he opened his eyes, wincing as pain lanced through his skull. He heard distant shouts. With an effort, he rolled over on his back. The first thing he saw was Jerome crouching over him.

"Praise the Lord," Jerome cried. "You don't be dead."

Hampton sat up. Even though Jerome's arm was supporting him, his head was spinning. He gaped in confusion at the conical hide lodges surrounding him. Where was he? The Delaware lived in log huts, the Potawatomi in round wigwams. These were tepees.

"They brought us here," Jerome reported. "Them painted Indians."

Hampton put his hands to his throbbing head. He couldn't remember what had happened. But both he and Jerome were barefoot and stripped to the waist.

"Old Three Buffalo, he get away. Most everybody else be killed." With a grimace, Jerome touched his white curls. "Get their scalps cut off."

We're prisoners, Hampton realized. Kept alive and brought here for God knows what.

An Indian woman dressed in fringed buckskin appeared between the lodges. Shyly she approached and offered Jerome a hide container. Jerome took it, in turn offering it to Hampton.

"What's that?"

"Water."

Hampton tipped the container up and drank.

The woman smiled at Jerome. She had a different look to her than the Potawatomi or Delaware women, Hampton thought. Wilder, despite her smile. Jerome smiled back and the woman ducked her head coyly and hurried away.

"She keep coming around, three times now," Jerome smirked. His voice held a tinge of gratification.

"God, I wish they'd stop those drums and that yelling," Hampton moaned, his fist to his forehead.

"They tied them bloody scalps to sticks. Be waving them like flags," Jerome said. "Reckon they're dancing with 'em now, having a jubilee, like."

Painted Indians. Scalping. Gradually Hampton began to recall the attack in the trees. Deer Track dead with an arrow in his chest. An attack by the Sioux, whose country they were in. Enemies of the Delaware and Potawatomi.

"The Sioux are very savage," Father DeSmet had told Hampton. "Completely heathen as yet. They war with other Indians and whites alike."

"Sioux," Hampton whispered to Jerome. "It's the Sioux who've captured us."

"River Woman say Sioux be rattlesnakes," Jerome confided. "Say they cook people." He glanced uneasily toward the sound of the drumming. "That Sioux lady seem like she want to be friends," he added hopefully.

Holding on to Jerome, Hampton got unsteadily to his feet. He closed his eyes momentarily against his dizziness. "We don't dare just sit back and wait," he declared. "Show them we're not afraid, that's what we'll do."

"We ain't got so much as a knife between us,"

Jerome told the staggering Hampton as they walked toward the sound of the drums.

"I thought of trying to make a run for it," Hampton confessed, "but that won't work. Neither of us know the country. Besides, we're unarmed."

A fine scout I make, he chided himself. Captured by Sioux. And poor old Jerome's in trouble right alongside me.

"Whatever you do, don't act scared," he warned. "We'll face them down."

"Gonna try."

Dogs slunk snarling from between the tepees. The sun was past meridian, but the shadows weren't long. The smell of stewing meat drifted by on the warm breeze. Hampton felt his stomach contract with hunger. Except for his beastly headache, he felt stronger every moment. Gingerly he touched the side of his head, grimacing as his fingers explored a large lump. His hair was stiff with dried blood.

The shouts grew louder. There was chanting. As if from nowhere, two Indians appeared in their path with their faces painted black. The taller one gestured at them.

Hampton wasn't sure, but he thought the Indian had made the sign for *go back*.

No, he signed. *We go to dance. I speak to chief.*

The men looked at one another. Hampton grunted, imitating a sound he'd often heard Three Buffalo and Deer Track make. "Go left around them," he muttered to Jerome as he swerved to the right, starting to step around.

One Sioux turned toward Hampton, the other toward Jerome. But they did nothing to stop them. When the two men walked together again, the Indians flanked them, keeping pace. Hampton forced himself to keep his eyes ahead. His face was expressionless as the chants and cries grew louder. He felt the throb of the drums in his bones. As they rounded the last of the tepees, he saw the dancers in the shade of cottonwoods. The women circled apart from

the men. They were near him, dancing without lifting their
feet, chanting, waving banners. Wait a minute. He remembered what Jerome had told him. Were banners what
they were waving?

Hampton's step faltered for a moment as he saw what
the women really carried. Scalps. Scalps tied to poles,
black hair blowing in the hot wind. He swallowed and
strode past the women toward the dancing men. Jerome
was still by his side as the two Indians escorted them.

He'd seen Potawatomi and Delaware dances often
enough, but these painted braves, their bare skins glisten-
ing with sweat, leaped and stomped in a wilder dance, the
drum's rhythm a counterpoint. He felt the hair on his neck
stiffen.

Older men, women and children stood or sat in a
scattered circle watching the dancers. The chief must be
among them, Hampton thought. I've got to pick him out
on my first try so I don't lose face.

He scanned the visages of the men who were seated
and narrowed the possibilities to three. Each of the choices
was an older man and each wore a war bonnet of many
feathers. The bonnets were decorated with painted symbols,
each different, but he had no idea what the symbols meant.
He kept walking toward them, knowing he had to make a
choice.

Suddenly a voice spoke in his head. It told him who
to pick and he didn't question his hunch. He made for the
man with the red circle on his forehead but veered off
slightly so he came up along the man's left side. Two feet
away he stopped to show respect. Then he turned to the Indian
following him and signed, *I sit beside chief. Watch dance.
Talk by and by.*

Without waiting for an answer, Hampton sat down.
Then he nodded for Jerome to sit, too.

The two escorts stayed on their feet, standing behind
their prisoners. The chief ignored them. Women had begun

bringing steaming containers of food. Most of the dancers
paused, crouching to eat. A rich, meaty aroma filled Hampton's nostrils, and when he was handed some food, he
took the horn holder eagerly.

"Good," Jerome mumbled into his plate.

Hampton nodded. He knew he might be eating dog
meat, but he and Jerome both had learned to do that when
they were in the Potawatomi camp. Whatever was coming,
he would face it on a full stomach. Glancing to the left, he
saw that a few women still danced with scalps. Suddenly
his appetite fled.

The Indian he had thought was the chief gestured in
words Hampton didn't understand. The guard next to Hampton prodded him with his foot and Hampton looked at him,
puzzled.

Go closer. Talk to chief, the guard signed.

Hampton rose. Indicating that Jerome should follow
him, he took two steps toward the chief. The Sioux got to
his feet. He was at least six feet tall. Though his lined
face revealed he must be about sixty, his hair showed no
grey. In his square face, his nose was large and hooked.
First he stared into Hampton's eyes. Then he studied Jerome. Other Sioux rose. Almost immediately, Hampton
and Jerome were surrounded by them.

You with enemy war party? the chief signed.

No. Hampton made his sign emphatic. *I come to*
. . . About to make the Potawatomi snake sign for Sioux,
he paused. What had Father DeSmet told him?

"The Sioux call themselves Dakota, a sign like this.
You know, almost all the tribes I've met call themselves
by a name other than what we commonly use. The Delaware,
now, are *Leni-lenape*."

Hampton made the sign for Dakota. *I want to learn
Dakota speech. Want to learn to scout like Dakota,* he
signed. *I meet Potawatomi. Meet Delaware. They many.*

We two. They take prisoner, me, black whiteman. Dakota come. Fight. Now we here.

The chief said nothing. As he stared once again into Hampton's eyes, Hampton kept his face impassive. Beside him, Jerome cleared his throat. At once, the Indian to the chief's left, a man with wavy yellow lines painted on his cheeks, broke into impassioned speech. Hampton understood none of the words, but the meaning was clear. He was urging the chief to kill them.

As soon as he finished, Hampton signed. *I want to speak.*

I listen, the chief signed.

I am Dakota. Father Dakota. Mother white. Mother, me, live with whites. Mother die. I come to Dakota. Bring black whiteman.

It might even be true, Hampton told himself. My father could be Sioux. I don't know what tribe he belonged to.

After what seemed like hours, the chief gestured for Hampton and Jerome to follow him. Along with seven of the elders, they entered the dancers' circle. The chief halted. Then he called out an order.

"That one don't like us," Jerome muttered. Hampton grunted in agreement as he saw the malevolent glare of the Indian with the wavy yellow lines on his cheeks.

The drums stopped beating. The dancers crouched, watching. A brave approached the circle, carrying something in his hand. All eyes shifted to him. Hampton let his breath out when he saw that the brave held a long-stemmed pipe. A smoke. He had convinced the chief.

I speak, the chief signed. *Black whiteman strongheart. He fight warrior who strike your head. Black whiteman has no gun. No knife. Fight hard. He not Dakota. You Dakota. All Dakota stronghearts. You strongheart? Show. We smoke after.*

The man with yellow cheeks removed thongs from a

bundle fastened to his waistband. A half-grown boy slipped among the men to set an animal's skull at his feet.

A buffalo skull.

The man grinned unpleasantly as he yanked a knife from its sheath and approached Hampton. Everyone except Jerome stepped back.

Hampton realized that Jerome must have saved his life when the Sioux attacked. But this time no one could help him. Jerome would be killed if he tried.

"Stay out of this, whatever happens," he warned Jerome, forcing the words through his constricted throat. The knife wielder frightened the hell out of him.

I'll be damned if I'll show them I'm scared, he told himself, tensing as the man raised the knife.

The sharp blade sliced into Hampton's chest. Once, twice. He clenched his teeth to prevent crying out as pain coursed through him and blood ran down his chest.

The yellow-cheeked man thrust a wooden skewer in through one of the shallow cuts, then out the other so that the skewer pierced an area of flesh under a flap of Hampton's skin and muscle. As the man attached long rawhide thongs to either end of the wood, Hampton realized that only a shaman would do this to anyone. A medicine man.

Don't show him your pain, Hampton thought to himself as he gritted his teeth. He wanted you to fail this testing.

The shaman tied the ends of the dangling thongs to the buffalo skull. Drums began to beat. Hampton fought dizziness as nausea rose to choke him. He clenched his fists, determined to stay on his feet. Then he staggered and tried to mask his weakness by taking several steps back the other way. The weight of the buffalo skull dragged at his flesh as he pulled it with him. He controlled his involuntary wincing as best he could and stared at the shaman through a blur of pain. Scars puckered the man's chest.

Hampton shifted his gaze to other braves. But he saw that most of them bore similar scars.

From this torture?

He knew the only way to get free was to tear loose from the skewer. He'd *have* to do that. He had no knife to cut the thongs. And even if he had one he knew that using it would doom him. Jerome's dark face wavered before him and he thought, Had each scarred brave torn himself loose?

More blood trickled down his chest. He saw it drip in the dust and he gripped the thongs, one in each hand, tensing himself against the pain. He pulled the thongs until the throbbing ache made him lightheaded. The skewer stayed firmly embedded in his flesh.

Taking a deep breath, Hampton waited for his head to clear. He'd never be able to yank the skewer free by pulling on it by himself. He looked around. Men circled him, all watching. The drum continued to beat in its slow tempo. And though he couldn't see the drummer, he did see a tall pole rising toward the sky above the men's heads.

Hampton thought a minute, deciding how to get to the pole. He knew he couldn't pick up the skull. That wouldn't be strong-hearted. So, satisfied he'd gauged the position of the pole exactly, he turned away from it and began to walk backward toward where it projected from the ground. As he moved, the skill dragged in front of him, tugging painfully at his chest.

Braves parted to let him through and followed him until his back touched the pole. Hampton stopped, then began to circle it. As he had hoped, the heavy skull on the ground allowed the thongs to wind about the pole as he went around and around. When there was no slack, he grabbed the pole with both hands to steady himself. Then he jerked back against the thongs.

The skull shifted, allowing the thongs to slacken. Hampton hardly faltered. Moving now as if he were apart from the pain in his chest, he stepped onto the skull, balancing, grabbing the pole again. Then he pulled back against the thongs and heard the skin rip on his chest. Pain knifed through him and he cried out despite himself, though he tried to mask the sound by bursting out with the first song he could think of.

> "Gonna run all night,
> Gonna run all day . . ."

Summoning all his strength, he jerked against the thongs again. More flesh tore loose.

> "Somebody bet on the bobtailed nag . . ."

He was half-shouting now, half-screaming. Jerome's deep voice boomed out.

> "I gonna bet on the bay."

The drum rhythm quickened. Through a haze of pain, Hampton heard Jerome singing, heard exclamations from the watching Indians. Giving a final, frantic jerk, he felt the skewer tear from his chest. Released from agony, he fell over backward, the skull sliding out from under him.

He grabbed it. Somehow he found the power to jump to his feet. He shouted as he held the buffalo skull aloft with bloody hands. "I did it! *Damn* you all! I did it!"

Chapter 8

"Heavy Pine says we travel south," One Claw told Stands Shining late in the Birth of Calves Moon. "The council has agreed."

No brave younger than thirty winters was asked to sit with the council. Usually the men were old. And they were leaders like One Claw.

"Do we go to Little White Man's trading lodge on the Arkansas?" Stands Shining asked.

"It is so. We will set up the village among the hills west of the trading lodge. Let Yellow Wolf's Cheyenne camp next to Little White Man if they wish. Our People don't care to sleep so close."

Stands Shining knew Little White Man had married women of Yellow Wolf's band—first Owl Woman, now dead, then her sister, Yellow Woman. He had many Cheyenne children.

"Little White Man has always kept his word to Our People and to the Cheyenne," Stands Shining said. "We can trust him."

"At least he'll trade us ammunition for buffalo robes," her great-uncle told her. "Broken Hand is there, too. Perhaps the Great White Father in the east has given Broken Hand more bullets for us."

Stands Shining nodded. Like every warrior in the village who owned a rifle, she needed ammunition. From the moment she acquired a white man's gun during the raid on the wagon train, she had practiced until she could shoot a bullet as accurately as she could let an arrow fly. But bullets could not be retrieved as easily as arrows.

"The buffalo return soon," Stands Shining noted. "We should have bullets for our guns."

"It is true. But I don't like to be near a trading lodge where so many white men come. Their bluecoat soldiers visit there too often. Remember four winters back when the bluecoat chief Fire Hair marched his soldiers into the trading lodge on the North Platte River? We were not there, but Our People who live in the north told us how he shot his big gun made of shiny metal and pulled on its wheels.

"They told about the terrible roar. The sand flew up and there was a big hole. Think how many warriors that big gun could kill with one firing."

"I have also heard many times," Stands Shining mentioned, "of how the Northern Arapaho trembled in fear at Fire Hair's warning. He warned them that if they killed any more white men, he'd destroy the Arapaho nation. Yet when they killed two white trappers in the spring, what happened?

"We both know four of their chiefs brought horses to the trading lodge to compensate for the killing. But the horses were refused. And the chiefs were also told not to bring in the Arapaho brave who killed the trappers. Yet the big gun was never used though four winters have passed. Fire Hair's threat was only words to blow on the wind."

One Claw frowned. "Don't be so sure. White soldiers can't be trusted. All whites are like our word for them—*niatha*, the spider, cunning and clever. They do not think like Our People or like any of the Buffalo People."

"I hear what you tell me," Stands Shining replied, "but I think of the many whites who have died from

Arapaho arrows since Fire Hair's visit. And he has never
come back to lead soldiers against us though other bluecoat chiefs harry the Comanche and Kiowa. Fire Hair is
afraid of the Arapaho.''

"No, he is not."

"Even so, the bluecoats won't bother us," Stands
Shining assured One Claw. "Chief Left Hand has urged
all of the Southern Arapaho to keep peace with the *niatha*,
the whites. Haven't we done so? Didn't I say no to Little
Bear? Didn't I tell him we wouldn't join the Kiowa raids
against the white traders on the Mexico Trail along the
Arkansas?

"Both he and the Comanche boast that white men are
easier to kill than buffalo and their captured wagons yield
much that is good. But Our People listen to Broken Hand
and to Chief Left Hand. We keep the peace."

"You do not see what is true, Stands Shining. You
listen to my words but do not hear." One Claw folded his
arms across his chest. "Bluecoats say all the Buffalo
People are the same. They see no difference between
Arapaho and Kiowa or Comanche. Our turn for trouble
may be next. It's best to avoid all white soldiers."

"We need bullets," Stands Shining reminded her
great-uncle. "Not only for the buffalo, but because the
Pawnee and Utes have rifles to use against us. But I agree
the village must be away from Little White Man's lodge.
Maybe the warriors won't trade for so many hollow-woods
full of the stinging water, the *veheomahpe*." She stared at
One Claw. "Why do they wish to drink such poison? I've
tasted it. Paugh!"

"Firewater changes the way a man feels," One Claw
said. "He becomes someone else and knows nothing of
what's happening around him."

"Why would a man wish to be someone else? I
would never be anyone but who I am."

"There were times in the past when I drank firewater,'' One Claw admitted, ''but that was before my medicine vision.''

''Crying Wind will grumble over the move,'' Stands Shining noted. ''It would be well if I helped her pack the tepee.''

''Some day you must bring back a Pawnee slave to help Crying Wind with the work.''

''I'll remember.''

Turning to enter the tepee, Stands Shining paused when she heard the Crier's voice calling a message at the far end of camp.

''Buffalo! Buffalo come. A herd of bulls.''

Stands Shining smiled. This time of the year, the bulls and the cows herded separately. Cows had more tender flesh, but any buffalo meat would be welcome in this moon. She turned back to grasp One Claw's hands. Her eyes were bright with anticipation.

''A sign,'' he whispered. ''The bulls come early as a sign we should remember how Second Hero gave Our People the magic arrows made from buffalo short ribs, and how he showed our ancestors how to use the arrows to kill buffalo.'' One Claw looked thoughtful. ''Perhaps we rely too much on the white man's rifles.''

Men hurried to check bows and tighten bowstrings. Women readied pack ponies. Boys raced to bring buffalo horses to the hunters. The animals had been trained to follow tight beside a running buffalo. In that way, a rider's hands were free to use his bow.

Stands Shining's buffalo horse was a pinto she called Clever Foot. She accepted it from a grinning boy of nine winters, Bear Fat, who had no father to hunt for him and his mother.

''Your mother's tepee will be full of meat,'' Stands Shining promised the young Indian boy. ''Tell her to look for my arrows after the hunt.''

The dogs, who'd been running with the children,

barked a warning. One of the men who guarded the village, a Coyote, loped in.

"A stranger approaches from the east," he warned. "He signs he comes in peace. He is alone."

Stands Shining joined the warriors near the edge of the village and watched the stranger ride toward them. His horse was black and white and he led a half-grown pure black colt. Though he carried a bow and quiver of arrows, they were on his back, not in his hands.

The man halted when he reached a distance of four horses from them. Then he raised his right hand in the sign for friend.

Stands Shining saw his eyes shift from one warrior to another. Then they fixed on her. He was Kiowa. He was—was it possible? Her heart leaped.

He was First Cloud! He had grown taller, grown from a boy to a man. How handsome he was!

She kicked her pinto, intending to go to him. Then she halted the horse abruptly in sudden shyness. The warriors shifted, upset by her movements. Some reached for weapons.

"He is a friend," Stands Shining reassured them hastily. "I know him."

The warriors closed in around First Cloud, escorting him into the village. But Stands Shining lagged behind, her heart pounding uncontrollably.

First Cloud had demonstrated courage and daring even as a boy. Now, Stands Shining noticed, his headdress showed he'd killed enemies in war. No doubt such a warrior would already have a Kiowa wife.

Yet he'd come here to her village. A true warrior never forgot a promise. But was it only to keep his word to a little girl that First Cloud had ridden so far? She'd seen nine winters since she was with him last. She made a face remembering herself, a scrawny child with tangled hair.

When she looked at her reflection in still water, she

calmed herself. Her face wasn't ugly. Her hair lay in sleek braids and her body was healthy and well formed, a woman's body.

Crying Wind's words echoed in her mind. "No man wants a warrior woman for a wife."

Stands Shining shivered. She urged Clever Foot ahead and trotted past the warriors. I'll tell Heavy Pine that First Cloud is my friend, she decided. I'll make certain he's invited to come wih us on the buffalo hunt so I can be with him, talk to him. I won't think of what Crying Wind says. First Cloud is Kiowa, not Arapaho, and he's come to see me.

The Arapaho Spear Men, Age Society men over forty, were responsible for policing the hunt. They had organized the braves into groups, reminding each one that no one was to rush toward the herd until given the word. One rash man, they were told, might scatter the buffalo before the rest of the hunters were close enough to make their kill. The Spear Men signed to First Cloud to obey them and he signed back that he understood, that he had hunted buffalo in a similar manner many times with his own tribe.

"Any brave who disobeys will be punished." The leader of the Spear Men spoke sternly, eyeing the younger braves.

Stands Shining watched First Cloud check his bowstring, but she turned her eyes away when he glanced in her direction. Her heart was fluttering as rapidly as the wings of a hummingbird. Why couldn't she bring herself to speak to First Cloud? No man had ever made her feel so strange.

A Spear Man directed Stands Shining to the north, away from First Cloud. She and her six companions were to stay far enough from the herd that the buffalo would ignore them. Her pinto, Clever Foot, was the finest breed of buffalo horse. He'd been a wild mustang and had been captured a year before.

The mustangs shared the prairie with the buffalo. They didn't fear the massive creatures as village herd-born horses often did. If a hunter couldn't urge his horse close to a buffalo, he had little chance of killing the animal.

When Stands Shining first learned to shoot buffalo, she'd been frightened to be among the herd. The bulls stood as tall as warriors. Their wicked curved horns were as long as two spans of a man's hand. When she'd lived among the Kiowa, she'd once seen a bull's horn catch a hunter's horse, carrying horse and rider aloft for many paces before hurling them to the ground. The disemboweled horse died on the spot. The hunter was mangled and crushed, but lingered for two suns.

The Spear Men signaled the charge. Stands Shining rode Clever Foot toward the mass of buffalo, urging him into a gallop. As the hunters rushed at the beasts from three sides, the buffalo turned to run. The sun shone dimly through a great dust cloud as the pinto dashed among the bulls. Stands Shining heard their horns rattling as the huge animals jostled one another.

She selected a bull. With her knees, she directed Clever Foot alongside while her hands nocked an arrow. The animal's coat was too spring-shabby to make a good hair robe, but even his tough meat would be welcome.

Aiming just behind the short ribs, she let her arrow fly. It sped true. Blood gushed from the bull's mouth and Stands Shining wheeled her horse away. She knew he was mortally wounded and would soon fall.

One by one, Stands Shining killed eleven bulls. Another, to her shame, ran out of sight with two of her arrows still in him.

Soon Bear Fat's mother, Snake Woman, and Crying Wind would be searching among the dead bulls for her arrows. Then they would butcher the animals. Stands Shining remembered helping with this task before she became a warrior. She'd slashed across the brisket and neck, folded back the hide and cut out the forequarters. Then she'd slit the hide down the middle of the back and peeled it to the ground so the meat could be laid on it and hauled away. After the hindquarters had been disjointed, she'd cut the flank open to remove the stomach and intestines. Cooked intestine with partly digested feed inside it was one of her favorite dishes.

The liver and heart belonged to the hunter to keep or give away. Stands Shining would make sure Bear Fat got a heart for bringing her Clever Foot. Crying Wind would smoke the tongues over a fire of buffalo chips. One Claw never got enough of that.

Stands Shining rode past the dead bulls looking for Kiowa arrows. "Nine," she counted under her breath. "Ten." Then, finally, "Eleven." She smiled, admitting to herself she hadn't wanted to kill more than First Cloud.

Her smile faded when she rounded an outcropping of rock and saw a bull down behind it, partially hidden from view. Two shafts protruded from his side. Her shafts. She'd killed twelve buffalo. First Cloud had killed only eleven.

After staring for a moment at the dead bull, Stands Shining glanced quickly behind her. Then she slid from the pinto, dropped to one knee and cut out her arrows. Remounting, she joined the hunting party.

When the counts were announced, she and First Cloud had killed the most animals with eleven each. Nothing was said about finding a dead bull with no arrows in him.

First Cloud approached Stands Shining at the evening's feast. Her pulse quickened.

"I have tethered the black colt beside your great-grandmother's tepee," he told her. "He is the son of the stallion you rode in my camp. I saved him to bring to you."

Stands Shining dropped her eyes as any maiden would before a brave. "I am pleased," she murmured.

"When I first heard about this brave Arapaho girl who rode a white war horse and brought luck to her every raid, I knew she must be my little friend, Pony Girl," First Cloud said. "But I find you are no longer little. Certainly you are no longer a girl."

Stands Shining raised her head and saw admiration and desire shining in First Cloud's eyes. Her face warmed and a quivering began in her stomach.

This handsome Kiowa warrior wanted her!

"I didn't know you'd heard of me," she whispered.

"All those who follow the buffalo know of Warrior Woman," First Cloud informed her. "Enemies of the Arapaho fear her."

"You have never been my enemy."

"Maybe I am a little bit afraid of you, just the same," First Cloud confessed, smiling. "I never thought to find a woman who could match me shooting buffalo."

A feather of uneasiness touched Stands Shining's elation. She thrust the twelfth bull from her mind and smiled. First Cloud was a few inches taller than she—not as tall as Arapaho braves, though taller than most Kiowa men. She was happy he didn't have hair on his face like Chief Sitting Bear.

"You have grown to be very pretty," First Cloud complimented her.

Stands Shining blushed. Other warriors had praised her prowess with the bow and the rifle. They had commented favorably on her horsemanship. But none had ever told her she was pretty.

"You would be welcome in my great-grandmother's lodge," Stands Shining told First Cloud, "for as long as you wish to stay."

"I can stay only one more sun," he answered. "I've promised to join a Kiowa war party."

Stands Shining tried to keep the disappointment from her face.

"How was I to know, without seeing you, how I would feel?" he asked, reading her thoughts.

"How do you feel?" Stands Shining's words were so soft First Cloud had to bend close to hear her.

"I want you for my wife," he whispered back, and Stands Shining sighed in relief, in joy.

"I'll return with many horses for your great-uncle," First Cloud swore. "You are worth every horse in my herd." He took her hand. "When the sun warms the morning, we will ride out together before I leave."

He wanted to be alone with her!

Stands Shining sighed. She knew that tonight was not the time. There would be ceremonies and the dancing to come after the feast. But in the morning . . .

"Yes," she responded, gently returning the pressure of his hand.

Never had she had such trouble sleeping. Tossing and turning, she waited eagerly for the sun to rise. First Cloud had not stayed in Crying Wind's tepee. Heavy Pine had taken a liking to him and offered the hospitality of his own lodge. A visitor did not refuse such an invitation.

By dawn Stands Shining had already been to the stream to wash. At the tepee, she had just finished braiding her hair when First Cloud whistled softly outside. She hurried to meet him.

A few clouds darkened the edge of the sky to the northwest, but the morning held the promise of spring. An undercurrent of coolness was the only reminder that Old Cold Maker from the north didn't give up easily.

First Cloud stood beside the black colt, patting its neck while the colt nuzzled his shoulder.

"He's more affectionate than his father," First Cloud observed, "but he'll be just as fiery. Wait and see."

Stands Shining untied Strong Heart and mounted him.

She realized her white stallion was getting too old to be a war horse. She would have to train the colt to replace him. A pang of grief gripped her as she imagined riding to war on any horse other than Strong Heart. The two of them were as one when facing the enemy. Strong Heart knew without direction what she wished of him.

"My heart is full of gratitude for the colt," Stands Shining declared, watching First Cloud vault onto the back of his black and white horse.

"How does your heart feel about me?" he asked as they threaded their way among the tepees and headed for the stream.

Stands Shining bit her lip. She was too shy to tell him. She'd had no experience with such a whirlwind of feelings as these that shook her when First Cloud smiled at her, when he touched her.

"We can ride to where my herd grazes," she suggested. "It's pleasant there."

And secluded as well, she thought. If Bear Fat came to check on her horses she'd send him away. No one else was likely to intrude. Her breath came faster as she considered what might happen once she was alone with First Cloud.

"You have brought your bow. Do you think you will need to use your arrows against me?" he asked.

Stands Shining flushed. It was second nature to her to arm herself when riding out of camp. It was expected of a warrior. Frowning, she observed that First Cloud carried his bow as well. But she mentioned nothing.

They dismounted near her horse herd. First Cloud took the robe from his horse's back and spread it on the ground. The location he chose was a protected spot slung against a low hill where the wind didn't reach but where there was warmth from the sun rising into the sky. He sat next to her.

"I have left my bow with my horse," Stands Shining pointed out, "as you have."

First Cloud had started to reach out to her and now he hesitated. "I forget you ride with the warriors," he murmured.

Stands Shining put her hand in his, smiling at him, and he took a deep breath.

"I never hoped to find such a beautiful woman to keep a lodge for me," he told her, swelling with emotion, "to fashion my moccasins and bear my children."

A chill spread over Stands Shining as though an unseen spirit cloud had darkened the sun. She swallowed. "I don't . . ." she began, then broke off. "I'm not good at women's work," she managed to get out.

First Cloud laughed. He put his arm around Stands Shining's shoulders to draw her closer. "It is easy to learn," he chuckled. "At least it's easier than learning to be a warrior."

First Cloud's manly smell excited Stands Shining. She snuggled against him. Naturally he expected her to do women's work. But she wasn't going to work at all the tasks of a wife. They must talk about this problem more. Now she would be silent. This was not the time for such discussion. This was the time to discover what it was like to have a man hold you in love.

First Cloud pressed her even closer to him. The feel of his arousal made a tremor of desire and fear tingle along her spine. She longed to merge with him. Yet at the same time she fought off an impulse to jump to her feet, to leap onto Strong Heart and flee.

"You will be mine," he rasped. His face was dark with desire, his breathing quick and heavy as he pushed her backward insistently until she lay on his robe.

The woman in Stands Shining responded to First Cloud's passion, but a part of her looked at him and saw a stranger who would never understand her. She closed her eyes, fighting away doubt. This man was First Cloud and she loved him, wanted him, but . . .

The warning howl of a Coyote made her start. She thrust First Cloud aside and sat up.

He stared at her, a question in his eyes.

"Listen!" she urged.

Another Coyote howled. Then he barked three times.

The hair bristled on Stands Shining's neck. "Don't you hear?" she asked, scrambling to her feet. "The Coyotes, the camp guards, warn of danger."

"I hear them!" First Cloud hissed in frustration. Rising, he adjusted his breechcloth.

Stands Shining leaped onto the white stallion.

"Bluecoats!" she cried. "Bluecoats ride against our village!"

Chapter 9

Stands Shining galloped toward the village, veering to join the group of mounted Arapaho warriors already leaving the tepee circle. First Cloud pounded up beside her as she slowed Strong Heart.

"Bluecoats came to my village twelve suns ago," he told her. "Their chief smoked with the council and they harmed no one."

"We cannot trust any white soldier," Stands Shining replied. Too well, she remembered One Claw's warning. "We go to meet them armed. We will be prepared to fight."

The sun dimmed as Stands Shining spoke. It was as if clouds to the northwest had sent scouts to cover the sun.

"The bluecoat chief sought to make peace with the Kiowa," First Cloud went on. "Perhaps this is the same man, now coming to the Arapaho. I do not like white soldiers but it is not wise to ride against them when they come in peace."

"I hear what you tell me," Stands Shining said. "There will be no fighting unless the bluecoats come as enemies."

First Cloud glanced at the unsmiling Arapaho warriors. Some had painted their faces for war.

"Do they heed the words of Warrior Woman?" he asked.

* * *

"These be 'Rapaho, not Pawnee," the black-bearded scout called Oregon Tom muttered to Lieutenant Cooper. Both men were staring as the Indians sat astride their ponies on the crest of the next hill.

"What difference does it make?" the lieutenant asked. "They're all horse thieves. You demand they return our horses and mules and we'll see what they do."

"Pawnee stole them horses," Oregon Tom countered stubbornly.

"Maybe so. Maybe not. I'm not so sure you can tell one from the other, like you claim. No one caught a glimpse of the bastards. Even if they were Pawnee, the damned Arapaho are like the rest of the Indians. They've got plenty of army horses in their herds. We'll get those horses back. Today."

"That 'Rapaho camp's got more warriors than we got troopers," Oregon Tom warned.

Lieutenant Cooper looked back at the double line of troopers on their horses. He grunted in disgust. One measly company was all they'd given him.

"See that the men have their rifles ready," he told his sergeant. "One trooper is worth twenty redskins any day."

But uneasiness touched him. At least half his men were green as grass. Some had been farmers less than six months ago.

"Be prepared to fight," he called, halting his troopers and turning to face them. "Rifles at the ready but no one is to fire unless I give the order."

"I don't like the sky," Winter Bull commented. "It is not a good sign." His gaze shifted from Stands Shining to First Cloud. "I wonder if we are wise to listen to Kiowa words."

Stands Shining narrowed her eyes as she stared at

Winter Bull. Why had he ridden with them? He was too old to be with the warriors.

"It is true the sky is dark. A storm approaches. Do you say we must attack the bluecoats because of this?" she asked.

"We ought to be ready to attack," he answered sullenly.

"Have I argued against being prepared? I will ride out ahead of the warriors and offer to parley with their chief. I know I have strong hearts and sharp arrows ready to come to my aid. Why loose the arrows unless we must?"

"The bluecoats won't parley with a woman," First Cloud argued, speaking in Kiowa so only she knew his words. "I have never seen a white woman soldier."

"I am a warrior," Stands Shining declared proudly. "They'll deal with me!"

"You are wrong," First Cloud stated determinedly.

She glared at him.

"Don't be angry. I speak truth. I will go in your place. I am Kiowa. We're at peace with the bluecoats."

Was First Cloud right? Would the bluecoat chief refuse to speak with her? Would he order an attack? The Arapaho had few bullets, the bluecoats many. The warriors' arrows would kill many white soldiers, but if fighting began now, the soldiers might raid the village where the women and children waited. A parley, successful or not, would give time for the helpless ones to flee to safety.

Before she could answer First Cloud, he signed to the warriors that he would ride ahead. Then he wheeled and kicked the black and white horse into a fast walk.

"*No,*" Stands Shining snapped under her breath. She remembered One Claw's insistence that bluecoats couldn't distinguish Kiowa from Arapaho. She urged Strong Heart after him.

"Will you ride with the Kiowa to protect him?" Winter Bull called, his voice heavy with sarcasm.

Stands Shining knew she couldn't do such a thing. First Cloud would never forgive her if he lost face. She yanked Strong Heart back abruptly, causing the white stallion to rear and dance. Then she soothed him while, apprehensively, she watched First Cloud descend the hill toward the bluecoats.

Lightning flickered out of roiling clouds that had advanced midway up the sky. The Thunderbirds were ready to fly. Could it be a sign as Winter Bull insisted? He envied her, she knew, but it was true her power came from Father Sun and the sun was gone from the sky.

"She's gonna be a bad one," Oregon Tom said. "You got to be careful when them clouds gets to looking green-black."

"The hell with the storm," Lieutenant Cooper swore. "What about that Indian coming this way?"

"I say it's a trap," his sergeant broke in. "Sir, the sneaky bastards mean to trick us into a parley so they can get close enough to kill us all. Seen it happen more than once."

The troopers muttered to one another. Horses snorted and stomped.

"He wants to parley, all right," said Oregon Tom. "I'd swear he was a Kiowa from the way he's dressed."

"Probably got Kiowas with the 'Rapahos hiding in back of that hill, waiting to fall on us, sir," the sergeant said.

Lieutenant Cooper turned a chilly glance at the man. He was a veteran trooper but too outspoken for a noncommissioned officer. Yet the lieutenant knew he needed the man's experience with Indians.

"Kiowa don't ally with 'Rapaho as a rule," Oregon Tom observed.

"Maybe it's a Kiowa camp," the lieutenant parried.

Tom shook his head. "Ain't. My thinking is you

ought to listen to this one them 'Rapaho sent out. You can
usually make peace with 'Rapaho. They fight when it's
needful but they ain't like the Cheyenne, always looking
for trouble. You want me to ride to meet him?''

Lieutenant Cooper hesitated. If anyone rode ahead, he
should. Yet he couldn't understand Indian gibberish. Both
of them ought to go, maybe.

Or should they?

Stands Shining forced herself to keep from clenching
her hands on the stallion's guide rope. First Cloud seemed
very small and alone as he headed toward the halted
bluecoats. Thunder growled far away and she shivered as
she felt more and more that something would go wrong.

Why hadn't the whites sent a man to meet First
Cloud?

I can't stay here and do nothing, Stands Shining
thought. I'll gallop ahead and join him. The two of us will
face the bluecoats together. But she didn't follow through
with her plan, though the horse moved restlessly under
her. It was right for her to wait. First Cloud would expect
her to do that.

Like a woman.

Why should she think such a thing? Hadn't he told
her he respected her as a warrior?

"I don't like this," Winter Bull remarked, interrupt-
ing her thoughts.

For once Stands Shining was in complete agreement
with him.

"Watch those rifles!" the sergeant called. "You heard
the lieutenant. No one fires until he gives the order."

I said "unless," Lieutenant Cooper thought, but he
issued no correction.

Some of the green troopers had been aiming nervously at the oncoming rider, fingers at the ready. Hearing

the sergeant's words, they had lowered their rifles. But almost immediately, some thrust the muzzles up again. Jesus, the lieutenant thought, they're jittery enough to shoot *me* in the back if I ride out to meet that damn Indian.

He turned to Oregon Tom, intending to order him to go ahead to try to talk to the Indian before one of those nervous bastards behind him did pull his trigger and catapult them into a battle.

A jagged streak of lightning struck the ground like a snake uncoiling. Stands Shining waited for the boom of thunder. It came, blotting out all other sound.

For a moment nothing changed. Stands Shining bit the inside of her lip, her eyes fixed on First Cloud, who was still riding toward the bluecoats. Slowly he began to slip sideways. She caught her breath. The warriors around her did the same.

She saw First Cloud fall, topple from the black and white horse. He made no move to catch himself. When he landed on the ground, he lay still, his riderless horse breaking into a gallop and racing to the south away from everyone.

Stands Shining blinked in disbelief. For a moment she connected the lightning blast with what had happened to First Cloud. But the lightning had been nowhere near him. The bluecoats milled about. She smelled the faint tinge of gunsmoke wafting toward her on the wind.

First Cloud had been shot! She understood that now.

With a shriek of defiance and rage, she urged Strong Heart ahead and galloped down the hill, bow in hand.

Kill them, she thought. Kill every bluecoat.

The stallion passed First Cloud's motionless body. Stands Shining saw the red stain on his breast and knew he was dead. Then she heard the warriors pounding behind her. Their war cries rode the rising storm.

Thunderbirds flew across the sky, their wings making

bone-shaking thunderbolts. Rain pelted down. The entire world was noise and darkness lit erratically by the white flame of lightning. In the garish brilliance, Stands Shining saw the bluecoats' rifles pointed at her. At once she heard the crack of gunshots between roars of thunder.

The white soldiers wheeled. They fled as the wind screamed past Stands Shining, carrying shouts from the warriors behind her.

She couldn't make out their words. Not caring, she raced after the bluecoats. I'll never give up, she vowed. I'll track them down. Kill them. The wind seemed to suck at her breath. She felt Strong Heart strain under her, fighting its blast. The rain whipped at her with such fury she could no longer see the white soldiers, even when lightning streaked through the terrible darkness.

Strong Heart struggled on, slipping and sliding as the ground grew slick with water. There was no sign of the warriors. Had they sought shelter from the storm?

"Cowards," she muttered, and the wind picked up the word from her lips and whirled it away.

Strong Heart stumbled and Stands Shining heard a crack. The horse fell, throwing her forward. She tumbled into the mud. The wind howled like a wolf, shoving her away from the downed stallion as she struggled to crawl toward it.

In desperation she placed her hands on the horse's foreleg and felt the shattered bone she had hoped she wouldn't find. Slowly she inched her knife from its sheath.

"Brave spirit," she whispered into the stallion's ear. "Wait for me in the Land Beyond."

Then she cut his throat.

Tears streamed down her face and mixed with the rain as she stumbled away. She felt hopelessly lost. All landmarks were hidden by rain and darkness, so she went with the wind, pushed along. She had no strength or will left to fight it.

Strong Heart was dead. No longer would he carry her into battle. Never again would his great strength pour into her, help her arrows fly true, send her bullets straight.

She couldn't think past his death, or past the memory of First Cloud and what she had lost when he died.

Suddenly she was ankle-deep in swirling water. Muck caught at her moccasins. She fought to free herself, stumbled and fell headlong as water swirled over her head. She struggled to escape the raging torrent and caught a branch. Painfully she pulled herself up until her head was above water. She took a breath, but the branch snapped and the flood waters swept her away.

For long moments she didn't resist the pull of the current. What was left for her? First Cloud and Strong Heart waited for her in the Land Beyond. There they would be happy together.

But as water rushed over her head, Stands Shining held her breath. Her ears thundered and she thrust desperately upward until her face rose above the water. There she gasped for air, forgetting all thoughts of death. Her body seemed to her to be acting without her will, clutching at branches, beating its way to the surface each time she went under.

For some reason she didn't understand, she was refusing to die.

Chapter 10

Hampton found that escaping from the Sioux was going to be more difficult than being accepted by them. Lost Hunter, the chief, valued Skull Singer, as he named Hampton. He even gave him back his chestnut, Ares, and assigned him to the Wolves—the Sioux scouts—for further training.

Jerome was renamed White Hair and taken into the tepee of the ferocious medicine man, Grey Spider, who believed Jerome's black skin held special power.

"Old conjure man ain't never gonna take to you," Jerome told Hampton. "Trouble be, he take to me so much he watch everything I do."

Hampton knew that he and Jerome had little chance of escaping. No sooner did he learn about the lay of the country that surrounded the village than the tepees were taken down and hauled by travois to another location. He and Jerome might be able to slip away undetected but soon they would get lost and be recaptured. Maybe killed.

As fall slipped into winter, snow and biting cold isolated the village. In the spring, the Sioux moved again, seeking buffalo. Halfway through June, the Sioux Moon of Making Fat, Hampton was with the Wolves outside the village when they saw strangers riding into their lands. White men, a party of fifteen.

Two of the Wolves howled, then raced to warn the village. Hampton stayed with the third scout. On foot, and keeping in the shelter of a shallow ravine, they crept closer to the travelers. Hampton noticed one of the fifteen men was wearing black. He risked discovery to get a better look and froze when he saw who the man was.

Father DeSmet.

The other scout also recognized the priest. "Blackrobe comes back to us," he said.

Stepping into the open, Hampton walked toward the priest's party. When he had signaled that he was a friend, the white men slowed their horses and advanced cautiously.

"Father DeSmet!" Hampton called.

Despite a shouted warning from one of his companions, the priest urged his horse toward Hampton. Reluctantly the others followed and soon surrounded him. The priest slid off his horse and held out his hand, but he gave no sign of recognition.

Hampton glanced down at himself and smiled ruefully. Breechcloth, moccasins, bow and quiver of arrows slung on his back, hair long and braided. An Indian.

"I'm Hampton Abbott," he stated quietly, the name sounding strange to him.

The priest stepped back in shock. "I was told you were dead!" he gasped.

When Father DeSmet rode away from the Sioux camp a week later, Hampton was with him, riding Ares. Jerome rode by Hampton's side until the tepees were almost out of sight. Then when he slowed, Hampton slowed too.

"I just plain don't want to leave that woman," Jerome admitted, looking back.

Hampton hesitated only a moment before he spoke. He knew Grey Spider's daughter and Jerome had been married in Sioux fashion and that Jerome's Sioux wife was expecting a child in the summer. He smiled, remembering how she'd offered water that day that seemed so long ago.

"Do you want to go back?" he asked Jerome. "Do you want to live with the Sioux?"

He saw the longing in Jerome's face and continued speaking before the black could answer.

"You're free to do what you wish." Hampton grasped Jerome's arm in friendship. "But know that I'll miss you."

"Free?" Jerome echoed in disbelief. "Free," he said again, feeling the full impact of what that word meant to him. Tears flooded his eyes when after a moment he covered Hampton's hand with his own. "The good Lord bless you," he whispered. Then, wheeling his horse, he galloped away.

"Good-bye!" he shouted as he raced back toward the village.

Hampton blinked away tears of his own as he hurried to catch up to DeSmet's party. Jerome had more than earned the right to be his own master but he was, Hampton realized with a shock, the only person in the world he'd ever called friend.

Certainly, Hampton reminded himself, he had learned to get along with the Sioux. But they didn't understand his aversion to raiding enemy villages as well as to killing and scalping.

It had taken Father DeSmet many hours to convince Lost Hunter that Hampton had obligations to the Great White Father in Washington and must leave to fulfill his vows. The chief viewed keeping a vow as a sacred duty, that ill luck would plague anyone who failed to do so. Reluctantly, he'd let Hampton and Jerome leave the village.

Jerome may have gone back but I never will, Hampton told himself. He laughed scornfully, remembering the dream he'd had as a child that he wanted to be an Indian again. But after so much time spent with the Indians he had seen he didn't fit in. What he longed to do was return to St. Louis. He wanted to see Roseann. Hampton shook his head. He knew he couldn't do that. As Father DeSmet had convinced Lost Hunter, there were obligations. And he would meet them.

Three Buffalo greeted Hampton as one returned from the dead, but Hampton declined his offer to stay in the Potawatomi village.

"I must see the commander at Fort Leavenworth," he told his friend.

At Leavenworth, Hampton found that the fort commander had no record of a Hampton Abbott who was supposed to have reported to him the previous August. He advised Hampton to return to St. Louis and consult with the superintendent of Indian Affairs.

St. Louis, swollen and noisy with growth, seemed unfamiliar to Hampton. Strangers had bought his grandfather's house. When he tried to visit the Youngs, he was told that the colonel and Roseann were living temporarily in Washington, D.C. He tried to see Superintendent Harvey, only to find out that a man named David Mitchell was the new superintendent. Mitchell would see him the next day.

Hampton rode past the Youngs' again. He stopped for a moment, staring at the side veranda where he'd last seen Roseann. She was far away from him still. At least she wasn't in New York and near Chambers at West Point. Next year Chambers would graduate and be an army lieutenant.

What was *he*?

The following morning, he met Superintendent Mitchell. "I found a memorandum mentioning you, Mr. Abbott," Mitchell told him. He eyed Hampton's buckskins and his moccasins. "You were to live with friendly Indians and learn their languages. Apparently you have done that."

"I speak Potawatomi, Delaware and Sioux, sir. And I

know the sign language. I have learned to scout with both Delaware and Sioux."

"It's hard to believe the army didn't snap you up."

"They seemed to think I belonged to this office, sir."

"Tom Fitzpatrick out at Fort Laramie could use a Sioux interpreter. I'll try to get authorization from Washington for you to join him, Mr. Abbott. It may take some months though, so leave word with me where you can be reached."

Hampton had no money and found work as a blacksmith's assistant. He didn't mind helping to shoe horses and the smith treated him civilly enough, but as summer edged into fall, fall to winter, he chafed at the waiting. He'd come to hate the city and longed to ride the hills in the west where greenery didn't close him in.

In March, his patience dissolved completely, and he went to Mitchell's office. "I've been waiting a long time, sir," he told the superintendent.

"Washington does move at a snail's pace," Mitchell admitted. "I can give you a letter releasing you to enlist at Fort Leavenworth as a scout. Would that help?"

"I'd be grateful, sir. I'd like to work as an interpreter among the Indians, but . . ." Hampton hesitated, searching for words. He could find none to tell how trapped he felt in the city.

Mitchell nodded understandingly. "If I hear anything from Washington I'll send word to Tom Fitzpatrick. You can stop in at Fort Laramie if you're sent that way or at Bent's Fort on the Arkansas. Tom's usually at one or the other of those places."

In late April, Hampton enlisted as an Indian scout at Fort Leavenworth. He was issued army blues and black boots as well as the regulation army percussion musket. Only the sharpshooter units got rifles.

Lieutenant Owens was in charge of the scouts. He paired Hampton with an Osage and assigned the two men to a company of troopers who'd been instructed to guard a train of traders' wagons going west on the Santa Fe Trail.

During the second week out from the fort, a man in the lead wagon complained of violent stomach cramps. Within two hours he was dead. His companion died that evening while the train was camped along the Arkansas River. Three more men took sick before midnight. Hampton saw one of them clutching at his stomach and groaning.

The Osage scout motioned Hampton away from the wagon. "Big sickness," he declared in English. "Very bad. We go."

Hampton watched in surprise as the Osage scooped up his belongings and headed for his horse.

"You stay, you die," the Osage warned, for Hampton had made no move to accompany him.

As the Osage rode away, the hair on the back of Hampton's neck bristled as though an enemy were stalking him. He whirled to look behind him but nobody was there. He crossed to one of the army campfires, deliberately not hurrying. He wouldn't let the Osage spook him.

"Cholera," he heard a sergeant mutter as he approached. "I tell you it's cholera. I seen it in St. Louis in '49 and that's what we got here."

The enlisted men listening to the sergeant glanced about uneasily.

"Why they was burning barrels of tar and sulphur on every street corner in St. Loo that year," he went on. "The death wagons was carting corpses off like cordwood, fifty or more every day."

One of the men rose, a blond private Hampton thought looked hardly sixteen. Without warning the soldier staggered, his eyes rolling back in his head. Then he fell heavily to the ground. His arms and legs jerked uncontrollably.

"Jesus!" the sergeant cried. "The damn cholera's got Johnson."

Except for the sergeant, the men around the fire fled. "You, there, come and help," the sergeant ordered Hampton as he darted away. "I'll fetch the doc."

Hampton walked closer. There was bloody foam on Johnson's chest. There was no rise and fall. The private was dead.

Shouts rose from the tents. Hampton waited, but no one came to look at Private Johnson. A wail of grief and terror came from the wagon camp. A woman's voice was suddenly cut off as if someone had clapped a hand over her mouth. Hampton turned from the dead man and moved quickly toward the army tents. Soldiers milled about, their voices high and excited.

A man with a fiery red beard was arguing with the captain in command of the troopers.

"I don't give a hoot what your orders are," Redbeard yelled. "Me and my friends are taking our rigs and hightailing it out of here. Damn your eyes, the army promised to help us."

"If you'll just wait until morning—" the captain began.

"Be dead of cholera by then. Now's when I'm skedaddling."

The captain's eyes lit on Hampton. "A scout," he said. "That's all I can spare." He jerked his head at Hampton. "Go with this man," he said. "Up the Arkansas as far as Bent's Fort. Wait there for orders."

"One man?" Redbeard exclaimed incredulously.

"You want the scout or not?" the captain asked. "I've no time to argue." He turned and strode away without waiting for an answer.

"Hundreds of hostiles out there and he gives me a scout. One goddamned scout." Redbeard peered closely at Hampton. "A half-breed," he muttered. "I hope to hell you're not like most of 'em. Half Indian, half white, all devil."

Hampton forced himself to stay quiet.

"Well, come on," Redbeard ordered. "I ain't staying to wait for the cholera to catch me. Rather take my chances with Kiowa and Comanche."

Hampton saddled Ares under a gibbous moon, then rode out with Redbeard, four other men and three wagons. Bent's Fort was on the Arkansas River. He'd be able to find it.

The California-bound Redbeard and his four companions drove their mules hard through the night, stopping to rest at dawn. Less than three hours later the three wagons were on the trail again, despite the fact that the animals obviously were tired.

"No point in killing your mules," Hampton advised Redbeard.

The man looked him up and down. "Who asked your opinion? The damn mules can rest all they want to once we get to Bent's. I hear tell a man can trade for fresh stock there."

By nightfall it was obvious the mules were played out. The men grumbled and set up a night camp.

"You take first guard," Redbeard ordered Hampton. "Wake me for second."

Hampton nodded and walked away to stand by Ares. He leaned his head against the chestnut's neck and the horse nuzzled him.

Near midnight he awakened Redbeard, then slept beside Ares for a few hours. He woke when Redbeard roused another of the men to take his turn as guard. Hampton dozed again, woke, and when he looked for the man who was supposed to be guarding the camp, saw him slumped asleep by the coals of the fire. Upon waking the man up, Hampton got cursed for his trouble.

Though he tried to stay awake after that to keep an eye on the irresponsible guard, Hampton kept dozing off. A whuffle from Ares woke him near dawn and he came awake with the feeling something was wrong. Instead of jumping to his feet, he grasped his musket, eased up and stood listening.

He heard nothing except the snores of the men. Even the guard was asleep. But he knew he should have been hearing the shrill of frogs, too. What had silenced them?

Hampton peered carefully about. The sky was still dark, but the blackness of night had lifted and he could make out vague outlines of wagons and trees. Slowly he edged closer to Ares, crouching so that anyone watching would see only the outline of the horse.

Was anyone watching? Hampton couldn't see anyone, but felt eyes on him. He gathered breath to shout a warning to the men. Before he could call out, one of the mules brayed, the raucous sound slashing into the quiet and startling him.

Redbeard cursed. But his words were cut off by screeches that seemed to come from every side at once.

Indians!

Hampton vaulted onto Ares' bare back. He had learned from the Sioux that the first move to make when attacking the enemy was to steal his horses. He turned the chestnut toward Redbeard and the other men. Screeching painted warriors blocked his path. He swung the musket up. As he fired, Ares reared and snorted. Then he bolted, racing out of the camp, pounding west along the riverbank.

Hampton struggled to turn the horse around. Looking back, he saw six mounted warriors pounding after him. A rifle cracked. Another. He heard the zing of the bullets. As luck would have it, he hadn't had time to reload his gun. Hastily he kicked Ares into a gallop.

I'll lose them and circle back somehow, he told himself. But deep within he realized his plan was useless. His year with the Sioux had taught him that attacking Indians gave no quarter. Redbeard and the other four men hadn't had a chance. By now all five had been scalped and the mules driven off as booty.

He'd be damn lucky to save himself with six warriors after him. Ares could outrun most horses, but the big chestnut had been ridden hard the day before. Hampton leaned forward, talking to him.

"You can do it, boy. We'll show them you're the best. You're the fastest, too. You can do it."

They pulled steadily ahead until only one brave was able to keep up the chase. Ares couldn't shake the spotted horse he rode. Hampton had seen only one other horse like that, spotted, with a short tail and scanty mane. It had been owned by Lost Hunter, who'd traded for it, he'd said, with the Pierced Noses who lived beyond the mountains.

Hampton felt his chestnut's energy waning. The spotted horse edged closer. A hundred yards. Eighty. He'd have to fight. He'd known all along it would come to that. There was no way to reload at full gallop. He had his knife. Spotted Horse had a rifle. Was it loaded? Two shots already had been fired at him. Had one been from Spotted Horse's gun?

Hampton scanned the terrain ahead in the grey dawn light. Straggly clusters of cottonwood grew along the riverbank. The hills rolled green and treeless providing no adequate cover. Hampton slowed enough to wheel Ares.

"*Hoka hey!*" he yelled, issuing the Sioux war cry. Then, while his pursuer was startled momentarily, he drove Ares straight at him.

Spotted Horse fired and, to Hampton's dismay, Ares staggered. The chestnut had been hit.

"Damn you!" Hampton shouted at the Indian.

Ares recovered his footing. As Hampton forced him on, he lagged, but strove gamely forward. The warrior tried to swerve to one side, but Hampton was too close and the chestnut rammed the other horse hard, both animals reeling back, scrambling to stay on their feet. Hampton launched himself off Ares at the Indian, knocking him from his horse. They both slammed to the ground.

The warrior was small, but tough and wiry. He was quick, too, and grabbed for his knife. Hampton clamped his wrist just in time to stop him from using the blade and the Indian raised his other hand to jab outspread fingers at Hampton's eyes.

Hampton jerked his head away, at the same time lunging for the warrior's neck. Red clouded his vision. His ears still echoed with the shot that had wounded Ares. He dug his fingers into the Indian's flesh. Not until much later did he realize that the Indian no longer struggled. He took his hands away and stared down through the blur of red. Then gradually his vision cleared and he rose, taking a deep breath.

The warrior was dead. But when guilt spread through Hampton, it came with a fierce feeling of elation. Why? He'd won! Battled the foe and killed him. Why should he feel guilty? It had been his life or the warrior's and he was the conqueror.

He looked east. There was no sign of pursuit. Ares waited, head drooping, only yards from him. But the spotted horse was farther away, ears pricked alertly, watching. Hampton walked over to Ares and examined him. The bullet had gone into the chestnut's right shoulder. Blood oozed from the wound. He patted Ares' neck.

"Poor old boy," he soothed.

Then, hoisting himself onto the chestnut's back, he coaxed him into a walk. As he'd hoped, the spotted horse stayed put as they approached, less alarmed by a rider than he would have been by a man on foot. Moments later he held the horse's trailing bridle rope in his hands, and he leaned toward him, talking softly.

"Fast as the wind, aren't you?" he murmured. "A beauty you are, fast and lovely."

He went on talking as he slid off Ares and climbed onto the spotted horse, careful to mount the Indian horse from the right instead of the left.

As he quieted the uneasy animal, it occurred to Hampton to name the horse, as the judge had always done, after a Greek god.

He looked upriver where the sun rose behind him and illuminated green and brown hills rolling westward. Layers of clouds settled above them. A damp breeze lifted a strand of Hampton's hair.

"Westwind," he announced tenderly. "That will be your name."

Hampton recovered his gun and the Indian's. Riding Westwind and leading Ares, he headed west. To go back would be certain death. The Indian warriors would be searching for their comrade. If he could get far enough ahead of them they might decide not to trail him. There was a chance they would consider the scalps of Redbeard and the other men vengeance enough.

Chapter 11

For many minutes the flood rushed Stands Shining downstream. She was bruised and shaken from being buffeted against trees that had been torn from the banks and swept into the swollen stream. She had barely enough strength to keep her head above water.

Grasping a large floating limb, she manipulated her fingers until she managed to take firm hold. The sound of roiling water filled her ears. She could hear nothing else. Lightning still flickered even though the sky was less dark. Stands Shining was cold, chilled to the heart.

With a bone-shaking crunch, the limb hit an obstacle. Clutching the slippery wood frantically, Stands Shining heard the limb grate against rock. She caught a glimpse of a boulder. Through a tangle of branches, she clawed her way to it. She huddled there, shaking.

The sky lightened. The angry clouds raced southeast. The rain lessened. To her dismay, Stands Shining discovered that her boulder was surrounded by flood water. Land was too far away on either side for her to leap to. Dropping her head, she shut her eyes. Winter Bull had seen true. She had misread the signs. Her power was gone.

Suddenly brightness swirled behind her closed lids. Her body grew numb, then strangely light. She felt transported to another place. The brilliance blinded her as if she dwelt in the heart of Father Sun himself. With difficulty she made out a dim shape, a tiny dot of darkness approaching her.

It was a horse. A spirit stallion.

Stands Shining watched, her own spirit exalting as the horse galloped, head high, mane and tail flying, black as coal. He circled her four times. Then, though the light persisted, he was gone.

When she opened her eyes, Stands Shining saw that the sun had broken through the clouds. A shaft of light touched the southern bank of the stream. Then, even as she looked, the sunlight disappeared. The sky was dark again. Rain drops sprinkled her face.

The sun had been a sign that power waited. Stands Shining was sure of that.

Teeth chattering from the chill, she pondered her vision. She had seen the colt First Cloud had brought her. He had grown into a magnificent steed, her war steed.

She must live. If not for herself, for First Cloud. She must ride the black horse to seek those who had murdered him. She must kill bluecoats.

Vengeance would be the stallion's name.

Feeling stronger, Stands Shining stood and surveyed the flood waters. She was closer to the south bank than the north. But it was twice as far as she could jump and the swift current made swimming impossible. She eyed the mass of broken trees caught against the boulder. As she studied it, a clump broke free and swirled downstream to the north of the rock.

What would happen, she wondered, if she could maneuver a large clump into the south channel? Would it be large enough to span the space from boulder to south bank? And even if it did that, would it hold long enough for her to scramble across?

The rain had stopped, but the rock was wet and slippery. Stands Shining slid time and again as she pried and prodded the debris, trying to force branches toward the south channel. Splinters tore at her hands until her blood stained the wood.

She was breathless until at last a mass shifted and was caught by the current. It spun into the south channel and Stands Shining flung herself at the debris when she saw it reach the bank. For the moment it choked the stream.

Halfway across, she felt the wood shift under her. Faster and faster she crawled over the intertwined limbs. The debris was moving. Desperately, Stands Shining climbed onto a projecting branch. There she stood for a moment, balancing, then leaped for the bank just as the water snatched her bridge from under her.

She landed half in the stream. The current tugged at her legs, pulling her back into the water. But she dug her fingers into the mud and dragged her body onto the ground until finally she was able to stumble to her feet. Staggering away from the stream, she leaned against a cottonwood trunk.

"Man Above, thank you for helping me," she whispered, and after a time she pushed away from the tree and made her way out of the cottonwoods to open country.

Once there, she scanned the horizon. Thinning clouds revealed patches of blue. Far to her left was the tall thrust of Spirit Peak, always a landmark for Our People. But it likely was as far as two sleeps away.

After shaking and squeezing as much water as she could from the tunic she wore, Stands Shining untied her leggings and wrung them out. She had lost both her moccasins, so she fashioned coverings from the leggings and bound them to her feet with thongs.

Heading upstream, she shivered. On foot and weaponless, she was extremely vulnerable. To add to her uneasiness, she was wet and cold.

But soon the sun broke through. Light poured onto the muddy ground. As she crested a rise, Stands Shining saw a glint of white in the distance. She slowed. White was a color to be wary of. Few things except snow were naturally that color.

Whatever this was, it didn't move. It was not an animal, Stands Shining decided. She ducked among the cottonwoods straggling along the stream, still forging ahead, but more carefully now. Her path would take her near the white object that was at the edge of the trees farther upstream.

The cottonwoods fluttered new green leaves that were still pale and small. A washed-clean smell rose from the wet ground. And the patch of white grew larger.

Stands Shining stopped forty paces away from it. She discovered a wagon covered with white cloth in the manner of the palefaces. Her eyes narrowed, feeling frustrated to be without a weapon. After a moment she edged cautiously ahead, keeping in the cover of the trees.

Carefully she eased from tree to tree, but she saw no other wagons. This was strange. The *niatha* usually traveled with groups of wagons. Then she caught sight of a horse tethered close by. Its head was turned toward her. Its ears were pricked. The horse knew where she was.

Stands Shining waited, watching and listening. The clouds had rolled off to the southeast and the sun slid down the western sky toward his night lodge. Shadows thickened among the trees and still she heard nothing from the wagon except the whuffling of the horse. No one appeared.

There was no sign of mules or oxen that must have lugged the wagon to that spot. The horse, a brown mare with a white-starred forehead, was small. She was a horse to ride, not to pull a large wagon. Where were the white men? Inside, asleep?

At dusk, Stands Shining slid closer. Cautiously she circled the wagon, again keeping to the cover of the trees. The mare's ears twitched.

To the rear of the wagon, a white man's digging tool was shoved into the ground near a mound of mud. The hair prickled along Stands Shining's arms. The horse whinnied, making her start.

She wanted that horse, needed her. But was someone watching from inside the wagon?

Taking a chance, Stands Shining darted across the space between the trees and the wagon. She half-expected a challenge, a shot, but nothing stirred except the horse who tried to nuzzle her. She eased around to the front of the wagon and saw a booted foot thrust from under the board used as a driving seat. When the foot didn't move, Stands Shining stepped onto the wagon tongue to peer inside. A bitter stench made her grimace.

A man with a beard the color of straw lay on the floor of the wagon. He had been sick, and the odor was nauseating. His face was twisted in death. There was no one else in the wagon. Stands Shining stepped off the tongue and backed away.

Drawn against her will to the clump of mud, she hurried across the small clearing and stopped short at the edge of a partly filled grave. She bit her lip as she stared down at the muddied body of a child. A bit of red color in a clump of saplings nearby caught her eye. Reluctantly she walked to the trees, fearing what she'd see.

A woman wearing a red cloth over her hair lay face down among the cottonwood shoots. Despite the cleansing by the rain, the smell of vomit clung to her, too. She was dead.

Terror shot along Stands Shining's spine. She knew she faced an unknown evil. Backing away, she wheeled and ran to the horse. Her fingers fumbled frantically at the knot that tied the mare to the wagon. Once the horse was loose, Stands Shining vaulted onto her back and kicked her into a gallop. Only when she was out of sight of the wagon and its dead did she slow. The mud was making the going hard for the mare. Stands Shining knew she couldn't afford to have this horse stumble and break a leg as Strong Heart had.

Why had the white family died? What terrible disease had struck them down, killing father and mother before they'd finished burying their child? Smallpox was a white man's disease, one that caused ugly sores over the body. Few Arapaho or Cheyenne survived smallpox. She'd heard whites sometimes did. But these whites had no sores on their bodies.

She said a prayer to Man Above so that no bad disease spirit would follow her as she fled the wagon. She rode all night, drowsing when she could. At dawn she stopped to let the mare graze. She found herself wishing that dried grass and cottonwood shoots would satisfy her hunger as they had the horse's. After a brief rest she rode on, following the stream. Late in the morning she found a spot shallow enough to risk fording. The high water had already receded considerably. But still it came to the mare's shoulders.

The sun warmed Stands Shining's back as they rode west toward the Arapaho village. But her heart held the chill of dread. She was not able even to grieve for First Cloud, for an invisible menace hovered so close that she could feel its evil breath.

Something terrible would happen. Soon.

Near sundown, Stands Shining reached the bluff and looked down at the Arapaho camp. She gasped. Half the tepees were gone. At once she chided herself for being surprised. She had forgotten that the village planned to move. Some families had gone on ahead, that was all.

But no dogs ran barking to meet her as she approached. She smelled no meat cooking and saw no smoke rising from the cooking fires. An unnatural silence hung everywhere.

Fearfully, she rode toward Crying Wind's tepee. It was still in its accustomed place. But when she dismounted and pushed aside the tepee flap, again the sour smell of vomit struck her.

"Great-grandmother!" Stands Shining cried, seeing Crying Wind stretched on her sleeping mat beside the cold ashes of the fire.

Rushing toward the still figure, she stopped so abruptly that she lost her balance and nearly fell into the ashes. Hair rose on her arms.

Crying Wind was dead. And where was One Claw? Why had her great-grandmother been left alone on her mat when she should have been properly buried?

Terror-stricken, Stands Shining rushed among the remaining tepees, ducking her head inside each, smelling the dreadful odor, seeing the dead on their mats. She found other people sprawled among the lodges, filthy with vomit.

She'd returned to a village of death.

For only an instant, Stands Shining raised her head to shriek out her fright and grief. Then just as suddenly she choked off her wail. There was no time to mourn. Our People never left their dead unburied, but they'd never known such a frightening disease before, a disease that killed its victims before any medicine could help.

Those who remained alive must have fled.

This was a white man's disease, Stands Shining decided, this vomiting sickness. It had been brought to Our People by the wagons rolling to the west.

What would she do now? She couldn't leave Great-grandmother like this. The wind blew ashes from a deserted cooking fire to her feet. A coal glowed red. Stands Shining clenched her jaw. She didn't dare try to bury the dead, but she could prevent the wolves from mauling and eating them.

She could burn the village.

She dropped to her knees and blew on the ember, adding dried grass and a few buffalo chips until a fire was burning. After that, she ignited a stick and touched the flame to the nearest tepee. Flames edged along the hide covering.

Tepee by tepee, Stands Shining fired the village. Then she mounted the mare and rode to the crest of the bluff. Below her the village burned, the flames carried by a rising wind until the circle was bright with fire. The mare snorted and stomped.

Crying Wind was dead. Her great-grandmother, who'd scolded her and tried to turn her from her chosen path, was dead. Crying Wind, who had wanted her to be a woman, not a warrior. Crying Wind, who'd loved her even though she could never be a submissive Indian squaw.

She could have helped the old woman more. She could have brought her a Pawnee slave to assist with the work many winters ago. She'd been thoughtless. Too concerned with her own desires.

Now it was too late.

"Be happy in the Land Beyond," Stands Shining murmured sadly.

There Crying Wind would be young again. There her work would be easy. In the Land Beyond, First Cloud waited, forever young, forever handsome, a warrior forever.

But she, Stands Shining, lived.

The mare pawed the rocky ground and Stands Shining jerked her head upward as a hot ash blew against her cheek. The smell of burning hides fouled the wind. The grass on the hillside below was on fire and the flames wriggled up toward her like yellow snakes.

She retreated down the far slope, but the fire followed her. It swept over the rocky summit to catch the winter's dried thistles that were crawling downhill. Stands Shining kicked the mare into a trot, then a gallop. Still the flames pursued, flaring with the wind.

In alarm, Stands Shining veered north out of the path of the fire blown by the west wind. When she no longer

felt the pricks of burning ash on her skin, she looked for a
rise. She found one and rode to its crest and looked back.

A herd of horses was trying to escape. Arapaho
horses. The smell of burning grass had frightened them.

Stands Shining's heart beat faster. Her fire was out of
control, fanned by the wind. Let it burn, she thought. Let
it cleanse the village, cleanse the rolling plain, destroy the
whites in their wagons.

She squinted, then frowned. Had she seen a man? A
soldier wearing blue, thrashing in a stream? She could feel
hatred build within her. As if she had willed it, the trees
by the stream started to burn. While she watched, fire
leaped to the opposite bank.

"Let the white man die," she whispered. "The white
man *will die*."

Westwind moved ahead tirelessly. Hampton had taken
Ares off the lead. He kept looking back anxiously as the
chestnut fell farther behind. The clouds darkened and mul-
tiplied, climbing the sky.

Rain was coming. That was good. The storm would
wash away his tracks, Hampton thought. But as the clouds
rolled by overhead, they began to take on an ominous
greenish tinge. Hampton knew that look. Tornado weather.

He eyed the clouds, watching for funnels, casting
about for some kind of shelter. Trees were no good. What
he needed was a hole. Lightning was beginning to split the
clouds and thunder was all too close behind.

Ahead, a stream rushed into the Arkansas, its water
already high. Fifty yards back from the river, hills rose to
either side of the stream. That could be protection of a
sort. Yet if the ravine was too narrow, the rising stream
could drown him if he took shelter there.

Far off to the west, a whirling wisp of cloud reached
down to skip along the ground. Which way would the
funnel sweep? Hampton knew he couldn't risk waiting

around. He yanked Westwind's head toward the ravine and kicked him into a gallop. As he turned, he saw Ares swerve to follow.

Rain was pouring down by the time he reached the ravine. The force of the wind took his breath away. Hampton splashed through the creek, feeling the swift current tug at the horse. Driving for the side of the west hill, he dismounted and crouched beside Westwind. He could no longer see through the torrents of gusting rain and felt, rather than saw, a bulk loom up beside him. What he reached out and touched was Ares' wet flank.

The storm lasted for hours, the creek rising. Hampton was forced to climb higher up the steep bank. When at last the wind eased, he mounted the spotted horse and, leading Ares, threaded his way along the slippery bank in the rain until he was free of the ravine and near the Arkansas once more.

The rain gradually lessened as he and the two horses plodded west. By evening Hampton saw patches of blue between the clouds. He stopped for rest in a stand of cottonwood. I wish I had my buckskins, he thought, shivering in the damp wool of the blue army uniform and trying to sleep.

Sunshine awakened him the next morning, and hunger. Ares' wound had stopped bleeding and the horse acted almost like new. When Hampton mounted Westwind and tried to set the pace, Ares loped ahead. Then he looked back as if wondering what was keeping them.

In the late afternoon, Hampton started up a small herd of pronghorns and managed to shoot one. The next day he was tempted to ride Ares, but was afraid the spotted horse might not follow if he did. By the late afternoon both horses were growing restless. At first Hampton could find no reason for their uneasiness. Then his nose picked up what they smelled on the brisk wind.

Fire.

Shading his eyes, Hampton saw a single mountain peak rising to the west. Pike's Peak? He'd heard it could be seen from more than fifty miles away. Hills between him and the peak kept him from spotting the fire. But he knew approximately where it was because smoke clouded the western sky and was red in the setting sun. There will be plenty of time to turn aside when I see exactly where the fire is, he thought.

Minutes later a family of wolves trotted past him heading downriver. Hampton looked after them and wondered if they were fleeing the fire. Slowing Westwind, he noticed flecks of ash on the sleeves of his blue army coat. Ares ranged ahead, snorted, wheeled and came racing back.

Flames were spurting over the top of the next hill by then, fanning toward Hampton along the ground. They were being driven by the strong wind. The Arkansas, high and fast, was too dangerous to risk crossing. Hampton wheeled the spotted horse and raced northeast, hoping to angle from the fire's path and outrun the flames.

Small animals leaped from under the horses' hooves. There were rabbits, a fox and two coyotes. Smoke fouled the air. A spark tingled on Hampton's hand. Flames flared to the right between him and the river. Hampton was alarmed and tried to remember how far back the last feeder stream had been. Could they reach it in time?

The horses needed no urging and raced neck and neck through the choking smoke. Heat seared Hampton's back. He heard the crackle of burning bushes as the horses dashed among cottonwoods and splashed into a stream.

Hampton yanked Westwind to a stop, shouting at Ares, flinging himself off the spotted horse to try to stop the terrified animal, but Ares plunged across the stream and pounded on. Westwind jerked his bridle rope free and rushed after. Hampton was left on foot, stranded in the stream.

Throwing off his blue coat, he shouted after the fleeing horses. But soon they were invisible in the smoke and growing dusk. Casting himself into the stream as flames leaped up, Hampton lay prone in the shallow water. He held his breath. Feeling that he was being pushed downstream by the current, he tried to stop himself by grasping the small trunk of a sapling overtaken by the high water.

When he could stay underwater no longer, he raised his head. Smoke choked him. Glowing cinders singed his face. So he gulped air in and again ducked under.

The third time he came up, the worst of the flames had swept past. Though fires burned on both banks, it was safe to stay above water. He stood. His lungs felt clogged with smoke. He resisted the impulse to breathe deeply.

Then a blow struck him in the middle of the back, hurling him forward. As he fell, he twisted half around. In the fire's glare he saw the outline of a human arm upraised in attack.

Chapter 12

Hampton splashed sideways into the stream. Then he flipped onto his back and thrust his feet out of the water, kicking at his assailant's legs. This knife wielder must be one of the dead warrior's vengeance-seeking companions, he thought.

The Indian jumped back to avoid Hampton's kick, giving him time to scramble to his feet. But before Hampton could free his knife, the warrior leaped at him, knife raised, and screamed words Hampton didn't understand.

He knew how the Sioux used knives and evaded the thrust. They chopped downward, trying to stab behind an enemy's collarbone. Or they slashed sideways at the chest or stomach. Hampton knew he faced no Sioux, even though the Indian fought like one. Perhaps he was a Pawnee, a Cheyenne or Arapaho.

The fire flared to Hampton's left, red glinting from the knife blade as his attacker shifted position. Both fighters were slowed by the water, knee-deep on Hampton, above the knees of his shorter, lighter opponent.

The Indian shrieked defiantly and struck again. Hampton lunged for the warrior's wrist. Feeling the knife slash across his ribs, he caught the wrist and twisted.

The warrior jabbed with his free hand, but Hampton was ready, trapping the Indian's other arm. At the same time he jerked his head to the side to avoid the outspread fingers. His opponent writhed in his grasp, trying to kick but hampered by the water.

Hampton tightened his hold on the knife hand and wrenched it violently. The knife splashed into the stream.

"Now I've got you, you bastard," Hampton muttered.

As he spoke, a horse whinnied, and then another. Hooves pounded nearby.

Ares?

Hampton shook the warrior in frustration. What the hell was he to do with this Indian? Kill him in cold blood? If he didn't, the warrior would stalk him again.

The Indian spat angry words. Hampton didn't understand even one of them.

To his left he thought he saw new flames flare, but a quick glance told him it was the moon rising, full and blood-red. Fire red.

He stared at the warrior, who glared back. A horse snorted somewhere close. Hampton started as a bush on the edge of the water crackled into flame, the branches sounding like tiny pistols.

In the fiery glow, Hampton got the first good look at his opponent. His captive was a woman! In surprise and shock, he nearly let go.

Hooves plunged frantically to his right. The woman's head turned toward the sound. Flames darted a hundred hungry tongues toward the stream again as though the wind had shifted. Smoke watered Hampton's eyes.

He released his prisoner and stepped back, signing *Horses. Get horses.*

The woman hesitated, then turned away and plunged across the stream into the smoke on the right bank. Hampton hurried after her, groping toward the terrified horses that were stomping and snorting somewhere in the murk.

"Ares!" he called. "Ares!"

He caught a glimpse of movement and raced ahead,

stinging cinders falling on him from every side. The big chestnut stood trembling, eyes showing white. His reins were caught in the twisted branches of a smoldering bush. Hampton slashed the leather with his knife, then crooned into Ares' ear, trying to persuade him to move. He could hear other horses to his right.

Where the hell has the Indian woman gotten to? he wondered. He couldn't leave her there, despite the fact she'd attacked him.

"Ho!" he shouted. "Ho!"

There was no answer but the sound of hoofbeats. Mounting Ares, he urged the horse ahead. Moments later he found Westwind. He'd just managed to grab the spotted horse's bridle rope when the Indian woman's voice called urgently through the smoke.

Hampton shouted again and she appeared, running, slapping at a smoldering hole in her buckskin tunic. Without hesitating, she leaped onto Westwind's back and tugged impatiently at the rope Hampton held. He released it and she drove the spotted horse into the smoke.

Hampton followed as she plunged into the water, heading Westwind upstream. It was a good plan. But he frowned when she splashed out again onto the right bank some distance ahead where flames licked out. He heard the desperate scream of an injured colt and urged Ares from the water.

In a moment he discovered Westwind and the woman among a group of panic-stricken, rearing horses. A black colt was down. The Indian was trying to drive the other horses toward the stream, but most were too frightened to obey.

Hampton coaxed Ares into the struggle, urging the chestnut to nudge the other horses. Together they forced the little herd toward the water. Hampton rode behind the horses, shouting at them. His throat was raw with smoke. The taste of ashes was on his tongue. He reached the stream just as Westwind splashed into the water beside Ares—riderless. When he looked back, he saw only red-tinged smoke.

Damn that Indian woman!

Ares fought him as he tried to force the chestnut out of the water. Ahead, the horses splashed upstream and Ares struggled to follow.

Finally Hampton slid from the chestnut's back and waded to the bank. The Indian would be the death of both of them, he thought angrily as he sidestepped new flames.

She was with the black colt. Somehow she had gotten him to his feet and was coaxing him to move.

Hampton reddened with rage. The woman was risking her life—his, too—over an injured colt. But even as he grumbled to himself, he strode to her and reached under the colt's belly, heaving the little horse into his arms. His chest ached as he staggered toward the stream. An ember landed on his shoulder and the woman darted to him and beat out the fire. She walked close beside him as he struggled to carry the colt through the thickening smoke.

At the stream, he eased the frightened animal into the water. Grasping its mane firmly, he pulled the colt upstream. To his surprise the colt made an effort to forge ahead, even though it was up to its belly in water.

Hampton's head buzzed dizzily as he waded upstream. Keep going, he urged himself. He could hardly force his legs to push against the current. His hand fell from the colt's mane.

He was scarcely aware of the smoke thinning and submitted dazedly when the woman led him from the stream. Once on the bank, he slumped to the ground. He knew the Indian had left him alone, but couldn't bring himself to care what she was up to. He drifted into sleep.

A pounding in his head roused him. But it was not in his head. It was in his ear when he pressed it to the ground. Hooves. Feeling less dizzy, Hampton sat up. The moon was still flame-red and rode higher. Fire swept to the southeast but he felt unburned grass moist under his fingers.

He forced himself to his feet, watching for the riders he had heard. Were they armed braves from the woman's camp? He fumbled with his knife, had it half out of the sheath when he saw Westwind. The woman was riding him and leading a riderless horse. The colt was tagging behind.

Hampton waited for her approach, his hand still on the handle of his knife. Only when he saw that the horse she led was Ares did he slide the knife back into its sheath.

As he climbed onto the chestnut, he felt his skin rip. Pain lanced across his chest. He touched his breast, felt the slash cut in the army coat and remembered the knife the Indian woman had wielded. He hadn't thought about being hurt by her attack until that moment.

As Ares followed Westwind, Hampton slid a hand inside his coat. He felt the wetness of blood and winced as his fingers found torn skin. Carefully he traced the edges of the cut along his ribs. It was a hand span long, but shallow.

Despite his determination to stay alert, he slipped into a doze as they rode to the northwest. By the time it was dawn and the Indian woman halted among cottonwoods, many hills were between them and the fire. Hampton could no longer see if it still burned.

He did see, maybe twenty miles west, the solitary peak he thought was the one he had spotted while farther out on the prairie. Beyond it, many peaks were etched darkly against the greying sky.

Fatigued as he was, his heart lifted at the sight. The Rockies, he told himself. He looked at the woman. She sat erect on the spotted horse gazing east. Her face was upturned. He knew, like the Sioux, she waited to offer a prayer at sunrise. Somehow he realized now she'd had no connection with the Indians who had killed Redbeard and his companions.

It made little difference that her buckskins were burned and dirt-smeared—she carried herself like a princess. Hampton watched her, fascinated. Never had he seen a lovelier Indian woman. Her high cheekbones and oval face, her large dark eyes and slender, curving form made her the rival of any white woman. Tired as he was, desire mixed with his admiration. He couldn't take his eyes from her.

Ares shifted under him and the motion sent a stab of pain across his ribs, reminding him who his attacker had been only hours before. He'd do well to remember that the Indian had tried to kill him.

She ignored him, lifting her arms as the first rays of the sun shot the sky with light. Then she began to chant.

When she finished her morning prayer and turned to him, Hampton blinked. He pulled himself straighter as she looked him up and down, then signed that he should dismount. When he hesitated, she made the sign again, impatiently, as though accustomed to being obeyed.

As he slid warily from Ares, Hampton decided this was no shy maiden such as he had seen among the Sioux.

She dismounted. *You are hurt,* she signed. *Rest.*

He stayed on his feet.

Rest, she signed again. *I tend your wound.*

She walked away to gather leaves from a plant growing almost under the water of the creek that ran among the cottonwoods. She put the leaves into her mouth and began to chew them, motioning to Hampton to come to the creek.

He walked slowly toward her, finding when he stood beside her that she was only half a head shorter than he. When she began to unbutton his coat, the rising sun touched her, turning her skin to gold. He sucked in a breath.

She glanced into his face inquiringly. *Pain?* she signed.

He stepped back and finished taking off his own coat and shirt, alarmed at the surge of desire that had nearly made him take her in his arms. He stared down at the blood-encrusted knife slash across his chest to the left and below the skewer scars.

When he was stripped to the waist, she gestured for him to sit by the stream. She knelt next to him and pushed at his shoulder until he understood she wanted him to stretch out on his back. He hesitated and she frowned.

As he lay back, he felt his muscles tense. Over and over the Indian woman scooped water from the stream and let it pour onto the wound. The chill was uncomfortable at first, but the flow of water became soothing as she persisted. Soon the dried blood and grime had been washed away.

Leaning over him, the woman spat the chewed leaves into the knife slash. Carefully she distributed the pulp with her fingers. For a moment her fingertips rested on the skewer scars. Then she pointed at his knife, indicating that he should give it to her.

Deciding to trust her, Hampton signed, *Take the knife*.

She slid it from the sheath, rose, took his shirt and slashed off a strip of cloth. Then she knelt and bound it carefully over the leaf pulp, making him sit up so she could tie the cloth behind his back. She returned his knife. Then she stood up and faced him.

He got to his feet. *Thank you*, he signed. *Friends now*.

No. Her sign was emphatic. *Bluecoats all enemies. Forever*.

He looked down at his army issue trousers and boots. *I'm not a soldier*, he signed. *I'm a scout*.

You work for bluecoats. Only Arapaho badhearts work for bluecoats.

Hampton puzzled over the meaning of her signs. She'd made the circling motion at her breast that meant

Arapaho. Was she saying he was a badheart? An Arapaho badheart? He didn't understand.

You are Arapaho? he asked.

You see I am. She turned from him and ran to Westwind. She vaulted onto the horse and then looked back. He hadn't moved. A shadow crossed her face and she scowled. *Come with me,* she signed.

Go to hell, he thought at first. She acted like she owned the world. But he had no choice other than to follow her. He needed food and Ares needed rest. Most likely there was an Arapaho village nearby. He walked slowly to Ares. In his hand were his damaged shirt and torn coat.

As he mounted and followed, he admitted to himself he wanted to go with her no matter where she was leading him. He wanted her with an intensity as hot as the flames that had nearly destroyed him.

They traveled toward the solitary peak as the sun climbed the sky behind them. When it reached the zenith, she stopped to rest the horses among a few cottonwoods that showed where a creek ran. Here she dug into the bank with a stick. After washing off the tuberous roots she uncovered, she offered him one. He took it, watched her eat hers, and bit into his. It was slightly bitter, but juicy. After eating it all, he drank from the stream.

He and the woman rested only briefly before she rose and remounted. And again he followed her as the sun slid down the other side of the sky. When it was hardly above the mountains, she halted at the crest of a hill. He rode up beside her, stopped and looked down.

Below him thirty tepees circled in a small valley between the hills. By the tepees, smoke rose from cooking fires that women tended. Horses grazed nearby. Two boys ran, chasing a dog.

Hampton gazed down hardly able to draw breath. It

was as though he'd ridden to this hill before and was now looking at a familiar village. His heart pounded.

Sioux, he told himself. This reminds you of a Sioux village. It was true. The Sioux raised their tepees in similar circles, but he knew his feeling had nothing to do with them.

This was different.

He sensed somehow that he had come home.

Chapter 13

Stands Shining eyed the stranger. She was puzzled. He wore the bluecoat clothes but bore Sun Dance scars on his chest. His face had a faraway look, as if he'd been subject to a vision. She heard a Coyote announce her approach with the call of the prairie lark.

Below her, women left their kettles, and pointed to the crest of the hill where she waited. Men emerged from tepees to look up at her. It was time to go among the lodges and find One Claw.

Never had Stands Shining felt she needed the advice of her great-uncle as she did now.

Her heart was troubled. First Cloud was dead, also Crying Wind. Yet this stranger stirred her in a way that made her ashamed.

He was still staring at the village below and hadn't moved. She leaned to touch his arm and felt the tensing of his muscles. He looked at her.

Come, she signed. She kicked the spotted horse and headed downhill.

A good mount, this horse, as were all the spotted horses raised by the Pierced Noses. But she knew it belonged to the stranger. He had been riding the horse when she first saw him trying to outrun the fire.

A faint echo of the fury she had felt then touched her

and she scowled. She had meant to kill him as she would have killed any bluecoat she had met. She had failed, then. Now it was too late because the stranger had saved Vengeance, the colt she prized above all her horses because he had been First Cloud's gift to her. She would have died with the colt rather than leave him to the mercy of the fire. So the stranger had saved her life as well.

Children ran up the hill, dogs racing ahead of them, barking. Stands Shining recognized Bear Fat and smiled. She was happy he had survived the sickness that had killed so many of Our People.

"My heart is glad to see you," Bear Fat called to her. "The warriors returned and said the storm had killed you." Trying not to stare, he kept glancing at the man riding beside her.

As a token of affection, Stands Shining reached a hand down to Bear Fat, lifting him up behind her on the spotted horse. She would ask his mother to share her son. It was a warrior's right to choose a boy to train and she would never have a son of her own. First Cloud was dead. Crying Wind was dead, too. Stands Shining's throat choked with grief.

Women with short-cropped hair and gashed faces hurried to meet her. Old men with blackened faces stood by their tepees. All were grieving for their dead. Stands Shining didn't see certain faces—Heavy Pine, Keeps Moving. Dead? She had been too shocked in the deserted village to note all whom the white man's disease had taken.

And she didn't see One Claw.

"My great-uncle?" she asked Bear Fat.

"He rode north after his mother died and you didn't return."

Stands Shining knew One Claw had lived before with the Northern Arapahos. An icy sense of loss touched her spine for a moment and she shivered. She had counted on

One Claw's good sense and on the comfort of mourning with him. Now she would be alone.

Bear Fat's mother, Snake Woman, touched Stands Shining's makeshift moccasin. "You are welcome to my tepee," she said. "I will make you new clothes."

Stands Shining thanked her. She sat straighter, stiffening her back. She was a warrior, the only woman among the Star Falcons, the second of the Age Societies. She would prove her strength of will by refusing to mourn until the fate of this stranger was settled.

As she feared, Heavy Pine was dead. Bobcat was now chief. Winter Bull sat on the council. After she had led the stranger inside the council lodge, Stands Shining told her story with him standing beside her. She took full responsibility for the fire.

"I went after the horses," she explained, "and this man helped me rescue them under a Fire Moon. If not for him, we would have lost all the ponies left behind at the old village. We owe him rest and food."

"He is a bluecoat," Winter Bull sneered. "We don't welcome bluecoats in this village."

"He is a *scout* for the bluecoats," Stands Shining corrected, the words bitter on her tongue. She resented having to defend the stranger, resented Winter Bull's words. In her heart, she knew they were really directed against her.

"He will not be denied hospitality," Bobcat put in. "We will smoke with him. Does he speak our language?"

"Signs only," Stands Shining answered.

"It is odd," Bobcat remarked. "The stranger looks much like one of us. It is only his eyes that prevent me from believing it. They are the color of rain clouds."

White man's eyes, Stands Shining thought, though she didn't speak aloud. She was very conscious of the man standing silently beside her, face so impassive as they discussed him. She thought some of the blood running in his veins must be Arapaho, for she recognized the resemblance to Our People. Yet he was taller than any man in the village and handsomer, too, with his strong nose and chin, his well-formed body.

She knew he didn't have the Arapaho chest tattoos, sky circles within circles, one above each nipple. In truth, she didn't trust him at all. He was a stranger whose white man's eyes looked at her from an Arapaho face. She hoped no harm would come to her village because she had brought him there.

Bobcat asked Stands Shining to stay and light the pipe and her heart eased at this sign of respect. With the metal tongs bought from a white trader, she picked a coal from the council fire. Then she touched the coal to the mixture of tobacco and kinnikinnick in the red-stone bowl of the long-stemmed peace pipe held by Bobcat. He drew in and the tobacco mixture glowed and caught.

She glanced quickly at the stranger without turning her head. He was not looking at her. His eyes were fixed on the pipe. Quietly she withdrew from the lodge.

Stands Shining found the spotted horse tied to a pole outside Snake Woman's tepee. She hesitated, then called to Bear Fat.

Bear Fat poked his head past the tepee flap.

"Wait with this horse by the council lodge," Stands Shining requested. "He belongs not to me but to the man who smokes with the elders."

"He's a beautiful horse," Bear Fat remarked as he came out and untied the rope. As he stroked the animal's neck, Stands Shining saw the longing in his eyes and knew he had fallen in love with the horse.

She smiled a little, understanding how he felt, but said only, "Go."

Inside the lodge, Stands Shining sat as a guest was expected to on the hide-covered willow backrest at the rear. Snake Woman offered her dog stew and Stands Shining accepted gratefully. She was very hungry.

No doubt the stranger is equally hungry, she thought, then grimaced. Why did she persist in thinking about this man? He was *niatha,* white man. Clever as the spider, *niatha,* but treacherous. His appearance was deceiving, but the truth was there for all to see in his grey eyes. White man. Scout for the bluecoats.

Paugh!

"Does the meat taste bad?" Snake Woman asked.

Stands Shining realized her face must have shown her distaste. "It's not your good food," she explained, "but my thoughts that trouble me." She finished her portion and refused a second, knowing Snake Woman's kettle must be nearly empty.

Snake Woman was a Ute. She had been captured in a raid by an Arapaho warrior who had married her, only to die two years later. Because she was Ute, she wasn't as tall or good-looking as women of Our People. No other man had offered to marry her. Yet her tepee was neat and her son, Bear Fat, was well clothed and healthy.

Perhaps now that I have no tepee, Stands Shining thought, Snake Woman and I might share one. I would keep the kettle full and she could cook for me as well as for the boy. She could make my clothes.

"I have been wanting to speak to you," Snake Woman murmured hesitantly. "It seems there is a man of our allies, the Cheyenne, who wishes me to come to his tepee. He has small children who are motherless and he seeks a wife."

"Do you wish to go?" Stands Shining asked.

"It is pleasant to have a man in the tepee," Snake Woman replied. "But I think my son will be sad to leave this village, especially because of your kindness."

"I had meant to ask you about Bear Fat," Stands Shining interjected. "If it meets with your approval, I would like to call him my son and train him as a warrior."

Snake Woman's face brightened. "He'd be so proud

to have you choose him. And I, too. Very proud. I will stay in this village."

"No, you don't have to. Why not marry the Cheyenne if you like him? When I set up my own tepee, Bear Fat can return to the village and live with me. Afterward, he can visit back and forth."

"I will think about what you say," Snake Woman answered pensively. "It's been long since a man wanted me and I . . ." She cast down her eyes like a maiden.

"Take him, then," Stands Shining urged. "Don't wait." The blood rose in Snake Woman's cheeks, a sign that she and the Cheyenne had already lain together.

Pain stabbed at Stands Shining. She and First Cloud had come so close to being lovers. She had almost discovered what women knew and maidens did not. If the bluecoats hadn't come, hadn't robbed her of the man she loved . . .

Bear Fat ducked into the tepee.

"Fire Moon stands outside. He wishes to talk," the boy announced.

Snake Woman's eyes grew round with surprise at the sound of the unfamiliar name, but Stands Shining knew that name was what the council must have given the stranger.

"He's the *niatha* who rode with me into camp," she explained.

"He's welcome to enter," Snake Woman offered.

"Thank you. But it is better I speak to Fire Moon outside."

He stood next to the spotted horse and signed to Stands Shining that she should accept the horse as a gift from him. Stands Shining felt her face grow warm. Did he mean to court her? A spark flared in her loins and she fought to keep her face expressionless. Why should she feel as she did? She didn't love this man. She could never love one who rode with bluecoats.

Fire Moon stood waiting for her response, his light eyes fixed on her. He doesn't know the ways of Our People, Stands Shining reminded herself. He doesn't even speak Arapaho. The gift of a horse from a man to a maiden means nothing to him.

Nevertheless she wouldn't accept.

She had just begun to make the sign of refusal when she remembered Bear Fat. She turned and called the boy to her. Then she put her arm around his shoulders.

"I accept the horse," she signed to Fire Moon. "Thank you."

She took the rope Fire Moon handed her and put it into Bear Fat's fingers. "I give you this horse for your own," she told the boy.

Bear Fat stood motionless for a long moment, his face blank with astonishment. Then he grinned widely. Taking a deep breath, he threw his arms about the neck of the spotted horse and hugged him. Fire Moon stared from one Indian to the other while Bear Fat turned to Stands Shining, words of gratitude pouring from his lips.

She held up her hand. "You understand this is a warrior's horse. It is important to learn to be worthy of him. I believe you can do that and so I will teach you."

Bear Fat took a step toward her, arms reaching as though to hug her as he had hugged the horse. Then he paused and stood very erect.

"Thank you, Warrior Woman," he said formally. "I will do my best."

"I know. That's why your mother and I have agreed to share you as our son."

She saw that Fire Moon was signing to her.

The boy is your son?

Yes, she signed.

Fire Moon faced the boy. *You have a fast and strong horse,* he signed. *I have named him Westwind.*

Bear Fat looked from the *niatha* to the horse and

back. *It is a good name,* he signed. He could wait no longer, scrambling onto the back of the horse and racing off, shouting to his friends.

He is a handsome boy, Fire Moon signed.

He will be a warrior like his father was.

His father is dead?

Yes.

Fire Moon was silent for long moments. At last he signed to Stands Shining, *I wish to learn to speak Arapaho. Will you teach me?*

She hesitated. *Do you stay long in our village?*

For two or three suns. Then I go to the trader's lodge on the Arkansas.

You cannot learn many words in three suns.

Fire Moon smiled. *I am coming back here. Will you teach me?*

Stands Shining knew she should say no, but she couldn't bring herself to sever the only bond between her and this man. Somehow he stirred her against her will.

I mourn my dead this moon, she signed. *When you return you may ask me again.*

The council had smoked with the stranger, and had named him. One of the men must have offered Fire Moon the hospitality of his tepee. Stands Shining knew her responsibility for him was dissolved. She was free to go off by herself and weep for First Cloud and for Crying Wind. She turned and walked quickly away from Fire Moon, moving toward the grassy bottom to the south of the village where the horses grazed. She would seek the black colt to be with her when she mourned.

To her distress, Fire Moon caught up and fell into step beside her. She waited until they were among the cottonwoods and out of sight from curious eyes before she stopped.

Go back, she signed. *I have no more to say to you.*

I ask a gift in return for the spotted horse, he signed. *Your name.*

Stands Shining almost smiled. She didn't resent Fire Moon's request. For a *niatha* it was courteous. Besides, the white man set great store in names, as if they never changed.

Stands Shining, she signed, then started to turn away. But Fire Moon touched her arm.

Say the words, he signed.

She did so.

Your name is beautiful, Fire Moon signed. *A good name. You shine as bright as the sun. You warm me like the sun.*

Stands Shining's lips parted as she looked into Fire Moon's eyes. His face was only a breath away and she wanted him to put his arms close around her, to hold her. She wanted to feel his body against hers. His nearness seared her blood with a fire heat until she couldn't catch her breath.

"Stands Shining," Fire Moon whispered in Arapaho.

She had only a moment to think that his first words in her language were her name. Then he bent his head and touched his lips to hers.

Chapter 14

When Fire Moon kissed her, Stands Shining felt herself melt as the ice of the Arkansas melts when Father Sun routs Old Cold Maker. She clung to him, feeling his desire for her, wanting him so desperately that nothing else existed for her.

A high, keening wail cut into her haze of desire. A woman's cry of mourning. Stands Shining pushed herself away.

"No!" she cried. She was trembling. How could she have forgotten she had come to this place to mourn?

Fire Moon stepped toward her and she scowled at him, fiercely gesturing for him to go from her. She yanked the knife Snake Woman had given her from its sheath. Watching her warily, Fire Moon stopped.

Stands Shining gashed both her arms with the sharp blade. With blood from the slashes dripping onto the dirt, she stared at Fire Moon and saw his face change, saw that he understood. Then she whirled from him and ran toward the horses.

When he didn't follow, she sighed in mingled relief and disappointment. He was truly *niatha*, the spider who'd caught her in his web. She was held fast, against her will.

"No!" she cried aloud. "I am Stands Shining. I am a warrior. I belong to no man."

She slowed her pace as she came from under the trees into the meadow where the horses grazed. Vengeance, his dark coat gleaming in the sun, stood beside the mare she had taken from the wagon of the dead whites. Stands Shining walked toward them. Then she hesitated.

If she came too near, her mourning might disturb the colt. The knife cuts on her arm had begun to close over and she pulled at them to start the bleeding afresh. She undid her braids and grasped a handful of her long black hair, holding the knife ready. She must cut her hair short for Crying Wind, for First Cloud.

With the blade touching a strand, she paused. Warriors kept their hair long. It was true, she was a woman, but she was also a warrior. Long hair was a sign of defiance, a taunt to the enemy. Who would want a scalp of cropped hair? Only a coward would ride to war with short hair, for no enemy warrior would ever try to count coup against such a man. He would be safe from the lances and arrows of the enemy.

A warrior challenged death, he didn't hide from it.

She returned the knife to its sheath.

Hearing faint wails drifting on the wind from the village where other women mourned, Stands Shining raised her face to the sky and added her plaint to theirs.

"*Maheo*, Man Above," she chanted, "do not force First Cloud to take the long trail east to the Land Beyond, up the steep hill with the rocks at the crest. He died bravely, a warrior's death. Allow him the privilege of the warriors' road in the sky where the stars dance. Do not make his ghost wander unhappily, whirling in the dust of the plains. Let him join the spirits of all those who have gone before. Let him be happy in the Land Beyond."

Stands Shining slashed four shallow cuts in each leg. As her blood ran, she prayed again.

"*Maheo*, Crying Wind is old, with bones that ache.

Give her my white war stallion, Strong Heart, to carry her over the long trail to the land of the rising sun. There she will rest and be young again.''

For three days Stands Shining remained among the horses, mourning her dead. Bear Fat brought food and water, putting it near her and going away without speaking. On the fourth day, Bobcat came to her.

"Our hearts are weighted with sadness," he told her. "We have lost those we love, many of them children. We have few horses. Many were lost to Pawnee raiders when we fled the death camp."

Stands Shining had been listening to Bobcat with bowed head. Now she raised her eyes to meet his.

"I haven't heard of this Pawnee raid," she replied.

"The young warriors know your medicine is powerful," Bobcat went on. "You must lead them soon against the Pawnees to regain our horses. Such an event will lift our hearts."

"What you tell me is true," Stands Shining agreed.

Bobcat nodded once, then turned to leave.

"The *niatha*," she asked. "Is he gone from our village?"

"He left when this sun rose," Bobcat informed her.

Stands Shining followed Bobcat back to the tepees. She took the finely quilled buckskin tunic and leggings Snake Woman had made for her to the pool where the women bathed. She washed herself, then cleaned the dried blood from her arms and legs before donning the fresh clothes.

Bear Fat was waiting at the tepee with a bow and a quiver of arrows. "These were my father's," he declared. "I have tried to care for them as my father did. Now they are yours."

"Thank you. I will use them," Stands Shining answered.

The bow was too long for her, but by tightening the sinew and practicing, she adjusted well enough to the slight awkwardness. The arrows were soundly made. On the shaft of each one was the distinctive mark of Bear Fat's father.

I won't change his mark to mine, Stands Shining decided. The dead warrior's spirit will help the arrows shoot true. They will bring me success. Bear Fat's father knows his son is now also mine.

Three days later, Stands Shining led fifteen warriors from the village. Also with them were two scouts and a boy. Stands Shining rode Westwind. The tassels Bear Fat had braided into the spotted horse's mane fluttered gaily in the breeze. Across her forehead was a green band with a single feather fastened to the back. She had lost her war bonnet in the burning of Crying Wind's tepee and the feather in the band represented her first coup.

Yet despite the borrowed horse and weapons, despite the lack of a war bonnet, power tingled through Stands Shining. Her band of warriors felt her power and rose proudly. They were certain that as long as they followed their warrior woman, they would be invincible.

The small size of the raiding party made the element of surprise paramount. Because she realized that, Stands Shining had chosen her two scouts carefully. Half Horse and Curly would find the enemy and return to report their whereabouts. Then the raiding party would surprise the Pawnee village by counting coup on stray Pawnee encountered along the way.

The Pawnee lived to the northeast, five sleeps from the Arapaho camp. On the fourth sun, Half Horse brought news of a Pawnee village half a sun away.

"Sixty earth lodges," he reported, "and the warriors are in the camp."

Stands Shining listened carefully. Unlike Our People,

the Pawnee had permanent round lodges made of earth. They lived in these villages each spring while planting maize and each fall while harvesting it. Winter and summer they hunted buffalo and lived in movable hide tepees similar to Our People's.

"The women are digging among their maize plants," Half Horse mentioned. "The warriors smoke near the lodges."

"How many warriors?" Stands Shining asked.

"More than sixty. It is a large village."

And Our People were only fifteen. Stands Shining had hoped to find at least some of the Pawnee men away on a hunt. She raised her face to the sun and closed her eyes. Bright yellow swirled behind her lids for long moments before darkness came. She opened her eyes to see a white cloud passing across the sun.

It was a sign.

"While we have light, we'll approach as close as we can without being discovered," Stands Shining declared. "We won't make a dawn attack. We won't attack at all. Instead, we'll creep into the village after darkness sends the Pawnee to sleep."

"Night is a time of ghosts," Little Owl protested. "Night is a time of dampness, when bowstrings grow limp."

"We are fifteen against sixty," Stands Shining reminded him. "At night we may not have to use our bows."

"I am not afraid to die," he boasted.

"Nor am I. No warrior among us fears death. But Our People need horses. And they need children. What will it avail them if we don't return? This is not a time for glory. Too many of Our People have died this past moon. We must bring life back with us, not death."

She turned from Little Owl to look at Half Horse.

"You and Curly will go after the horse herd tonight," she told the scout.

Then she faced the warriors. "Let it not be said that counting coup kept any warrior from bringing a captive back with him."

"What will keep the ghosts with their invisible poison arrows from us while we prowl in the night?" Little Owl asked.

"My medicine," Stands Shining answered boldly. "It will protect you. It will protect every one of you as it protects me. Father Sun has shown me this is so."

All except Little Owl raised their lances with exclamations of approval. Little Owl's stare verged on insolence. Stands Shining did not trust him, remembering all too well how he had tried to force her to lie with him one night when the warriors had been drinking *veheomahpe*. She'd had to strike his head with a rock to keep him from her. The *veheomahpe* had made him wild and mean as a grizzly.

She knew Little Owl had been taunted for his rashness and shameful failure. Even his brother-by-choice, Black Deer, had chided him. Ever since that time, Little Owl had looked for ways to challenge her and prove himself. She hoped he wouldn't endanger their party by a reckless thrust for glory.

At sundown the raiding party rested some distance from the Pawnee village, hiding themselves among the trees beside a stream. Unwilling to risk a fire, they chewed on dried meat. Stands Shining spoke to the boy who was riding with them on his first raid.

"You must keep our horses together," she told him. "Do not be tempted into any rashness. We cannot count on returning with Pawnee horses even though we plan to raid their herd. How will we escape the enemy if you lose our mounts?"

The boy was a nephew of Bobcat. He clutched his bow tightly. "No enemy will find our horses," he said fervently.

"Good. You are a man to be trusted."

The boy stood even straighter and Stands Shining resisted the impulse to smile, knowing he wouldn't understand. She looked forward to the day when she would bring Bear Fat on his first war party. Perhaps by then the black colt would be old enough to go along as a second horse. That way he could grow used to the shouts and smells of war.

The raid that night was no war party. Horses, lances and all ornaments that might click or rattle would be left behind when the warriors crept on foot into the Pawnee lodges.

Stands Shining walked away from the rest. Painted red by Father Sun as he slipped into his evening lodge, she faced the western sky and chanted.

> As a panther I go
> Swift and silent
> Stealthy the mountain cat
> Even as I.

She repeated the words four times. When she finished, she checked her bow and went to stroke the neck of Westwind. As she touched the horse, she thought of the man who had given him to her.

Fire Moon. He had promised to return to the Arapaho village. But would he keep his promise? She remembered how he had come to her. Then she turned away from the spotted horse, angry at herself for thinking of a *niatha* in that way. Fire Moon would never come back and she didn't care. She didn't care if she ever saw him again.

*   *   *

Darkness robed the land. Stands Shining struggled with her impatience as she waited for the scouts to come in and report. She had to be certain the Pawnee slept before she led the warriors into their village.

Half Horse appeared before her, his approach so silent she was forced to conceal her start.

"Curly is near the Pawnee horse herd," he informed Stands Shining. "I have killed and hidden a Pawnee scout. I found one only. They do not worry much, these Pawnee."

"All their warriors are still in the village?"

"All."

"There is no feasting or ceremonies this night?"

"None. We come at a good time."

Half Horse drew a map in some dirt explaining to Stands Shining and the warriors where the herd grazed. Next he described the terrain and suggested the best way to approach the village without being spotted. He pinpointed which lodges held children.

"The sky has clouds," Stands Shining noted. "We will wait for them to cover the moon and use darkness to help us. All the signs are favorable. Half Horse, you go to Curly now. When you hear the owl call three times, then two, start the Pawnee horses running toward our home."

Half Horse seemed to melt into the night and Stands Shining waited among the warriors until the moon had traveled a hand's width across the sky. Clouds passed over the moon's face.

"We go!" Stands Shining rasped in the darkness.

The party crept forward cautiously. They emerged from the trees, then trotted to a shallow ravine that led between two hills. There Stands Shining halted the warriors. Nestled between these hills was fertile bottom land sloping off to the stream. On the land was the Pawnee village.

"Wait for my return," she commanded softly. Then

she retraced her steps until she was at the top of a small rise. Cupping her hands around her mouth, she faced south where the horse herd grazed. Then she hooted three times, paused, and hooted twice more. As she hurried back to the warriors, she recalled One Claw teaching her to call as the owl calls.

How she missed her great-uncle. When he learned she still lived, perhaps he would travel south again.

Before she led the warriors into the sleeping village, Stands Shining touched each man on the shoulder. When she came to Little Owl, she whispered, "Do not forget what we seek."

He did not reply.

They crept through the valley, following its curve around a hill. Moments later the Pawnee lodges appeared as dark mounds. Each Arapaho warrior carried dried meat to fling to any dog that challenged him. The men scattered among the earth lodges. Stands Shining chose one of those Half Horse had seen children enter.

When she touched the flap, a dog snarled at her heels. She dropped a chunk of meat in back of her and eased the flap aside. She knew she must crouch to pass through the covered passageway into the lodge itself, and she wondered as she made her way how people could bear to live under dark earthen domes.

Coals from the fire in the center of the lodge winked their redness at her. She looked from one sleeping Pawnee to another, counting five in all. Only one was small, a child. Stands Shining slipped a wide thong from her belt into her hand to tie across the child's mouth.

Silently, she knelt beside the small sleeper. Raising the child's head, she quickly slid the thong into position, tied it, then lifted the child and hurried as quietly as she could from the lodge. The child awakened and tried to scream. Stands Shining could feel him struggling, but with the gag in his mouth and his head muffled against her breast, scarcely any sound escaped.

She raced toward the ravine. Just beyond the rise she had climbed to signal to Half Horse, the boy would be waiting with their own horses. While listening for an outcry in the dark village behind her, she heard a dog bark and tensed until it quieted.

Somewhere to the north a wolf howled. Stands Shining sucked in a breath. Was she hearing an animal or a Pawnee scout? In that instant someone ran behind her. She glanced back, then shifted the struggling, grunting child to reach for her knife.

A woman's voice called out words she didn't understand. Without thinking, Stands Shining stopped and made a shushing sound. To her surprise the woman said no more. Stands Shining saw as she came close that she was a small woman, even for a Pawnee. In fact, there was a chance she was only a teen-age girl.

Instead of killing the girl, Stands Shining held out the knife so it glinted faintly in the moonlight. Then she pressed the blade to the throat of the child in her arms. The child stopped moving and so did the girl.

The moon drifted free of the clouds and Stands Shining gestured with her head for the girl to go in front of her. She hurried her along by kicking her legs until she ran. Once the two of them were out of sight of the village, Stands Shining grabbed her prisoner to stop her. Then she handed her the child to carry, her knife touching the girl's side, and marched her toward the rise where Bobcat's nephew should be waiting. The welcome whicker of a horse reached her and she smiled. Bobcat would have reason to be proud of the boy.

Four of the warriors had returned. All were mounted and holding a captive child. Stands Shining started to take the child she had captured. But shouting and screaming erupted from the village. Leaving the Pawnee captive in the girl's arms, Stands Shining whirled and stared toward the noise, then quickly turned back. Seeing that one of the warriors carried a very young child, she changed her mind again. Snatching her own captive from the arms of the girl, she handed the infant up to him.

"Ride back to our village with these children," she ordered the four warriors.

As they hesitated, three more warriors came over the rise. All carried children.

"To your horses," she told them. "Do not worry. I will return for the other warriors. My medicine is powerful enough to protect me. Go now, hurry. I foresee that this is good."

With the Pawnee children still in their arms, the seven braves wheeled their horses and pounded off to the southwest. Stands Shining told Bobcat's nephew to bind the hands of the girl she had captured.

"And watch her," she warned, vaulting onto Westwind.

A rifle cracked, the sound echoing in the night. The Arapaho warriors had no guns with them, so Stands Shining knew a Pawnee had fired the shot. She kicked Westwind into a canter and headed toward the lodges.

On her way, she passed a man running from the village. Another. Her warriors.

"Head for home," she called to them.

Shrieks of defiance rose from behind the hill that hid the village. Dogs yelped. A woman screamed. There were six men left to account for.

Two warriors ran toward her. Arapaho. Four left.

She pounded along the ravine. A horseman rounded the curve of the hill and galloped toward her. Stands Shining nocked an arrow, shouting her war cry.

"Don't shoot," the rider called in Arapaho. She recognized Little Owl's voice.

They both halted.

"Where are the others?" she asked.

"Big Buffalo is dead," Little Owl told her.

"There are two of our warriors in the village," she told him. "We will go back for them."

Little Owl hesitated. Each one heard the clatter of stones scattered by racing hooves. Another horse dashed around the hill. Bow ready, Stands Shining shouted at the rider.

"Black Deer," he announced. As he came up to them, Stands Shining saw a body slung over the horse in front of him.

"Stone Man stopped a bullet," Black Deer explained.

Seeing that all the warriors were accounted for, Stands Shining wheeled Westwind and followed the other two horses to the rise. As they reached the Arapaho mounts, she heard Black Deer mutter to Little Owl, "So. Big Buffalo's scalp will decorate a Pawnee lodge. Are you happy?"

It was Little Owl's doing that Big Buffalo had died? Stands Shining frowned in frustration. There was no time to learn more. Little Owl and Black Deer had taken two of the war horses tethered beside the lodges, but there would be others that the Pawnee could ride in pursuit.

They galloped toward home, the girl captive riding with Bobcat's nephew. The wounded Stone Man had been tied onto his own horse, which was led by Black Deer. The three riderless Arapaho horses ran with them.

For a time shouts were heard back along the trail, but long before morning the Pawnee gave up the chase. Near dawn, Stands Shining halted to rest the horses and asked Bobcat's nephew to untie the Pawnee girl. "Take a fresh horse," she told him. "I'll be responsible for the Pawnee now."

Stands Shining asked the girl what her name was.

"Sweet Water," the girl replied. Her face was sullen in the grey light.

Stands Shining saw she was verging on womanhood. "Why did you chase me?" she asked.

"My little sister was gone from her sleeping place. I left the lodge to find her. I saw you. I did not know you were Arapaho."

Stands Shining nodded. This was certainly true or the girl would have screamed instead of following her.

"You will ride with us. If you give trouble, your sister will suffer," Stands Shining lied. She would never hurt the child.

Though she hadn't meant to capture this older girl, Stands Shining knew that Sweet Water and her younger sister would be useful workers. She would be able to set up her own tepee and have someone cook for her and make her clothes.

They reached the Arapaho village one sun after the other warriors arrived. Stone Man was very weak. He died before sunset. His wife mourned, as did Big Buffalo's mother and father, but seeing the ten captured Pawnee children lifted the hearts of the Arapaho. All were eagerly adopted.

Little Owl and Black Deer had brought no children back, but each had captured a well-trained Pawnee war horse. Stands Shining noticed how Black Deer avoided Little Owl. That was peculiar, she thought. As brothers-by-choice they had always been inseparable. Black Deer did not speak to Stands Shining of what had happened in the Pawnee village, so she let the matter alone. Secretly, however, she was curious. She had never before lost warriors in any raid.

To take her mind off her failure, she prepared to hunt buffalo. Skins were needed to make her new tepee. Before she rode out, Stone Man's widow came to see her.

"I go to Little Raven's camp," the widow told her. "That is where my parents are. I came to tell you I know you were not the cause of my husband's death and that I wish you to have my tepee."

"I was the war leader," Stands Shining said. "I am at fault. But I accept your offer."

"I have eyes in my head to see with and ears to listen," the widow continued. "I know who rides a fine war horse, who thought only of himself."

"Black Deer did everything possible to save your husband. He carried him on the horse he took from a Pawnee lodge. He delivered him from the enemy."

"I do not speak of Black Deer," the widow explained. "He is a brave warrior. I speak of the other. I do not wish to say his name. I do not wish to live in the same village as he does. May the whirlwind find him and suck out his spirit so that he twists in the dust forever."

As she watched the widow walk away, Stands Shining reminded herself that it was not up to her or to Stone Man's widow to punish Little Owl. Only the council had that power and they had chosen not to use it.

The widow's tepee wasn't new and the skins were smoke-blackened near the top. But Stands Shining didn't mind. She set the Pawnee sisters, thirteen-year-old Sweet Water and eight-year-old Bending Reed to work—cleaning the robes the widow had also left and making new backrests from willows.

It felt good, she thought, to have her own tepee. Stone Man had painted symbols of his coups on the skins outside around the door flap. She did not disturb these symbols, for he had been a courageous warrior. Adding to them, she painted her own design alongside. A green bear paw with black claws, and a red band to signify the grizzly she had faced as a child. Then stars in a night sky to represent her first night raid when she had trailed the war party. Carefully, using the tiniest stick she could find, she painted four-pointed stars. Completing ten, she stood back to examine her work. No, she needed more. She reached out with the paint stick to add another star.

''The stars are falling,'' a man's voice said lightly in halting Arapaho.

Stands Shining whirled around, her heart pounding. She knew the voice.

It was Fire Moon's.

Chapter 15

Stands Shining gazed at Fire Moon and her thoughts were as scattered as cottonwood in blossom time.

"Stars," he noted again, looking from her to her paintings on the tepee. "Falling."

"Not falling," Stands Shining corrected, gathering her wits. "Stars shining on the night of my first raid."

Fire Moon shook his head and made the sign for not understanding her speech.

But you spoke Arapaho words, she signed.

Words from long ago. From the time the stars fell, he signed.

Stands Shining had been told of the night many winters before when the stars fell from the sky but she had been too young to remember seeing them.

I ask again if you will teach me your language, Fire Moon signed.

Stands Shining felt a quiver of excitement picturing his being near her. It was possible, she supposed. Already she had been working with the Pawnee sisters, insisting they learn Arapaho words for everyday tasks. Fire Moon could join them. Surely he'd be harmless enough. Yet she hesitated. Although she didn't fear this handsome man who stood before her, she feared herself.

If you remain in our village, she signed, at last deciding he could stay, *I will teach you.*

I stay.

By the way he looked at her, Stands Shining realized that Fire Moon hadn't returned just to learn the speech of Our People. She couldn't ignore the rush of warmth flooding her body in response to what she saw in his eyes.

He was wearing a Cheyenne-made buckskin shirt. His moccasins were also Cheyenne. He still wore the bluecoat pants. It would be better, Stands Shining decided, if Sweet Water made him proper Arapaho clothes.

She shivered and had to fight to look away from him. Being so close made her tremble. Deliberately, she turned her head toward the tepee.

"Sweet Water, Bending Reed," she called. "Come outside."

Sweet Water popped through the opening so quickly that Stands Shining knew she had been standing beside the flap listening. Bending Reed followed her more slowly. Both girls stared at Fire Moon, but where Bending Reed gaped, Sweet Water lowered her eyes. Then she raised them, tipping her face so she glanced sideways at him.

She was flirting with him!

Fire Moon smiled at the Pawnee girls, his gaze lingering a bit longer on Sweet Water.

You will make him clothes, Stands Shining signed to Sweet Water. Her gestures were abrupt. *Arapaho clothes, not Pawnee.*

Sweet Water signed that she understood.

Go now, Stands Shining ordered. *Fetch fresh water.*

Sweet Water smiled a little, as though she understood why she was being sent away. Stands Shining forced herself not to scowl at the girl. She would not be jealous of her own servant!

Pawnee? Fire Moon signed when the sisters were gone.

My captives, she signed.

I have heard you ride with the warriors. He grinned at her more warmly than he had at the sisters. *You are a very beautiful warrior.* He paused, then spoke her name. "Stands Shining."

She was a warrior, yes, but now she felt only as a maiden felt when a brave courted her. Why had Fire Moon come back to tempt her? She could never marry a *niatha*. She shouldn't even allow a *niatha* to touch her.

"Why do you stay in our village?" she asked. "Do you not have to scout for the bluecoats?"

"I bring a message from the Indian agent to the council. I go now to tell them the words of Broken Hand."

Stands Shining watched him stride away. If One Claw were here, he'd warn her not to trust Fire Moon.

"A *niatha* learns to twist words as soon as he's taught to speak," her great-uncle had told her. "A few white men learn to straighten their talk as we straighten bent wood for arrow shafts—with difficulty and much labor. Most don't bother. They say one thing and mean another. Remember this."

Yet One Claw had words of praise for Broken Hand. "He is *niatha* and sometimes he thinks like a white man, but he has taught himself to live like us and he also tries to think like one of us. I would listen to his words and consider them. Perhaps believe them."

Stands Shining decided she would listen to Broken Hand's message when Bobcat told her what he wanted. She would consider it. But her advice would depend on whether she believed the white man's words.

It was true she wasn't on the council, but the young warriors heeded her words. She was young, as they were, and her blood ran fast and hot, not slow and cool like an old man's. Peace was what the old men advised more and more often.

What did a warrior want with peace?

                    *   *   *

Fire Moon sat to the left of Bobcat in the council tepee. Though the pipe was in his hand, he was feeling more like Hampton now than part Indian. It was difficult, he thought, being of two origins. To the white man he was Hampton. To the Indians, Fire Moon. And to himself? Sometimes he didn't know.

He bade proper homage to earth, sky and the four directions. Then he took a puff and passed the pipe to the next man. He knew he couldn't speak until the pipe had been passed through everyone's hands and back to Bobcat.

He hoped that when he did speak, they would listen. Fitzpatrick's message was urgent. This he understood, even though he hadn't spoken to the agent himself.

When, as Hampton, he had arrived at Bent's Fort among the giant cottonwoods along the Arkansas, William Bent had been cordial. He had been surprised seeing the small wooden buildings, however. For years he had heard of Bent's huge trading fort. Later a grizzled mountain man called Old Jack had told him what had happened to the original great adobe fort some miles upriver.

"Army wanted to buy it," Old Jack explained. "Offered chickenshit. Will wasn't about to take it. On t'other hand, he'd been brooding about his brothers dying. George died of consumption in that 'dobe fort. Then those Taos bastards murdered Charles. Robert got hisself killed and scalped by the Comanche years back. And Will's first wife, Owl Woman, died there in childbirth. Must've seemed like the best way he could get shed of all them bad memories was to blow the place to high heaven. So he done it."

Hampton recalled how well Bent had fed him. And Bent's wife, Yellow Woman, had made him moccasins and a shirt, clucking at every opportunity over the healing wound on his chest.

They had gotten along well, Bent and his Cheyenne

wife. Stands Shining's face flashed into his mind when he thought of that. He shook his head. He wanted her, God, yes, but marriage? That was another thing entirely.

He'd had no money to pay for the clothes or the gun Bent had given him to replace the ones he'd lost in the fire. Bent had merely shrugged at Hampton's apology.

"You can do me a favor in return," he'd suggested, "a favor to me and to Tom Fitzpatrick. You've been with Bobcat's Arapahos and I know Tom hadn't located their new camp before he left for Laramie. You go back and talk to Bobcat. Tell him what Tom wants and find out how he feels. Let me know and I'll see Tom's notified. I was going to send a man anyway and if you go, it'll save me the trouble."

He had been glad to carry Bent's message. "In fact," he said, "after I come back with their answer, I plan to return to Bobcat's village and stay there for a while. I want to learn to speak Arapaho. The problem is, I was told to wait for orders here at your place."

"Hell, *I've* given you an order," Bent had told him. "You might as well stay with Bobcat's band as here with me. Don't worry. If the army comes looking for you, I'll get word to you quick enough."

Bent had examined Hampton critically. "Got some Arapaho blood in you, I'd say."

"My father was Indian. He could have been Arapaho. His name was Bad Hawk."

"Never heard of him," Bent had replied. "But that doesn't mean much, the way warriors change names. About Tom, now, the Indians call him Broken Hand on account of the fact he lost two fingers on his right hand some years ago when his gun blew up. This is their sign for him."

Hampton sighed and made the sign now to Bobcat and the council. *Broken Hand sends a message*, he told them. *The Great White Father in Washington wishes a peace council with all the tribes who follow the buffalo. Broken Hand asks if you will come to Fort Laramie before the leaves turn color and meet with the other tribes and with him.*

None of the Arapaho spoke or made any gesture to indicate they understood his signing. Finally Bobcat grunted.

Pawnee comes? Ute? he signed.

Broken Hand asks all tribes to join the council, Hampton signed.

I would like to see peace with our enemies, Bobcat signed.

Ho's of approval came from the others.

We will do as Broken Hand asks, Bobcat signed. *We will go to the soldier lodge at Laramie. We will listen with good hearts.*

I will carry your message, Hampton signed. *After I do, I want to return and stay in your village. I want to learn your speech.*

Bobcat glanced around the circle of men. No one spoke against this even though Winter Bull scowled. *It is good for you to live among us,* Bobcat signed.

Stands Shining frowned at Bobcat. "Peace council?" she said. "How can Broken Hand ask us to make peace with Utes and Pawnees?"

"Our young men die fighting and our children die of new sicknesses," Bobcat answered her. "Soon there will be no Arapaho left."

"I led warriors to bring Pawnee children to our village for us to raise."

"The Pawnees suffer, too, enemies that they are. When they have no children for us to capture, what then?"

"You speak of things that have not happened. There was no sickness at the Pawnee village. Even if we make peace with them, how can we tell if they'll keep the peace? Pawnees can't be trusted."

Bobcat sighed. "We must try. The white man's wagons scatter the buffalo and the pronghorns so far they are hard to find. His guns kill our game. More white wagons cross our lands every summer. We know the wagons cross the lands of our allies, too, the land of the Sioux and Cheyenne, of the Kiowa and Comanche. They cross the land of our enemies as well. The whites are like bees swarming to a new hive. They are as many as bees while we are few, even with our allies."

"Our People are stronghearts," Stands Shining cried. "They are afraid of nothing."

"Stronghearts can't prevail against hunger. The buffalo are less every year and the white wagons more. Every tribe hunts the buffalo. Soon there will not be enough buffalo for us all. What then?"

Stands Shining's eyes glittered. "Fight!"

"Will we kill each other so only a few remain to feed off the few buffalo?" Bobcat asked. "It is clear we cannot fight the whites. You are young and cannot see. We must go and listen to Broken Hand. He tries to help us."

"He does have a good heart," Stands Shining agreed reluctantly.

"We must go and listen," Bobcat repeated.

Stands Shining knew he was asking her to convince the warriors.

"I hear what you tell me," she responded finally, remembering how One Claw had taught her to see into others' hearts. "I, too, will listen to the words of Broken Hand. But I make no other promise."

When Bobcat left her tepee, Stands Shining expected to see Fire Moon again. When he didn't come and she soon heard he'd headed back to Little White Man's lodge, she knew she must not think about him again.

The next morning she took Bear Fat to the horse herd.

"I'll show you how to train a war horse," she told him, and she selected a likely looking buckskin from the

Pawnee horses allotted to her. "We will discover, first of all, if he's too skittish to carry a warrior into battle."

Leaping on his back, Stands Shining issued a war cry. When the buckskin didn't falter or try to throw her as she urged him forward, she wheeled him back to Bear Fat and dismounted. "Soon we'll find out how he will act when his rider fires a rifle."

"It is true a war horse must be fast and strong, but he must also be dependable. Many times a wounded warrior is saved when he falls during a battle because his horse knows how to drag him to safety with the rope tied to both of them. Every warrior must spend hours training his horse to do this."

Bear Fat's eyes shone with excitement as Stands Shining showed him the best way to tie the rope around himself and the horse. He rode the buckskin a distance away and threw himself from the horse to the ground so enthusiastically that Stands Shining was forced to hide a smile.

"That's a good sign," she called to the boy as she strode to him. Gently she encouraged the horse to walk away from Bear Fat until the rope grew taut and pulled the boy along the ground.

They repeated the lesson.

"That's enough," she advised, after the third time. "A horse learns by doing something over and over just as we do, but just as we do, he grows tired. Come every sun and practice, but not too often each time."

"My Westwind already knows how to be a war horse," Bear Fat insisted.

"What is more important is that when you have finished training the buckskin, *you* will have learned what it is like to be a war horse," Stands Shining replied. "If you don't learn, you will never be a good warrior."

Each sun Bear Fat was off early to train the horse and each sun Stands Shining taught him another maneuver. The horse learned even more quickly than she had hoped and she decided she would ride him herself and use him to help train the black colt.

Her life was good now. She was fortunate to have an adopted son as capable as Bear Fat. His ability and persistence made her proud. Her tepee was comfortable. She found herself growing fond of little Bending Reed. Even the flirtatious Sweet Water was often enjoyable to be around. The sisters not only kept her comfortable, but even seemed happy in the Arapaho village.

Stands Shining sighed. Why, then, was she so restless and discontented?

Ten suns came and went. On the morning Snake Woman was to move her tepee to the Cheyenne village, Bear Fat came to Stands Shining's lodge and woke her. The sky had scarcely greyed.

"I want to work with the horse once more before I bring him into the village to show my mother. I want her to see what I have taught him. Will you come and see I make no mistakes?"

Stands Shining knew that Bear Fat would miss Snake Woman very much. She had reared him alone and they were close.

"I'll come with you to the herd," Stands Shining agreed. She was confident Bear Fat would make no mistakes, but she knew he wanted to be perfect when he showed off for his mother. Though he'd be visiting Snake Woman in the Cheyenne camp, in many ways this was their final parting.

Stands Shining took her bow from the tepee wall and slung the quiver of arrows over her shoulder. She had tried to impress Bear Fat with the importance of always going armed even though she, like most of the warriors, didn't always bother when close to the camp.

Bear Fat carried his own small bow and blunt arrows. Perhaps later this sun she would make a target for him as

One Claw had once shown her how to do. Improving his aim might take his mind off Snake Woman's departure.

The horse herd seemed nervous, but Stands Shining found no trace of wolves or mountain cats that sometimes stalked the animals. Bear Fat scrambled atop the buckskin while she searched for sign. Uneasy, though she found nothing suspicious, she located Westwind and mounted him.

"The horses tell us something is wrong," she informed Bear Fat as he began to put the buckskin through his paces. "I'm not sure what's bothering them. But while you work with your horse, you must remain alert. Watch. Listen."

It was possible, she thought to herself, that a rattlesnake may have spooked one or two horses and they in turn had disturbed the entire herd. There might be no more to it than that. But the hair prickled on her neck.

The herd was grazing in bottom land near the stream to the west. A steep bluff rose to the south, extending through the strip of cottonwoods along the stream. To the east lay another bluff, not as steep, but difficult to climb. The village was to the north, hidden from her sight by a rise.

Stands Shining could see nothing out of the ordinary in any direction. She glanced at Bear Fat. He was fifteen paces from her, racing the buckskin in a circle while hanging over one side of the horse and pretending to shoot under his neck. Danger seemed to vibrate in the air like the tail of a rattlesnake.

The Coyotes who guarded the village had given no warning. Was there no danger? Or were the scouts silent because they were dead?

A jay rose out of the cottonwoods. It called harshly.

"Bear Fat," Stands Shining snapped, "ride to me. Quickly."

The boy pulled himself up and turned the buckskin. A

second later he pitched from the horse to the ground. Stands Shining kicked Westwind into a canter. She hoped Bear Fat was only teasing her by letting the buckskin drag him to her, but dread gripped her stomach.

In just such a way had she watched First Cloud die.

Something struck her shoulder lightly, flying past.

An arrow!

Stands Shining flattened herself against Westwind's neck, at the same time yanking her knife from its sheath. She urged the horse in a circle around the buckskin, who was pulling Bear Fat's limp body toward the trees.

"No!" she screamed at the buckskin. That was where the arrow had come from.

As Westwind made his second circle, Stands Shining slowed him, then leaned and slashed the rope that held Bear Fat to his horse, snatching the end of it in her other hand. She yanked on the rope and Bear Fat helped her pull him onto Westwind. An arrow shaft thrust from his thigh.

Stands Shining urged Westwind into the herd, holding Bear Fat across the horse and crouching low herself. She slid off her horse and pulled the boy down. He leaned heavily against her and all around them horses milled uncertainly.

"I fell off so they couldn't shoot me again," Bear Fat explained while Stands Shining was examining his wound. His face was pale with pain. "That was right, wasn't it?"

"Yes."

"Who attacks?" he asked.

Stands Shining studied the arrow shaft to be certain. The head was deeply embedded in Bear Fat's flesh. She had no time to remove it. "Pawnee," she told him.

Stands Shining knew the Pawnee must have hidden among the cottonwoods during the night in order to steal the horses at dawn. They hadn't attacked the village though. She'd heard no outcry.

She could not go south—the bluff there was impass-

able. The east bluff could be climbed, but the going would
be so slow she'd be as full of arrows as a porcupine had
quills before she reached the top. Nor could she cross the
stream and circle to the village. She knew the Pawnee
waited among the cottonwoods. The only possible way to
get to the village was to ride directly there, heading north
over the rise. It was unlikely she would make it. Even if
she did, Bear Fat couldn't and would be killed.

Yet they couldn't stay like this. The horses would
trample them when the Pawnees stampeded the herd. She
helped Bear Fat onto the back of a small pinto.

"Lay along his neck," she cautioned. "He's smaller
than the other horses and they won't see you if you stay in
the herd. If the Pawnees run off with the herd, try to get
away and hide."

It was the best she could do for him. Stands Shining
knew she must get to the village and warn the warriors.
The Pawnee would be watching for the spotted horse. She
couldn't ride Westwind.

She forced herself to turn away from Bear Fat. Crouching so she wouldn't be seen above the horses, she made
her way to the buckskin, who had followed them into the
herd. She eased onto him, holding to his mane and hanging to his side, concealing herself from those who might
be watching from the trees.

Slowly she coaxed him away from the other horses
until he was free of the herd. She whistled softly into his
ear then as she'd taught Bear Fat to do. The buckskin took
off at a gallop, pounding for the village. Hanging on by
one leg, Stands Shining gripped his mane with one hand.
With her other hand she held her bow. Her body was to
one side, protected by the horse from Pawnee arrows.

She could see the cottonwoods by looking under the
buckskin's neck. Five riders broke from cover. Two raced
toward her. The other three angled ahead of her to cut her

off. The buckskin ran all-out, but he didn't have the speed of Westwind. Stands Shining knew she would be overtaken.

Raising herself onto the horse's back, she kept low along his neck and nocked an arrow.

"Hiyah hi!" she cried, swerving the buckskin and driving directly at the two Pawnees heading for her. "Hiyah hi!"

Her arrow flew true. One Pawnee slumped and rolled off his horse. The other ducked to the side of his mount. She shot again, hitting the horse.

An arrow grazed her face. It had been shot by one of the warriors to her right. Others raced from the left.

Stands Shining shot her arrows as fast as she could, but she knew she couldn't kill all the Pawnees who rode at her.

She began to sing her death song.

Chapter 16

Hampton pushed Ares north through the darkness. He knew both he and the chestnut should be resting, but when he had tried to make a night camp, he couldn't sleep.

The terrain was difficult. He was near the foothills of the mountains where the rolling swells of the plains along the Arkansas thrust higher and rockier. Streams trickled through boulder-littered canyons deep enough to make it a chore to get to water. Stark and treacherous hogbacks challenged the traveler.

Yet Hampton rode steadily on. It was his fourth trip over the same territory, so at least he knew the lay of the land. He crossed a pine ridge, descended to a grassy meadow, then climbed again. He would reach the Arapaho village by dawn if all went well.

As he traveled upward, a faint scent of wild roses drifted to him on the night breeze. He thought of Roseann. But as he tried to picture her fair beauty, a darker face flashed into his mind. The woman who rode with warriors, who drew him to her through the night. His blood was hot with his need for her.

Stands Shining.

He sighed and leaned forward to pat Ares' neck. "You're a good boy," he told the animal. "I've given you a rough time since we left Missouri."

Ares' bullet wound had healed cleanly even though the bullet remained inside him. That night Ares was carrying his heaviest load since he'd been shot.

Hampton was concerned. In addition to the rifle Bent had given him earlier, the trader had turned up a Walker Colt for him and given him ammunition. "The Indians never have enough bullets," he'd said. "You'll need these."

Yellow Woman had insisted on giving him another pair of new moccasins and a parfleche of food. He wondered how she felt when Bent journeyed to St. Louis, leaving her and the children behind. And Bent himself— did he sometimes wish to stay in the city and never return west? Or was it the other way? Did he leave his trading post and his family reluctantly?

Since he'd first seen the Arapaho village, Hampton had thought less and less of St. Louis. Every morning when he rose, he looked not to the sunrise but to the beckoning blue mountains that rose against the western sky.

His Arapaho blood?

But the blood of his mother and grandfather flowed in his veins, too. He was Hampton as well as Fire Moon. He was both. And he was neither.

An owl swooped over his head in a flight more felt than heard. Ares tossed his head and snorted. Soon he and his rider were descending into bottom lands again. The piping frogs shrilled, fading as they passed, rising again behind them.

Toward dawn a wolf chorus made Hampton tense. He listened, searching the darkness to try to tell if the wolves were human. There were others besides Arapaho and Cheyenne who roamed these foothills. He might convince warriors from those tribes he was a friend, but what of the Utes who camped in the mountains? He'd been told more than once that he looked like an Arapaho, and the Utes were their blood enemies.

He decided finally that the wolves were not human. Still, he rode more cautiously. He reached the cotton-woods near the stream that ran past the Arapaho village. A slight noise made him stiffen. He halted Ares.

A man had coughed. Hampton was certain of that. He slid quietly from Ares' back and stood beside the horse, listening. Perhaps he'd heard only a scout guarding the village. But no, there had been something wrong with the cough. Hampton searched his mind, trying to pinpoint the reason for his uneasiness.

He remembered Wolfing with the Sioux, his companion coming on a Crow scout. A quick kill, up from behind, the knife blade across the Crow's throat, blood spurting. A gurgling final cough.

That's what he'd heard.

A whisper of motion came from the cottonwoods ahead. Like the owl's flight, it was more felt than heard. There were faint splashes as the stream was crossed.

Enemies. Hampton was certain of it. He waited until all the sounds around him were the normal night noises: frogs, the rustle of leaves overhead, the scamper of a small animal along the ground. As silently as he could he tied Ares to a sapling. Then he eased his way in the direction of the sound he'd heard.

He found a dead man concealed among the bushes. From the feel of the scars on the man's chest and the shape of his moccasins, Hampton knew he was Arapaho.

He returned to Ares, his first impulse being to race to the Arapaho village to give warning. But stealth would get him past the enemy, not speed. A galloping horse would alert them and could easily, depending on their number and location, get him killed before he came near the tepees.

At that moment he had the advantage. No one knew he was there. He backtracked, leading Ares away from the stream until they both were out of the cottonwood grove. Then he mounted the chestnut and circled wide under a sky growing pale with the coming of dawn.

Climbing the rocky hill northwest of the village gave him a devil of a time, but finally he crested it and rode down toward the tepees. No scout challenged him. The enemy had been thorough.

As he drove Ares toward Bobcat's lodge, dogs sprang up to snarl at him. Bobcat was on his feet. He had reached for his bow by the time Hampton thrust the tepee flap aside.

"It is Fire Moon," Hampton announced, ducking back outside.

Bobcat stepped out to greet him. Other faces gaped from nearby tepees.

Enemies, Hampton signed. *They killed the scouts. Crossed the stream. They are south of the village where the horses graze.*

Bobcat shouted and men darted toward their horses. Hampton didn't wait but hurried to Stands Shining's lodge. The Pawnee girl, Sweet Water, greeted him with wide eyes. Stands Shining, she signed, had gone to the horses with Bear Fat some time ago.

Hampton flung himself onto Ares and raced from the village, rifle clutched in his hand. Mounted Arapaho warriors called to him. He paid no attention and forced the big chestnut to his utmost. Plunging up the rise that screened the meadow from the village, he dashed down into the open green field. Mounted warriors, Pawnee, dotted the meadow. Most of them rode with the Arapaho horse herd, driving it toward the stream. Stands Shining's war cry could be heard above the snorts and whinnies of the frightened animals. She was in the knot of Pawnees to his right. When Hampton shouted, his words were a scream of rage. Galloping at the men attacking Stands Shining, he raised his rifle, aimed and fired.

*   *   *

Stands Shining, her last arrow nocked in her bow, heard a rifle shot. One of her attackers toppled sideways off his horse. She let the arrow fly and saw it strike the side of a Pawnee as he whirled at the sound of the shot.

A warrior raced toward her, shouting, and the Pawnees turned from Stands Shining, scattering to meet the new attack. She saw the chestnut. Fire Moon! He dashed among the Pawnees, firing right and left with his pistol.

Quickly, Stands Shining recovered from her shock and kicked the buckskin in a half-circle to join him. Behind Fire Moon she saw Little Owl. He was leading the Arapaho warriors down the rise, whooping and brandishing bows.

A Pawnee thrust his horse toward Fire Moon and flung himself, howling on Fire Moon's back, knife raised.

Fire Moon fell from the chestnut and the Pawnee brave tumbled with him to the ground. Stands Shining sucked in her breath. Knife in hand, she urged the buckskin through the Pawnee horses toward the downed men. From the right, a Pawnee drove his horse across her path, leaning to swing his war club at her head. She ducked desperately, feeling the wind of the blow. He raised the club again as another Pawnee pounded alongside to her left, an arrow nocked in his bow.

Stands Shining threw her knife at the club wielder, but her aim was hurried and the knife buried itself in his thigh. He yelled and swung viciously at her with his club. She tensed for the blow.

It never came. The Pawnee toppled backward off his horse. An Arapaho arrow was deep in his chest. The other Pawnee wheeled away from Stands Shining, his arrow flying instead at an Arapaho brave. As she jerked the buckskin aside, she saw the arrow pierce the eye of the warrior who'd saved her. She knew he was dead even before he plunged from his mount.

Little Owl. He'd given his life for her.

By the time Stands Shining reached Fire Moon, the Pawnees were fleeing from the battle. Fire Moon was on his knees astride the Pawnee who had attacked him. He held a bloody knife in his hand. Stands Shining slid from her horse and called his name. Fire Moon turned, but his grey eyes were blank and cold. It was as though his spirit dwelt elsewhere.

She thought suddenly of the river ice that her long-ago ancestors had crossed. Fire Moon's eyes were like that ice. Stands Shining remembered how the old ones had spoken of the young maiden who had found a horn in the ice and tried to pull it out. In horror the maiden had watched as a water monster broke through, drowning her and many others of Our People. Stands Shining shuddered.

"Fire Moon," she whispered urgently. "It is Stands Shining."

Fire Moon repeated her name and warmth flickered in his eyes. Stands Shining knew his spirit had come back to him. He turned from her to stare down at the dead Pawnee. Then he leaped to his feet, away from the body. Glancing at the Pawnee, Stands Shining saw that Fire Moon had begun to scalp him.

Go ahead, she signed. *Take his scalp.*

Fire Moon grimaced. Kneeling, he thrust the blade into the dirt to clean it. Then he sheathed the knife. After standing once again, he crossed to Stands Shining and touched her face. She felt the sting of a wound and recalled the arrow that had brushed her cheek. But her heart pounded so at Fire Moon's nearness that she dismissed the cut and forgot about the four scalps that were hers to take. She could only gaze at him.

The sudden thought of Bear Fat brought her out of her reverie. She whirled and vaulted onto the buckskin. Fire

Moon followed on the chestnut as she dashed among the scattered herd, searching for the pinto.

"The boy is safe," Black Deer called to her as she passed him. He pointed toward the rise where village women had appeared dragging travois to carry the wounded and the dead. "I found him and brought him to Snake Woman."

Stands Shining saw Black Deer was waiting beside Little Owl's motionless body. She wheeled and brought the buckskin back.

"Little Owl saved me," she told Black Deer. "He is a strongheart. He died without shame. Your brother-by-choice will walk the warrior's road along the sky."

That evening Fire Moon refused to dance with the triumphant warriors. Instead, he chose to sit and watch with the old men. Stands Shining danced, leaping like a man. More than ever, she knew she was a warrior. Bear Fat, the Pawnee arrowhead cut out of his thigh, sat with his mother and the Cheyenne brave who was Snake Woman's new husband.

Stands Shining glanced at him while she was dancing. She was grateful the boy would not be permanently lame from his wound, though he would have a lasting scar. It was a scar, she thought, he could wear proudly. He had clearly shown himself to be brave and quick-thinking. He was a true Arapaho warrior. She had chosen well when she had picked him for her adopted son.

The drums throbbed. The fire flared. Life beat strong within Stands Shining. She had stood against the enemy without flinching. She had faced death with courage and acceptance, but now was glad to be alive, to be dancing. And she knew that Fire Moon watched, watched and waited.

He was truly the one who had saved her from the Pawnees, warning the village, leading the warriors. He had saved her and Bear Fat as well.

The keening wail of the women mourning the dead scouts and Little Owl rose over the chants and shouts of the dancers. In dying, Little Owl had redeemed his honor.

Women walked among the watchers with wooden bowls of meat and Stands Shining felt her stomach contract with hunger. She left the circle of dancers. Sitting with a bowl in her hands, eating, she tensed in anticipation.

It did her no good to plan how she would act when Fire Moon approached her. Whenever he was near, her wits deserted her. She shook her head impatiently. She was a seasoned warrior, not a silly girl like Sweet Water. She would do nothing foolish.

"Stands Shining."

Fire Moon had come up beside her without her seeing him. As before, the sound of her name on his lips made her breath catch. She turned to him and he held out his hand. She reached out to grasp it.

He led her away from the dancers, from the feasting, from the drums and the firelight. They passed among silent tepees, left them, then climbed the rise that led to the meadow. Fire Moon stopped halfway down the other side. The throb of the drums and shouts of the dancers and wailing women could only be heard faintly now. The hill blocked the sounds coming from the village.

Scouts who trailed the surviving Pawnee had reported them fleeing eastward. There was no sign of enemies, no reason to be afraid, yet Stands Shining was not able to relax. There was still danger shimmering around her, the danger of Fire Moon. Again she thought of the old story of the foolish maiden crossing the ice.

The night was brilliant with stars. Stands Shining listened to the whirling swoop of a nighthawk as it dived for an insect. The summer wind was soft against her face. All the sensations of the night were familiar and yet somehow different because this man she both wanted and feared stood next to her.

She'd seen the desire in his eyes. But did he also fear her in some way? She sensed his tenseness.

On nights such as this, Arapaho braves played love flutes in the darkness, calling to the maiden they longed for, luring her with high sweet notes. Fire Moon had needed no flute to call to her. He had reached out his hand and she had taken it.

Now she turned to him. He touched her cheek, his fingers gently tracing the shallow cut the arrow had made there. He drew back and signed to her.

You will come with me to Little White Man's Lodge. Leave the Arapaho village.

Stands Shining's heart leaped. Fire Moon wanted her with him. Thoughts whirled in her mind as wildly as cotton in a spring wind.

With me you can stop being a warrior, he signed. *You can be safe.*

She stared at him. *No!* she signed emphatically. *I remain a warrior.*

Fire Moon started to sign again, but Stands Shining turned away. She began to climb the rise, intending to go back to the village. No man would ever keep her from being a warrior.

From behind, Fire Moon's hands closed over her shoulders and jerked her around to face him. She twisted free, glaring.

I don't want you, she signed. But the gestures were inadequate to express her fury. How dare he force her to stay with him when she meant to go. How dare he object to her being a warrior. He had no right!

Fire Moon muttered words Stands Shining didn't understand, *niatha* words. She longed to throw her own angry words in his face but clenched her teeth to keep from speaking. What use would that be? Fire Moon knew only the babble of white men.

Stands Shining frowned angrily. Her being with Fire Moon was an insult to First Cloud's memory. She began to whirl away from him, but he gripped her arm, stopping her.

"Don't touch me!" The words flew out despite her promise to herself to be silent. "You are no Arapaho. You are an ignorant *niatha* and I hate you."

Fire Moon grasped Stands Shining's other arm and shook her.

She struggled to free herself but Fire Moon pulled her to him so violently that her breath went from her. His mouth met hers in a savage kiss. Flame seared through her. The smell of his maleness came to her, became a part of her. She tried to clutch at the remnants of her fury, but instead her arms went around him, holding him close. Her lips parted so that his tongue met hers.

Yet the ice of anger rose to fight her fiery need. Her hands clenched into fists. She beat at Fire Moon's back impotently, the intensity of her own desire keeping her pressed to his hardness.

Fire Moon lifted her. As he eased her onto the ground, Stands Shining burned inside as though the flames from the village celebration fire were consuming her. When he pulled off her tunic and his fingers caressed her bared breasts, even her bones seemed to melt.

Then she was naked beneath him. His bare flesh was hot against hers, and his hand ran along the curve of her hip. Nothing existed except Fire Moon and the fire his touch fed within her. She opened to him.

A flash of pain made her cry out. He hesitated, then groaned, plunging harder. At once the pain faded into a torment of wanting that made her writhe against him, her fingers digging into his shoulders.

He thrust savagely and she met his rhythm, a strange and wonderful exhilaration building inside her, rising as flames rose when fuel is poured onto a fire, rising higher, higher, to touch the stars.

She heard Fire Moon cry out, felt his body convulse. Then she, too, seemed to explode, fragments racing down the sky like falling stars.

Chapter 17

Hampton woke at dawn with a feeling of weight on his chest. He found himself looking into the bright eyes of Bobcat's two-year-old grandson who crouched on top of him. Plucking the boy off, he sat up. Except for the child, he was alone in Bobcat's tepee.

Hampton stood up and stretched, smiling as the two-year-old imitated him. He ducked out of the tepee and the boy toddled after him until his mother, cooking at the outside fire, scooped him up.

I'll wash at the stream before I go to Stands Shining, Hampton decided. At the pool where the men bathed, he met Winter Bull standing naked in the water, soap root in his hand. The brave offered half the root.

Hampton took it signing his thanks.

I see you follow her, Winter Bull signed. *Will you marry that woman who leads the warriors?*

That was the question Hampton had avoided asking himself. He still wanted Stands Shining. His desire was stronger than ever after last night, but until then, he'd thought she was a widow with a child. Now he knew he was the first man who had ever made love to her.

She calls Bear Fat her son, Hampton signed, avoiding Winter Bull's question.

She shares him with his mother. She trains him as a

warrior. A woman training warriors. Winter Bull shook his head and grimaced.

She fights bravely.

Winter Bull scowled, then glanced slyly at Hampton. *No Arapaho will marry such a woman.*

Hampton didn't reply, busying himself instead by scrubbing vigorously with the root, then rinsing by splashing in the shallow water before leaving the stream. Winter Bull's opinion was an exception, he told himself as he pulled on his clothes. Other Arapaho men, young and old, looked up to Stands Shining and admired her abilities.

But it was true that none had married her and twenty was old to still be a maiden. How, Hampton wondered, could any man have resisted her heart-shaped face or her challenging eyes that passion turned as soft as velvet? He found her beautiful. Her form was magnificent, high-breasted. There was a sweet curve to her hips. Just thinking about her brought a surge of desire.

Yet no man had lain with her before him. She must have had suitors but discouraged them. Certainly she had fought him. At first. He would never forget how she felt in his arms and how wild her response was when she stopped resisting his lovemaking.

Marriage was another matter entirely. Marriage was Roseann and St. Louis. A big white house like the judge's. Flower gardens. Servants. And that took money. Hampton scowled. He had none.

He remembered the Pawnee who had jumped him the day before. He had come out of the blind redness of rage and found himself set to scalp the dead warrior. He'd acted like a savage.

Like an Arapaho.

Hampton shook his head, water spattering from his wet hair. Now his hair was long enough to braid. When he had worked in St. Louis with the blacksmith, he'd avoided anyone who might recognize him. No one had.

"Ho," Winter Bull called to him from the stream where he still splashed. Hampton turned to face him.

"Marry Stands Shining," Winter Bull advised. "Make her a woman, not a warrior. Women who lead men are bad medicine for Our People."

Hampton made the sign telling Winter Bull he had heard, then he set off for the village. He didn't agree with Winter Bull's reasons. Stands Shining should give up being a warrior, yes, but for her own safety. As for convincing her of this. . . . He sighed and shook his head.

What did he want? Marriage was for the future and he was no hypocrite. It would be dishonest of him to enter into an Indian-style marriage with Stands Shining that she believed in and he didn't. Yet he wanted her with him, wanted to protect her.

At the tepee, Sweet Water smiled demurely and handed him a buffalo robe. Wrapped in it were a breechcloth, leggings and moccasins newly made of beautifully tanned elk skin. Sweet Water had used colored quills to decorate the moccasins and leggings in geometric designs. She was a pretty little thing and he smiled back at her.

Sweet Water made signs that he should put on the clothes.

Why not? The wool army trousers were torn and too hot for summer. He shooed Sweet Water and her younger sister from the tepee. They went out giggling.

He hadn't worn a breechcloth or leggings since his year with the Sioux. He found them as comfortable as he remembered, though the same feeling he'd had then of being undressed plagued him. He left his shirt off. Then, rather self-consciously, he emerged from the tepee naked to the waist.

Sweet Water pressed her hands together, giving a soft "ho" of approval.

Hampton started off to find Stands Shining, but he was intercepted by Bobcat's daughter. She signed that a man waited with Bobcat to speak to him. He went with her to the chief's tepee.

Hampton recognized the man sitting with Bobcat as Old Jack, the trapper who wore his long grey hair tied back with a thong. They'd met at Bent's Fort.

"Well, looks like you took to tepee life pretty quick," Old Jack said to Hampton. "Got yourself a squaw and all, I bet." He winked. "Always liked them 'Rapaho squaws myself."

"You sent for me?" Hampton asked abruptly.

" 'Taint me what sent for you. 'Twere Tom Fitzpatrick hisself, back to Bent's. Wants to talk to you. I was passing through on my way to Laramie. Gonna be big doings up there come September with all them tribes trailing in for the council. Anyways, I said I'd stop by here and give you Tom's message." Old Jack nodded. " 'Sooner the better,' Tom says."

"Fitzpatrick's at Bent's Fort?"

"What I said, ain't it?" Old Jack shifted position. "Getting hard on these old bones to squat and smoke in tepees anymore."

"Thanks for bringing me the message," Hampton said.

He'd have to go, of course. But first he'd find Stands Shining and explain.

She was with the herd, examining her horses to see if any had been injured. Her face lit up when she saw him. For a moment he thought she meant to run to him. But she checked herself and he slid from the chestnut to go to her.

Two are lame, she signed.

It took him a moment to realize what she meant.

Damn the horses.

He reached for her and she stepped back.

You wear Arapaho clothes, she signed. *You look Arapaho. Is your heart Arapaho?*

He found he couldn't answer. Annoyance flickered in

him. Why such a question when all he wanted was to hold her close?

I must ride to Little White Lodge, he signed. *Broken Hand sends for me. I will come back.*

She sighed. When he reached out for her again, she came into his arms. For a moment she returned his embrace. Then once more she pulled away, gazing at him with an expression he couldn't interpret.

Anger? Disappointment?

Abruptly she vaulted onto the back of a buckskin horse and loped toward the village.

He didn't want to leave her like this. He wanted to let her know with caresses how he hated to go away from her. Was there to be a struggle every time he tried to make love to her? Frustration and anger simmered in him as he mounted the chestnut.

She could be damned annoying. What right had she to ask him what his heart was? But for a time after he'd ridden south from the village, he felt as though he had no heart at all, that he'd left it behind with her.

Hampton's first sight of Thomas Fitzpatrick startled him. He knew about the injured hand and he'd been told Fitzpatrick was in his early forties, but he hadn't expected him to have pure white hair. Otherwise the Indian agent looked hale and fit, a tall man who moved with energy that belied his age.

"So your name is Hampton Abbott," Fitzpatrick remarked, examining Hampton with keen blue eyes.

Hampton wondered if he disapproved of the Arapaho clothes, although Fitzpatrick himself wore moccasins and a buckskin shirt.

"Hampton Abbott. You know, I recollect that name. Will says you're from St. Louis."

"Yes, sir. My grandfather—"

Fitzpatrick held up his hand. "I don't need any sirs,

lad. Makes me downright uneasy. Call me Tom. Go on with what you were saying.''

"My grandfather was a judge in St. Louis. His name was Douglas Hampton.''

Fitzpatrick nodded. "Your age is about right. I'd say the boy I'm thinking of was about five on the night the stars fell.''

A chill shot along Hampton's spine. He stared at the white-haired man, speechless.

"Your mother was Elizabeth Abbott,'' Fitzpatrick went on. "Never forgot her name.''

"Yes,'' Hampton confirmed in a whisper.

"What did your mother tell you about your childhood?'' Fitzpatrick asked.

For one terrible moment, all Hampton could remember was his mother's contorted face as she made him promise to kill his father.

"She . . . my mother died soon after we went to live in St. Louis.'' Hampton swallowed. "I do know my father was an Indian named Bad Hawk. I think he may have been Arapaho.''

Fitzpatrick nodded. "Must have been. I found your mother and you by a northern Arapaho village after a Ute attack. Brought you to St. Louis to the judge.''

His grandfather must have known Fitzpatrick's name, Hampton thought, yet he never told me, wouldn't speak of the rescue.

"Where was this village?'' Hampton asked. "Is my father alive? Did you see him?''

Fitzpatrick shook his head. "Wait. Easy, lad. Told you all I know. The village was in the foothills of the Rockies up near Laramie. It won't be there now. Your mother told me a bit about Bad Hawk . . .'' Fitzpatrick broke off. "Not enough to mention.''

"Is he alive?''

Fitzpatrick shrugged. "Was then, far as I know. The

Arapaho warriors were away hunting when the Utes attacked."

"I mean to find him if I can."

"Don't believe that's a good idea."

"I know his name and now I know where his village was."

"Indians change their names almost as often as a cottonwood sheds leaves. I told you where the village was in '33. This is '51 and there won't be a trace of it. You must know how Indian villages move."

"I intend to learn," Hampton declared stubbornly.

"That's up to you." Fitzpatrick smiled at Hampton. "I'm happy to see you've turned out to be a fine young lad, though I'm sorry about your mother."

Hampton forced himself not to blurt out the questions rising inside him. What had his mother told Tom Fitzpatrick? He burned to know. But he doubted Fitzpatrick had summoned him here just to talk about the night the stars fell.

"Sir, I mean Tom, I came as quickly as I could after Old Jack brought me your message."

"As long as you're hereabouts I can use another interpreter at the peace council," Fitzpatrick said. "Will says you're handy with signs, used to scout for the army."

"I didn't scout long for them. But I do know scouting. Learned from the Delaware and the Sioux."

"Speak any Sioux?"

"I'm pretty fluent. I know Potawatomi and Delaware, too, but no Cheyenne or Arapaho. I'd like to learn. Superintendent Mitchell has been trying for a year now to have me appointed as your interpreter."

Fitzpatrick nodded. "You're just the lad I've been looking for. I'll see if I can't push Washington to agree. I'll be going east when the council's over."

"I'd like very much to work with you," Hampton told the Indian agent. "But I did enlist as an army scout."

"Don't worry about that. Washington will handle it."

Fitzpatrick thrust out his hand. "We'll shake on working together."

Hampton glanced briefly at the other, mutilated hand, then shook the one that was offered to him.

"We're off to Laramie tomorrow, then," Fitzpatrick concluded.

Hampton found the country between the Arkansas River, where Bent's Fort stood, and the North Fork of the Platte River much like the foothill country he already knew. There were ravines, hogbacks and grassy bottoms hot under the summer sun.

Late on the day Fitzpatrick told him they would reach Fort Laramie, their party crested a rise and Hampton saw great circles of Sioux, Cheyenne and Arapaho lodges nestled around a hill. On top of the hill was a stockade, Fort Laramie.

"I thought the council was scheduled for the first of September," he remarked to Fitzpatrick. "It's still July."

"You've been among Indians long enough to know time doesn't mean much to them."

"There must be five thousand here already," Hampton observed. He thought of the raids when he had lived in the Sioux camp, of the Pawnee attack on Stands Shining's village. "Will they get along peaceably for six weeks?"

"These will. Sioux, Arapaho and Cheyenne are what's here so far. They're allies. The chiefs will handle any petty quarreling. Besides, there's nearly two hundred dragoons at the fort. And the cannon. The Indians respect and fear the fort's 'big gun.' They don't want to hear it speak. But I'm hoping the mountain Indians—Utes, Shoshones, Crows—don't arrive early. They're age-old enemies of these Plains tribes. If any fights start, then I don't know if a thousand dragoons could stop them."

Hampton stopped a lone warrior galloping toward them. Arapaho, he thought. He glanced at Fitzpatrick, who peered intently at the rider. Other men in the party fingered their rifles.

Fitzpatrick broke into a grin. "Put the guns away, lads, I know who he is."

The Arapaho, a young man of about Hampton's age, halted his horse and jumped to the ground. Fitzpatrick slid from his own mount and the two hugged each other, laughing.

"That's Friday," one of the party whispered. "I recognize him now."

"Hampton, come here," Fitzpatrick ordered.

Hampton dismounted and approached.

"This is my adopted son, Friday," Fitzpatrick told him. "Friday Fitzpatrick. Friday was the day I found him twenty years ago on the *Jornado del Muerto*, the Journey of Death, on the Santa Fe Trail. What were you, lad, about five?"

"Five or six." To Hampton's surprise, the Arapaho spoke perfect English.

"Never did find his folks," Fitzpatrick went on. "Brought him with me to St. Louis and put him in school there." He looked at Friday with obvious pride.

"Glad to meet you." Hampton extended his hand.

Friday couldn't quite mask his own surprise. Because *I* speak English, Hampton thought with bitter amusement.

Fitzpatrick touched Hampton's arm. "This is Hampton Abbott. Rescued him and his mother during an Arapaho-Ute battle not too far from here."

"I grew up in St. Louis with my grandfather," Hampton informed Fitzpatrick's son. He tried not to stare at Friday, but wondered how the Arapaho's St. Louis schooling and his Indian life mixed. Still, Friday belonged somewhere. He was all Arapaho.

After shaking hands, the three remounted, descended the rise and trotted toward the clay walls of Fort Laramie. A sentry recognized Fitzpatrick. He came to attention, saluted and permitted them to pass through the gate under the blockhouse. The fort was much smaller than Leavenworth, even with its inside livestock corral. Soldiers were everywhere, as well as buckskin-clad men, traders and Indians.

For the next few weeks, Hampton was kept busy visiting the Sioux tepees, meeting their chiefs, smoking with them. He was asked to do some translating, too, for Fitzpatrick, though he noticed the agent was quite proficient in sign language.

He kept an eye out for Lost Hunter's Sioux band, hoping to see Jerome again, but those tepees weren't among the Sioux circles. And he waited impatiently for Stands Shining to arrive with Bobcat's Arapahos.

The late-August days were unpleasantly hot and the Indians complained that their ponies lacked forage. Fitzpatrick decided to move the council to a grassy valley some thirty miles down the Platte where Horse Creek entered the wide river. Hampton was in the Sioux circles talking to the chiefs about the move when excitement rippled through the camp.

Scouts had ridden in to report that mounted bluecoats and wagons were only a half-sun away. Superintendent Mitchell would be coming to the conference from Washington with presents for the tribes.

A Sioux brave thrust his hand in the air, saying, "No more wagons than I have fingers on this hand. We are many. Our allies are many. What are five wagons of presents for all of us?"

Hampton noticed a cloud of dust to the south. "What others approach?" he asked the scout.

"Arapaho," the Sioux scout replied.

It had to be Bobcat's band, Hampton was certain. Eagerly he mounted Ares and galloped toward the dust cloud. He smiled as he thought of Stands Shining's surprise when he spoke to her in Arapaho. He'd found an old

Arapaho woman living in the Sioux camp who spoke both languages and had been learning the more difficult Arapaho as quickly as he could from her.

What would he say to Stands Shining?

"My heart fills with sunshine to see you," he murmured. Yes, but there should be more. He must tell her how lonesome the nights had been, how he longed to have her in his arms, how lovely she was, how often in his mind he relived the times they'd been together. If he were only fluent enough to say it all.

When he finally caught sight of old Bobcat, the chief was dressed in his silver armbands, feathered bonnet and pipestone breastplate. Seeing him riding at the head of the band, Hampton whooped for sheer joy.

Stands Shining rode with the warriors who flanked the columns of women and children. Ponies pulled the travois loaded with tepee gear and toddlers too little to walk. He pounded to her side and wheeled Ares to fall into step next to her buckskin horse. His chest tightened as he gazed at her and he fought to bring the Arapaho words to his mind.

"I have waited long for you," he managed to say.

Her eyes widened and she smiled a little. "You have found a teacher."

She rode fully armed with lance, bow, war club, arrows, rifle. Her shield hung at her side. He had never seen her this way, a woman ready for war. Yet she didn't look masculine. Nor did she seem out of place, for she carried herself with the assurance of a successful warrior.

He could find no words to tell her how much he admired her.

"If that is all you learned, you need a new teacher," she teased.

You be my teacher, he signed, giving up on words. *We can start tomorrow.* He leaned toward her, longing to touch her, aware he should not. Not now, not here.

"Perhaps," she replied. But the promise in her eyes told him she felt as he did.

He saw Bobcat motioning for him to ride at the front of the column. Stands Shining gestured with her head that he should go.

Bobcat had many questions regarding what was going on in the camps around the fort. He also wanted to know about the council. By the time Hampton finished telling him all he had learned, the campgrounds were in sight. Bobcat pointed out the proper spot for his band and everyone scattered to set up tepees among the Arapaho circles.

Hampton tried to talk to Stands Shining again, but she was busy instructing Sweet Water on how an Arapaho tepee should go up. By the time the tepee was finally in place, it was past midday and the dust of the approaching dragoons and wagons was visible over the eastern hills.

I must go to the fort to be with Broken Hand when he greets his Chief, Hampton signed to Stands Shining.

Bobcat rides to greet Broken Hand, she signed. *I will join him.*

He clasped her hands for a moment, but she pulled away.

At the fort, Fitzpatrick had no immediate need for Hampton. So he stood watching as the honor guard of Laramie cavalry escorted the eastern party into the fort. Bobcat and Stands Shining had come inside and he tried to catch Stands Shining's glance. But she wouldn't look at him.

As Superintendent Mitchell passed Hampton, the official smiled and raised his hand. The dragoons behind Mitchell tried to stay in formation, but the inner square of the fort was jammed with people. One of the officers directed them to the right and left with abrupt gestures as a covered wagon drawn by mules rolled through the gate. At once the dragoons scattered to get out of the way.

Hampton stared at the officer in disbelief. It couldn't be! The man, a lieutenant, turned fully toward him, his eyes passing over Hampton without recognition.

It was Steve Chambers!

Hampton couldn't look away from Chambers. Only when he heard the surprised exclamations from the fort soldiers and the ho's from the Indians around him did he turn to look at the wagon.

A woman had appeared in the front of it. A white woman. She wore a violet traveling dress and, as Hampton watched, her matching bonnet slipped back to reveal strawberry-blonde hair.

"A real beauty, by God," the private next to him exclaimed, awe-stricken.

Hampton couldn't speak.

The private was talking about Roseann.

Chapter 18

Roseann's face glowed pink as she smiled at the men below her. Hampton broke out of his paralysis of shock and elbowed his way toward her.

She had come to him! Somehow she had discovered where he was and had braved the dangers of travel over the plains to seek him out.

He was within a few steps of the wagon when Chambers cut in ahead of him and reached up his hand. Roseann grasped it.

Chambers caught Roseann about the waist and lifted her down. Hampton ground his teeth as he watched them hug briefly.

"Roseann!" Hampton called.

They both turned to face him. Roseann blinked, her face blank. Chambers stared, scowling for a moment. Then he grinned.

"Look, Roseann," he chuckled, "there's Hamp Abbott, of all people. And dressed exactly like all the rest of the Indians."

Hampton saw uncertain recognition cross Roseann's face as he reached for her hand. Chambers pulled her aside, his arm around her.

"Hamp," he said, "I'd like to introduce Mrs. Steven Chambers."

Hampton didn't move or speak. He stared at Chambers, seeing his face through a growing reddish haze. At his side, someone spoke, then spoke again. The words hovered just beyond understanding. A hand clamped on his wrist.

"Fire Moon!"

He broke free and whirled toward the intruder. Through the fog he made out a woman's face. She spoke again.

"Fire Moon!"

The pressure on his wrist returned, preventing him from leaping at Chambers. He bared his teeth at the woman, yanking his arm from her grasp, and he had already started to turn back toward Chambers when he realized she was Stands Shining.

He faced her again. Behind her, he saw Fitzpatrick standing on the steps leading up to the officers' quarters. Fitzpatrick was speaking urgently to Superintendent Mitchell on the step above him and paying no heed to what was going on below.

Hampton did his best to shake off his anger. He swallowed and turned stiffly to Chambers and Roseann. "My congratulations to you both."

Roseann's lips parted as if she wished to speak, but Hampton bowed, wheeled and forced his way through the crowd toward Fitzpatrick. He knew Stands Shining was keeping pace beside him, but he didn't look at her. As he reached the steps, she leaned close and stared directly into his eyes. Then she was gone. He stood gazing after her, his mind a whirlwind of confusion.

Fitzpatrick's voice rose and Hampton knew immediately that the usually soft-spoken agent was furious.

". . . a week? We can't hold the tribes off another week waiting for the damn wagons. And this woman . . ."

Superintendent Mitchell broke in. "Her father's a colonel, a friend of General Scott's. She's married to one of the junior officers and wanted to 'see the West' with him, of all fool things. I tried, Tom. As for the wagons, God knows you can't control what the army does.''

Fitzpatrick waved an arm. ''Sorry, Dave, I don't mean to sound as though I blame you. I'll do what I can with the chiefs.''

Jim Bridger pushed by Hampton and mounted the steps. Bridger was another of the mountain men who had trapped with Fitzpatrick years before. Old Gabe, as Fitzpatrick called him, had a trading post on the Green River and had helped convince the Shoshone to come to the council.

''Don't mean to interrupt,'' Bridger said to Fitzpatrick, ''but Chief Washakie is camped a day away with his Shoshones.''

Fitzpatrick nodded. ''Thanks Gabe.'' As Bridger left, Fitzpatrick caught sight of Hampton below and motioned to him.

''Come on up and say hello to Superintendent Mitchell, Hampton. Then we'll ride over to the Sioux circles and ask the chiefs for a bit more patience with the Great White Father, as well as a firm rein on their warriors when the Shoshones ride in.''

After the ritual smoke, Fitzpatrick and Hampton spoke to a gathering of the Sioux chiefs. Among them was Crazy Horse, a medicine man who was chief of the Oglala Sioux. During the meeting, he kept his eyes on Hampton rather than on Fitzpatrick.

Along with the other chiefs, Crazy Horse assured both men that the peace would be kept. Fitzpatrick rose to leave. As Hampton followed him, Crazy Horse spoke.

''I have heard of a man with rain-cloud eyes. He is called Skull Singer by Lost Hunter's band of my people.''

''I was named Skull Singer,'' Hampton told him, stopping.

"You are welcome in my tepee," Crazy Horse declared. "It would be good to speak with you."

Hampton accepted the invitation and spent the night in Chief Crazy Horse's tepee. As they talked, the chief's ten-year-old son sat by his father, solemnly listening. The boy, smaller and lighter-skinned than most Sioux children, was an obvious favorite of his father's.

"I have heard of the black whiteman in Lost Hunter's camp," Crazy Horse reflected. "It is told that he has great medicine."

"Yes," Hampton agreed. "He possesses power."

It was true enough, he thought. Without Jerome, he would never have had a friend in the judge's house and certainly would have died when the Sioux attacked the Potawatomi raiding party. He owed Jerome more than he could ever repay.

"You, too, have power," Crazy Horse asserted, "perhaps because of those." He gestured toward the scars on Hampton's chest made by the skewer. "I feel this power in you."

"I am not aware of power."

"Be careful you don't misuse it. Used wrongly, it turns back on the one who possesses it and destroys him. Listen. I speak truth."

The boy listened wide-eyed to his father's words. The lodges surrounding them were still, for it was very late. Even the dogs slept. Frogs shrilled in the distance. A fox barked. Hampton tried to feel the power Crazy Horse thought he had.

"How does a man know he has this power?" he asked.

"When you need it, it is there. It is different for every person. Sometimes I see power shining in my son here, but I do not know what form it will take. I try to teach him so he will know when the time comes for him to use his power." He smiled and touched the boy's head.

Strong medicine for a ten-year-old, Hampton thought.

Later, as he lay on his sleeping robe, Hampton tried to clear his head of the jumbled images of Roseann, of Stands Shining, of Chambers. He'd meant to kill Chambers earlier that day during the red rage that commanded him. And he would have killed him had it not been for Stands Shining. Somehow she had known his intent and had stopped him. He was grateful. Yet in his heart he still wished Chambers dead.

Outside, a wolf howled. Others joined in until the sound seemed to come from every side of the camp. If Roseann, in her room at the fort, woke to the wolf chorus, would she turn to her husband for comfort?

Hampton grimaced at the thought of Chambers' hands caressing Roseann's fair skin. His blood pounded in his temples. Chambers was a man whose heart was bad, as the Indians would say. A man who could never be trusted. A man to hate.

Yet Roseann had married him.

Hampton sighed, feeling confused. He wasn't even certain why Roseann had meant so much to him. What was there about her, really, that he respected or loved? Yet he knew he must stay clear of both her and Chambers while they were at Laramie or there would be trouble.

Near dawn, Hampton finally fell asleep, only to jerk awake and bolt upright with a shout. He was fumbling for his knife when someone shook his arm.

"*Sacré bleu!*" a man cried out. "*C'est moi*, La Bonte."

On his feet, Hampton took a deep breath, his pulse still racing. Backed against the tepee wall, the Frenchman who interpreted for the Sioux stood wide-eyed.

"Sorry, La Bonte," Hampton managed to say, speaking in French. "I must have been dreaming."

"A bad dream, no doubt. I came to wake you. The Shoshone are on their way in." He shook his head. "Me,

I don't like it, Sioux and Shoshone camping next to each other.''

"Both tribes agreed to the peace council."

La Bonte shrugged. "Chiefs and old men agree. The young warriors lust for blood, for glory."

"Crazy Horse has his people under control."

"I hope you're right." La Bonte cocked his head. "Listen," he whispered.

Hampton heard a bugler from the fort sounding "Boots and Saddles." The notes were faint on the warm morning air.

"The army is nervous, too," La Bonte reported. "What can two hundred soldiers do if Shoshone and Sioux decide to fight? Will the dragoons shoot the warriors to prevent them from killing one another?"

When La Bonte and Hampton joined Bridger, Friday and the other interpreters at the edge of the camp circles, the first of the Shoshone were cresting a low-lying hill northwest of them.

"That's sure enough Washakie hisself," Bridger said. "Damned if he ain't in full battle dress. Looks grand, don't he?"

The Shoshone chief rode ahead and his warriors followed. All were garbed in magnificent feathered war bonnets and fully armed with rifles. Many of them rode spotted war horses like Westwind.

As the Shoshone came closer, a Sioux woman began to wail in the high-pitched keening used for mourning. Another woman joined in, then another. Hampton knew the women grieved for relatives slain by the Shoshones. The sound set his teeth on edge.

Suddenly a brave behind him shouted, "Hoka hey!" Recognizing the Sioux war cry, Hampton raced toward Ares, who was tethered beside a nearby tepee. Slashing the rope with his knife, he leaped onto the chestnut. A mounted Sioux brave, waving his bow, was galloping toward Chief Washakie. Hampton recognized La Bonte on a pinto trying to cut the warrior off.

Hampton kicked Ares into a run and raced toward the Shoshone chief. His plan was to get between Washakie and the Sioux. The Shoshones halted. Their war cries rose above the keening of the Sioux women. Washakie brought up his rifle.

Ares ran as hard as he could, but the Sioux had too much of a head start. Hampton yanked out his pistol. Then he hesitated. He couldn't shoot the Sioux. There wasn't a man in the Sioux camp who would understand or ever forgive him. He thrust the gun under his belt, watching La Bonte's pinto. "Go!" he shouted. "Get him!"

La Bonte closed in as the Sioux nocked an arrow into his bow. The Frenchman flung himself from his horse at the Sioux, knocking him off his mount.

Hampton reined in Ares and leaped off. La Bonte had seized the Sioux's bow and Hampton grappled with the young warrior, finally getting an arm across his throat from behind. He forced him to his feet.

"Let me go!" the Sioux gasped. "I will kill the murderers of my father, kill them all." He writhed and twisted, but couldn't break Hampton's hold.

La Bonte fastened the warrior's wrists and ankles with thongs. Under the muzzles of readied Shoshone rifles, he and Hampton threw the Sioux across Ares' back. Horses pounded toward them. Hampton looked up. Fitzpatrick and Crazy Horse were being followed by the other interpreters. A line of dragoons marched between the Sioux camp and the Shoshones.

"All over but the haranguing," La Bonte muttered to Hampton as Fitzpatrick rode up to greet Washakie. Crazy Horse gestured to Hampton that he should bring the captive warrior back to the Sioux camp.

Hampton spent hours with Fitzpatrick, Crazy Horse,

La Bonte and Bridger, assuring Washakie that such an act wouldn't be repeated.

"I came to seek peace," Washakie assured finally. "I will stay to seek peace."

Fitzpatrick, however, made certain the Shoshones camped near the dragoons.

Hampton saw neither Roseann nor Chambers during the next two days. He stayed away from the Arapaho circles. What was between him and Stands Shining had been set aside because of Roseann's presence. Yet both nights he dreamed of her, not of Roseann.

Fitzpatrick turned the relocation of the camp to Horse Creek into a parade led by the dragoons. Superintendent Mitchell and Fitzpatrick came next, followed by a wagon with gifts scrounged by Fitzpatrick from the fort's stores—blankets, beads, knives, coffee, tobacco and flour. There was only enough for the chiefs, but at least it was a token, Hampton told himself as he followed the wagons. He knew the missing presents from Washington had finally been located on a loading dock along the Missouri. At the earliest it would take two weeks to get them to the council site.

Behind Hampton and the other interpreters came the tribes—the Sioux with Crazy Horse in the lead, the Cheyenne, then Arapaho, Arikara, Shoshone, Atsina and Assiniboine. At the last minute the Crow had ridden to join them and they brought up the rear.

The caravan extended for miles along the Platte, raising clouds of dust. They reached the new campground at Horse Creek after a day's travel. While the women set up the camps, Fitzpatrick met with the chiefs and distributed the gifts.

"The council will begin in two days," he had the interpreters tell the assembled chiefs. "Meanwhile we will feast."

That evening the dance drums began. They throbbed in every circle as warriors painted their faces and bodies. Dog meat bubbled in every kettle except in the Shoshone camp, where it was taboo.

Hampton had been dismissed for the day by Fitzpatrick and was walking toward the Sioux camp through a stand of cottonwoods when a voice halted him.

"Well, I do declare, Hampton Abbott, the least I expected was that you'd stop in and say hello to me."

He turned slowly. "Hello, Roseann," he said. But he made no move to take her hand.

She looked charming in the fading daylight. She wore a green-sprigged gown of some thin white fabric, the tight bodice outlining her breasts.

"Marriage agrees with you," he told her.

She gazed at him through lowered lashes. For some reason she reminded him of Sweet Water.

"Well, after all, you never did come back like you promised," she said, pouting.

Hampton's heart began to thud in his chest as she moved closer and laid her hand on his arm. She smelled of lilacs.

"I did come back," he managed to say, "but you were in Washington."

She ignored his words. "I could hardly believe it was you at the fort," she murmured. "You look so different in those clothes. Exactly like an Indian." She pretended to shiver. "Should I be frightened of this savage Indian?"

"I'm the same Hampton you've always known." Even as he spoke the words, Hampton knew he lied. The boy he had been at Judge Hampton's house seemed a stranger.

Roseann tilted her head and examined him. "No," she declared, "you're different." She reached to touch the scars on his bare chest with her fingertips.

He controlled his shiver at her touch.

"I'm certain you could be very dangerous. Could take anything you wanted by force. Could be devastatingly cruel." She moistened her lips with the tip of her tongue.

"Are you happy?" he asked abruptly.

She drew back. "Of course," she answered.

"Then why did you come to Fort Laramie?"

"I would have had to stay in St. Louis and it's so dull there. Besides, there was always the chance I'd find you. And I have."

He had difficulty breathing. "Did you really come looking for me?"

She smiled slowly, dreamily. "What do you think?"

"But you married Chambers."

"Well, really, a girl doesn't get any younger sitting and waiting."

"Leave him," Hampton said hoarsely. "Stay with me."

Her eyes opened wide. "Out here?" She looked around. "With Indians? With wolves? Oh, no. Besides, it would wound Daddy terribly. Think of the scandal."

"Then what do you want with me?"

"Why, just to be friends. Don't you want to be friends with me, Hamp?" She pouted, her lips close to him.

And then he knew he could have her. She might pretend to struggle, but she wanted him to take her. Force her. Desire flared in him. She was so pretty, so softly curved. And he'd wanted her for so long.

Anyway, it would serve Chambers right.

That thought cooled him like a wind from the north. Is this what he intended? To strike at Chambers through Roseann? His hands, already reaching for her, dropped to his sides.

"Go back to your camp, Roseann," he requested coldly. "It isn't safe for you to be wandering about with so many Indians here."

Silently he chided himself. He knew no brave would
come near Roseann unless he was drunk, and there was no
liquor in the camp. Fitzpatrick had made certain of that.
Roseann was safer with the Indians than she would be with
the dragoons.

"You'll take care of me, won't you?" she asked.

"I have to go into the Sioux camp," he told her,
knowing he must get away from her before he lost his
head.

"Promise me you'll come and visit? Steve is so busy."

He took a deep breath. "I'll see."

She raised on tiptoe and kissed him quickly. Then she
turned and hurried off in the direction of the army tents.

He watched her go, bemused, remembering how she'd
done the same thing in St. Louis, kissed him and run
away. Teased him. She was a flirt as she'd always been,
he saw that clearly. At the same time he knew it was
different now. Anything between them needn't end with a
kiss.

And he still wanted her.

Chapter 19

Stands Shining put the last touch of red paint on her face and leaned forward to examine herself in the narrow looking glass. The mirror had helped her make every line, every circle on her forehead and cheeks perfect. Truly, some of the devices of the *niatha* were useful.

Rifles. Kettles and awls of iron. Blankets.

One Claw had always advised her to take what was good from the *niatha* and reject the bad. The northern Arapaho bands were all at the council and she had hoped to find him among them. That didn't happen.

"He had a bad medicine dream and would not travel with us," she had been told.

Stands Shining stood up and left her tepee. Outside, in the warm morning, Bear Fat braided thongs decorated with feathers and fur into Westwind's scant mane. Since he could not yet ride with the warriors, he had begged her to take his horse that day. The night before, like the night before that, she had thrown herself into the dancing and celebrating, singing until she was hoarse, even forgetting Fire Moon for a time.

She would not think about him now nor about how he had looked at the white woman at the fort. The woman had hair the color of the strange metal pebbles One Claw had

once shown her. He'd explained that years before Chief
Whirlwind and a war party—that had three guns but no
ammunition—had found just such shiny metal pebbles in
the mountains behind Spirit Peak. The pebbles had been
soft enough to be worked into bullets. The Arapaho had
defeated a large Pawnee war party with these magic bullets. They were strong medicine. But Whirlwind had never
told exactly where he had picked up the shiny metal. And
he had never gone back to find more.

Fire Moon wanted this woman whose hair was the
color of the magic bullets. Stands Shining was as certain
of this as she was that he'd meant to kill the bluecoat with
the yellow-haired woman. His spirit had left him just as it
had when he killed the Pawnee. She would not have
interfered otherwise. But when a man's spirit is elsewhere,
who knew what took its place?

It was likely to be a malicious ghost who meant harm
to the body it invaded. If Fire Moon wanted to kill the
bluecoat, she could understand that. She herself hated
bluecoats. But when his spirit had returned, he did not
attack the white man. He had turned away. And he hadn't
come to seek her out.

She would not let herself care. If Fire Moon preferred
the white woman, he could have her.

"The horse looks brave and beautiful," she complimented Bear Fat, laying her hand on Westwind's neck.
"I'm proud to ride him."

She mounted and turned the horse toward the grassy
flats that stretched along Horse Creek where the Cheyenne and Arapaho warriors were gathering. As she approached them, she looked across the stream where Sioux
warriors were forming into ranks, four abreast. There were
almost twice as many of them as Cheyenne and Arapaho
combined.

How magnificent they looked, true stronghearts, nor

afraid to die. The sun glittered off their guns and metal-tipped lances as though touching them with power.

She looked back at her own warriors. Her heart swelled. They were fewer, it was true, but fierce and proud in their war paint and decorations. Little Raven, chief of all the southern Arapaho, rode among the warriors, silver hoops swinging from his ears.

"Ho, Warrior Woman," he called as he caught sight of her. "Come and join us. We will show everybody Our People are so stronghearted that one of our women can outfight their warriors."

Crow and Shoshone braves began to gather farther upstream. The Sioux rode off, shouting and singing, heading for the council area where the women of the tribes had erected a huge brush-roofed lodge with open sides for the peace ceremonies.

A big gun spoke and the roar echoed from the surrounding hills. Stands Shining concealed her start and directed the nervous Westwind into place beside the warriors from Bobcat's band. The Cheyennes trotted off after the Sioux, two abreast. Soon they disappeared over the rise that hid the council area from sight, and Little Raven raised his lance. The Arapaho moved out.

As they crested the rise, Stands Shining saw the red, white and blue banner of the White Father fluttering atop a tall pole near the brush lodge. The Sioux chiefs had spread their robes to sit on in front of the meeting place and the warriors had dismounted. Boys took away the horses. The Cheyenne chiefs were even now spreading their robes on the ground.

When the Arapaho reached the council lodge, Stands Shining dismounted and gave Westwind to Bear Fat, who had been waiting to turn out the horse to graze. Stands Shining took her place in the ranks of warriors back of Little Raven's robe. Arapaho women and children gathered behind them.

Stands Shining could not see Fire Moon through the open sides of the lodge because too many sat in front of her. But she knew he would be there with Broken Hand. After all of the tribal chiefs were seated in a circle in front of the council lodge, Broken Hand's chief from St. Louis spoke and Friday repeated the words in Arapaho. He was there in good faith, the white man assured everyone, and wanted only those whose hearts were free from deceit to smoke the pipe of peace with him.

Crazy Horse of the Sioux filled a long-stemmed redstone pipe with tobacco and kinnikinnick. When it was lit, he handed it to Broken Hand's chief, who puffed before handing it to Broken Hand. Broken Hand offered the pipe to the sky and earth and the four directions as was proper, puffed and gave it back to Crazy Horse.

The Sioux chief drew his right hand slowly along the stem from the bowl to his throat in the sign swearing honesty by the pipe. After he smoked, the pipe was passed to the other chiefs, who repeated the pledge. Then it was handed back around the circle.

The white chief spoke again. "The Great White Father wants peace," he pledged, "wants to pay your tribes for the damage done to your lands by the white wagons. In return he wants the wagons to roll west without being raided. He wants to build bluecoat war lodges to protect the white wagons."

Stands Shining bristled as she pictured more bluecoats coming among the tribes.

The white chief asked the tribes to make peace among themselves by deciding for now and forever where their hunting lands would be. He promised that wagons with many gifts were on their way.

Broken Hand spoke next, advising the chiefs to talk to one another about these matters until the next sun, when they would meet again with him and the white chief.

For ten suns the chiefs talked with the white men. Stands Shining heard every speech. When Cut Nose of the Arapaho told the whites, "We have to live on these streams and hills, and I would be very glad if the whites would pick out a place for themselves and not come into our country," she added her "ho" of approval to the others.

But Cut Nose's words could not stop the wagons. And the Great White Father would not stop them, Broken Hand told them. They were there to make peace with the whites. Peace with each other. In the morning the treaty would be ready to sign.

Stands Shining hadn't spoken to Fire Moon in all these many suns, and she lingered as the others dispersed. He will leave with Broken Hand, she told herself, and I will never see him again. She tried to think that it would be for the best, but her heart yearned for him.

Her breathing quickened when she saw him walking slowly from the council lodge with the blackrobe who had joined the whites after the council had begun. Many of the Arapaho had listened to this blackrobe and brought their babies for him to touch with his spirit water. Even Broken Hand had brought his small son.

Fire Moon hesitated when his eyes fell on Stands Shining. He turned to the blackrobe and spoke. Then they both approached.

"Stands Shining," Fire Moon began, "this is Father DeSmet, my friend." Except for the blackrobe's name, Fire Moon spoke in Arapaho.

The blackrobe nodded greetings to Stands Shining and spoke words she didn't understand.

"He asks his Man Above to be kind to you," Fire Moon explained.

Stands Shining signed to the blackrobe that this was good. The blackrobe smiled and, after saying more words to Fire Moon, walked off and left them.

"You have learned many words," Stands Shining told Fire Moon.

"I have spent much time with my teacher."

Stands Shining could think of nothing more to say. She stood mute with downcast eyes as if she were an awe-stricken maiden summoned by a seasoned warrior. But *she* was a warrior herself. She would *not* act so submissive. Raising her chin, she stared directly into Fire Moon's eyes.

"What did you think of the council?" he asked.

"I believe the white chief means to help us," Stands Shining answered. "But I don't know if the treaty will help Our People. How can more bluecoats coming among us help?"

"Their war lodges will be on the wagon trails. The Arapaho must learn to stay away from those trails."

"Now you speak as a *niatha*. The trails cross our lands."

"With the treaty, there'll be peace with the white wagons. Broken Hand plans to seek the Pawnee and Kiowa and Comanche, too, so all tribes will be at peace."

"For a time, maybe. Pawnee and Arapaho are never at peace for long."

Fire Moon made a gesture of impatience. "That will change."

"Can the whites send us more buffalo to take the place of those frightened away by their wagons? Will more pronghorns appear in place of those killed by their hunters?" Stands Shining spoke sharply. And they both knew such a thing was impossible.

"All the tribes will get food from the Great White Father. Food and clothes and other supplies. Plenty of everything. We will pay you these things for fifty years."

"This is good," Stands Shining agreed reluctantly. "Still it is not buffalo."

She noticed that when Fire Moon spoke, he put her and the Arapaho on one side and himself on the other, with the whites. It twisted her heart to hear him do so, even though she'd known from the beginning he was *niatha*, like his eyes.

Still she was confused. He had told her he wished to be Arapaho. Had he lied?

Fire Moon drew back, suddenly standing very straight. He gazed over Stands Shining's head and she turned to follow his look.

It was the woman with yellow hair. She was walking arm in arm with the bluecoat Fire Moon hated. Stands Shining tensed.

In a hushed tone, Fire Moon said something she didn't understand. She glanced at him to make certain his spirit hadn't taken flight again, but he was himself. She turned back to face the bluecoat and the woman, her arms folded tightly across her breasts.

The white woman spoke in a high voice that set Stands Shining's teeth on edge. She watched as the woman fluttered her eyelashes and flirted with Fire Moon. Then she felt the bluecoat's eyes on her. She drew in her breath.

She had seen that look many times in the warriors' eyes when they took captive women. She was as brave as any warrior, but she was not a man. This look of lust she did not like to see.

She would not tolerate a bluecoat looking at her in such a way.

She didn't have her bow. All the warriors had gone unarmed after the opening ceremony to show their peaceful intentions. But her knife was belted to her waist and her fingers touched the hilt as a warning. She glared angrily at the bluecoat.

He followed the motion of her hand to the knife and his expression changed. He spoke to Fire Moon. She didn't understand the words, but the tone was taunting.

The yellow-haired woman turned her head to stare at Stands Shining and Stands Shining knew the bluecoat had spoken of her to Fire Moon. The woman's pale eyes examined her from head to foot. Stands Shining gazed back coolly.

It was obvious that the woman was soft, unused to work. Used to having her way. Her appearance, Stands Shining thought, was strange and pallid. Did Fire Moon like such looks?

"Stands Shining, this is Lieutenant and Mrs. Chambers." Fire Moon spoke as though the words hurt him when they passed between his lips.

"They are married?" she asked.

"Yes."

She didn't think the bluecoat's wife acted married. She heard Fire Moon say something to them and the man tilted his head toward her briefly. To her surprise, the woman held out her hand.

After a slight hesitation, Stands Shining touched the white woman's fingers. They felt like cloth, she thought. She looked more closely. The woman wore thin mittens on her hands. Why? The sun was very warm.

The bluecoat spoke again to Fire Moon. Stands Shining could tell that the words meant to hurt. Then the bluecoat took his wife's arm and led her away. She glanced back once to wave her hand, but it was clear that the gesture was meant for Fire Moon.

"He has a bad heart toward you," Stands Shining commented. "And he has one toward me in a different way."

Fire Moon blinked in frustration.

"His wife flirts with you," she added.

He looked down.

"They come from your village?" Stands Shining asked.

"From St. Louis, yes." Fire Moon's mouth tightened. "It is no longer my village."

I will walk away, Stands Shining told herself. Fire Moon makes no sign that his heart is tender toward me. His eyes follow the white woman. There is nothing left to say. Forcing herself to turn her back, she started for the Arapaho camp.

"Stands Shining."

The sound of her name from Fire Moon's lips twisted like a knife inside her. She stopped and looked back.

"I'm heading east with Broken Hand. Going with him to Washington to see the Great White Father."

Friday was going there, she knew, and Arapaho chiefs Tempest and Eagle Head. Sioux and Cheyenne chiefs, as well. Bluecoats would travel with Broken Hand's party as guards. No doubt the bluecoat who was Fire Moon's enemy would be one of them.

And his wife.

Stands Shining said nothing, turning away again, hurrying her footsteps. Fire Moon called her name once more, but this time she did not stop.

If he wanted the yellow-haired woman, let him have her.

Hands grasped her shoulders, fingers digging in. Jerking her around to face him, Fire Moon hissed, "We are not through with one another!"

Stands Shining felt the blood pound in the hollow of her throat. She hoped Fire Moon wouldn't notice its throbbing. But because she was angry at the way his touch affected her, she allowed the hot words inside her to boil up.

"I do not choose to notice a man who cannot decide what he is," she told him resolutely. "I do not like Winter Bull even though he is one of Our People. But I respect him, for he knows who he is. He is Arapaho.

"I hate all bluecoats and I despise this badhearted one you told my name to. Still, he is *niatha*. He cannot change the way he acts. He knows, unlike you, where he belongs."

With a sudden twist, Stands Shining freed herself from Fire Moon's grasp.

"I know who I am," she proclaimed. "I am Arapaho. I am a woman who chooses to be a warrior. What are you?"

Fire Moon stared at her.

Stands Shining whirled and raced away from him, afraid that if she stayed a moment longer she would be unable to resist both the lost look in Fire Moon's eyes, and the temptation to cry.

At last I have cut the thongs binding us, she assured herself.

Yet instead of heading for her tepee, she found herself approaching Bobcat's lodge. Bobcat sat outside with two of the elders. He gestured for her to sit and she settled herself on the ground beside them.

No one spoke for some time. Stands Shining's face was as dark as a storm sky as she battled with her thoughts.

It was true, she decided, she was a warrior. But there were ways to fight without knives and bows and guns. Women's ways. She was as much a woman as the palefaced one who eyed Fire Moon so boldly.

It was true a warrior is proud. Yet Stands Shining's heart told her that if she did not fight for Fire Moon, he would be lost to her. She could shout to the winds that she did not care, but she would be lying.

She turned to Bobcat. "The Woodlodge band sends a chief to Washington," she remined him. "The Red Willow band sends a chief. We do not."

"That is true," Bobcat agreed.

"When Tempest returns, you will listen to him. You will listen to Eagle Head. You will wait for them to tell you of the meeting with the White Father."

"They are good men. Truth-tellers."

"It is so. But you will not be the first they speak to. Our band will be the last to hear about the journey. What if, after they leave, you have questions to ask about the trip? Who will answer them?"

"I do not care to travel so far," Bobcat argued halfheartedly. "Besides, I was not invited by Broken Hand."

"I was not invited either," Stands Shining admitted. "But if you asked me to go, I would be willing."

Chapter 20

The gift wagons arrived the next morning, twenty-seven of them. And they were heavily loaded. The chiefs were the first to receive presents. There were uniforms of bluecoat chiefs with swords and tasseled hats, also medals to hang about their necks.

Stands Shining watched Bobcat pull on a coat adorned with shiny metal buttons. He slashed his sword through the air. Though he looked warlike, she turned away, disturbed that he had put on any part of the bluecoat uniform. She saw that all the chiefs were trying on similar coats, and a chill seeped into her despite the warm sun shining down on her back.

Were these the good things One Claw meant they should accept from the whites?

It took two days to distribute all the gifts. Then a cry was raised reporting buffalo on the south fork of the river. Hastily the tribes broke camp to hunt.

When Bobcat's band feasted the next night on their share of the buffalo meat, they were camped to the south of the council place on their way to their home grounds near the Arkansas.

"I have talked to the council," Bobcat informed Stands Shining. "It would be a good thing if you went east with Broken Hnad. You will bring us back the words of the Great Father in Washington. Try to count the whites while you are there to see if almost all of them have come through our country on the trails. Truly, there must be only a few left, for we've seen so many.''

Excitement raced through Stands Shining. Not just because she would be with Fire Moon, but because on the journey she would be traveling over unfamiliar country. Who knew what magic she would see in the white man's land? No expression showed on her face as she told Bobcat, ''I hear you and will do as you say.''

Stands Shining never thought she would be in a Pawnee village on a peace mission. As Broken Hand led their party among the lodges of Big Fatty's Pawnees, she stepped cautiously, sensing the tension of the other Arapahos.

Alights On The Cloud, a Cheyenne chief, scowled darkly. He fingered his bow. But an older Cheyenne chief, White Antelope, spoke to him sharply and his hand fell away. The scowl on his face, however, remained.

Broken Hand signed to the Pawnee chief that they came in peace.

''My heart leaps with joy,'' Big Fatty said, speaking and signing simultaneously, ''because I find myself in the presence of those that from my infancy I have been taught to consider my mortal foes.''

Stands Shining thought his words were straight and true and wondered if she had been wrong. Perhaps Pawnee and Arapaho could truly live at peace.

All present smoked the pipe except Alights On The Cloud, who agreed only to refrain from war while he was on this trip to the east.

While they had been traveling, Stands Shining had kept with the Arapaho or the allies, occasionally speaking to Broken Hand's young wife, Margaret, whose mother was Arapaho. She stayed as far as she could from the bluecoats guarding the party and from Fire Moon, who rode with Broken Hand. What she couldn't do, though, was stop herself from watching him.

By the time the party arrived at what Friday called St. Mary's Mission, Stands Shining was convinced that even though the yellow-haired woman rarely spoke to him, she wanted Fire Moon. Her husband kept too close an eye on her. As for Fire Moon, Stands Shining thought he was avoiding both her and the yellow-haired woman.

The chief of the village of Potawatomis that lived near St. Mary's Mission greeted Fire Moon with cries of delight and embraced him.

Friday told the Arapaho that Broken Hand wished to show them what excellent food the Potawatomis grew. That evening they feasted on food Stands Shining had never tasted before. In their fields, the Potawatomi grew food such as maize and pumpkins. Every mouthful was sweet to Stands Shining's tongue.

"My ears are open," Eagle Head remarked. "These people who dig in the ground eat well and their food is good. Perhaps our way should be the same."

Stands Shining studied the Potawatomi villages. It was true that even the dogs looked well fed, but these people lived in permanent lodges. They stayed in one place forever. Even the Pawnees left their home villages for moons at a time, living in skin tepees and hunting. How could anyone stand to live in the same place moon after moon, winter after winter?

No, she would never submit to it.

When the Moon of Falling Leaves was half-finished, they came to a large white village where Broken Hand led them aboard a walk-on-the-water. Stands Shining was embarrassed by the stares of the white passengers and the comments she didn't understand. During the voyage, she shrank behind the other Arapahos, but noticed Friday seemed pleased by the attention. With great ease, he talked and stood among the whites.

I must learn to speak the *niatha* tongue, Stands Shining told herself. I must know what they say and not have to wait for another to tell me what their words are. The whites are very many and very powerful. It is well to understand them firsthand.

Even before they arrived in St. Louis, she gave up trying to count the white people as Bobcat had asked her to do. They were so many! And Friday said St. Louis was still a great distance from Washington and that all the country in between was filled with whites.

When Friday brought her a message that the yellow-haired woman wished to speak with her, Stands Shining did not tell him no, as she might have a few suns before.

"If this wife of a bluecoat wishes to talk I will listen," she told Friday.

The white woman was in a small wooden lodge built inside the walk-on-the-water. There were many of these lodges, but Stands Shining and the other tribe members preferred staying in the open air.

"She says her name is Roseann," Friday translated. "She wants you to come with her to her father's lodge in St. Louis. She wants to be your friend."

That one will never be my friend, Stands Shining thought. She eyed Roseann, who smiled at her. Tentatively, Stands Shining smiled back, signing yes. The best way to learn the strengths and weaknesses of an enemy was by close observation. No doubt the white woman, too, knew this was true.

"Tell Roseann I would like her to teach me to speak her tongue," Stands Shining told Friday.

They arrived in Washington on what the whites called Christmas. It rained and a cold wind blew, but there was no snow. Old Cold Maker did not control the land here.

Roseann, who had insisted Stands Shining stay close beside her for most of the trip east from St. Louis, informed her, "Daddy is taking me to stay at Colonel Hansen's plantation in Maryland."

Stands Shining understood most of what was said to her in English now, though she spoke it poorly.

"Mr. Fitzpatrick says you must stay with the other Indians at Maher's Hotel." Roseann pouted, as she always did when denied her own way. "I wanted to show you off to the Hansens and their friends. Now I can't."

Stands Shining had come to understand this white woman well. She was generous and cheerful if everything went as she wished. "I stay with tribesmen," she replied haltingly.

"Those fierce warriors respect you," Roseann told her. "I see the way they look at you, hardly as if you're a woman."

"I prove myself in war," Stands Shining declared. "They know my heart."

Roseanne sighed. "I could never do that."

Roseann would never have to. Stands Shining had known that right away. She had a husband to protect her and the ability to entice other men to her side. Some man would always stand between Roseann and danger. No man would ever forget she was a woman. Still, Stands Shining would not want to be like Roseann.

"Well, I think it's mean of Mr. Fitzpatrick, just the same," Roseann went on. "He knows I'm lonesome without Steve."

Lieutenant Chambers had been sent ahead to Fort McHenry with his company. He was to join his wife in Washington soon.

"I'll invite the Hansens to tea at the hotel," Roseann stated suddenly. "It's one of the most fashionable in Washington, you know. You'll join us, of course. And perhaps Hamp." Her voice was carefully casual. "His grandfather knew the Hansens."

Stands Shining understood perfectly that Roseann was

arranging all this to see Fire Moon. He had remained persistently aloof as far as either of them was concerned, but Roseann was not the type to give up on anything she wanted.

After departure, Stands Shining rode with Broken Hand and the others through the streets of Washington. She had seen many large villages on the journey, but had not grown used to the number of people in them.

Their carriages rolled into a wide street with tall lodges on either side. Broken Hand pointed to a white lodge where the street ended. "The Capitol building," he said. "The old and wise men sit in council there and make laws."

When Broken Hand was satisfied the proper arrangements had been made in the Maher Hotel, he left them, saying he would be back. Black-skinned men appeared to show them where they would sleep. Stands Shining had grown used to being shut into rooms with glass windows, but she still didn't like the feeling. She followed the others along carpeted halls. Two by two, the chiefs disappeared into the rooms pointed out by the black men.

"Eagle Head and Stands Shining," one of the black men said, gesturing toward a room. By now, all of the tribesmen knew how their names sounded in English. She and Eagle Head looked at one another.

"I not wife," she said in English to the black man.

"You two in this room, all's I know," the black man told her.

"Friday," she answered. "Friday talk you."

"Ain't Friday. Today's Thursday."

Stands Shining started to repeat her words, then realized that it would do no good. "Hampton Abbott," she declared instead, giving Fire Moon's white name. He would make this black man understand.

"Abbott?" he asked.

"Yes."

The black man nodded and opened the door of the room. Eagle Head went in. Farther down the hall, the black man opened another door. "In here," he said to Stands Shining.

She entered the room, walked over to the bed and sat on it, marveling at its softness. She had grown to like the white man's beds quite well.

Unlike their allies, the Arapaho had raised beds in their tepees. They were not so high as white ones, nor so soft, but comfortable with buffalo robes and willow backrests. Although she'd rather have been in her own Arapaho bed, the white beds would do until she returned to Our People.

She lay back on the pillows, thinking how difficult it was going to be to try to explain to Bobcat the number of whites who lived in this eastern land. It was hard to think that perhaps the East had belonged to Our People long ago. Yet some of the old Arapaho stories told of living far to the east.

Other stories said it had been far to the north where they lived. No one, not the oldest in the tribe, knew what was true. Crying Wind had once said that the Arapaho had lost their history. Many believed Our People had lived from the beginning by the blue mountains between the Arkansas and the river the whites called the Platte.

It was winter in Arapaho country now, time for storytelling since the snakes were asleep and so wouldn't hear and come to punish the storyteller. Perhaps the Keeper of *Hehotti*, the Sacred Wheel, had chosen a successor and was preparing him by telling how the world came about and how Flat Pipe had created land and all the people.

She had heard only the part of the story that children heard, not the Sacred one only the Keeper knew.

"In the beginning there was nothing but water. Flat Pipe floated alone on the water. There was nothing else.

" 'Man Above,' Flat Pipe prayed, 'I am lonely.'

" 'Call on helpers,' Man Above said. 'Talk to them.'

"Flat Pipe called to the water people and a duck appeared. 'Dive to the bottom of this water and bring me what is there,' he said to the duck.

"First a little teal tried but came up nearly dead, having found no bottom. Then the mallard tried but he came up the same way. Flat Pipe called the geese. They tried and failed. He thought of the swans and called them. They tried and failed as well.

" 'You can only summon one more kind of water people,' Man Above warned.

"Flat Pipe thought a long time. He and the birds floated and floated and still he thought. Finally he called to turtle. 'Dive to the bottom of this water and bring me what you find there,' he said.

" 'I can only try,' the turtle said. She dived and was gone for a very long time.

" 'Don't give up hope,' Man Above advised.

"At last turtle's head rose above the water and, exhausted, she spat a tiny piece of dirt onto Flat Pipe. He made the dirt expand and it grew and grew until it was large enough for the birds and for the turtle to walk on. Still it grew.

" 'I have made a world,' Flat Pipe said. He took some dirt and made the first man and woman of Our People. Then he made other people, some even with light skins. He made all the animals, everything that walks or flies or crawls or swims.

"Our People were given Flat Pipe himself. He instructed us never to let our hearts grow tired of giving. 'To give,' he said, 'is the greatest gift of all.' "

The northern Arapaho had Flat Pipe now. Stands Shining knew that, for they were the original Woodlodge people he had given himself to. The southern Arapaho kept *Hehotti*, the Sacred Wheel, but still honored Flat Pipe as their creator.

Stands Shining covered her face with her hands, tears filling her eyes. She was lonesome for her village, for those she knew, familiar voices and familiar ways.

She heard the door open and close. Hastily she sat up. Before she could stand, Fire Moon was at the bedside.

"Stands Shining," hĕ murmured, his eyes soft. He eased onto the bed and put his arms around her, held her close.

Her pain and loneliness fled as quickly as a prairie dog disappearing into his burrow. She pressed against his comforting warmth and her need for him flared hotly through her.

His mouth was on hers. His tongue met hers. His hands stroked her hair.

"I've wanted you so much. So many times," he whispered.

"Yes," she murmured. So had she wanted him.

"I thought you'd never come to me," he breathed into her ear. His breath made her shiver.

She wanted nothing more than to lie with Fire Moon on this soft bed. Yet she struggled away from him.

"I didn't come to you," she advised Fire Moon. "The black man said this was my place to sleep."

"It's my room," he told her, reaching out his arms. "Never mind. You're here."

Stands Shining scrambled to the far side of the bed and stood up. "I didn't come to you," she repeated.

He stared at her.

"The black man has made a mistake," she snapped.

Fire Moon stood on the opposite side of the bed. "We can share this room."

"No."

"Don't try to act like a village maiden. You want me as much as I want you."

There was no point in lying. "Yes."

"Then why . . . ?"

Her knees felt like water as his grey eyes held her gaze. She longed to have his arms close about her again, to feel the thrust of his passion. But extricating herself from his web had brought her much sorrow and she would be a fool to fly into it once again, to be bound by the spider in a cocoon of desire where she had no control, where she was trapped.

If he loved her, it would be different, *niatha* though he was. "I will not stay in this room with you," she announced again.

"I could make you stay." He started around the bed.

She hesitated a moment, remembering the night they had come together, how she had fought him at first. But he had been stronger and she had been betrayed by her own need.

As she would be now if he touched her.

She ducked away and fled toward the doorway. He cut her off. Reached for her.

Someone knocked. Roseann's sweet, high-pitched voice called, "May I come in?"

Stands Shining pushed past the frozen Fire Moon and opened the door. Roseann, starting to step inside, stopped, staring at Stands Shining. Her eyes darted to Fire Moon.

"Oh!" she said.

"Mistake made," Stands Shining told her, feeling heat rise to her cheeks.

"Yes. Quite a mistake," Fire Moon acknowledged.

"Will you help?" Stands Shining asked Roseann. She knew she could never make the hotel men understand what was wrong.

"I came back to help," Roseann said after a moment. "I said to myself, this is Christmas Day and here you are, Roseann Young Chambers, acting like you didn't know what Christian meant, leaving that poor girl alone in a hotel filled to bursting with men."

Stands Shining blinked. This was far from true. She

had seen white women in the hotel, and the two Oto tribesmen who joined Broken Hand when he stopped at their village had brought their wives.

"I mean to take you with me," Roseann proposed. "Mr. Fitzpatrick be damned!"

"I not go with you," Stands Shining snapped back, but for some reason she felt Roseann had expected her to refuse again, had counted on it.

Roseann's eyes slid to Fire Moon and her lips tightened. "I understand," she said coolly.

"No." Fire Moon strode to the door. "I'll go to the hotel desk and explain their mistake. You keep this room, Stands Shining." He stepped around Roseann and into the corridor. Roseann looked after him.

"Black man show rooms," Stands Shining said. "Not understand."

"It looks like I arrived just in time," Roseann responded, turning back to Stands Shining. She smiled.

Stands Shining didn't smile back. Roseann had been surprised to see her. Roseann had come to this room expecting to find Fire Moon. Alone.

"If you're quite certain you won't come . . . ?" Roseann asked tentatively.

Stands Shining wondered what Roseann would do if she suddenly consented. She could not go because she had told Broken Hand she would stay in the hotel, and she could not break her word.

"I stay here," she stated.

Roseann left without further protest.

Stands Shining walked slowly back to the bed, but didn't feel like resting on it again. She peered through the window at the street below. Shouts of men selling food mingled with the rattle of carriages. Women in bonnets and wide skirts hurried past, clinging to the arms of men holding umbrellas.

She had seen similar sights in St. Louis. There they

had seemed beyond understanding. Now, though Roseann had taught her much, what she saw was still as alien as the harsh English words were on her tongue.

She had encountered many marvels in the East—the steamboats, the fire horse that rides on metal. A train, Roseann had called it, a railroad train.

"Daddy says someday the tracks will run clear to California," Roseann had told her.

Across Arapaho land? Certainly across the land of the Sioux and Cheyenne allies. The peace treaty mentioned nothing at all of railroad trains, but Roseann's father was a big chief of the bluecoats, a colonel, and he spoke truth, Stands Shining believed.

In this hotel in Washington, whites were all around her, more of them than stars in the sky. Suddenly she felt she couldn't stand her room one moment longer. She must find a fellow tribesman, any one of them, to talk to. Deep within her, she needed reassurance she was not alone with people as alien as whirlwind ghosts.

She hurried down the corridor, trying to recall which rooms she had seen the Arapaho chiefs go into. This one? That? She knocked on several doors, but there was no answer and the doors did not open. Coming to another hall which crossed hers, she walked along it and recognized coming toward her the unwelcome figure of Lieutenant Chambers.

The lieutenant called her name and walked faster. "Where's my wife?" he demanded when he had reached her.

Stands Shining had never spoken to the lieutenant, avoiding him whenever possible. "I not know where Roseann," she replied carefully.

He stared at her a moment. "She's in the hotel. She came to see you. Where is she?"

"Roseann see me. Leave. I not know where."

Stands Shining turned to get away, planning to head

back toward her room. Chambers grabbed her arm and whirled her around.

"You're lying!" he charged.

She jerked away. "You not touch me!"

Broken Hand had talked long and sternly to them all about how they must behave on this journey. "You must bring honor to your tribes," he'd told them. "Keep your knives in their sheaths, your bows in their carriers. Turn a deaf ear and a blind eye to bad manners. It is best to act as I say when in my villages."

Stands Shining knew she must not pull her knife, must not even threaten to do so. She glared at the lieutenant.

"Regular little spitfire." He smiled one-sidedly. "You're covering up for Roseann. Don't lie to me. If she isn't with you I know damn well she's with Fire Moon."

He turned on his heel and strode to the right down the intersecting corridor. A terrible suspicion drove Stands Shining to follow him.

She was at his heels when he flung open a door halfway down the hall. From inside the room, Fire Moon's startled face stared at the lieutenant. At her. He stood beside the bed, Roseann clasped in his arms.

Chapter 21

For a moment no one moved. Roseann, still standing close to Fire Moon, stared at her husband. Chambers' hand reached for the small gun he wore at his side. Before Stands Shining could spring toward Chambers, Roseann screamed and ran to her husband, flinging herself at him.

"I couldn't help it," she cried. "He forced me!"

Roseann lied! was Stands Shining's first reaction. She took a step forward, then hesitated. Might Roseann be speaking part of the truth? It could have been as it was between Fire Moon and herself.

She looked at Fire Moon. He hadn't moved. He was unarmed except for the knife at his waist, but he made no effort to reach for it. Chambers tried to put Roseann aside, but she clung to him, weeping. Doors along the corridor opened and men looked out curiously.

"I challenge you," the lieutenant said to Fire Moon.

"I accept." Fire Moon's voice was uneven.

Stands Shining understood that the two men planned to fight one another at some future time.

"Oh no, no, you can't!" Roseann wailed, but Stands Shining thought the anguish in her voice was not genuine. She wanted these two men to battle over her.

Stands Shining listened to Fire Moon and the lieutenant speak curtly to one another, talking of seconds.

"Friday," Fire Moon said.

"An Indian." The lieutenant's voice was scornful.
He shrugged. "What else could I expect?" Putting an arm
about the weeping Roseann, he led her down the hall.

"When you kill him, will you take Roseann?" Stands
Shining asked.

Fire Moon blinked, seemingly aware of her for the
first time. "No," he answered. "No, not likely." He
laughed harshly. "Actually Chambers is apt to kill *me*.
He's a crack shot."

Stands Shining stared at Fire Moon, seeking to know
if he spoke truth. She had heard so many lies and half-lies.
"When do you fight?" she asked finally.

"Friday. Chambers' second will arrange the time and
place." He eyed her sternly. "You are not to involve
yourself in this. Is that clear?"

"I hear what you say to me," Stands Shining replied.
She turned away and walked back the way she had come,
ignoring the men who gaped at her from their doors. By
the time she reached her own room, she had made up her
mind what she was going to do.

Two suns after Christmas Day, the weather changed.
The cold wind eased and the clouds parted. Father Sun
shot his red rays up the eastern sky. Stands Shining, alone
among the trees, stepped into the open area along the
Potomac River. She faced east and raised her hands.

> Take pity on me
> Father Sun, have pity
> Pity me, your daughter
> Father Sun.

Four times she repeated her prayer.

"I vow to hold an Offering's Lodge when I return to
the land of Our People," she said. "A Sun Dance when

the moon of summer returns to us. Grant only the favor I
have asked of you. Grant me this favor, Father Sun. After
the Moon of Thunderstorms I will dance in the Sun Lodge.
This is my pledge.''

When she finished, she bowed her head. Hearing the
clop of approaching horses, she slipped among the trees
again. Truly the trees of the white man's land were many
and varied. Some had leaves even in this winter moon just
as the pines of her mountains kept their green needles.

She peered around a trunk, watching as two men
dismounted—Fire Moon and Friday. Hoofbeats pounded.
Holding her breath, Stands Shining sighed when she recognized that one of the approaching riders was Lieutenant
Chambers. The others would be his bluecoat friends.

With growing apprehension, she watched as one of
the uniformed strangers talked to Friday. During that time
Fire Moon took up a position at one end of the clearing
while the lieutenant took his place at the other.

Silently, Stands Shining pulled her bow from the
carrier, nocked an arrow and waited. Friday approached
Fire Moon with two small guns. The lieutenant examined
his.

Lifting her bow, Stands Shining aimed at Chambers'
chest. If Fire Moon died, the lieutenant would not live, she
had already made that vow. What she really wanted was to
let the arrow fly now and strike him down just as a
bluecoat's bullet had once struck down First Cloud. Without warning. But Fire Moon would never forgive her for
taking his honor from him. She could not do such a thing
before he'd had his chance to shoot Chambers. It was not
her right.

The sun's rays touched the dew on the brown grass
and Stands Shining murmured under her breath, ''Father
Sun . . .''

Suddenly her head turned fractionally to the left. Did

she hear a sound? With her eyes fixed on the lieutenant, she listened.

Hoofbeats.

In the field, Fire Moon and Chambers now stood back to back, pistols in their hands. Stands Shining stared in fascination as one of the uniformed men shouted and Fire Moon and the lieutenant began to walk away from each other. How many paces would they take before they whirled and fired?

Soon others heard the galloping horse and glanced around. Stands Shining did not look, her arrow point following the lieutenant.

A horse pounded into the field and raced between the two men.

"Stop! Stop this nonsense!" Colonel Young shouted. "Lieutenant Chambers, Hampton Abbott, that's an order!"

The two men surrendered their pistols and Stands Shining lowered her bow. "Thank you," she whispered. "Thank you, Father Sun."

President Fillmore was white-haired and moved with the kind of dignity that befitted a Great Father. Stands Shining did not care for the white mustache on his upper lip, but she knew the *niatha* did not feel the same as Our People about hair on the face.

One of the President's aides spoke earnestly to Broken Hand, gesturing at the Sioux chief, One Horn, who held a pipe ready.

Broken Hand signed to One Horn that white men never smoked the pipe with ladies present. One Horn glanced at the President's wife and daughter and grunted assent. He replaced the pipe in its pouch.

"I'm happy you have come to the White House to visit me," President Fillmore greeted them. "I know you want peace between the white and red brothers as much as I do."

One Horn responded, then White Antelope.

The President spoke of his wish that the tribes would turn to farming so that no one would go hungry. He smiled at another chief's request for the present of a horse for each of them.

"The white man's iron horse will take you to the steamboat faster," he responded. Then he handed out silver medals and small flags and the meeting ended.

What message will I carry back to Bobcat? Stands Shining asked herself as she followed the Arapaho chiefs from the President's white lodge. It is clear Our People, even with the help of the Cheyenne and Sioux allies, can never prevail against the white man. They are too many. More than stars. As many as the green blades of prairie grass in the spring. And they own wonders that Our People cannot even imagine how to fashion. It is best to honor the treaty and keep peace forever with the whites, she decided, if we can.

The fire horse of iron took them to the steamboat and they journeyed down the Ohio River into the Mississippi, then into the Missouri. They disembarked at the village Stands Shining knew was Westport and Broken Hand found them horses for the trip across the prairie.

Stands Shining was pleased that Roseann had remained in Washington with her father and her husband. Now, to her joy, no bluecoats rode west with Broken Hand's party. Fire Moon had been like a man in a dream all the way from Washington, speaking rarely. But once their horses trotted away from the lodges of Westport, he seemed to come alive.

On the second sun westward, he slowed his horse, falling back to ride next to hers. For a long while he said nothing.

"I was there," she admitted finally.

He raised his eyebrows.

"By the river in Washington."

"Oh, the duel. Yes, I thought you might be. I knew you'd talked to Friday."

"It still troubles you, this duel?"

Fire Moon scowled. "I hate Chambers."

"But not his wife."

He shrugged. After a time he sighed and shook his head. "I thought she was something she wasn't, but, no, I don't hate her."

After they'd ridden in silence for a time, Fire Moon exclaimed, "She came to me in that hotel room. I thought she had made a choice. I was more surprised than Chambers when she claimed I'd forced her. It troubles me less than I thought it would. Roseann has always been a flirt. She's always tired of what she has and wants something new. Chambers is welcome to her." Fire Moon frowned. "But you shouldn't have interfered. I thought at first Roseann had told her father, then I decided it had to be you. Roseann wanted us to fight."

"Whatever happened at the duel—if it had taken place—Roseann would have won," Stands Shining explained. "I couldn't let her win."

"You should have let me kill him," Fire Moon chided. "I'll never rest easy until that bastard is dead."

"It is over."

Fire Moon shook his head. "You're wrong."

"You don't plan to return east?"

"No. No, what I mean to do when Broken Hand can spare my services is to search for my father. I think he's still alive. Tempest told me of a man who once lived with the Ugly Men band near Laramie who lost his white wife and their son during a Ute raid. An evil man, Tempest says, with a squint in one eye. But he didn't remember the Indian's name."

"Why would this be your father?"

She listened as Fire Moon told her Broken Hand's

story of rescuing him and his mother on the night the stars fell.

"Tempest says the stars fell on the night of the Ute raid. So when we get back to Laramie I plan to begin my hunt."

"Even if he is evil as Tempest says?"

Fire Moon's eyes narrowed. "I will find him."

"More than one man among us has a squint-eye," Stands Shining pointed out. "What's more, what you speak of took place long ago."

Fire Moon's hand clenched the bridle rope. "I have pledged myself to search," he insisted. "I have made a vow."

Stands Shining realized that vengeance was Fire Moon's right. Even so, a chill struck through her.

"Nothing will stand in my way," Fire Moon vowed. "Nothing."

Though he rode with her every sun and they talked, Fire Moon seldom spoke of anything else than his intent to find his father. Stands Shining thought wistfully of the time he had pursued her with equally single-minded purpose. Gradually her heart hardened toward him.

When they came on Little Raven's Arapaho band heading south to the Arkansas, Stands Shining left Broken Hand's party without a backward glance. Her life did not depend on whether or not Fire Moon wanted her. Let him search all he wished for this long-lost evil father who, more than likely, was in the land of the ancestors by now. She could get along without Fire Moon.

Along with seven warriors, Little Raven escorted Stands Shining to her home village. He had listened carefully to what Tempest and Eagle Head had been saying about the Washington visit. After they continued north with Broken Hand, he questioned Stands Shining at length, withholding his questions only as they neared Bobcat's village.

Stands Shining smiled at Bear Fat and the Pawnee

sisters who walked by her horse. All the village trailed
them to the council lodge. Inside, the pipe was passed.
Stands Shining began to tell of her trip, all the wonders
she had seen, in addition to what the Great White Father
had spoken of.

"We can do nothing but respect the treaty," she
concluded. "Even if Our People and the allies united with
the Shoshone, the Crow, the Comanche, the Kiowa and
the Pawnee, the white men would still be more numerous.
Not braver but more powerful."

"The Pawnee. Paugh!" Winter Bull glared at her.
"How can you speak of uniting with such enemies?"

"They signed a peace treaty with Broken Hand," she
reminded him. "We were in Big Fatty's village and came to
no harm."

"The Pawnees raided our horses only two suns ago
and carried off the boy who guarded them. True, he was
once Pawnee, but now he is Arapaho." Winter Bull's voice
rose. "A Pawnee can never be a friend of any of Our
People."

"I hear Stands Shining's words," Bobcat said. "I
agree we must keep peace with the whites, but the Pawnees
are another matter." He looked at her.

Winter Bull's antagonism annoyed her, as always.
But Stands Shining grew excited at the idea of painting
for war again. Her heart leaped as she thought of leading
a raid against the Pawnees.

"Yes," she agreed with Bobcat. "The Pawnee broke
their word first. Why should we honor ours?"

As soon as the council was finished, she took Little
Raven aside. "I have a request," she told him.

"I will listen."

"Tell the Keeper of the Sacred Wheel that I will
come to him soon. Tell him I have pledged a Sun Dance
when the Moon of Thunderstorms is finished."

Little Raven studied Stands Shining a moment before

speaking. "I will give your word to the Keeper," he told her. "When the bands assemble in the summer it will be good for us to honor Father Sun by our Offerings Lodge. It is well you have made this pledge."

Stands Shining's heart lifted at Little Raven's approval. She would do what she had never yet dared. Though she'd danced in the Lodge with the warriors the last two summers, she had never offered her own flesh and suffering to Father Sun.

The Moon of Thunderstorms had begun by the time preparations for the raid against the Pawnee were complete.

"It is time for you to come with us. To carry water and to help with the horses," Stands Shining informed the delighted Bear Fat.

Before all the arrangements were complete, Fire Moon rode into the village. Stands Shining could not control her own delight at seeing him. When he took her hands and looked into her eyes, she felt her knees grow weak. How long it had been since he'd looked at her in such a way!

"Come with me," he ordered quietly.

She was struck dumb. She'd given up thinking he cared for her, that he wanted her at his side.

"I started north," Fire Moon went on, "but I couldn't go on without returning and asking you to please come with me. You've told me you have a relative in the north. We can locate him and he may be able to help me find my father."

Stands Shining jerked her hands away. "What you want of me is to travel north with you to help you to find your father."

"Yes."

"You came to my village to ask me such a thing?"

At once Fire Moon's face changed. "Not only that," he murmured. "You know how I feel. I want—"

"I am leading a war party against the Pawnee at

dawn," Stands Shining retorted coldly. "I go there and nowhere else."

Fire Moon stared at her. "But the treaty, the peace pledge . . ."

"The Pawnee broke their word first. They are the ones who broke the peace."

"That's no cause for you to lead warriors against them. Let Broken Hand talk to them. You must keep the peace as you promised."

"You reason like a white man," Stands Shining accused. "Pawnee and Arapaho are enemies, but neither of us think like the *niatha*. If we don't attack, the Pawnee will believe we are weakhearted and not to be feared."

"You can't go."

Her eyes widened. "You can't stop me."

Fire Moon took a step toward her and Stands Shining crouched, reaching for her knife. "Do not think to lay hands on me. You have no right. Go back to the whites and do not bother us. You will never understand."

Fire Moon's eyes flickered from her face to her hand on the knife hilt and back again to her face. "You're a *savage!*" he shouted in English.

"I'm proud to be a savage," she lashed back in the same language, her eyes flashing.

He glared a moment longer, then strode away.

The war party rode out at dawn. Before the sun reached the top of the sky, one of the scouts came to Stands Shining.

"Someone trails us," he told her.

"Who?"

"Fire Moon."

"Let him follow if he must."

Stands Shining had trouble falling asleep that night. When she did, she dreamed of rifles pointing at her from the sky, more guns than she could quickly count. She woke before dawn, shivering.

"The dream means nothing," she comforted herself. "My medicine is good."

When they moved on, she tried to spot Fire Moon following them. But she could not. He wouldn't turn back, she concluded. He must be concealing himself, remaining somewhere behind and trailing them. Did he think to stop her at the last instant?

"When we come near the Pawnee village, watch Fire Moon," Stands Shining ordered the scout that night. She didn't really believe Fire Moon would warn the Pawnees but it was well to take no chances.

The next morning he rode up as they were starting off. He carried his rifle and small gun along with ammunition.

"Do you mean to fight along with us?" Stands Shining demanded.

"Not unless I have to," he answered grimly. "I am against this raid."

I'll watch Fire Moon myself, Stands Shining decided.

Her plan was to camp that night and attack just before dawn. But in the late afternoon both scouts came hurrying in.

"We spotted a hunting party of Potawatomi," one reported. "There were ten braves and two boys."

"Where are they heading?"

"Toward the Pawnees," the other said. "They go too fast. They may have crossed our back trail, know who we are and have circled us. By now they may be racing to tell the Pawnees where we are."

Stands Shining turned to the other scout. "Is this your belief?"

"Evening nears," he replied. "They may be eager to enjoy themselves among the Pawnees for the night. They do not travel as though they feel an enemy's nearness."

Her warriors looked at one another.

Stands Shining reviewed what she knew. The Pawnee

village was one of hide tepees, a hunting village of about thirty warriors plus women, children and old ones. The Potawatomi ten would bring their strength to forty warriors. She herself led only twenty-five, so the element of surprise would be important.

"We are close," Stands Shining stated. "We will attack tonight. Even if the Pawnee are warned, they will have little chance to be ready. These are my words."

Stands Shining frowned. The ho's of approval were not loud enough to satisfy her. Some of the warriors glanced toward Fire Moon. He had stood apart from them, but not so far that he couldn't hear what was being said.

Stands Shining instructed Bear Fat about their horses. The scouts were to stampede the Pawnee horse herd. As it grew dark, the Arapaho warriors painted themselves. Before the moon rose, Stands Shining led them in on foot. Fire Moon, unpainted, trailed behind.

Stands Shining had never felt so uneasy about a raid. It was nowhere near her moon time so she was clean of any blood taint. She had prepared properly back at the village. All omens had been favorable. Except her dream. But she wouldn't think of that now. Nothing would occupy her mind except what lay ahead.

They crept through the darkness toward the village. Stands Shining's uneasiness grew as time passed. Was it Fire Moon behind them that made her feel so uncomfortable?

Suddenly the night erupted with noise. War cries. The crack of rifles. Torches flaring. A Potawatomi warrior raced toward Stands Shining, rifled leveled. But her arrow took him in the chest and he fell.

Beside her, Two Toes went down. She let fly one arrow after another. Mounted Pawnee warriors dashed shrieking out of the darkness. Stands Shining realized that her own warriors had little chance on foot against a mounted enemy. Their own horses were too far away to reach. The Pawnees would run them down.

Someone shouted Stands Shining's name. A moment later, Bear Fat pounded up to her on the buckskin, leading Westwind. She vaulted onto the horse, shouting defiance, seeing her warriors running for their mounts as Fire Moon, riding his chestnut, drove the Arapaho horses in front of him.

Outnumbered and outgunned, the Arapaho warriors fought as they retreated. But by the time the enemy gave up the pursuit, two Arapaho were dead. Ten were wounded, three of them so badly they had to be tied onto their horses.

Stands Shining knew that Fire Moon had raced back and helped Bear Fat bring their horses. If he hadn't they might all lie dead, the Potawatomis and Pawnees dancing with their scalps. But she had failed. She was disgraced. Only once before had she lost men to the enemy and that time because Little Owl had gone against her plan. This time she alone was to blame.

Fire Moon eased his chestnut next to Westwind. He said nothing, but Stands Shining couldn't hold in her anger and despair.

"You didn't join us as a warrior," she accused Fire Moon. "You turned my medicine bad by trailing us."

Tears started to her eyes and she clenched her teeth to prevent herself from sobbing.

"I'm dishonored," she cried. "Why didn't you let me die fighting?"

Chapter 22

After the Pawnee battle, Fire Moon was angry and rode north. Stands Shining stared after him as he left camp. Her heart was sour with blame for him. It was better to have him gone. Why, then, did she long for him so much as the suns passed without his return?

Her spirits plummeted even lower when Little Raven sent a messenger to her saying that this year's Sun Dance had already been pledged by another. Was this a sign, Stands Shining wondered, that Father Sun no longer favored her?

She did not dance in the Offerings Lodge. The summer moons passed. The fall moons passed and Old Cold Maker blew his icy breath from the north. Before the deep snow fell, Bobcat's village moved to their favorite winter campsite along Cherry Creek in the foothills where bluffs broke the sweep of the north wind.

Other Arapaho bands wintered along this stream as well. A hundred tepees were strung along the icebound water.

One of the Seven Old Women, Moon Dog, came to Stands Shining's tepee to tell tribal stories to Bending Reed. How Found-in-Grass made buffalo come forth from a hole in the ground and tales of *Nihansan*, Spider Above, who, despite his powers, was always getting into trouble.

Last of all, Moon Dog told the story of the son of Moon, a favorite of Stands Shining's. As she listened to the familiar words, she felt as young as Bending Reed.

". . . and so Moon, seeing his wife and child climbing down through the hole in the sky on a sinew rope, threw a stone and killed her. His little son fell down and down into the leafy embrace of a cottonwood tree.

"Old Woman Night found him there. 'You are Little Star,' she said. 'Come, grandson, to my tepee.'

"She made him a bow and arrows and with them he killed a horned monster with eyes that blazed fire. This was Old Woman Night's husband, but she did not blame Little Star, though she turned his bow into a lance.

"With the lance, Little Star pierced six evil serpents that threatened him. Then he tired and fell asleep on the prairie. The seventh and last of the snakes crawled into his ear as he slept and coiled inside his skull."

Stands Shining shuddered as though she felt the cold evil of the seventh serpent creeping inside her own head.

"All the flesh fell from Little Star until he became a skeleton. But he was the son of Moon and so prayed to his father for rain and to his father's brother, Sun, for heat to follow the rain. His prayers were answered. Rain fell. Then Sun sent his hottest rays down onto the bones of Little Star.

"The snake grew very warm until at last he thrust his head from Little Star's mouth. Little Star grasped the serpent's head and pulled and pulled until all of the evil snake was in his hands. Instantly flesh grew over Little Star's skeleton.

"He killed the serpent and put its skin on his lance to bring home to the dark lodge of Old Woman Night. When he handed her the lance, she lifted her grandson up, up, up until he reached the sky to shine forever as the Morning Star."

Bending Reed and Sweet Water sat without moving,

filled with the magic of the story. But Stands Shining felt strangely oppressed, as though she had followed Little Star to the night lodge and dwelt there still.

The winter passed. Another, then another, until five winters had gone by. With a heavy heart, Stands Shining saw the Moon of Thunderstorms begin again. The streams, swollen by melting snow, raced and roiled. Flowers began to paint their pink and yellow among the new green of the grass.

Stands Shining kept herself busy hunting. Sometimes she went along on a raid, though not as war leader. This moon and the next were the hardest to bear. It was the time when lovestruck braves played their flutes in the evenings hoping to lure the maidens from their tepees.

Though the flutes wailed outside her tepee, Stands Shining knew they weren't for her. Sweet Water was the most sought after maiden in the village. Cheyenne as well as Arapaho braves courted her, journeying from their camp near Bent's Fort.

The women of the village thought Stands Shining refused to let Sweet Water marry because she herself had no husband. Stands Shining knew that was not true. For three summers she had told Sweet Water that she was free to marry.

"But the man I wish to marry does not court me," Sweet Water had replied each time. "I will wait."

"Every eligible brave has waited under his blanket for you on the path to the stream," Stands Shining reminded Sweet Water. "Each sun it takes longer for you to return to the tepee. Yet you say you want none of them."

Sweet Water smiled patiently. "It is courteous to talk to each man. Perhaps someday the right one will wait there."

"Do you speak of a certain man or do you long for a dream lover?"

Sweet Water clasped her hands together. "I know who the man is. He'll come for me one sun."

The words each spoke were little changed in those three summers. Stands Shining was tired of the evasion. Both she and Sweet Water knew which brave the girl meant.

"Do you really believe Fire Moon will return?" Stands Shining demanded. "Return and marry you?" Her voice was harsher than she had intended, for she knew Sweet Water had seen Fire Moon two summers ago and she, away on a Ute raid, had not.

Sweet Water sighed, her eyes reflecting her memory back to that time. "He smiled at me when I gave him the new moccasins I had made. He told me I sewed more beautifully than any Sioux or Cheyenne woman. He praised my stew when I fed him."

Stands Shining felt her heart turn bitter as she looked at Sweet Water. Sweet Water's face was the prettiest of any of the maidens living either in allies' villages or in the southern villages of Our People.

I have never made him moccasins, Stands Shining admitted silently. I have never cooked for him. I have only found fault. She raised her chin defiantly. If he preferred Sweet Water, then let him take her.

Sweet Water lifted the water paunch and left the tepee. Bending Reed had been stirring meat into the kettle over the fire. After a moment she straightened and faced Stands Shining.

"I have made Bear Fat new moccasins for his journey," she declared, her face flushed.

Stands Shining looked closely at Bending Reed. Was her flush from the fire or for another reason? At thirteen winters Bending Reed was a shyer girl than her sister. She was pleasant-looking rather than pretty.

"Bear Fat prefers my moccasins," Bending Reed announced harshly, as if anticipating an argument.

Did the girl imagine herself in love with Bear Fat? Stands Shining wondered. It was true Bear Fat had counted coup on three raids and was well on his way to becoming a good warrior, but he had seen only fourteen winters. He was far too young for marriage. Perhaps it was wise he was journeying to the Cheyenne camp to visit Snake Woman. In that way he and Bending Reed would be separated for a time.

That evening the insistent notes of the flutes drove Stands Shining from the tepee. She climbed to the top of a bluff north of the camp and tried not to think of Fire Moon. But she failed.

Did he still search for his father? She knew Broken Hand had died three winters before in Washington. Fire Moon rode with a new agent named Whitfield, whom the Arapaho did not trust.

Stands Shining did not believe Fire Moon would come back to this village to make a wife of Sweet Water. Most likely, she imagined, he had decided to follow his *niatha* blood and so would not take an Arapaho bride. Certainly he would never return to seek her out. Then why was it she couldn't forget him? She closed her eyes.

"Old Woman Night," she chanted, holding her arms outstretched. "Grandmother Night, must I stay within your dark lodge forever?"

Fiery circles began to spin against her closed eyelids, combining into one great circle, a snake of flame with its head devouring its tail. Around the fiery snake spun tiny stars and small Thunderbirds. At once she realized she was looking at *Hehotti*, the Sacred Wheel none but the chosen ever saw.

It was a sign. She had never honored her vow to Father Sun, her pledge for an Offerings Lodge.

Stands Shining rode into her village from the south in the middle of the Moon of Thunderstorms. Her heart was lighter than it had been for a long time. In Little Raven's village, the Keeper of the Sacred Wheel accepted her pledge. This summer, when the bands gathered into one great camp, she would offer herself to Father Sun.

Sweet Water hurried to meet her. "Sioux and Cheyenne chiefs are in the council lodge," she reported. "All the warriors are there."

Stands Shining slid off Vengeance, who by then had grown to be a sleek black stallion. She handed his bridle rope to Sweet Water. As she walked toward the council lodge, she heard hearty ho's of approval. She entered and stood with the other Arapaho warriors. Four Sioux and six Cheyenne chiefs sat in the circle with Bobcat and his council.

"The tribes who live to the east hunt our buffalo," Bobcat said. "This is what you have told me and it is true. They must be stopped. The buffalo grow fewer each winter."

Ho's of agreement came from everyone.

"We must join our friends in battle. The Arapaho must send a war party against these people who invade our hunting lands. Against Potawatomi. Against Delaware. And against Pawnee."

The roar of agreement shook the lodge.

"Our Sioux allies will lead this party. It is good that they do this." Bobcat's eyes slid along the ranks of his warriors as Stands Shining added her ho of approval to the others. She would have a chance to redeem her honor.

Seven suns later, two hundred and fifty warriors met near Pawnee Forks on the Arkansas. Forty of them were Arapaho. Full of confidence, the war party set off to vanquish the encroaching eastern tribes once and for all.

Stands Shining rode astride Vengeance at the head of the Arapaho. She was surprised and proud they wanted her there. But she was uneasy, too. At dawn, she had prayed to Father Sun, but as he sent forth his rays into the sky, clouds blanketed them. The eastern sky turned the color of blood. For Stands Shining whose power came from Father Sun, it was not a good sign, particularly since they rode east.

As they traveled, the cloud cover increased, threatening rain. The next sun was also cloudy, and the rain that would have cleared the skies did not come.

The following sun, a thin drizzle dampened spirits. But the sight of twenty Pawnee warriors watching them from the crest of a hill heartened the warriors.

High Eagle led a party of fifty Sioux tribesmen against the Pawnee. They galloped off, the Sioux in pursuit. Pursued and pursuers disappeared over the hill.

The main party followed at a lope, halting just over the rise. The Sioux were pounding around the side of a steep bluff.

"Do not ride into an ambush," older warriors warned.

The main party listened to their advice and rode cautiously, but the younger Arapaho warriors glanced at one another, muttering.

Gunshots echoed from the other side of the bluff. Groups of young Cheyenne and Sioux warriors broke away, galloping ahead, yelling and brandishing bows and rifles. Stands Shining glanced at her warriors. She recognized the eager gleam in their eyes and knew she might not be able to hold them back.

Yet the bluff could conceal waiting enemies. Never had she felt so indecisive. Her urge to pound ahead was checked by the awareness that her medicine might be bad.

"Do we leave the allies to fight alone?" Spotted Horse asked. He was a warrior with but a single coup to recommend him and was impatient.

"Hiyah hi!" Stands Shining shouted, making up her mind. Kicking the buckskin into a gallop, she led the Arapaho warriors toward whatever waited.

Chapter 23

"General Smith sent out the order," Superintendent Mitchell told Hampton as they sat in Mitchell's St. Louis office in April of '57. "Colonel Sumner will be riding west from Fort Leavenworth with eight companies of cavalry and instructions to whip the hell out of the Cheyenne this summer. The Indians need you, Hampton. I know you haven't been happy working with John Whitfield, but I think you'll get along with this new agent, Miller."

"I've met Mr. Miller," Hampton replied. Robert Miller was an ex-sailor with ships tattooed on his arms. Hampton realized that whether or not he and Miller got along made no difference. It was too late to undo the damage Whitfield had done. It was too late to stop the army.

Since Fitzpatrick had died so unexpectedly in February of '54, nothing had gone well for the Indians. Whitfield had no feeling for them and they knew it. Hampton had read the report Whitfield turned in to Mitchell two years ago.

"We can deal with the Plains Indians by exterminating them in all-out war," Whitfield had written. "We can wait for them to die natural deaths from starving or from disease. Or we can feed them until they adjust to the change and can care for themselves. Being a humane man,

I recommend this last option, though the tribes will first have to be whipped into submission by the army.''

"I don't like to think of Sumner's cavalry fighting the Cheyenne," Mitchell grumbled.

"And any other Indians the troopers come across," Hampton added bitterly. "I know the northern Cheyenne have made trouble. Something should be done about their raids on white wagons. But sending cavalrymen who don't know a Cheyenne from a Kiowa is bound to bring worse trouble."

Mitchell spread his hands. "I'm afraid you're right," he agreed. "But there's not one damn thing I can do about it."

Hampton left St. Louis the next day and rode into Bent's Fort before the first of May. The new stone fort had been built four years before to accommodate the growing emigrant trade. After warning Bent that Sumner would be on the march, Hampton headed for Laramie to tell the northern chiefs to try to avoid the bluecoats that were riding against them. Then he headed for Bobcat's camp.

He'd sworn never to go back there again. Two years ago his longing to see Stands Shining had driven him to her. And where had she been? Off with the warriors on a Ute raid.

What *did* he want? To go on interpreting for one Indian agent after another? He could admire none of them as he'd admired Fitzpatrick. And he knew he couldn't tolerate St. Louis for more than a few days at a time. City life would be the end of him.

What then? He wasn't an Indian, either. Hadn't Stands Shining told him he had the heart of a *niatha?* Yet here he was riding to her village again.

It was true the Arapaho had to be warned about Sumner and his cavalry. He grimaced, thinking especially of Stands Shining with her grudge against bluecoats. Yet Bent would send messengers to all the southern camps.

Why did he feel compelled to deliver the message personally? Face it, he told himself. He was headed this way because he wanted to see Stands Shining again.

He pushed his horse, traveling all night. What would this woman be like whom he hadn't seen for five years? Would she still be as beautiful? The Sioux and the Cheyenne told many stories of her sorties against enemies. He pictured her riding her black war horse, the invincible warrior woman no man could best.

If Roseann hadn't come to Fort Laramie, would everything have turned out differently? He hardly thought of her now. When he did, it was never with desire. And always he dreamed of Stands Shining.

He cantered into the Arapaho village as children and dogs ran beside his horse. Out of courtesy, he knew he must greet Bobcat first. Then he'd be free to go to see Stands Shining.

After the pipe had been passed, Hampton told Bobcat the bluecoats would be marching against the Cheyenne.

"Little White Man sent this message," Bobcat noted.

"It is well to avoid the bluecoats when they ride to punish a tribe," Hampton cautioned. "They do not always distinguish friend from foe."

"You speak truth," Bobcat agreed. "Our People will be careful. We have tried to keep peace with the whites ever since we promised Broken Hand."

"But not with the Pawnee and Ute."

Bobcat grinned. "Even now our warriors ride with Sioux and Cheyenne against Pawnee, also against Potawatomi and Delaware. Those tribes would hunt our buffalo."

Hampton had heard that the Sioux were on a war party. He hadn't heard the Cheyenne and Arapaho had joined them. "Who leads the Arapaho warriors?" he asked, certain he already knew.

"Stands Shining leads our warriors," Bobcat said. "They left one sun ago."

Ares had been pushed too hard and needed a rest, so Hampton rode out of the village on a fresh horse from Bobcat's herd, a fine roan. By the time he passed Pawnee Fork, the leaden sky drizzled rain.

He scowled upward, muttering to himself as he continued following the warriors' trail east. "Damn weather. Damn fool war party." He knew he was the biggest fool of all, going after a woman who didn't want to see him.

But in his mind was a terrible vision of Stands Shining on her black horse, riding defiantly into the fire of bluecoat rifles. No matter how he assured himself it wouldn't happen, he knew the cavalry could already have marched from Leavenworth. And certainly the Pawnee villages were to the east in the probable path of Sumner.

Could he make Stands Shining listen to him when he caught up to her? She never had before. Bad medicine, she called him. He set his jaw. Damn it! He'd *have* to make her listen!

How? By beating her as his father had beaten his mother? A spur of hatred dug into him at the thought of his father. For the past five years he'd spent all his free time searching for Bad Hawk. Finally he had found the northern band of Arapaho Bad Hawk had lived among in '33.

"You were called Rainy," an old man, Knows Medicine, had told him. "Your mother was *niatha*. You both disappeared on the night the stars fell and it was thought the Utes had taken you."

"My father?" Hampton asked.

"That man was a badheart," Knows Medicine said. "Everyone knew how harshly he beat the *niatha*. Though she tried to learn Arapaho ways, she was slow and clumsy with her crippled arm and he had no patience. He was a war leader until his party rode against the Utes. That night thirteen out of twenty died. After that his spirit became twisted until he grew as gnarled and tough as manzanita wood.

"He had no tenderness for you, even though you were his son. Our People do not hit children. We know it makes them liars and cowards. Yet Bad Hawk struck you more than once. As for the *niatha*—it is well she was taken from him. She had no family to interfere in her behalf and he would have beaten her to death sooner or later. We were glad when he left us and never returned."

"You don't know where he went?"

"Some say he stalked the Ute raiding party and was killed."

"Do you think this is what happened?"

Knows Medicine didn't speak for some time. "In my heart I believe he still lives," he admitted at last. "I do not know where. I do not wish to know, for never again do I want to see his bitter face with the one eye that looked elsewhere."

The rage Hampton felt when he heard of his mother being beaten had simmered within him ever since. No wonder she had asked on her deathbed that he kill his father. No wonder she had made him promise. Hampton inhaled deeply, staring into the grey sky.

I will keep my promise, Mother, he swore silently. You will be avenged.

As if in answer, a rifle cracked in the distance, followed by a fusillade of gunshots. Hampton kicked the roan into a gallop. Inside him, anger at Stands Shining flared hotly. Mixed with his anger was fear. Had the warriors met Sumner's cavalry? Was he too late?

He knew the Indians living close to the whites along the Missouri were better armed than those who lived farther west. Both Potawatomi and Delaware owned many excellent rifles. Every brave had a gun and ammunition.

He would be in as much danger from them as he would from the cavalry. The eastern Indians would believe him to be Arapaho—after all, he was dressed like one. As for the cavalry, it would be enough for them that he looked like an Indian.

"To hell with all that!" he grumbled, as he thundered over a hill. A fifty-foot bluff rose ahead of him. He heard the terrible scream of a stricken horse. It was hair-raising even at that distance. Gunfire popped from behind the bluff. Hampton could see nothing.

He urged the roan on. Rain began to fall heavily. A premonition of disaster struck him with such force that he gasped. Stands Shining? Her name played over and over in his mind.

Indians appeared on top of the bluff. The opposite side must not be as sheer as the one he was on or they couldn't have climbed it. He was close enough to see that the Indians were attempting to pile rocks into a barricade. Arapaho? He thought so.

The shots dwindled to a few and then they ceased. Hampton stopped, staring at the bluff top. Had anyone up there seen him? Quickly he turned the roan and rode in a circle four times. If anyone watched from the bluff, this would alert them. He jerked his rolled blanket from the back of his saddle. Shaking it out, he waved it in the air in the sign for "friend comes."

There was no time to watch for an answering signal. Hampton drove the roan into the shelter of a clump of small cottonwoods growing along a stream. He and the horse had hardly concealed themselves before four warriors on horseback appeared from behind the bluff. Hampton saw the identifying crest of ornamented hair. The Indians were Delaware.

So it wasn't Sumner's troops who fought the Arapaho. Still, the Delaware were deadly foes for anyone to have against them. Hampton watched as the warriors wheeled and returned the way they had come, disappearing once more behind the bluff.

He nodded, realizing there was no need for them to

bother with guards at the bottom of a sheer drop of at least fifty feet.

If those on top could hold out until nightfall, he might be able to help.

When it was completely dark, he led the roan to the base of the bluff and tethered him there. Then he removed the coiled rope he'd brought. Draping himself in his army blanket, he made his way around the rock wall until he saw the gleam of campfires. Drums had begun to beat despite the rain. Would the Indians dance with scalps already captured? With any luck, the combination of rain and celebration would get him past them without being challenged.

He stepped boldly on, blanket folded close about him. Keeping in the shadows as much as possible, he began to climb the slope leading to the top of the bluff. He had gone only a few yards when a man with a roached head-piece rose to block his way.

The man was a Delaware.

"They are quiet up there," Hampton reported in Delaware. "I go to see why." His hand clenched the rope under the blanket as he waited for a response.

The Indian grunted and stepped aside.

Hampton continued upward. Even on his side it was not an easy climb. He knew those on top would hear him coming. Stones rattled down the slope. He tried not to think about the arrow that might be speeding silently toward him. He didn't dare call out lest he alert those below that he wasn't one of them.

He crouched and began to whisper in Arapaho, then in Sioux, the same message he'd signed with the blanket. "Friend comes, friend comes."

"Who?" a Sioux voice demanded.

"Fire Moon," Hampton replied. "Arapaho."

Hands grasped him and pulled him over a rocky barricade. Hampton heard the snort of a horse as he scrambled to his feet. Good, they'd brought some of their mounts up with them. He'd counted on that.

"Arapaho," he repeated. "I must see Warrior Woman."

"She was shot," an Arapaho warrior told him.

"No!" Hampton answered involuntarily in English.

"I, Spotted Horse, carried her to this bluff myself when she fell."

Hampton grabbed Spotted Horse's arm. "Where is she? Take me to her."

Stands Shining lay on a robe near the horses. Hampton knelt at her side. He spoke her name, and she answered.

"Fire Moon." Her voice sounded weak.

"Where were you hit?" he asked.

"In the thigh. Much blood flowed."

"The bone?"

"Not broken." She spoke with effort, yet she managed to lift her arm and touch his face. He caught her hand and held it.

"You have come to die with me?" she asked.

"You're not going to die," Hampton said. "Neither am I." He laid her hand gently on the robe and stood, turning to Spotted Horse.

"I'll need all the ropes you can find, bridles from the ponies, everything. Get others to help you. Bring them to the cliff edge."

When the ropes had been tied together Hampton went down the sheer rock face, Spotted Horse following him. They reached the bottom and split up, each searching for stray ponies while the others on top of the cliff began lowering themselves down.

By the time Hampton brought his fifth pony back to the base of the cliff, those still on top were lowering the wounded—three Sioux, two Cheyenne and Stands Shining. Spotted Horse drove in two more mounts. That made twelve in all counting the roan.

"A man must ride with each of the wounded," Hampton ordered. "I will take Warrior Woman on my horse. Those without horses must find their own mounts or go on foot. It is dangerous to delay any longer."

Not all the warriors had roped down by the time Hampton headed the roan west. He held Stands Shining in his arms. Even wrapped in his thick wool blanket she felt very small. It was awkward for him to hold her and he knew that such a position was certainly painful for her. But she was too weak to sit astride.

As they traveled on, Hampton felt a wetness on his thigh. Fear struck him. Stands Shining's wound was bleeding again. It was saturating the blanket and his buckskin leggings.

"Sun Dance," she mumbled.

"What?" he asked, uncertain he'd heard her right.

"I was going to dance. Make an offering."

"Don't worry about that."

"I promised," she whispered, her voice so feeble he had to bend low to hear her.

"Next year," he soothed.

She said nothing.

"Stands Shining?"

There was no response. She lay, a dead weight, in his arms. A lump rose in his throat. He couldn't tell if she breathed or not.

"Don't die," he begged her, choking out the words. He looked from her face to the night sky. Rain blinded him. Almost involuntarily he gripped Stands Shining more firmly. The Episcopalian God of his grandfather seemed impossibly remote, too far away to listen to one man's pleading voice. Here on the western plains the Arapaho Great Spirit seemed closer, more accessible. He took a deep breath.

"Man Above," he began tentatively.

A single star sparkled through a rent in the clouds. Fire Moon shivered. It was a sign.

"Grant her life," he begged hoarsely. Then he waited, feeling something more was needed.

A vision of himself in the Sioux camp flashed before him, the shaman's knife cutting into his chest, inserting the skewer, attaching the buffalo skull. He had never known such pain.

He swallowed.

"Man Above," he began again. "Hear me. It is I . . ." He paused. Hampton Abbott had nothing to do with this. "It is I, Fire Moon, who speaks," he went on. "Grant this woman life and I will dance in her stead. My chest will bear the skewer. My flesh will be the offering."

Chapter 24

Before the Moon of Juneberries was full, Bobcat's band moved south to the great camp where the tribe was gathering for the summer. Stands Shining was still weak and listless. She had to be pulled on a buffalo-robe-padded travois.

At the site of the gathering, she lay propped against her willow backrest under a cottonwood. As she rested, she watched the women busily raising their tepees. The dogs were discovering old enemies to challenge while the children shouted at friends they hadn't seen since the summer before.

Stands Shining felt isolated from the excitement. More troubling was the separation she felt from her own body. To be so helpless frightened and angered her. She felt that her body had become her enemy.

She knew that Fire Moon had rescued her from the bluff where the Pawnee and Potawatomi, along with the Delaware, had trapped the Arapaho warriors and their allies. She'd been told he had carried her in his arms to her own tepee.

But her memories drifted and were insubstantial ghosts in a shining land of rocks and sand where nothing grew. There was no pain, no hunger, no fear. How restful it would be to float forever in this sunlit country, Stands Shining imagined. But the voices wouldn't let her.

"Daughter," the first voice told her, "you have not reached the end of your journey."

A spirit spoke from regions where light was so intense she could not bear to look at it. Then another voice, high and shrill, came from the rocks below her.

"Daughter, remember me," it whined.

Stands Shining recognized this voice as Turtle's, Turtle who had brought the mud so Flat Pipe could create the earth and all who lived there. Turtle, who lived forever.

Feeling herself whirling backwards and drawn out of the shining land, Stands Shining spun faster and faster until pain struck her. It was a throbbing ache starting in her left leg and spreading upward. She opened her eyes to the greyness of a dimly lit tepee. Someone was bending over her.

Fire Moon. He was there every time she drifted into awareness. Then he was gone and she saw only the troubled faces of Sweet Water and Bending Reed or the wise eyes of Moon Dog, the healer of the Seven Old Women. It was Moon Dog who laid cool leaves on her burning wound.

"I have opened your medicine bag," Moon Dog told her. "It is hanging above your head and will help you to grow strong again."

Stands Shining wanted to ask where Fire Moon had gone, but it was too much effort to speak. And later, when she had gained strength, she was too proud to ask. Now, watching the bands gather under the tree, she told herself she didn't care.

Nothing mattered. How could it? Tribesmen and allies lay dead in enemy country, their scalps taken, their fingers worn as necklaces by Pawnees and by the other enemies whose guns had slaughtered the Arapaho, the Cheyenne and the Sioux as if they were pronghorns trapped in a pen.

The eastern tribes had conquered them even though they'd had fewer warriors. Stronghearts could not prevail against bullets. Stands Shining knew she had failed a second time. After all, she had not heeded the signs warning that her medicine had weakened.

The camp circles grew as the suns passed, the southern Arapaho congregating in one vast village along Fox Creek where it joined the Arkansas. Stands Shining sat listlessly in the shade of her tepee. When four warriors of the Club Carriers came to join her early one morning, she greeted them without enthusiasm.

The Club Carriers were the third of the Arapaho Age Societies. Men over thirty belonged to it. After them came the Spear Men, who policed the tribe. The Moths or Lime Crazies were next. They were men over fifty who learned to dance in and out of fire without being burned. Councilmen were at least Moths, and usually were Dog Men, the next society up. Last of all were the Water Sprinkling Old Men.

Stands Shining did not believe she would live long enough to be a Water Sprinkler.

"We have talked," Water Snake, the eldest of the Club Carriers, said to her. "It is true you have seen but twenty-six winters."

True, Stands Shining thought, her age made her a Star Falcon. She was well accepted among the men in the society. Had she not proved herself many times over as a warrior?

"When your wound is healed," Water Snake continued, "we wish to invite you to join the Club Carriers."

Stands Shining looked from Water Snake to his three companions. One by one they signed approval.

"I am honored," she told them. "I must look into my heart to see if I am worthy."

"It is good," Water Snake agreed. "Will you come

with us now? The Keeper of the Sacred Wheel begins his prayers. This is the first sun of the Offerings Lodge.''

"I cannot," Stands Shining answered.

When they'd gone, Stands Shining told the Pawnee sisters to go to the ceremony. Then she pulled herself to her feet. Using a stick for support, she could walk a little. But she hated to have others see her so drained of strength and power. The Keeper would be painted red and wear red robes. He would call on Man Above, asking for peace and happiness as he did on the first sun of each summer's Offerings Lodge, the Sun Dance.

Stands Shining knew she could not keep her promise and take her place in the Sun Dance. She was too weak, so she would not go at all. On their return to the tepee, she forbade Sweet Water and Bending Reed to speak of the ceremony.

On the second sun, the warriors erected the Rabbit Lodge. She did not leave her tepee to see the Sacred Wheel taken inside.

During the third sun, willow canes were bent to form a frame over which buffalo robes were thrown to make the Sweat Lodge. Stands Shining recalled the many times she had watched the Sacred Wheel removed from its place of honor atop the buffalo skull which faced the Sweat Lodge entrance. Next it was taken inside by those who purified themselves for the Dance.

Stands Shining stubbornly remained in her tepee during the next sun while the cedar tree was brought in, trimmed for its use as a center pole, then "captured" and dragged to the middle of the camp and raised. In her mind's eye, Stands Shining visualized the offerings tied in the fork of the center pole—a buffalo robe, a bundle of willows, a digging stick, moon shells and eagle tail feathers.

She pictured the other poles being put up for a frame, then the beams for the lodge, and the brush halfway up the sides. She saw them fashioning the altar, laying out the buffalo skull, the straight pipe, the rattle, the badger pack and the paint sacks. Ceremoniously the Keeper would approach with the Sacred Wheel and place it on the altar.

The drums began, their beat vibrating their rhythms into the tepee where she sat, summoning her. Stands Shining closed her eyes as though that could keep the sound away.

"Stands Shining!"

Startled, she sat up and stared. She saw no one, though the bottoms of the tepee hides were rolled up to allow the air to pass through.

"Come forth!"

It was a voice she knew. Scarcely believing what she heard, she grasped her stick and rose. Pushing through the opening, she blinked in the unaccustomed light and was blinded for a moment.

"What is wrong that I must come all this way to tell you what to do?" the voice asked.

She saw him then. One Claw stood to her left and a twinge of her childhood fear of him sent a chill along her spine. He looked much the same as he had when she had last seen him. She started to reach out her arms, then stopped. Was he really before her in the flesh or did his spirit stand beside her?

"Great-uncle?" she whispered hesitantly.

"Have you lost your voice as well as your senses?" One Claw asked.

He grasped her hands and pulled her to him, embracing her. Tears came to her eyes. "I thought I'd never see you again," she cried.

"I have only now recovered from the coughing sickness or I would have come sooner," One Claw reassured her. "It was long before I heard you were alive and then I heard you went off to visit the Great Father in the East. Soon after, other matters kept me away."

"I've missed you."

He held her at arm's length. "Why do you sulk in your tepee while we prepare the Offerings Lodge? You are not so ill as that."

Suddenly Stands Shining was ashamed. "I couldn't keep my vow to dance," she replied in a low tone.

"And did you think Man Above couldn't see that was so?"

I failed as leader of two war parties, she wanted to say. My medicine no longer brings victory when I head our raids. I have no power. Everyone knows this is true. I am weak. I cannot fight.

She had forgotten how piercing his one eye was and how intimidating the other wandering eye was. None of the excuses she wanted to make would stand up under the gaze of such eyes.

"Because you do not dance is no reason to hide away," One Claw reprimanded. "Besides, haven't you been replaced?"

She didn't understand. Seeing this, he suddenly smiled. "You must come to the lodge with me," he coaxed gently. "You must be there."

Stands Shining heard the singing as she and One Claw neared the Lodge.

> May he take pity on me
> Father Sun
> My Father Sun.

All the people of the village were pressed close around the lodge. She was not tall enough to see over their heads. One Claw touched the arm of a man in his path, saying, "She must go inside."

The man recognized Stands Shining and stepped back. She wanted to tell One Claw not to do this thing, but knew her words would have as little effect as trying to catch the wind. She watched One Claw clear a path for her to the entrance of the lodge. Then she followed him.

She had not walked this far since being shot. She feared her leg would not support her as she passed through the crowd toward the entrance. Pain radiated from the wound, making her jaw clench unnaturally to keep her from wincing with each step.

The singing grew louder, the drum beat faster. The aroma of sage filled Stands Shining's nostrils as she passed between the poles of the entrance. Before her the Keeper of the Sacred Wheel held his knife raised to the sky. Sun shining through the open beams of the room glinted off the blade.

Slowly the Keeper's arms came down and he turned to the man covered with white paint who stood waiting. Stands Shining's heart leaped like a startled doe's. One Claw put an arm about her shoulders and she leaned against him. It was Fire Moon who waited for the Keeper's knife.

"It is as I said," One Claw murmured. "This man offers himself in your place."

Stands Shining wanted to cry out Fire Moon's name, to rush to him, embrace him. Never had she thought any man would do such a thing for her.

The Keeper's knife sliced into Fire Moon's flesh, the skewer was thrust in and he was attached by a thong to the center pole of the lodge. The other Dancers, who were not attached to the pole, began blowing the eagle wing-bone whistles they held in their mouths. The shrill sounds mingled with the drumbeats.

All night they would dance—Fire Moon, his chest pierced by the skewer, and the others. Their whistles would blow while silent prayers rose in the darkness to Man Above.

"I will remain here," Stands Shining told One Claw.

One Claw smiled in approval and handed her a small pouch of leaves. "To keep you strong," he advised.

Stands Shining did not use the leaves. Despite herself, she fell asleep, then woke before dawn and rose from the robe One Claw had brought for her. Facing the center of the lodge, she fixed her eyes on Fire Moon, who still danced in place, his steps slowed almost to a stop. Blood trickled down his chest and along his legs.

It was the fifth sun of the Offering. The Dancers greeted Father Sun as he rose. Then the Keeper began preparing the lodge once more. Warriors dug a shallow trench and planted small trees. The Keeper set the buffalo skull in place. It was painted with dots—red to the north and black to the south. The Sacred Wheel was positioned at the west end of the trench so the head of the serpent it formed faced east.

Then the Keeper painted the unattached Dancers yellow. Fire Moon danced on, drinking the water One Claw offered him, but refusing food. Stands Shining watched, stifling her urge to run to him. It was not yet time.

She passed an uneasy night as the irregular piping of the eagle-bone whistles awakened her time and again.

When the sun rose on the sixth day, Fire Moon had not yet torn loose from the skewer. He shuffled in place. This time he shook his head when One Claw brought water, refusing it.

Stands Shining put some of the leaves One Claw had given her into her mouth. She got to her feet as she chewed them. Leaving her support stick behind, she limped to Fire Moon. His eyes were glazed. He did not seem to see her. She reached up and took his face between her hands. Then she raised herself on tiptoe, heedless of the lance of pain in her left leg.

Behind them, the Dancers formed their semicircle and

the eagle-bone whistles shrilled in the dawn. Stands Shining put her lips to Fire Moon's, forcing the leaf pulp into his mouth. Then she eased away.

"Chew!" she demanded fiercely.

Fire Moon stared at her as if in a trance. His jaw moved as his teeth bit into the leaves. As she watched, Stands Shining felt the juice from the leaves course through her. She felt her blood race to the pound of the drums. When she was certain Fire Moon also felt the effect of the juice, she leaned toward him.

"Pull," she ordered. "Pull. Now."

Fire Moon threw himself backward. His lips drew away from his teeth in a rictus of pain as the skewer tore at his flesh. Bright red blood ran down his white-painted torso, but the skewer still held.

"Pull," Stands Shining ordered again through clenched teeth.

The drummers speeded their rhythm. The observers outside the lodge began to chant.

"Pull!" Stands Shining shouted. "Pull, pull, pull!"

Sweat dripped from Fire Moon's forehead. He fixed his eyes on the fork of the center pole where the offerings were tied.

"*Maheo!*" he cried. "Man Above!"

Then he flung himself back, the thong holding him to the center pole stretching taut. Suddenly he was falling. The skewer had torn free. The crowd shouted approval. Fire Moon tried to rise, but the Keeper held out a restraining hand. He knelt beside Fire Moon and severed the piece of bloody flesh that dangled on his chest. Next the Keeper rose and held it up for all to see. He raised it to the sky, then placed it on the altar next to the buffalo skull.

Fire Moon rose slowly. Stands Shining tried to lead him to her robe at the side of the lodge, but he refused to come with her. After a moment he walked to where the

Dancers stomped in place. Facing the center pole, he, too, began to dance.

Ho's came from the onlookers as approval of his strong heart. To Stands Shining, Fire Moon seemed to gleam like the Lone Star of the north, the son of Mother Earth and Moon.

Beside her, One Claw murmured, "The man you have chosen is very powerful."

Chapter 25

Stands Shining's wound healed before the Moon of Juneberries ended. As she exercised with her black stallion, her strength returned and grew with every sun.

One Claw had moved into her tepee, and though Sweet Water served him with unconcealed fear, Bending Reed grew used to his strange eye and giggled when he teased her.

Stands Shining was with her horses when Fire Moon returned from Fort Laramie. He seemed withdrawn, so she checked her impulse to rush into his arms.

"We will go into the mountains to hunt, you and I," he told her.

Her heart leaped. They'd be together, just the two of them. "It is good," she answered.

"I'll leave Ares here and ride one of your ponies. Don't take Vengeance. Let me choose your horse."

Stands Shining was surprised at this request but agreed quickly.

She and Fire Moon rode west in the bright hot morning, stopping to rest past midday in the shade of trees along a stream. The new scar tissue on Fire Moon's chest was pink. She wanted to touch it gently, but did not.

In his breechcloth and moccasins, Fire Moon was the handsomest of Arapaho men. Though his eyes would always be grey, they were no longer *niatha* eyes. He had shown the Arapaho how important Stands Shining was to him by taking her place in the Sun Dance.

Stands Shining smiled as secretly she looked at Fire Moon. She would never forget what he had done for her. But why didn't he touch her now that they were alone?

Not once since he had danced had he held her in his arms or kissed her. Now, sitting next to her under a cottonwood, he avoided her eyes and looked to his right where the drying grass moved slightly in a rippling motion.

"Snake," Stands Shining remarked.

"Rattler. I've been watching to see if he'd wriggle off rather than make a stand."

Stands Shining had been so preoccupied with thoughts of Fire Moon that she hadn't even noticed the rattlesnake. She smiled a little, excusing herself. This was a magic time. No snake would intrude now. No enemy would come near. She knew this was true.

Did Fire Moon?

They went on in the late afternoon and made a night camp where a few pines clustered among the cottonwoods. After Fire Moon lay on his own robe and slept, Stands Shining listened for a time to owls calling to one another. Their melancholy cries echoed in her heart.

Had Fire Moon's feelings for her so changed that he thought of her only as a companion? He had called their excursion a hunting trip. Was that really all it would be? Lonesome and uncertain, she fell asleep.

They greeted the sunrise together. All day, as they climbed and traveled through pine and cedar, the air was heavy with fragrance.

"We will soon reach the hunting lands of the Utes," Stands Shining cautioned near evening.

"The Utes will not find us," Fire Moon declared. "Not this time."

Even so, Stands Shining watched and listened carefully. It was always wise to keep alert.

She knew they were near those green and game-filled mountain valleys where the Arapaho sometimes wintered. But Fire Moon headed for none of them. Instead, he led her up a rocky incline so steep the horses labored as they climbed. They came out atop a bare rock outcropping.

"Look," he told her.

Ahead and below them she saw the spikes of pine tops and the trembling leaves of aspens. Far below them the sun was behind the peaks to the west, shadowing the valley. Stands Shining imagined she saw a stream in this valley surrounded by high cliffs.

"I have never seen this place before," she told Fire Moon. "Is there a way down?"

"A secret way," he whispered. "We will look for it tomorrow."

They slept under the stars on the outcropping of rock. Again he did not come to her. But, tired from the trip, she slept well.

The morning sun warmed the rocks around them as they breakfasted on pemmican and water. They had climbed far and the air was cool.

Stands Shining stood near the edge of a cliff. She gazed down to where a stream weaved like a sinew through brilliant green grass before disappearing into the pines. A golden eagle soared over the valley. Then he rose in a spiral until he was even with her. For an instant, before he shrieked and angled away, his yellow eyes stared into hers.

The harsh scream echoed in Stands Shining's ears. The eagle had been a sign of Thunderbird. He had warned her. She knew that and turned away from the cliff edge, shaken.

"Broken Hand told me this valley saved his life one winter," Fire Moon recounted as they mounted their horses.

"He believed he was the only one who ever found the way in."

Stands Shining shook off her uneasiness. She wanted nothing to keep her from enjoying this time with Fire Moon.

"Broken Hand honored you by giving you his secret," she said.

Fire Moon glanced at her. "Broken Hand felt as you did about my quest for Bad Hawk," he admitted reluctantly. "When I traveled with him the year before he died, he spoke many times of the futility of revenge."

Fire Moon mounted and started downhill, retracing their path. Stands Shining followed, wondering about Broken Hand's talk of revenge. When they were down the steepest part of the slope, Fire Moon veered south, moving slowly, hesitantly. After they passed a large boulder split open by a pine growing in its center, he turned again. This time he headed west.

Ravines cut into the rocky slopes. Fire Moon led Stands Shining into one of them, stopping at a dead end. She looked at him. He tried to keep his face impassive, but she noticed a tiny quiver of his lips and guessed that he was suppressing a smile. She frowned.

"You think to make me ask if you've lost the way," she observed. "Yet I don't believe this is true."

"No? Then how do we get to the valley from here?"

Stands Shining slid off her horse and walked along the rock-strewn chasm. To either side, twisted pines clung to the uneven walls. They grew sideways. They grew downward. The pileup from a huge landslide cut off any farther advance. Yet there must be a way out of the ravine other than turning back. Where was it? She saw Fire Moon smile as he watched her.

"I see no way," she concluded finally.

Fire Moon dismounted and climbed an arm's span up to two gnarled and contorted pines. He motioned to Stands

Shining to follow. She scrambled up beside him and he forced branches aside to reveal a narrow, dark opening barely large enough for a pony. She peeked in. Then she looked back at Fire Moon.

"There's a turn," he told her. "The passage comes out into the valley. Ares and Vengeance would never have gotten through, but Broken Hand said his pony did."

They had to lead their mounts into the opening. Stands Shining followed Fire Moon without hesitation. But once she was inside, her spirit quailed. She sensed rock was all around her in the darkness, pressing closely. When the tunnel curved to the left, she felt better. Dim light filtered down from a thin crack that rose to the very top of the cliff. The rock under Stands Shining's feet angled down abruptly and she trod carefully to keep from sliding.

In truth, she did not like the passageway any better than the ponies, who whuffled uneasily as their sides scraped against the stone.

At last she saw the brilliance of sunlight ahead. And moments later she was looking out into the valley, its greenery beckoning. Below her, Fire Moon and his horse scrambled down a slope, heading for the valley floor. Fire Moon's rifle cracked before she was halfway down. A bighorn that had been racing away from him dropped.

They built a fire and cooked a haunch on the spot. Both welcomed the fresh meat. After they'd eaten, they separated the ponies, who were grazing on the juicy grass. Then they rode across the valley floor toward the stream. Hundreds of yellow and black butterflies danced above the grass like flitting flowers. Near the pine grove, Fire Moon stopped.

"We will camp here," he announced.

When her pony was unpacked, Stands Shining unbraided her hair and walked to the stream to wash. Fire Moon joined her as she reached the bank, and watched as she kicked off her moccasins and bent to feel the water. It ran clear and cold, she discovered when she thrust in her hands. She had meant to undress and plunge into the stream, but Fire Moon's presence made her shy.

"Stands Shining."

She caught her breath at what she heard in his voice. Still crouched by the water, she looked up at him.

"Come to me," he ordered gently.

Stands Shining rose and walked to where Fire Moon stood. His eyes seemed to be lit from within. They glinted like the sun-touched water. He reached for the thongs fastening her tunic. Then he tenderly untied and unlaced them. As he pulled her tunic off, a breeze caressed her bared breasts and her nipples firmed. In an instant his hands were on her skin.

He knelt to untie and remove her leggings, then rose to look at her. Warmth rose inside her, but she didn't move.

"You are beautiful," he complimented her, his voice rough with passion. "You shine in the sunlight." Keeping his gaze on her, he took off his clothing.

She saw he desired her, but still he did not touch her.

"We must go into the stream," he told her.

She understood then why he had brought her to this place and why he had not taken her into his arms before. Tears came to her eyes. But she blinked them back and walked into the water, forcing herself not to gasp at its chill. She waded to the middle of the stream where the water rose to her waist.

Fire Moon followed, coming to stand in front of her. He scooped water into his hands and trickled it onto her shoulders, over her back and her breasts until she was completely wet. He pulled a piece of soap root from where he'd tucked it into his hair. Dampening the root, he began washing her arms, her breasts, her back, her stomach. His hands dipped below the water as he crouched to wash her buttocks. He washed her thighs. Last of all, he rubbed her legs and then between them.

Her entire body tingled from the iciness of the water. Yet she wasn't cold. Her need rose with the touch of his hands until she was aflame.

Then Fire Moon offered her the soap root. She took it and began to wash him slowly and carefully. She saw his eyes darken with desire.

Taking the soap root Fire Moon tossed it onto the bank. He reached for Stands Shining's hands and she came into his arms.

He kissed her hungrily, consuming her mouth with his as she pressed herself to him. He scooped her up and carried her into the shallows where he knelt and set her down so she was lying half in and half out of the water. He stretched beside her.

His fingers touched her face, moved down her throat to linger at her breasts. Then they traveled down, now under water, along the curve of her hip to her thigh and moved to her loins. He caressed her gently, wonderfully, so that she moaned with pleasure and longing.

Her hand crept down to his maleness and the feel of it, hard and alive. It made her quiver with eagerness to join with him. But just as she was about to pull him to her, he held her away and bent his head so his lips touched her throat.

His mouth caressed her breasts. His tongue was warm on her nipples. She grew limp with wanting.

He eased his body over hers, his maleness probing, finding the secret part between her legs. She gasped as he entered her.

She clung to him, moving in rhythm as he thrust into the very center of her being again and again, making the fire inside her flare wildly.

His lips sought hers and every part of them burned.

She was no longer Stands Shining. He was no longer Fir
Moon. They were one.

A throbbing pain began in her loins. It rippled ou
ward until she cried out. She felt him shudder in her arm
and call out, too, clutching her tightly to him.

They lay close for a time. Then Stands Shining slippe
away and eased deeper into the water. Looking back ;
Fire Moon, she saw he hadn't moved. On impulse sh
scooped her hand to spray water on his face.

"Aaagh!" he shouted, plunging in after her.

She laughed and swam downstream. Fire Moon caug
her foot. Pulling her back, he ducked her head under th
water. She came up sputtering and he laughed.

Quick as a dart, she dived down and jerked his fee
from under him. He fell backwards, then scrambled up an
reached for her. In a moment the water games had change
to caresses and desire. Again there was passion and lov
making, this time in the soft grass bordering the stream.

Stands Shining and Fire Moon spent four suns in th
secret valley discovering the wonders of one another. Neve
Stands Shining was convinced, could such a place exist fe
anyone else. Never could any other couple have enjoyed
place where the grass grew so green, where the pin
smelled so fragrant, where the water ran so cold and clea
She knew she would be content to stay there forever wi
Fire Moon. No other man was his equal.

On the fourth night Stands Shining dreamed that Fi
Moon was gone. When she awakened, he was not at h
side and her heart beat with fear. Telling herself she w:
foolish, she rose to look for him.

She found him sitting beside the stream at the sp
where they'd washed one another in the old way of O
People. She sat beside him without speaking.

Fire Moon sighed and turned to her. "I had a ba
dream," he told her.

Stands Shining was chilled by his expression. Sl

knew his dream had not been a good one. A wave of sadness passed over her. Bad dreams had no place in this magic valley.

"I dreamed I woke and found myself embracing not you but a skeleton," Fire Moon droned ominously. "The skeleton contained my father's bones. When I tried to roll away, I found I could not. My father's empty eyes stared into mine. His icy breath froze my cheek. The harder I tried to escape, the closer his bony arms held me."

"A frightening dream," Stands Shining whispered.

"We must leave in the morning," Fire Moon told her reluctantly.

Much as she wanted to, Stands Shining could not protest. Such a dream was a very bad sign. They must leave as Fire Moon had ordered.

"Do you still seek your father?" she asked.

Fire Moon sighed again. "I told you. The reason Broken Hand gave me directions to his secret valley in the first place was so I could find my father. It was later he said I should give up my quest and come here with the woman I loved.

" 'I meant to take the time to bring my wife here when we first married,' Broken Hand told me, 'but somehow I never had the chance. Go there, lad. Give up this pursuit of the past and find your future in my valley.' "

Stands Shining was silent for a moment. "But you haven't given up hunting, have you?" she asked.

"How can I? My father held my mother captive. He beat her, though she did her best to learn to please him." Fire Moon flung out an arm and flexed his fingers. "He broke her arm so she could never use it again. She was scarred from falling into the fire during a beating. . . ." Fire Moon put his hands to his head.

"What good will it do to find such an evil man?" Stands Shining pressed.

Fire Moon jumped to his feet. "I'll kill him!" he shouted. "Kill him for what he did to my mother!"

Stands Shining said nothing. Revenge. She could understand revenge.

"My father believed my mother and I were captured by the Utes who attacked the Arapaho camp the night the stars fell. He doesn't know who I am. I will hunt him down. Before I kill him I will force him to taste the agony my mother suffered." Fire Moon raised both arms to the thin disc of the new moon. "I vow it."

As Stands Shining washed in the stream the following dawn before packing the pony to leave the valley, she saw something glinting yellow at her feet. She reached into the water and picked up a pebble as shiny and yellow as the sun. Casting it away, she heard it splash farther downstream. Only later, as she and Fire Moon climbed from the passage into the ravine, did she remember Whirlwind and his magic bullets.

Had Whirlwind found what she had found? She did not believe Whirlwind had been in that secret valley. That meant the shiny yellow metal could be found in more than one place in the mountains. The thought was somehow frightening and Stands Shining decided she would keep it secret.

Three suns later, she and Fire Moon were nearing her village along the Fox when they met a band of Arapaho hurrying their travois-laden ponies northward. A scout thundered up to them on his pony.

"Do not go there," he warned, gesturing south. "Death hangs over the camp. We flee to stay alive."

Chapter 26

Fire Moon saw Stands Shining stiffen as the scout rode off. "I must go into the camp," she declared. "One Claw is there, the two girls, also."

He studied her for a moment, then nodded. "I'll come with you."

Mourning wails could be heard even before they entered the village. Women with sheared hair and bleeding faces wept in the entrances to their tepees. Other women were hurriedly dismantling their lodges and packing them on waiting travois.

"The many sores sickness is here," one of them cautioned as Fire Moon and Stands Shining passed.

"Smallpox," Fire Moon spat angrily. Then he sighed. "You're in no danger then. Broken Hand had you vaccinated in St. Louis."

Stands Shining well remembered the little sore the white doctor had made on her arm. Broken Hand had insisted on vaccinating all the tribesmen who went with him to Washington.

"And you?" she asked.

"I was vaccinated a few years back."

As Stands Shining and Fire Moon entered her tepee, Bending Reed staggered up from her robe. Crusted sores marred her face. Bending Reed burst into tears. "My sister," she sobbed. "My sister."

Sweet Water lay on her robe. Without going to her Stands Shining could smell the odor of death.

"Utes! Utes!" One Claw shouted from his robe at the rear of the tepee. Stands Shining hurried to him.

His face was covered with yellow, running sores and his skin was as hot as sun-baked rock. His eyes were glazed. He didn't recognize her, Stands Shining realized. Thrashing on his buffalo robe, he tried to rise.

"My shield!" he cried. "My war pony!"

By singing a lullaby, Stands Shining finally calmed him and he settled into an uneasy sleep. By the time she stood, Fire Moon had wrapped Sweet Water's body in her buffalo robe and closed the robe with thongs.

"Do you want me to bury her?" He spoke loudly to make himself heard over the pitiful wails of Bending Reed, who rocked back and forth on the ground.

Stands Shining took a deep breath, gagging from the stench of death that lay heavy in the tepee. She crossed to kneel by Bending Reed. Then she raised the girl's head and looked at her.

"We must bury your sister," she stated determinedly.

Bending Reed howled in agony. "Yes, bury her," she told Fire Moon as Stands Shining held her. "It is fitting. For many years my sister has loved you." Both Bending Reed and Stands Shining lowered their eyes. Then Bending Reed said to Fire Moon, "Bring water on your return. The pouch is empty."

After Fire Moon left carrying Sweet Water's body, Stands Shining brought Bending Reed back to her robe and made her lie down. Though the girl was warmer than normal, her few sores were healing and she seemed to be past the worst of the sickness. She would live.

"The stars," One Claw moaned from the back of the tepee. "The stars fall."

Stands Shining had been reaching to brush Bending Reed's hair from her forehead. Hearing One Claw's words, she hesitated, her hand poised in the air. Then she rose and went to him.

"Hush," she comforted softly. "Hush. I am here to care for you." But as she crooned, she darted a look over her shoulder to see if Fire Moon had returned.

She did not explore the fear that lay just under the surface of her thoughts. One Claw is very ill, she told herself firmly. He speaks nonsense.

Fire Moon came back with a filled water paunch, but did not stay.

"I must hunt," he informed Stands Shining. "Many lie sick and there is little food in the village."

Before the sun had set, he was back with a freshly killed dog and regretful he could find nothing else near the camp. The evening was warm, but because One Claw had been shivering and babbling about snow, Stands Shining had already lit a fire. She dropped meat into the boiling water and later fed One Claw a dipper of the broth.

Fire Moon slept in the tepee, but he and Stands Shining did not lie together. After seven suns all the stray dogs had been caught for food and Fire Moon left with five other men to try to find buffalo.

"I'll be back as soon as I can," he promised. Then he kissed Stands Shining and held her close.

No sooner had he ridden off than One Claw called, "Utes!" and demanded that Stands Shining fetch his bow.

"His spirit has been gone from his body for many suns," Bending Reed observed. "Before I got too sick, I tried to help, but One Claw did not acknowledge his own name. He accused me of stealing his wife and little boy. I was afraid of him."

Bending Reed's words fell on Stands Shining's heart like stones. But she disguised her shock and continued spooning broth from the kettle into One Claw's mouth. His sores had crusted over. Some of the scabs had even dropped off, but he was still very weak.

"He didn't know who I was," Bending Reed whimpered, her voice breaking. "He even called me *niatha*. Sweet Water was as sick as One Claw and she died. Is One Claw going to die, too?"

"I think he will live," Stands Shining told the girl. But, she asked herself, what then?

That night One Claw recognized Stands Shining for the first time and called her by name. Despite his weakness, she felt compelled to question him.

"You must tell me," she urged, "were you once called Bad Hawk?"

One Claw closed his eyes. After a long time he whispered, "I buried that name."

His words exposed Stands Shining to the raw truth and shattered the shelter of love she and Fire Moon had built in their valley. She remembered how One Claw had warned her so many times to be certain that she tread the right path lest she become twisted. Now she understood that by doing that he'd hinted to her about what had happened to him in his youth.

She sighed, sinking back on her heels. The One Claw she knew wasn't an evil man, his heart was good. He'd helped her find her true place. He'd defended her when everyone had laughed at her. She loved him.

It was as he said. Bad Hawk was dead. Buried.

But how could she convince Fire Moon?

The next sun he returned triumphant with the other men. They had killed two buffalo cows and a calf and their horses were laden with meat. While they'd been gone, however, three more of Our People had died in the village and Fire Moon helped with the burials. When he returned to the tent, he was exhausted and fell asleep.

By the next sun Bending Reed was recovered enough to tend to One Claw, so Stands Shining rode out with Fire Moon to check on her horses.

"I've been thinking about your dream," she told him. "About the skeleton. I believe the dream means you should give up this vow to kill your father. What is such a vow but a rope around your neck that keeps you tied to the past? Bury the past. Lay Bad Hawk to rest forever."

Fire Moon shook his head. "I can't. I made a promise. I mean to find him and when I do—"

"No!" Stands Shining fired the word like a bullet and Fire Moon glanced at her in surprise.

"For me," she whispered hoarsely. "Will you give up your revenge because I ask you to?"

Fire Moon was silent for so long that Stands Shining's heart began to beat faster with hope.

"I love you," Fire Moon told her, "but you must not take advantage of my love and ask this of me."

They found the horses and examined them in silence. Even as they rode back to the village, Stands Shining did not speak.

"We hunt again at dawn," Fire Moon told her. "Will you come?"

There were others who lay recovering in tepees and needed meat. Stands Shining knew that Bending Reed could care for One Claw if she went on the hunt. But she could not go.

"Not yet," she informed Fire Moon, hoping he would think she held back because of One Claw's condition. It was important that he never suspect what she intended to do.

She lay awake in the darkness listening to the sounds of sleep from the others in the tepee. Fire Moon kept to his own robe and she was glad. Her heart was too troubled to welcome him.

If she did nothing, Fire Moon would surely look one day on One Claw when he was better and wonder. Others might know of her great-uncle's past and might tell Fire Moon. She loved them both, but she could not live with Fire Moon if he killed One Claw.

"Mother Night," she prayed under her breath, "how can I stop Fire Moon?"

After a time she sighed and closed her eyes. There was nothing she could do but what she had first thought of. She must move One Claw from her tepee and take him to a place where Fire Moon could not find him. When the sun rose, she would decide where to go.

At dawn she stepped back from Fire Moon's farewell embrace as he prepared to leave on the hunt. His eyes questioned her, but she turned her head. If he held her again, her tears would flow, and that must not happen.

When he mounted Ares, she could tell by his abrupt movements that he was angry with her. She knew he'd be angrier still when he returned.

Bending Reed's eyes widened when Stands Shining told her to ready the travois. "Where do we go?" she asked.

"North. The travois is for One Claw. He is weak and I do not know how long he can ride. We will not take the tepee because it will slow us."

One Claw didn't argue. Stands Shining helped him mount his pony. Her heart was troubled at how he slumped atop the horse. But she clenched her jaw. There was no choice.

No one came to ask them where they were going. It was expected that each family, as soon as they could travel, would leave the ill-fated camp.

One Claw said little as they rode north. Even when the climbing sun beat relentlessly down he didn't complain. But after midday he had trouble keeping his seat. He swayed, nearly falling. Stands Shining knew it was too soon to stop. Besides, there was no shade. So she kept the horses moving and watched One Claw worriedly.

When they came to a clump of cottonwoods by a nearly dry stream, Stands Shining made camp, though she would have liked to go on.

At dawn One Claw couldn't sit his horse, so Stands Shining strapped him to the travois. She had planned to ride to one of the northern Arapaho camps above the Platte, but as she watched the travois bump along the ground, she knew One Claw needed to rest and grow stronger before he'd be able to survive such a long journey.

There was no going back, so they would veer east. It was true they would come upon the Cheyenne village where Bear Fat was visiting his mother and that Fire Moon warned of bluecoats riding against the Cheyenne in that area, but she would be alert for sign and take the chance.

"We go toward the Kansas River," Bending Reed remarked after they changed direction. "Do we vist Bear Fat?" Her voice was colored with hope.

Stands Shining smiled a little as she signed yes. At least one person in their little party would be happy.

Before midday on the following sun, Stands Shining found the huge camp where both northern and southern Cheyenne had gathered. Boys tending the horse herd raced ahead with word of her arrival and Stands Shining was surprised to be greeted by Grey Beard, one of the Cheyenne medicine men. He helped One Claw off the travois and welcomed him into his own tepee.

"When he has rested, we will talk," Grey Beard told Stands Shining. "You and the girl may stay in my tepee as well."

Stands Shining frowned, but only for a moment. She had planned to stay with Snake Woman, but could not decline the honor Grey Beard extended to her. Soon One

Claw was able to prop himself against a willow backrest and smoke. White Bull, a northern Cheyenne medicine man, joined him and Grey Beard. Bending Reed sat with the women, but Stands Shining was invited to smoke with the men.

After the pipe had gone around and the ashes had been extinguished, Grey Beard spoke.

"Bluecoats ride against us."

A thrill of anticipation rippled through Stands Shining. She was certain that her path had been fashioned by Man Above for this reason.

"I have dreamed," Grey Beard declared. "My colleague, White Bull, has had the same vision. Thunderbird showed us a medicine lake whose waters would be a shield for our warriors against bullets." He looked at One Claw.

"My medicine has not been strong this moon," One Claw told them. "The white man's many sores sickness struck my village with suffering and death."

"We had no such sickness among us," Grey Beard put in, "perhaps because our warriors bathed in the sacred water."

"It is good," One Claw acknowledged.

"While you recover your strength in my tepee, perhaps you, too, will dream," Grey Beard suggested. "All know that the man whose medicine changed a woman into a warrior has powerful spirit helpers."

Stands Shining longed to offer to join the Cheyenne warriors, but said nothing. She had not been to the sacred lake and her presence might interfere with the medicine. If Grey Beard asked her, she would gladly fight the bluecoats.

He did not ask.

"Your warriors have faced bluecoats before?" One Claw asked.

"No. But it does not matter. Bullets cannot wound them."

"When do the bluecoats come?" One Claw inquired.

"Before three suns pass. They left the big war lodge in the east two moons ago to ride against us."

Later that afternoon, when White Bull and Grey Beard left the tepee, One Claw motioned for Stands Shining to come to him.

"You take the Pawnee girl and ride from this camp," he ordered. "Go back to the Arapaho village. Or north, if you choose. Go tonight."

"You are too weak to—"

"I will stay here. But you must go."

"Why?"

"While I rode on the travois, I saw this camp in flames. It will come to pass. You have no magic. It is dangerous to fight alongside men protected by magic. Go."

"But I won't leave you!" Stands Shining protested. "Not with bluecoats coming. No!"

One Claw's good eye gazed at her. "I saw you in my vision," he told her. "Your hands were bound. You were a prisoner. I tell you to go."

Stands Shining remembered a dream One Claw had told her of years before, a dream of her in darkness, weeping. The dream had come before First Cloud was killed and she was lost in the storm. Stands Shining grimaced. One Claw's dreams were not to be taken lightly.

She drew herself up. "I will die fighting before I will ever be a prisoner of bluecoats."

One Claw sighed. "I have not asked why we left our camp as though pursued by evil spirits. I thought I knew. Now I wonder if anything I see is true. I am old. A man should not live as long as I have lived. He should die bravely in battle before snow touches his hair and his strength fails."

Stands Shining said nothing. Whatever One Claw

believed about their hasty departure, he couldn't suspect the truth. She couldn't tell him about Fire Moon. If she did, One Claw would insist on returning to face him.

"I will stay here with you," Stands Shining asserted. "But because I am warned, I will be watchful."

Before dark, Bear Fat came to the tepee. Though he greeted her warmly, Stands Shining noticed the eager look in his eyes when he saw Bending Reed seated among the women. Surely these two someday would marry.

Grief stabbed her heart as she thought how she had left Fire Moon behind, perhaps forever. How could she bear the loss of him in her life?

"I have bathed in the medicine lake," Bear Fat told her. "I will ride with the warriors against the bluecoats."

"It is good," Stands Shining answered, proud of this handsome youth. At fourteen, he stood almost as tall as a man, and his courage matched any warrior's.

She woke before dawn to the howling of wolves. The hair on her neck stiffened as she slipped into her moccasins. Listening carefully, she knew she was hearing scouts, not animals.

Soon the rim of the sun shone in the eastern sky. Warriors painted and feathered for war were gathered west of the tepees. They checked their weapons and their horses. One Claw had left the tepee to watch the preparations. He leaned heavily on Stands Shining.

Bear Fat was on Westwind. He sat straight and proud and Stands Shining pointed him out to her great-uncle. How she longed to be among the warriors, shield on her shoulder, arrows on her back, gun in her hand. When she looked, she did not see many guns among the Cheyenne. Those she did see were old. Arrows would be enough, she thought, since the bluecoat guns couldn't harm them.

"You wish you were riding with them," One Claw noted.

"Yes."

"Are you so certain war is still your path?"

Stands Shining hesitated. War had always been her way. But what of the warning signs and her bad luck when she paid no heed? What of the eagle who had stared at her in the mountains?

"Take care lest you blind yourself to what is true," One Claw warned.

The last of his words were drowned in the shouts of the Cheyenne warriors as they rode four abreast up the river valley. Women ran beside the horses, urging the men to be brave, cheering for them to bring bluecoat scalps home.

According to the scouts, the bluecoats were marching down the valley less than half a sun away. They arrived earlier than predicted. Surely these three hundred stronghearts galloping to meet them would put the bluecoats to rout.

"I want to see the battle," One Claw burst out suddenly. "I want to see with my own eyes this magic that Grey Beard and White Bull speak of. Where is my horse?"

Stands Shining protested, "You're not well enough to—"

"No!" he boomed. "I will go!"

Stands Shining brought Bending Reed with them and warned the girl, "If danger comes and I must fight, you are to take One Claw to safety."

Despite her worries, Stands Shining's excitement grew as they raced after the warriors. Her heart pounded in her ears when they sighted the Cheyennes forming their battle line.

One Claw pointed to a bluff rising along the river. "We can see better from up there."

Stands Shining hesitated. If the Cheyenne were to fall back, the three of them might be trapped on the bluff. All sides were steep but one, and that one dropped off into the river. But One Claw had already started his horse climbing and she followed him. The medicine water protected warriors so they could not fail, she told herself.

From the top of the bluff, Stands Shining could see an officer leading the mounted bluecoats. There were over a hundred, she thought, but not so many as the Cheyennes who charged them, singing their war songs. What a proud and wonderful sight they made, Stands Shining thought. Their feathers fluttered. Their bows and guns were ready.

Now we will see the magic, Stands Shining reassured herself. The bluecoats will aim their guns and fire, but their bullets will fall harmlessly to the ground. No Cheyenne will die as First Cloud did.

She heard the call of a bluecoat battle horn. The officer raised his sword and shouted. Faintly his words came to her. They were carried on the wind.

"Draw sabers! Charge!"

As Stands Shining watched, gaping in shock, the sun glittered on the naked steel of a hundred curved swords as the bluecoats whipped them from their scabbards. One Claw groaned as the bluecoats thundered toward the warriors, swords upraised.

"Shoot!" Stands Shining screamed. "Fire your arrows!"

Instead the Cheyenne line faltered. Stands Shining stared in horror and disbelief as one warrior after another wheeled his horse and veered to the south. Before long, three hundred Indians were scattering before the bluecoats like a herd of pronghorns chased by wolves.

"Stand!" Stands Shining commanded. "Stand and fight."

The faster bluecoat horses rode beside the warriors' ponies. Sabers slashed. Cheyennes fell.

"There is no magic against bluecoat swords," One Claw announced sadly.

His voice returned Stands Shining to thoughts of their own misfortune. "We must go down," she urged, "take the easier side toward the river. We can't stay here waiting to be discovered."

Though the slope to the river wasn't that steep, it was covered with loose rocks that slid out from under the horses' hooves. Some bounced downhill. Others bounded across the narrow strip of level rock between the river and the bluff and splashed in the water.

Stands Shining led the way. She was followed by One Claw and Bending Reed. They would have to cross the river. There was no other way. After all three of them were across, they would head north. In that way, perhaps, they would be able to keep ahead of the bluecoats. . . .

A rattle of stones prompted Stands Shining to look back. Bending Reed's pony had lost his footing. He scrambled to regain it, but fell against One Claw's mount, who stumbled sideways and then slid down the slope. One Claw was thrown free and rolled all the way into the water.

Bending Reed's pony struggled to rise. Doing that, it knocked loose a small avalanche of rocks and fell with the stones down, down, down, Bending Reed still clinging to its mane.

Stands Shining knew if she tried to hurry her black horse, she, too, risked falling. She let him pick his way, trying to see through the dust. As it thinned, she spotted Bending Reed struggling to get out from under her horse. There was no sign of One Claw.

When she reached the water's edge, Stands Shining flung herself off the black horse and grasped Bending Reed's shoulders. After tugging her free, she helped the girl to stand and was thankful no bones were broken.

Stands Shining scanned the rocks and the river. One Claw was nowhere in sight. She heard the shouts of white soldiers, but the steep walls of the bluff prevented her from seeing them. Bending Reed's pony was still down, its foreleg shattered. But One Claw's mount struggled to his feet and splashed out of the water.

Hurrying the dazed girl to the trembling horse, Stands Shining boosted her on top of him. "Cross the river," she ordered. "Hurry." But when Bending Reed showed no sign of obeying, Stands Shining yanked the horse's head around until he stood facing the stream.

"Cross the river," Stands Shining repeated. Pulling her quirt from her belt, she slapped the horse sharply across the haunches.

At once he snorted and plunged into the water. Hoping he wasn't favoring his right rear leg, Stands Shining vaulted onto Vengeance. She urged the black horse into the stream.

"There goes one!" a voice shouted in English. "I'll get him!"

Vengeance plunged after the other horse. Now clear of the concealing rock wall, Stands Shining saw the bluecoat who had spoken. He was upstream, his horse in the water. His saber was in his hand and he fixed his eyes on Bending Reed. Her mount was floundering in midstream.

Stands Shining turned Vengeance sharply. Her plan was to intercept the bluecoat. She reached hastily for her bow and nocked an arrow. As she let it fly, the soldier saw her and ducked. Instead of piercing his heart, the arrow struck his shoulder. He yelled with pain and his saber splashed into the stream.

Bending Reed screamed. Stands Shining whirled and saw the girl's horse struggling. She wheeled Vengeance around to help, then heard more shouts behind her. When she reached the girl, she pulled her up in front of her quickly and glanced around.

Two bluecoats were driving their horses into the stream

where the wounded soldier had gone down in the water. The bluecoat horses were fast, she knew that. Vengeance could outrace them, but not if he carried two. Stands Shining spoke into Bending Reed's ear.

"Give him his head. Go southwest."

The moment the black horse reached the far side of the stream, Stands Shining slid off his back and whistled the run signal. Vengeance was trained to obey and galloped off with Bending Reed on his back.

On foot, Stands Shining turned to face the onrushing bluecoats.

Chapter 27

The mounted bluecoats splashed across the stream. One rode after Bending Reed. The other rode at Stands Shining, who raised her bow. But the bowstring was damp and loose. Thrusting the bow away, Stands Shining grasped her knife and glared up at the bluecoat.

He held not a sword, but a pistol. She tensed for the bullet. But to her surprise, the soldier reined in his horse. As he did, her gaze shifted from the pistol to his face.

"I thought that was you up on the bluff," Lieutenant Chambers chuckled evilly.

Stands Shining's grip on the knife tightened.

"Throw the knife into the stream, Stands Shining," the lieutenant ordered, his pistol aimed at her heart. "I kill women only when absolutely necessary."

A horse splashed to the left of Stands Shining and she glanced sideways. The bluecoat who had gone after Bending Reed was returning.

"Stop right there, Sergeant," the lieutenant told him. "Keep your gun on the Indian and don't shoot unless she attacks me."

At least Bending Reed got away, Stands Shining thought spitefully as she glared at Chambers.

"Why don't you finished her off, sir?" the sergeant asked. "Old Jeb's back there with an arrow in him on account of her. Ain't no difference between Injun braves and squaws. The devil's spawn is what they is. Kill 'em all, that's what I say. Get rid of the red-skinned bastards so decent men can ride in this land.''

"I don't want to hurt you," Chambers told Stands Shining, ignoring his companion. "Be a nice girl and toss that knife away."

A flicker of motion to her right among the hillside rocks caught Stands Shining's eyes. She glanced first in that direction, then immediately to the left and behind her to mask what she had done.

A feather had disappeared behind the rocks, the old and battered feather One Claw wore in his hair. He was alive. Stands Shining was certain of it. She was also certain that he was unarmed or injured. Otherwise he'd have put arrows into Chambers and the other bluecoat.

They will kill One Claw if they find him, Stands Shining thought. Taking a deep breath, she dropped her knife into the water as a distraction.

"Very good," Chambers encouraged. "Now the bow and arrows."

After Stands Shining obeyed, Chambers ordered her to get up in front of him. She waded toward him and he reached his hand down to help her.

She ignored it and pulled herself onto the bay horse by grasping the stirrup strap. Then she clutched the bay's mane and held herself away from Chambers.

"But, sir, the colonel's orders . . . we wasn't to take prisoners."

"Thank you, Sergeant Oates. I'm aware of the orders. But Colonel Sumner could hardly expect me to kill an old friend of my wife's, could he?"

"Uh, I guess not, sir."

"And I'm certain you won't upset him by rushing to inform him of this little adventure, will you now?"

"Ain't never been a tattletale," the sergeant muttered.

"Good."

Chambers did not enter the soldiers' camp until the blue shadows of evening lay thick among the hills. Stands Shining's wrists were bound behind her, but she held her head up and stared straight ahead as she was pulled from the horse and pushed ahead of Chambers toward his tent.

"The looie's gonna have his blanket warmed tonight," one man said softly. Others laughed.

Once they were inside the tent, Chambers gagged Stands Shining. Then he bound her ankles and fastened the rope to the one holding her wrists together so she lay on her side curved backward like a bow.

When he left the tent, she tested the strength of the knots and rope. There was no give. She was helpless. From time to time men passed the tent and she strained to hear every word.

"The colonel says we did for nine of the bastards, that's all."

". . . march to burn their village in the morning . . ."

". . . sure skedaddled. Ain't an Injun in miles . . ."

It was dark by the time Chambers came back into the tent. Her back was to him. She couldn't see what he did. But she saw light flare and heard the rustle of clothing. In another moment she felt hands on her legs and breathed in relief as the rope slackened so she could straighten. Chambers untied her. Then he flipped her onto her back. Yanking her hands in front of her, he retied them, but did not remove her gag.

"I've waited a long time for this," Chambers sneered down at her. He was naked except for a shirt.

Stands Shining drew up her legs. A kick in the proper spot. . . .

He shook his head. "Don't do it. I'll beat you unconscious if you fight me."

Don't fight? She couldn't let this man put his hands

on her! Yet she needed her wits about her. If Chambers was at all careless, she would find the means to kill him.

Stands Shining swallowed. She knew she must not struggle but the bitter taste of humiliation stayed on her tongue as her leggings were yanked off and her bound arms were pushed up over her head.

Chambers shoved her tunic above her waist. She looked away from his lust-filled eyes as he stared at the secret part of her no man but a husband should see. After extinguishing the lantern, he grasped her legs and jerked them apart. She felt the weight of his body and the hurtful thrust of him against her. With her bound hands, she tried to find a weapon above her head to strike him. But there was nothing within reach.

Cold numbed her as he forced himself inside her. It was a deadly rage, one that would lay heavy in her heart until she killed this man.

At last he grunted and rolled away. When she heard him breathe deeply in sleep, she sat up, located her moccasins and slipped them on. It would be difficult to get into her leggings because her hands were bound. Cautiously, she stood and pulled her tunic down to cover her.

Chambers' hand reached out without warning and clamped hard onto her ankle. He yanked her to the ground.

"Be still or I'll tie your legs again!" he warned.

She lay rigid, waiting, but he did not force himself on her. Only when she was sure he was asleep again did she relax. Each time she moved, his breathing lightened. She knew he'd awaken if she tried to get up.

Earsplitting shrieks jolted her. A gun cracked. Chambers sprang up at once.

"Indians!" a man shouted outside the tent. "Indians after the horses."

Chambers pulled on his clothes. Stands Shining heard him plunge into the night. She got to her feet and groped for a knife. Deciding he must have taken it with him, she walked to the tent flap and listened.

Chambers shouted for Sergeant Oates, his voice some distance away. Men cursed and called to one another. Stands Shining poked her head through the flap opening.

Circles of light bobbed in the darkness as soldiers rushed here and there with lanterns. The stars and moon were covered by clouds.

Stands Shining heard gunshots to her left. A horse whinnied. Hoofbeats pounded close, then faded away. Stands Shining darted from the tent and ran. She felt awkward with her hands tied. Trying to avoid the lights, she stumbled and fell to her knees more than once. She didn't dare take the time to search for a knife. And with the gag in place, she couldn't use her teeth to try to loosen her bonds. Her only hope was to get away from the camp and hide before she was caught.

"Whoa there! Goddamn you critters!" a man shouted off to the right. Horses snorted.

Stands Shining headed for the sounds. Then she stopped when she heard hoofbeats trotting toward her. From the way the horse ran she knew he carried no rider. She could neither speak to it nor tell it to come to her. Instead she crooned deep in her throat.

There were only the two of them in the night—she and the horse. Stands Shining sensed he would listen and come to her if she willed him to.

His pace slowed. She heard the whuff of his breath close by. She didn't move, didn't stop her wordless crooning. The horse loomed beside her. In one motion she grasped his mane with her bound hands and pulled herself onto his back. He quivered with surprise and she leaned forward to soothe him as her knees urged him forward.

"Halt! Halt or I'll shoot!"

Stands Shining kicked her mount hard. Her bound hands twisted in his mane. She had no saddle, no bridle.

She'd ridden bareback many times, but on horses she knew, and always with her hands free.

The horse reared and she almost slipped from his back. He was a white man's horse and much larger than she was used to. It was difficult to grip him with her knees. When he came down, she kicked him again. He stretched out to gallop and headed straight back into the camp. With every fiber of her strength, she fought to turn his head back toward the stream.

A rifle cracked behind her. She leaned low along the horse's neck, still crooning to him, still trying to turn him. Finally he altered course and aimed for the water. Plunging across the stream, he galloped west.

Stands Shining gave him his head. She wanted distance between herself and the bluecoats. As for Lieutenant Chambers, she would meet him another time. She'd make certain of that.

The moon floated from behind the clouds. Stars finally peeked through. Hearing a horse's hoofbeats, she looked behind her. The horse's rider waved.

"Stands Shining?" he called.

Her alarm changed to disbelief and then to joy as she recognized the voice.

"Fire Moon!" she cried, half choking on her gag and trying without success to slow her mount.

Fire Moon pounded up behind her. He passed her horse, then cut in front of it. "Whoa!" he shouted. "Whoa!"

Her horse slowed. Stopped.

Lifting Stands Shining from the horse, Fire Moon cut the rope that bound her hands together. He took away the cloth that gagged her and put his arms around her. But she pulled away.

"Was it you who spooked the soldiers' horses?" she asked, the words coming with difficulty from her dry throat.

"Yes," he answered. "I've been trailing you. Hiding from the cavalry. When Bending Reed showed up on your black horse, I didn't know if they'd killed you or taken you prisoner so I stampeded the army horses as a diversion, figuring while they chased the horses, you might escape." He grasped her arms and shook her. "Why did you leave me?"

Stands Shining looked away without answering. "Where are Bending Reed and Vengeance?" she asked.

"I sent Bending Reed west with the Cheyenne women who were fleeing from the village. Vengeance is tethered nearby."

"I must have my horse. And I will need your gun."

"Why the gun?"

"I am going back to kill"—she hesitated briefly—"the man who captured me. I will dance with his scalp."

"You will be killed before you get near him. Or be recaptured."

"No. That will not happen. I will kill him," she maintained.

"If you do kill him, you will doom Our People. Shall they lie in blood because of your selfishness? You know the army will burn Arapaho villages if you kill a white soldier."

Stands Shining's heart beat faster. Fire Moon had said "Our People." Never until now had he used that term.

"Stands Shining, you asked me once to give up my vow to kill my father," he reminded her. "Now I ask you to give up yours in exchange. Both of us will deny ourselves vengeance."

Stands Shining realized it made little sense to rush back and try to kill Chambers. If she succeeded, Cheyenne and Arapaho villages would be destroyed because of her. It would be better to wait, to stalk him, to shoot from ambush, to deny herself the sweetness of having him know she was his killer.

But Chambers must not live! If her vow to see him dead doomed One Claw to Fire Moon's vengeance, then that must be.

"Do you know the name of the man who captured you?" Fire Moon asked.

Stands Shining knew she dared not tell him it was Chambers. If Fire Moon learned what Chambers had done to her, he would demand his own revenge and hang if the white men caught him. She could not risk such a thing.

"Was it Chambers?" Fire Moon demanded, his voice thickening with anger. "I know he's been with Sumner. I've kept track of the bastard." His grip on her arms tightened until his fingers hurt her.

"If he touched you, if he dared to touch you . . ."

Wings seemed to beat inside Stands Shining's head, the wings of Thunderbird.

". . . I'll kill him," Fire Moon vowed. His voice came from very far away.

Stands Shining felt Thunderbird grasp her in his strong talons and whirl her upward. Higher and higher they rose until they were so far above the land she could look down and see all the way from where Father Sun rose in the morning to where he disappeared into his lodge in the evening.

A stream of blue rolled from east to west. It flowed ceaselessly. She saw that the stream was not water but many bluecoats, as tiny and as numerous as ants. There was no end to the marching bluecoats. The Buffalo People, the Arapaho, the Cheyenne, the Sioux allies and even the enemy tribes were surrounded by them.

All of this Stands Shining saw as Thunderbird carried her aloft. And she knew it was true. Hadn't she seen for herself how many white men lived to the east?

"Daughter, look into your heart," Thunderbird warned her. Then he let her go and she tumbled from the sky.

Opening her eyes, Stands Shining saw that the sky

had paled to grey. She stared into the concerned face of
Fire Moon.

She realized what she'd been shown. She understood
Thunderbird's warning. She had been chosen and felt no
regret. Only her hatred of Chambers remained to sadden
her heart.

"I thought you had left," Fire Moon murmured gently, "never to return."

"I was on a spirit journey," Stands Shining replied.
"My great-uncle had just such a journey on the night the
stars fell."

Fire Moon's hand stopped stroking her forehead.

"My path changes," she told him. "No longer will I
ride to war. Thunderbird's path is the medicine path. Now
his path is mine."

"One Claw was once a warrior?" Fire Moon asked,
rising to his feet.

Stands Shining could tell by his voice he suspected
the truth. She sat up. "I have known my great-uncle only
as a medicine man and teacher. He is a good man, not
evil."

"But he was once Bad Hawk." Fire Moon's words
were firm. There was no doubt in his voice.

"He buried the name when he set foot on his rightful
path."

"He killed my mother."

"Bad Hawk may have done what you say. One Claw
did not."

Fire Moon gazed at Stands Shining, his nostrils dilated
in anger. Gradually his face softened. His fists unclenched.
He took a deep breath and sighed.

"One Claw does not know why I rode from the
Arapaho village," Stands Shining told him. "Now he lies
injured near the bluecoat camp. I heard the white soldiers
say they ride to burn the Cheyenne village this sun. I mus

go back and find One Claw when they break camp.'' She rose and looked into Fire Moon's eyes.

"I cannot find it in my heart to hate an old and feeble man," he told her. "You are right. My father is dead. Bad Hawk is dead. I will go with you."

"I give my word I will not try to keep my vow of revenge," she told Fire Moon, though her hatred of Chambers choked her.

They rode to the cottonwoods where Fire Moon had left Stands Shining's horse. She put her arms around the black stallion's neck. "I give you a new name," she whispered to him. "You will be Night Runner."

Then she mounted him and Fire Moon led the army horse behind his own.

As they set off for the bluff where she had last seen One Claw, dust rose from in the valley, telling them the soldiers had broken camp. There was no sign of One Claw. But Stands Shining scanned the rocks where she knew he had been hiding and found a mound of pebbles.

"He's left a message," she told Fire Moon. "He's following the bluecoats."

"He isn't crazy," Fire Moon said slowly. "He must believe you're still a prisoner."

"I made him travel this road to the Cheyennes because I feared you would learn of his past," Stands Shining replied. "Now he is weak and hurt. I must ride after him."

Fire Moon nodded without speaking. The two set off along the valley, taking care to stay out of sight among the trees bordering the stream. The sun climbed fierce and hot into the sky.

Night Runner seemed more and more uneasy and Stands Shining slowed to study the ground. "A horse has passed here," she observed, "a horse with iron shoes."

Both she and Fire Moon knew it was possible that One Claw had captured an army horse as she had, or that a bluecoat might have come to get water. It all meant little, yet Stands Shining's hair began to prickle at the back of her neck.

Fire Moon rode past her. Ahead of them, huge boulders blocked their path. They would have to leave the cottonwoods or go into the water to skirt them. Fire Moon glanced back and pulled Ares to the right. As he did, Stands Shining saw that a narrow passage threaded between the huge rocks.

A good place for an ambush, she thought, and she was not armed. They would do better to risk taking to the water.

"Wait," she began to call. The she froze with the word on her lips. A horseman suddenly appeared from behind a boulder. His rifle was aimed at Fire Moon.

"Hello, Hamp," Lieutenant Chambers sneered. "I was certain you'd come after me. It's about time we took care of our unfinished business."

Chapter 28

Without thinking, Stands Shining reached for a bow that wasn't there. Seeing her futile gesture, Chambers laughed. Then he sobered when Fire Moon's hand dropped toward his pistol.

"Not a chance," Chambers told him. "My bullet will be in your heart before that pistol's halfway out."

Stands Shining's attention shifted from the rifle Chambers kept pointed at Fire Moon to his sheathed saber and the pistol strapped at his belt.

"I've always hated you," Chambers told Fire Moon. "Passing as white, what a farce. You've never been anything but a savage. Roseann told me how you terrorized her in her own home before you left St. Louis, how you dragged her into your room in Washington when she went to visit your Indian slut." He gestured toward Stands Shining.

Chambers grinned lewdly. "You don't know what a pleasure it is to be able to kill you, Hamp. Think how I'll be praised for ridding the West of another redskin." His eyes slid to Stands Shining. "Or two."

Fire Moon tensed and Stands Shining feared he meant to fling himself at Chambers, hoping to sacrifice himself so she could get away.

"No!" she cried.

Chambers glanced at her, but his rifle didn't shif from Fire Moon's chest.

"I might not shoot you, at that," he said to her "Squaws do have their charms."

Stands Shining gauged her chance of making Chambers shoot at her instead of Fire Moon. She could not urge Night Runner to charge Chambers—Fire Moon blocked her path. But pressuring with both her knees while she pulled back on the bridle rope would make the black horse rear and paw the air. She frowned. That probably wouldn' distract Chambers either.

"I trust you've said your prayers to the Great Mani tou or whatever heathen god you worship," Chamber sniped. He raised the muzzle of the rifle slightly and aime it. Just as his finger tightened on the trigger, a dark figure swooped shrieking from the top of the boulder and fell or him.

Thunderbird has come to save us! Stands Shining thought.

The rifle blasted. She heard a zing as the bulle ricocheted off rock. Chambers and his assailant crashed to the ground while Fire Moon flung himself off Ares.

Stands Shining leaped from her horse. She saw tha Chambers struggled not with Thunderbird but with a war rior whose face was painted black. She ran toward them Fire Moon held his fire, unable to shoot for fear of hitting their rescuer.

Chambers wrenched his knife from his belt and sank the blade into the warrior's side. The warrior twisted as h was struck and the knife hilt jerked from Chambers' grasp The black-faced warrior yanked the knife free of his flesh Blood gushed from the wound and he faltered. Chamber lunged for the knife, but the attacker eluded him an brought up the blade. In a second he had slashed acros Chambers' throat.

Chambers let out a hideous, gurgling cry. Blood spurte

from his wound, spattering the warrior's black face with red. Chambers slumped and fell backwards, his head half-severed from his body.

The warrior raised himself from the dead body and stood, wavering. Instantly Stands Shining recognized who he was. She sprang forward along with Fire Moon, but the warrior held up his hand.

"Do not touch me," he cautioned, "lest you injure yourselves. My spirit helper is within me. His power is great." With deliberation, the rescuer sat down on the ground next to the body. Very carefully he slid the knife back into the sheath on Chambers' belt.

Blood bubbled from the wound in the warrior's side. Stands Shining knew that the knife had pierced his lung.

"Daughter," One Claw said, "you walk the true path now." He looked at Fire Moon. "My son, you are with me as I sing my death song."

One Claw couldn't know who Fire Moon really was, Stands Shining told herself. Tears welled in her eyes. Fiercely she blinked them away. It was not yet time to weep.

She glanced at Chambers. He was dead, the knife slash in his throat looking like a bloody smile. She knew she did not want his scalp. There was no reminder of him that would please her.

One Claw closed his eyes and began his chant.

> The moons pass
> Swift as the wind
> Flowers bloom
> Flowers die
> Earth lives
> She lives forever
> I die
> With the flowers
> Die as the flowers die.

One Claw repeated the words four times before his head dropped.

Fire Moon fell to his knees beside him. He leaned forward, but touched nothing. One Claw's lips moved, but Stands Shining could not hear what he said because his body sagged and toppled to one side. She knelt next to Fire Moon.

"Do you know what he said to me?" Fire Moon asked. Tears ran along his cheeks.

"I did not hear," Stands Shining answered softly.

"He called me Rainy."

Fire Moon urged his chestnut into a stand of cotton-woods as the hills ahead turned to purple. Stands Shining followed.

Far behind them they had left the dead—one buried, one lying as he had fallen.

A stream flowed between the cottonwoods. The water was shallow, but also it was clear and inviting.

Stands Shining slid from Night Runner as the black horse headed for it. Hurrying upstream, she undressed and waded into the water. Moments later Fire Moon joined her, but they did not touch. Stands Shining washed herself completely. She stepped dripping from the water to let the warm breeze dry her.

There would be time enough to mourn for One Claw when they found the new place of Bobcat's village. One Claw trod the warrior's star path. Now was the time to celebrate life.

She opened her arms to Fire Moon.

He held her to him and they made love tenderly as the shadows of evening crept among the cottonwoods.

"You are my wife, now and forever," he murmured.

"As you are my husband."

"We will live with Our People on the land pledged to

us by treaty," Fire Moon vowed. "We will keep the peace as we promised."

Stands Shining stirred in his arms. "Willingly do I walk the path of peace," she agreed, "but will the *niatha* keep to this path?"

"We must keep many miles between them and us," Fire Moon declared. "They wish to cross the land to reach the far west. They don't want our mountains and foothills. There we can live apart from them."

Stands Shining frowned, looking past Fire Moon at the darkening sky. She pressed close to him once more. "We will be happy together, you and I," she said.

Yet the night's growing darkness felt like weight on her spirit. She sighed. A star shone brightly above the western hills. The memory of the shining metal in the magic valley crossed her mind. She suddenly recalled the *niatha* word Roseann had taught her for the yellow metal.

Gold.

She shivered.

Fire Moon held her closer. "Happy forever," he whispered, bending to kiss her.

Stands Shining forgot her foreboding. She forgot everything but Fire Moon and her love for him.

Yes, she thought hopefully. Happy forever.